WHILE DARKNESS GATHERS

A Sequel to The Edan Trilogy

PHILIP CHASE

PRAISE FOR THE WAY OF EDAN

In *The Way of Edan*, Philip Chase has written a highly accomplished first novel. The storytelling is top-notch. There's a gravitas in the writing that put me in mind of Tolkien, with definite shades of Katherine Kerr, along with John Gwynne. This is a novel born of love for the story.

— MARK LAWRENCE

What a wonderful read! Prose that is smooth and accessible, a world with a weight and depth to it, and a gripping and emotional story. There's a lot to love here. Lovely to see the Anglo-Saxon influences that gave me a real sense of time and place, and the storytelling was done with a deft, assured hand.

— JOHN GWYNNE

The Way of Edan encompasses an expanding war driven by voracious religious fanaticism. Young heroes emerge, bonded by loyalty, in an age of ripening prophecy. Traditional fantasy readers will find elves with a fresh spin expanding the familiar bounds of individuality, and women, old and young, who wield magic in positions of power.

— JANNY WURTS

For A.P. Canavan, best of Nemesisses

Grim
Outer Isles
Hemeldowns
Beoroth
Frost Bay
North Downs
Frones Sea
Vulpe
Farwich
hwitwater
Northweald
(Iltharwyn)
Norfast
The Marca
Rimdale
Fyrnhowe
Wolvendon
withweald
Kinsford
folkwater
folkmere
DWEORG BARROWS
DEL
Birch Bay
Southweald
(Iltharwyn)
anrod
theodamar
The Dweorghlithes
Etinstone
Ellordo
Woodburg
Torrlond
ORMETBERG
Bay of Harlon
Hasumere
Torrhelm
Gorifaen Hills
Sundering Sea
ea
Belzlam
stramas
Derwyn
Carrilion
glas
fahu
Gadomiel
Balnor Pass
Harlech
gilion
Iarfain
Marar Mtns
Culvor Sound
maranant
Adanon
Galad
Asdralad
Bay of Feradan
Briufa
Palahon
Dirgal
Dwarioth
Isles of Yaladir
Kiriath
Gulf of Gath
Ralion Sound
Firdal
Normenlond
or
Andumedan
Isthmus of Lod
Yalawyn
25 50 75 100 150 200 300
scale in miles

Enga Isle
ornholm
Savage Sea
OF
ra
Ironwood
The Wildlands
SIRUKINN'S WALL
Amlar Mtns
Edwend Downs
Sea of Morthul
kuralas
Slith
(The Great Fen)
nurgleth
Nahan
Shohan
diadas
Sildharan
Shinan
Holurad
sannodi
Golgar
ulnodi
lannad
Orudwyn
Sundara
Kelzaon
Gulf of Bahan
Glirdan
Tinubor
N
W E
S

A BRIEF NOTE ON THIS STORY

While Darkness Gathers follows sixteen years or so after the events of The Edan Trilogy, to which it is a sequel. While someone who has not read the trilogy could read this book and, I hope, enjoy the story for its own sake, it does spoil major events that occur in The Way of Edan, The Prophet of Edan, and Return to Edan. Also, a person who has read The Edan Trilogy, already knowing and perhaps feeling attachment to some of the characters who appear in this story, will have a reading experience that is different from that of someone who has not.

PROLOGUE

Flames roiled downward. The sky boiled with fire. A huge form blotted out the sun, its vast shadow slipping over the rugged, ruddied landscape. Like boulders grinding together, the beast's massive bellow drowned out the shrieks of burning and dying men, flooding Volund's ears and vibrating in his chest. In the air streaked sail-like, leathery wings and scales the color of blood clotted and dried, careening to a point a few hundred yards before him, where several warriors armed with bows and spears stood their ground, lobbing futile missiles at their attacker.

Death's maw gaped open. Rows of glistening, yellowed teeth surrounded a blackened tongue. A roar and then a bright burst of fire exploded from it, and even when Volund cringed down and shut his eyes, red pierced his eyelids while heat washed over him in a searing gust. When he opened his eyes, naught remained of the warriors save smoldering meat, bones, and ashes.

"Get back here or I'll kill you myself!" Yrsa's angry voice was small and dim beneath the ringing in his ears from the dragon's scream.

With smoke stinging his eyes and the nauseating stench of roasted flesh filling his nostrils, Volund straightened out of his crouch and glanced back toward the falls. His sister was sprinting toward him, her sword flashing as she brandished it.

"I can help!" He shook his head and turned his back on her. Grasping it by the tiller and taking care not to set off the trigger, he clutched his stirrup bow and ran toward the slaughter. He took care not to upset the nocked arrow in its groove, which slowed him down, but he needed only one clean shot before Yrsa caught him.

Before him, Valfoss burned in a conflagration that rumbled like a giant herd of galloping horses, making a mighty funeral pyre of the town. Choking smoke rose and billowed from the groaning bones of its buildings, and sparks cracked and danced out of the inferno as homes crashed inward. In the town's center, even Skjold, the ancient hall of Grimrik's kings and queens, was succumbing to flames as they surrounded it like dogs taking down a stag. No matter. The Thjoths were more than wood and stone. The folk of Grimrik, those few that had stayed behind, were safe in the caves behind the falls, where Volund's father had commanded them to seek shelter.

Beyond Valfoss, where the warriors his father had chosen had formed up to meet the flight of the dragon, the valley was churning in chaos. Men fled for their lives, most toward the Mjothelf, whose water granted the only safety from the lingworm's flames. One small ring of warriors remained around King Orvandil Dragonbane. Halvard, Bodvar, Hakon, Kialar, and a few others stood around Volund's father, each bearing one of the heavy, rectangular Dweorg-wrought shields and iron-shafted spears. The king was shouting something and pointing skyward with his spear. The warriors gazed up at the beast — so vast and old that her heat had baked her red scales nearly black, and yet so graceful as she twisted in the air to make another pass at the doomed mortals below her. Gorsarhad, eldest of dragons.

Volund slowed down and, steadying his heavy breaths, held up his stirrup bow to ready his shot. There had been little time to test it, but he knew it would work. More powerful than a normal bow, it could punch one of its steel-tipped arrows even through dragon scales. At least he hoped so. He raised it by the tiller with one sweaty hand, grasped the long trigger mechanism with the other, and, with his heartbeat throbbing in his ears, took aim at the monstrosity streaking toward his father.

Or, at least, he took aim where the beast should have been. Somehow, the huge terror had disappeared from the sky while he was focusing on his stirrup bow's trigger mechanism. *How can something that big simply vanish?*

Something slammed into him from behind, and a wave of heat like a thousand forges passed overhead with an orange-reddish flash and a deafening rumble. Volund grunted when the ground slammed into his chest and something heavy landed on top of him. His stirrup bow went flying from his hands. It seemed to hover in the air for a long moment before the bowstave clacked on the ground, and then it landed on the trigger with a loud click. The unseen arrow must have sped straight toward King Orvandil, whose Dweorg-wrought shield made a loud ping. With fury in his eyes, Volund's father scowled his way before screaming a command. The king and his warriors hefted their spears and launched them at the enormity hurtling toward them.

Disgorging a roar that bent the air with its heat, Gorsarhad unleashed her flames. King Orvandil Dragonbane yelled another command. He and his ring of warriors crouched and formed a protective shell of overlapping shields, with the king's shield at the top, as the huge column of fire washed over them. The iron-shafted spears they had cast toward the eldest of dragons glowed red in the heat of her fire before clanging off her scales, but a couple of them lodged in her. The massive lingworm emitted an ear-splitting bellow as she sailed over the cocoon of shields, kicking up a gust that tugged at the smoke curling from them. The king and his warriors leaped up and tossed aside their smoldering shields before sprinting toward the river. Aloft, the mother of dragons banked and veered toward them.

Volund's stirrup bow lay several feet in front him. His quiver of steel-tipped arrows was still strapped to his side. "I've got to reload it." He reached toward his weapon, but Yrsa was still on top of him, all the heavier in her byrny.

"Edan-cursed fool! I just saved your stupid hide." Yrsa clenched her teeth as she growled at him and yanked his collar. "Who'll fend off the dragon while you sit on your arse tugging at that thing? Get up!"

Volund's sister tried to haul him up by his arm, so he stood. Though he loomed over her and was much stronger, her age and fierceness counted for more. Burn marks spotted her cloak from the dragon fire that had passed over them, and the helm covering her auburn braids was slightly askew. She pulled him back toward the falls, but Volund planted his feet.

"The stirrup bow."

"Leave it!"

An enormous shadow winked over them even as a loud gust plucked at their cloaks.

Yrsa gawked skyward with widened eyes. "Run!"

Volund heeded her without argument.

"Only three with the gift have wielded the song of origin of dragons in the last several hundred years." Queen Sequara held up three fingers of her right hand to emphasize her point. "The Prophet Aldmund, who founded the Way in Torrlond, was one, and we believe he learned the song here on Asdralad, thus preserving it when it fell out of our lore. Some three hundred years later came the Supreme Priest Bledla, who made weapons of the serpents of the air in the War of the Way." She drew in a long breath and exhaled. "And then came the one we call the Prophet of Edan, who ended both Bledla's control of the dragons and the costly war he began. No others have had sufficient strength in the gift to wield this song of origin since the days when our ancestors set about founding our kingdoms."

The queen sat alone on one of the stone benches surrounding the garden pool as she lectured. The rest of them occupied the other three benches, one on each side of the rectangular pool. Riall sat beside Kara, who sat beside Iwan, emphasizing, as usual, that among the queen's nine pupils, only they three were not from Asdralad. And of them, only Riall came from Caergilion. Kara and Iwan, both from

Adanon, were always mooning over each other of late, leaving Riall feeling ever more the oddity. She shook her head and dismissed her resentment and self-pity with a crooked grin. At least she had Belu, who lay beneath the bench with her hind quarters sticking out and her black tail wagging.

You want to play, little one, don't you?

In response, Belu's tail swept back and forth with such force that her little bottom waggled along with it. *Play!*

Riall had been inside the dog's mind so many times that she had no need to sing a song of origin to share thoughts with her. She and Belu could sense each other with almost no effort, which the others might have found unnatural – not to mention unnerving – had they known the extent of it, but it was something Riall did not think about much.

Belu's whole body began to wiggle with excitement.

Not yet, Belu. The queen hasn't finished her lesson.

The dog's little bottom and tail both went still, drawing a quiet smile from the girl.

"Riall."

Riall's head snapped up. Queen Sequara was gazing at her. So were all her fellow pupils.

"Are you speaking to that dog again?"

"No, my lady."

The queen's dark eyes continued to stare at her, and they narrowed as her frown deepened.

"I mean, yes. My lady. In a manner. I was just telling her to wait for your lesson to finish. She wants to . . . play."

With that final word, Belu's tail and rump began wagging again.

Peeking down, Kara giggled at the dog's antics, and the others looked and laughed as well. But Queen Sequara kept her blade-like gaze on Riall, who made a helpless shrug and tried to shrink into the stone bench.

But then, the queen rolled her eyes and sighed, which she followed with a quick glance at Belu and something that might have been a grin tugging at one corner of her mouth. "Well, perhaps such a fine day should be for playing. *If* you and Belu can bear to wait until after the lesson. We'll keep it short."

Riall gave the queen a shy, awkward smile. "Thank you, my lady."

The day *was* beautiful, like most days at the palace, which perched on a height overlooking Kiriath, Asdralad's chief city. Its garden was one of Riall's favorite places, though she preferred being alone in it. Beneath the pool's clear water, which reflected the clean blue sky, the colorful stones of a mosaic glistened. The flowers on the two rows of hibiscus trees lining the gravel path seemed a more vibrant red than usual under the sun's warm touch. The myriad flowers elsewhere in the palace garden drank in the light and trembled in the gentle breeze laden with the sea's salty scent. *Sun is life,* thought Riall as she sensed the energy quivering within the flowers.

"Queen Sequara, how is it that all three with such strength in the gift came from Torrlond? Why did we Andumae lack the power?" Arvhan's piping voice brought them back to what the queen had been teaching them. At ten years of age, he was the youngest of those training in sorcery on Asdralad, and his curiosity led him to ask more questions than all the others put together. This time, Riall was grateful to him for returning everyone's attention to the lesson.

The queen directed one of her sad smiles, the kind that never reached the eyes, at Arvhan. "Aldmund and Bledla were Torrlonders, true, but the Prophet of Edan came from the Mark. Of course, he was a special case. As for us, there were those among the Andumae who could wield the song of origin of dragons. Ogmos the Wise, for one. A few more in the early years, when our ancestors first came to Andumedan and fought the dragons."

"What made the Prophet special?" pursued Arvhan.

Queen Sequara paused a moment as she gazed back at the boy. "The source and nature of his power were . . . different. He was far stronger in the gift than perhaps anyone else has ever been."

"And he used it to defeat the Torrlonders and to tell everyone about Edan," recited the boy as if proud of his knowledge, though every person on the streets of Kiriath knew the same.

The queen nodded. "That's right. The Prophet stopped the war, and he is the reason the people of all the kingdoms in Andumedan worship Edan, save the Ilarchae in the Wildlands. After the war, we survivors beheld a changed world. The Prophet gave us something to believe in, a reason to keep going. Even here on Asdralad, worship of Anghara and Oruma, the Mother and Father, has dwindled. In the east, the other Andumaic kingdoms follow only Edan now. And the folk of the northern kingdoms have abandoned their old gods. It is a twist of fate that this is exactly what the Supreme Priest Bledla and the Torrlonders wanted: to make all worship Edan. While fighting them, the Prophet unintentionally brought about their goal, though he preached about an Edan far different from Bledla's. But that is a topic for another day. Perhaps we will discuss it at our next meeting." She put her index finger to her lips as she regarded her pupils. "Yes, I think you're all due for a history lesson."

A few of them squirmed, and though none dared voice the groans Riall supposed they were suppressing, Deepala let out a quiet sigh.

Sequara raised a questioning eyebrow and directed it at Deepala, who took a sudden interest in her lap. The queen cleared her throat and sat even straighter, the faint trace of her smile disappearing. "For today, you will learn the song of origin of dragons. Though you might not possess the strength to wield it, in light of the attacks on the mainland, it's best to pass along this knowledge."

"Forgive me, my queen." Yudhiran inclined his head in a slight bow, as graceful and proper as always. At seventeen, he was the eldest of the sorcerers and sorceresses in training, and he was also destined to be Queen Sequara's chosen heir. Riall did not envy him such a fate since, according to ancient Andumaic law, he would have no lover, no spouse, and no children as Asdralad's sorcerer-king – the ruler was wed to the kingdom. Not that Riall could ever hope to have a family either.

"Yes, Yudhiran?" Queen Sequara's tone always seemed to soften a bit with Yudhiran, perhaps because he was her favorite, but perhaps also because she understood more than any other how lonely he would be someday.

"The attacks have all been in the north. The dragons are unlikely to fly all the way here, are they not?"

The queen paused just a moment before nodding. "True. But unlikely is not impossible. The best defense is to prepare for anything, and you play a vital role in preserving our lore."

Another fluid bow, this one a touch deeper. "Yes, my queen."

Queen Sequara waited while she scanned them all, commanding their attention with her eyes alone. "Now, I will sing the song of origin. You will repeat it until it is part of you. Release yourselves into the realm of origins, and listen."

Most of the pupils frowned in concentration. Riall, however, slipped into the realm of origins without thought. The world grew more vibrant to her senses. Light brightened. Colors leaped toward her. Scents of sea and trees and flowers and soil and bodies swirled around her even as she perceived that her body no longer contained her, and never truly had. All was crisp and keen, vibrating with life. The emotions of all those nearby, including Belu's eagerness to be off and play, eddied around the edges of her awareness as if they all emanated from one organism. At the same time, she could have focused on any of them, plucked them from the infinite dance all around her. Just as easily, she could have allowed herself to expand beyond the palace, beyond the city of Kiriath, beyond even the island of Asdralad – to dissipate and float wherever she would, perhaps even to the strange and beautiful forest she often glimpsed in her dreams. Instead, she listened to Queen Sequara intoning a song of origin:

Urkhalion an dwinathon ni partholan varlas,
Valdarion ar hiraethon im rhegolan wirdas.
Gholgoniae sheerdalu di vorway maghona,
Dardhuniae sintalu ar donway bildhona.

Again and again the queen repeated it, but the song was already part of Riall, and she began to sense what lay at its heart. Therein coiled a vastness of cold cunning and angry heat, a will both ancient and sharp. A keen, reptilian intelligence dwelled within the words, a foreign yet strangely familiar sentience. Most of all, its immense strength threatened to overwhelm her with the certain knowledge that the flesh housing her was but a small and fleeting thing.

One last thing Riall knew as she hovered dispassionately in the realm of origins, realizing none of the others sensed the song of origin's heart. Though the queen had acknowledged that the others lacked the strength in the gift to wield this song of origin, she did not mention what they all likely suspected – what they all must have known and on some level feared. *They needn't worry. I will keep Asdralad safe*, thought the tiny part of her that was still Riall. In the serenity and timelessness of the realm of origins, she knew it: If ever she met a dragon, she could master it.

2

As if frozen in the act of writhing, the ancient northern trees – oak, ash, maple, beech, elm, fir, and more – were twisted and gnarled into grotesque, watchful presences, while dark, fathomless gaps lurked between their lichen-crusted trunks. It was a deep, dim, and musty place, thick with untold years of growth and decay. And yet, a few slivers of sunlight, shimmering as the soughing breeze shifted the branches, penetrated the lush canopy to spot the forest floor. It was the slanted, soft-gold light of dawn, layering a keen amber aura over the greens and browns. One ray gleamed jewel-like where a dew-laden spider web caught it. Elsewhere, the stirrings of creatures were tiny drops in the endless, patient ocean of sylvan stillness. For the abiding forest, each passing season was a breath in the endless cycles of birth and death.

Riall had come to love this place where she often wandered in her dreams since she could remember having dreams. It was a haven that always seemed to wait for her, her secret place that life could not stain, and, to preserve its purity, she had revealed it to no one. What was more, the forest shared the same clarity that marked true-dreams, fleeting glimpses of what was to come that sometimes appeared to those with the gift. Memories of the future, Queen Sequara called them. That clarity convinced her that this place was likely somewhere real, perhaps even in Andumedan. Perhaps in some lost land far over the Great Sea. However, unlike in the visions that were true-dreams, nothing ever happened during Riall's visits to the forest. Instead, much like she might float in the timeless realm of origins, she merely dwelled in the rich soil, the tangled roots, the rough boughs, and the veins in the sun-kissed, translucent leaves as the wind sighed in the swaying canopy.

Until now.

It seemed to Riall that this time was different. She had some purpose. The play of light shifted, and the shadows of trees morphed as if she were ghosting through the forest. Almost as if she were looking for something. Or someone.

Trees rushed by faster, and Riall winced a few times in anticipation of crashing into one. Instead, she misted through bark and trunk, each time experiencing the slow, patient yearning for light and moisture that would allow her to reach up and branch out. Her speed increased until everything became a shadow-filled blur, and she passed through so many trees that they ceased to be separate entities. As she expanded and became the forest, her sense of time and place on a scale a human mind could wrap around diminished to a point where it almost disappeared. And then, abruptly, she stopped.

She expected her breaths to come in heavy gasps after such a burst of speed. But, of course, here she had no lungs, no throbbing heart, no weary flesh. She was in a different part of the forest, a place where the trees were thinner and the light stronger. Without knowing whence came the knowledge, she sensed she was close to the edge, where the trees gave way to . . .

A harsh, guttural sound drew her attention. At first, after transforming into sundry trees and then a forest for what felt like an age, she puzzled over the sound. But after a moment, she realized it was speech. Human speech. Voices called out nearby, shouting words of a language she thought she recognized. The Northern Tongue. In the back of her mind, she took note of the observation: *So, somewhere in the north of Andumedan, then.* Because of the trees being so different from those on Asdralad, and because of the snow and ice that covered them in the winters, she had often suspected as much.

The next shout was louder than the others, and its higher pitch seemed to convey a warning. A tortured groan and several sharp snapping sounds preceded a huge crash that shook the forest and caused the branches of the nearby trees to quiver. Had it not been a dream, Riall would have recoiled in alarm. Instead, a strange serenity pervaded her.

More voices shouted. Perhaps it was the distance or the effect of the trees, or perhaps she was still struggling to return to a human perspective, but the voices seemed fuzzy and distorted, like the gruntings and snarls of animals. Something more powerful than curiosity drove her to approach them. This was the first time she had ever experienced any human presence in her forest dreams. Perhaps they could tell her more about this place.

Feeling as if she were hovering more than walking, she glided by several trees until the light grew. The reason for the increased brightness lay on the ground ahead of her: Dozens of felled trees littered the earth, leaving splintered stumps where once there was forest. Plants that had sheltered beneath the trees were bent, trampled, and withered. The score or so of pale-fleshed creatures who had wrought this were still swarming over the trees, making thunking and thudding noises as they hacked and lopped off limbs with their sharp steel.

Most of the broad-backed men were shirtless, and sweat ran down their pale skin as they swung their axes under the early morning sun. A strange, deep urge compelled Riall to draw nearer to a group of them.

In addition to their pinkish skin, some of the men had straw-colored hair and beards, while a few even had fiery red hair. They were a strange sight to Riall, who was lighter skinned than most on Asdralad but still had the copper tone and dark hair of the south. She came up behind one, a big man whose corded back muscles bulged and slithered under his skin as he raised his axe.

The man stopped mid-swing. If Riall had possessed lungs in this dream world, she would have held her breath. Could the man hear her approach?

Goosebumps blossomed over his flesh. For a moment, he stood

frozen, but then, axe still raised above his head, he turned around. With sweat running down his face into his blond beard, he stared straight at Riall with his bright blue eyes, which widened with terror and seemed unable even to blink. His mouth gaped open, but all that came out was a choked off cry. Expecting his axe to crash down on her, Riall almost winced, but the man just stood there with his lower lip quivering. In his eyes, helpless horror yielded to wondrous bliss, which in turn gave way to a strange dullness – all in the space of a breath. The axe dropped to the ground, and the man, bathed in a cold light that seemed to emanate from Riall, stepped toward her.

At that moment, one of the man's companions turned toward him, jerked backward, and screamed. More screams followed, and Riall sensed the men were all dropping everything to scramble away as fast as they could. Horses whinnied in the distance, and the shouts receded. But the first man, the one who had looked in her eyes, only stepped closer with his arms held out as if to embrace her. His sweat-slickened chest squirmed where his heart throbbed harder and faster, and the veins in his forehead and temples protruded. Ineffable ecstasy beamed from his eyes, whence tears tracked down his cheeks.

I'm killing him, she thought. *I don't want to. Stop. Stop it!* She tried to recoil from him, but she could not. She tried to wake up, but instead she opened up to embrace him. She was a rip in the world's façade, behind which lurked an imperturbable and all-enduring void. Vast darkness awaited him behind her, and the light pouring from her bleached away his features, drawing forth the energy that had animated him and created the illusion that his flesh had possessed a will of its own. *He returns through me.*

No. He's dying. Stop! I don't want to!

With only the barest outline of his form to distinguish him, the man stepped into the blazing light and joined it.

No!

Darkness.

Something warm and wet and soft slathered her face. Riall groaned.

Eager licks continued to wet her cheeks, accompanied by soft whimpers.

"Enough, Belu."

The little dog, whose black fur camouflaged her in the morning dimness of Riall's room, kept at it. *Scared?*

"Ugh. I'm alright." Riall raised her hands in front of her face, but Belu's tongue managed to slip between them. "Stop it. Your breath reeks. Have you been eating rotten fish from the kitchens again?"

Belu made a little high-pitched whine as if protesting her innocence, and she batted Riall's face with her paw. *Not eating. Hungry.*

"Fine. But your breath still stinks." Riall sighed and shook her head in an attempt to dispel the tatters of the dream still clinging to her mind. She reached over to scratch the soft fur of Belu's neck and the top of her head, her favorite spots. The small dog leaned into the scratches, and one of her hind feet pattered on the floor in appreciation. "Well, fish-breath, I suppose I owe you for waking me from that one."

Belu's head cocked to the side. *Food?*

"Yes, little one." Riall cracked a fond smile at her friend. "Food. Then our morning stroll to the beach." She rose from her sleeping pallet and shuffled toward the window to open the shutters, allowing the light and a sea breeze to spill in. Then, at her writing table, she splashed water from a basin on her face.

The water trickled down her cheeks, tickling them before dripping from her chin back into the basin. With her eyelids clenched shut, the dead man's widened blue eyes flashed before her once again. When she opened her eyes, Belu was sitting next to her feet, looking up at her with mingled concern and excitement animating her bright brown eyes. *Food! And walk!* Her pink tongue poked out of her mouth as she panted in expectation.

Riall returned the dog's gaze and sighed again. "Yes. Best to forget about that one. Right? Just a dream anyway."

$\maltese$ 3 $\maltese$

Khel leaned his back against a palm tree and enjoyed its shade as he took in the dockside aromas of spices and fried fish mingled with Halion Sound's ever present salty scent. The cries of seagulls punctuated the market crowd's usual din, but an unwonted nervous edge tinged many of the people's voices. Along with most everyone else near the docks, Khel watched a certain ship glide closer to Kiriath over the clear azure waters. The sailors had already reefed the large square sail, and soon they would slip their oars out of the water to ship them.

He did not need the exclamations behind him to know it for one of the famed Thjothic warships. The clinker-built vessel was about ninety feet long. The rudder near the stern on the starboard side grew visible as the ship skimmed closer to the docks. Just above the oar ports, on the outer side of the uppermost strakes, shield-battens held rows of round shields. Atop the vessel's prow, a carved dragon's head gazed forth with mouth agape in a soundless scream.

The ship was a matter of curiosity, and no small amount of fear, in Kiriath. Though King Orvandil Dragonbane had put a stop to the Thjoths' predations at sea, it had not been so long since the warriors of Grimrik had sailed from their fjords to raid for plunder and slaves.

Those a generation older than Khel would remember. But then came the War of the Way, and the Prophet of Edan changed everything. All of which meant that, instead of running for their lives, the citizens of Kiriath pointed and gawked at the northern ship. Khel's interest, however, went beyond mere curiosity.

He was fairly certain he knew the reason for the Thjoths' arrival in Asdralad. Like Ellond and northern parts of Torrlond and Sildharan, Grimrik had suffered much from the dragon attacks of late. No doubt they had come to beg aid from the famed sorceress-queen of Asdralad. *They'll find little enough help here.*

When the ship docked and the sailors threw out hawsers to the longshoremen, Khel moved out from the palm tree's shade. Passing by some of the dockside vendor carts, he noticed one of the fruitmongers directing a stern frown his way. Khel gave the man a toothy smile. "Good day to you, Udil."

Udil's scowl deepened. "Piss off. And don't come near my cart, bastard boy."

Khel smiled harder. "Fear not for your wares, old man. No one cares for such moldy, wrinkly figs." He grabbed his crotch and gave it a conspicuous yank, provoking a chuckle from some of the other mongers.

Udil was yelling something about leaving honest folk to do their business, but Khel had already turned his back on the man and was striding toward the Thjothic warship. Tall, mailed warriors with the pale skin of the north clinked as they descended a plank onto the dock, and they spoke their strange, harsh language in loud voices. Compared to the colorful, long silks people favored in Asdralad, their garments were crude: wool cloaks, drab tunics over byrnies, sturdy helms with nose guards, rough breeches, heavy boots. Every one of them wore a sword or an axe hanging from a thick leather belt. The daggers Khel kept at his side seemed table ornaments in comparison.

The stories of the Thjoths' height were no exaggeration. At sixteen years of age, Khel was one of the tallest men in Kiriath, but he would not have been even average among the men of Grimrik. *Perhaps they send only the tallest ones abroad to impress everyone.*

But it was not the Thjothic men who drew his gaze. In their midst were three figures of special interest. One was much shorter than the rest, likely just under five feet, though broad-shouldered enough and wearing a full white beard. Though Khel had never seen one before, he supposed the fellow to be one of the famed Dweorgs that King Orvandil had allowed to return to Grimrik. Those Dweorgs were the reason the Thjoths were the best armed warriors of any kingdom in Andumedan.

Khel's interest in the second individual sprang from an altogether different source. She was an auburn haired woman dressed much like the male Thjoths. While he could not understand Thjothic, it seemed to him from her frown and the authority in her voice that this striking woman was the one giving the orders. The men hearkened to her and moved where she pointed. It was not hard for him to keep his eyes on her as he approached the group and deliberately bumped into the third person of interest, who was standing apart from the rest.

The blond boy whipped his head around, and intense blue eyes stared at Khel. He reckoned he *might* have about two years on the Thjoth, though that was a rough guess since the broad-shouldered lad was several inches taller than he was and more than a few pounds heavier. Smelling of leather, oil, and the sweaty body odor one would expect after a voyage, the lad appeared by his slightly finer garb – at least by barbaric standards – to be a young man of importance among the Thjoths.

Khel took his hands off the boy's chest and shoulder as he pretended to regain his balance. "A thousand pardons," he said in the Northern Tongue. "Quite clumsy of me."

The lad stared at him for so long that Khel began to wonder if he was some sort of idiot, or if he was about to introduce his sword's edge to Khel's neck. *Perhaps he doesn't speak the Northern Tongue.*

"No matter." The Thjoth gave the barest nod to dismiss the matter. His voice was beginning to show signs of a man's huskiness.

Khel gave a deeper nod, almost a bow. "Very gracious of you. In return, may I do you some small service? Since you appear a stranger to our city, perhaps you're in need of directions?"

Again the awkward pause with the hard stare, as if the boy were deciding whether he might slay Khel after all. "We're here to see

Queen Sequara." He spoke the Northern Tongue well enough, but his Thjothic accent was evident even to Khel, who was no native speaker of Andumedan's most common language of trade.

"Ah. Then I fear I am of little use. The queen is not hard to find. Just follow the main thoroughfare through the city and then climb the stairs." He pointed up at the distant palace on the clifftop overlooking Kiriath. Sunlight gleamed off the iridescent stone tiles of its roof and dome, far above the rest of city's buildings of tan stone with red terra-cotta roof tiles and the occasional white dome.

The boy's eyes followed the direction of Khel's finger, and then he turned back to Khel and nodded.

"Volund!" The woman with the braided auburn hair was glaring at the lad, who turned toward her as she shouted in Thjothic at him.

The boy turned back to Khel and gave another curt nod. "Thank you." He meant it as a polite dismissal, and he shifted as if to leave.

Khel held up a palm. "A moment, please. Are you *Volund*, son of King Orvandil Dragonbane?" His tone suggested he had not suspected as much all along.

The boy frowned and shuffled a bit as if he were uncomfortable. "I am. I must go."

"Of course, my lord." Khel bowed and presented Volund with his most gracious smile. "Has the great man come as well, then?"

Confusion took over Volund's frown as his eyes narrowed.

"Your father." Khel prompted him with a nod.

"No." Volund shook his head and lurched away to fall in with the auburn haired woman and a small group of the Thjoths as they plunged into the city, where folk gave them a wide berth. They soon disappeared into the throng around the dockside market.

Khel shrugged. "Quite the conversationalist." From his cloak he took out and examined the folded parchment he had lifted from an inside pocket of Volund's cloak when he bumped into him. "I wonder if he'll be needing this."

❧ 4 ❧

From Queen Sequara's attempt at a gentle smile – so unlike the formidable sorceress's wonted stoic frown – Riall sensed something was amiss.

"Thank you for coming, Riall. Please sit." Her smile faltering a bit, the queen patted the stone bench to indicate Riall should take a place beside her, on the other side of the pool.

Something's very wrong. Riall stepped toward the bench and eased down onto it, all the while keeping her eyes locked on the sorceress-queen. Even the palace garden's beauty beneath yet another sunny sky did not lessen the foreboding chill tingling under her skin. She blinked at Queen Sequara and waited.

The queen seemed about to speak, but then she sighed and swallowed before glancing down at her hands lying on her lap. Riall too peeked at the woman's hands, which turned upward and opened for a moment to reveal identical lines clear across each palm – dark, straight scars that, she supposed, the woman had acquired during the War of the Way. A hundred times Riall had been on the verge of asking Queen Sequara how she earned those scars, and each time the question had died in her throat.

She watched one of those scarred hands – a couple shades darker than Riall's, being the rich bronze tone found on Asdralad – reach out to grasp her own. It was warm and comforting. At the same time, the gesture frightened her more than anything. They broke their gazes from the queen's hand at the same time and looked each other in the eyes. A dozen small, dim scars marked the beautiful queen's face as well. Riall had always thought they looked like burns, but she had never dared to inquire about them either. As always, the woman's dark brown eyes seemed to weigh Riall, and more silver strands streaked her raven-colored hair than the girl recalled seeing before. Then again, it was rare for her to be this close to the queen, and much rarer for the woman to touch her.

"Riall." Queen Sequara seemed to be summoning the will to speak. She sighed again, and Riall said nothing.

"We've had a letter from Caergilion. I'm so sorry . . . It's Seren. She's dying." The queen's hand squeezed a bit tighter, but Riall had gone numb all over as soon as the words were out.

It was a long while before Riall could find her own words. "But . . . That's not possible. Her last letter said nothing of . . ."

"It's a wasting illness. It took hold of her many weeks ago, perhaps even months. For her own reasons, she chose to tell us only when she drew close to death."

"Why would she hide this from *me?*" Riall shook her head, willing it to be untrue. But her eyes betrayed her, going blurry with tears that spilled onto her cheeks, and her throat tightened so that nothing would come out. At once, an animal sound, half moan and half sob, forced its way from her mouth, and she folded in on herself as the queen embraced her. Racking sobs shook her. With the dam broken, her tears flowed freely, spilling and soaking into Queen Sequara's blue silk dress.

Even as she wept, a resolution formed within Riall. This resolution helped her to rein in her wild grief just enough to begin to suppress her tears. Her shaking diminished into trembling, which subsided at length. Once the storm abated, she sniffled a few times and wiped the snot from her nose with her sleeve. She separated herself from the queen, who released her, and then she set her jaw as she gazed at her mentor. "I must go to her."

A flash of pity escaped before the queen hardened her countenance. "I've already asked Yudhiran to travel to Caergilion and see what can be done. He'll depart on the morrow. He's an excellent healer."

"I'm better."

"You know you cannot go."

"What if he lacks the strength? What if just a little more power is all that's needed to save her? What if she dies because . . ."

"Riall . . ."

"Or *you* could go." Riall's hands balled into hard fists until her knuckles whitened, and she could not keep the anger from her trembling voice. "You're the most skilled healer there is. She's your friend too, after all. *Isn't* she?"

Queen Sequara drew herself up and gazed at Riall, who feared she had overstepped her bounds. But the queen sighed and gave the girl one of those smiles weighed down with all the sorrow of her past. "You know she is. That's why I'm sending Yudhiran."

"But you . . ."

"I must remain here."

Riall swallowed and wet her lips with her tongue, all the while looking straight at the queen. "To be my jailer."

Silence inserted itself between them, and when the queen reached out, Riall shifted backward. Sequara let her hand fall. "Is that what you think? My dear girl . . ."

"I'm not a girl anymore."

The sorceress-queen crossed her arms before her, but she appeared more composed than angry. "Very well. Give me a woman's answer, then. Why must you remain here on Asdralad? And why must *I* stay with you?"

"Because . . ." Riall's anguish gave way to fury at the unfairness of it all. Her long banishment from her homeland, of which only fragmented memories remained, her loneliness and isolation. She had done nothing to earn it other than to be born the way she was. And the only person who had ever truly loved her was dying far away.

So much power lay within her, waiting to leap out. It seemed absurd not to use it. She could save Seren. She *would.* That power beckoned to her, her vast strength in the gift, pounding on the crumbling edifice of her years of restraint. Swirling like an undeniable maelstrom, it mounted higher and higher. She was *strong,* much stronger even than Queen Sequara, who at once appeared smaller next to her. She did not need to remain a prisoner on Asdralad. The notion was intolerable, even unjust. With such might in the gift, she could go whither she would, and no one could stop her.

All she needed to do was reach forth. She did not even need to sing a song of origin. She could pluck the energy from the woman before her and grant her everlasting peace from the many trials she had endured. It would be a simple matter and even a mercy. The injustice of her captivity must end. It would end, and she would save *everyone* from their grief.

Just as she opened her mouth to rebuke the fleeting mortal before her, an image flashed within her. It was the northern man she had slain in her dream, his blue eyes wide in ecstasy. Riall's jaw worked for a moment, and whatever words were about to emerge from her mouth dissolved. Queen Sequara was staring at her.

Riall looked down at her lap, and her chest heaved as she suppressed her heavy breaths. "I'm sorry, my lady. I know why. It's just that . . . Seren is the closest thing I ever had to a mother. I wasn't thinking. I'm sorry." She glanced up at the queen, whose eyes had widened. Had the woman sensed the surge of power in Riall, how close she had been to unleashing it? Riall trembled at the thought of what she might have wrought. She could never forgive herself for harming this woman who had done so much for her, who had sheltered her and taught her what mastery of the gift she possessed.

Queen Sequara reached out to brush a lock of Riall's hair from her face and tuck it behind her ear. Was her hand trembling? "No. It is I who am sorry. Yudhiran will do what can be done for Seren." She did not say the words aloud, but Riall saw them in her eyes. *If she's still alive when he arrives.*

Riall peered down and nodded, but her head snapped up again at the sound of footsteps approaching on one of the garden's gravel paths.

"I believe I left instructions that we should not be disturbed," said the queen in her most formal Andumaic.

Taria, one of the household servants clad in a white robe, emerged from behind a rose bush and bowed low. "My apologies, my queen, but I'm instructed to tell you that envoys from Grimrik have arrived, and they are most eager to speak with you."

❈ 5 ❈

Volund scratched at the elusive itch that kept crawling all over the back of his neck. Beneath his cloak, kirtle, leather-lined byrny, and undershirt, sweat ran down his back. Not for the first time, he envied the Asdralae their strange, colorful garb, which suited the warm clime. Had circumstances been different, he would have asked someone about the process of making the silk, but he knew Yrsa would scold and mock him for such a question. They were here for different reasons.

When the white-robed servant reappeared, bowed, and beckoned for them to follow her, he swallowed and fell in behind his sister and Gnorn. The old Dweorg turned back and gave him a reassuring smile and a wink, deepening the web of wrinkles around his brown eyes. Yrsa, who had been cursing under her breath the whole time they were waiting, marched after the servant without a backward glance.

They emerged from the palace back beneath the hot sun to walk on a gravel path in the midst of an abundance of flowers, the like of which Volund had never before seen. The servant led them between two rows of trees brimming with red flowers to a pool in the garden's center. Sitting at the far end of the pool on a stone bench were two people, a woman and a girl. Volund did not need to guess which was Queen Sequara.

Setting his hands on his legs for balance, Gnorn grunted and eased down onto his knees, almost tottering over in the process. Volund knelt as well, and Yrsa followed a moment later. The old Dweorg cleared his throat and spoke in the Northern Tongue. "Your Majesty, thank you for granting us this audience."

Queen Sequara stood up from the bench and answered in the same language. "Rise, honored guests."

Volund was up in a moment, and, seeing Gnorn struggle, he offered a hand to his friend and allowed the Dweorg to lean on him as he stood, nearly staggering himself under the weight. Though he had witnessed it many times, the Dweorg's solidity always surprised him. Having worked countless hours at the forge with Gnorn, he well knew what strength lay in those arms, hard and knotted like fat tree branches.

The Dweorg stood straight and smiled up at Volund. "Thank you, lad. The knees aren't quite so sturdy as they used to be."

Queen Sequara approached. She was every bit as beautiful as the tales said, and the scars on her face rendered her more intimidating. She closed in on Gnorn and embraced him. "It's good to see you, old friend."

From stories Gnorn had told, Volund knew the Queen of Asdralad had fought alongside his father and the Dweorg during the War of the Way, but her gesture still surprised him.

Gnorn chuckled as he returned the embrace. "'Old' I am. Yes. So many years have passed since last we met, my good queen. But your friend I remain, and always will."

The queen placed her hands on the Dweorg's shoulders and smiled down at him. "I'll never doubt it, Gnorn. Had I known you were coming, I would have had an escort awaiting you at the docks." She glanced at Yrsa and then at Volund. "But you have brought friends with you. First, introductions, and then, something to refresh you before you rest. You must be weary after your journey."

Gnorn shook his head. "We've little time for rest, I fear."

Yrsa stepped forward. "Queen Sequara, our errand is urgent."

Gnorn cleared his throat and gestured toward Volund's sister. "My queen, this is Yrsa, daughter of Queen Osynia of Grimrik."

The queen beheld Yrsa and seemed to weigh her. For a moment, Yrsa locked eyes with the woman, but then she glanced down. Even Volund's sister, who relished sparring with men twice her size and was several inches taller than the older woman, seemed to shrink under Sequara's gaze.

As if unaware of the power of her presence, the sorceress-queen smiled gently at Yrsa. "I met your father, King Vols. He was a good king."

Yrsa bowed her head. "Thank you, my lady. He was a good man too. But King Orvandil has been just as much a father to me."

"I've no doubt he has." Queen Sequara turned to Volund, and a rush of warmth spread through his cheeks as they flushed. He blinked at her while she smiled at him. "And, unless I miss my guess, you must be Volund, son of King Orvandil and Queen Osynia."

"I . . . I . . ." Volund remembered to bow as he felt his cheeks go a shade redder. "Yes, your Majesty."

"You look so like your father. I would hear news of him. But first, your errand. Tell me why you've journeyed so far to Asdralad and honored us with this visit."

Gnorn released a long sigh. "In truth, my queen, King Orvandil sent us with two purposes. The first is to keep these two out of mischief for at least a short while." He pointed with his fat thumb at Yrsa, who glared down at him, and then at Volund, whose face went red all over again. "The second is to ask for your counsel and any help you can offer."

The sorceress-queen nodded. "Go on."

The Dweorg tugged his beard. "You're aware of Gorsarhad's attacks in Grimrik?"

"And in Ellond, Torrlond, and Sildharan. Yes, we've had tidings of them, and I am sorry to hear of your people's suffering."

Gnorn looked down for a moment. "She razed Valfoss. We lost our homes. But, thank the ancestors and Edan, only a few lost their lives. The attacks on the other kingdoms forewarned us, and King Orvandil ordered most folk away from the town. The beast has been assailing populated areas. I've seen nothing like it since the war."

Queen Sequara nodded. "Back then the Supreme Priest Bledla wielded dragons as weapons. Elsewise, for more than a thousand years, they have been solitary creatures that stay far from men. However, this time, I do not believe it is possible that someone with the gift could have mastered Gorsarhad."

Gnorn shook his head. "I watched the attack on Valfoss from the falls. She has some *purpose*, I deem, though what it is I cannot say."

The queen's eyes narrowed in concentration, as if she were bringing to mind some powerful memory. "Gorsarhad. The ancient dragon the Prophet of Edan used to fight Bledla."

"Yes, the very same, we believe. One such as I cannot know a dragon's mind, but they are cunning. When the Prophet wielded Gorsarhad, perhaps she *learned* what dragons can do to us when they are angry and determined. Perhaps it is vengeance for how she and the others of her kind were used. Why now, though? Some sixteen years have passed since the war. Whatever it might be, she's of a mind to destroy."

"Such a thing is possible. According to our lore, when we Andumae first came to these lands and struggled against the dragons, they fought much as men do: wrathfully and vengeance-blinded."

"We Dweorgs tell such tales as well, from before the coming of your people."

The queen took a deep breath and released it as a sigh. "You said there was loss of life. Tell me what happened."

Gnorn frowned. "King Orvandil would not abandon Valfoss without a fight. He tried the trick with the iron-shafted spear he used back during the war, when he earned the name 'Dragonbane'."

"And?"

Gnorn's cheeks puffed out, and he blew the air out in a sigh. "Didn't work this time. Might be he scratched old Gorsarhad's hide a bit. Made her angry, for certain."

"How many of your folk died?"

"A score of warriors. Good men. And these two almost joined them." Gnorn used his thumb again to indicate Yrsa and Volund.

Volund winced and swallowed down a surge of nausea as the stench of burnt flesh and hair resurfaced in his memory.

Yrsa scowled at Volund, who licked his lips and swallowed before he mustered the courage to speak while staring at the ground. "It was my fault. Yrsa was protecting me."

Gnorn grunted. "True enough. But then there's the *other* matter."

Queen Sequara raised an eyebrow. "The other matter? Did the dragon attack elsewhere?"

"Two villages burnt to the ground. Their folk hid. Save for some sheep and cows, none perished." Gnorn sighed again and shook his head. "But I speak of another thing. The pain is still fresh, so forgive me if I falter in telling of it."

Volund glanced at his sister. The cords of Yrsa's jaw muscles stood out as she ground her teeth.

The Dweorg cleared his throat. "After Gorsarhad destroyed Valfoss, the Thjoths and we few Dweorgs scattered to make ourselves less tempting targets. Unfortunately, while this thwarted the beast's large-scale attacks, it made us easier prey for other predators."

"What sort?"

"The worst. The sort that walks on two legs."

"The Ilarchae." Yrsa almost spat the word. "They sailed from the Wildlands and attacked in the dragon's wake. Like the cowards they are." Her knuckles whitened on the hilt of the sword she wore at her hip. "They took Sigra. They took our *sister*."

At Queen Sequara's puzzled frown, Gnorn explained, "The Ilarchae tribe called the Raven Eyes raided and came upon one of our small parties as we moved for shelter. They killed many, and they took a few hostages. One was Queen Osynia's eldest daughter, Sigra. Their war-leader, Bolverk, has made an offer of exchange to return Sigra and the others."

"And what does he demand for the hostages' freedom?"

Gnorn tugged at his beard and frowned. "The Ilarchae want Dweorg-wrought blades. They understand the advantage such weapons would gain them. And they want Dweorgs as slaves to forge them and share the secret of their making. We would never reveal our lore, but a few of us offered to go serve the Raven Eyes. King Orvandil forbade us."

"It's a hard choice." Queen Sequara frowned. "But Orvandil is wise not to give the Ilarchae what they want every time they raid. It would bring them back for more sooner rather than later."

"*I'll* give them a Dweorg-wrought blade." Yrsa's hand gripped her sword's hilt, and Volund feared she might draw the weapon then and there.

The Dweorg cleared his throat again. "No one blames you, lass, for your anger. We all want your sister back alive. But, as the king said, we will strike when the time for deeds is ripe." He looked at Queen Sequara. "Yrsa and a small band of followers set out for the Wildlands without the king's knowledge. Fortunately, before they could deliver themselves to the Ilarchae as additional hostages, he learned of their plans and found them just as they were about to set sail. That is why *she* is helping me on this particular errand."

Queen Sequara looked at Yrsa. "If I had a sister in such peril, I'm sure I would feel the same urgency." Though her face showed little emotion, compassion tinged her voice.

For this remark the queen earned a grudging nod from Yrsa, whose frown softened a little.

The sorceress-queen nodded back to her before turning her gaze again to Gnorn. "These are ill tidings, and I sorrow to learn of them. But tell me why King Orvandil sent you to me."

Gnorn glanced down for a moment before looking Queen Sequara in the eye. "The Ilarchae we will handle on our own. But it's no easy task with the dragon on the prowl. It's difficult to gather an army, which we must do to teach the Ilarchae to stay in the Wildlands."

The queen gave the Dweorg a slow nod, but she said nothing.

Gnorn cleared his throat. "As you recall, some with the gift have wielded dragons in the recent past, and . . ."

"Gnorn." The sorceress-queen shook her head, and she gazed at the Dweorg with something in her eyes that Volund could think of only as haunted sorrow. "You well know what happened during the war. I tried. And I failed. I could not wield the dragons with the song of origin."

The Dweorg gazed back at the queen with a carefully blank but tense expression, making Volund wonder anew what memories the two shared. "I have not forgotten what happened. But the king . . . Orvandil. He thought perhaps you of all people might know best if someone . . ."

Queen Sequara went stiff, and her eyes widened for a moment. "No. There is no one who can do this. Those who could are gone."

Gnorn stood still for a moment, and then he sighed before nodding. "We thought as much. But still, the king wanted to be sure." He gave a sad smile. "And at least we've kept these two from mischief for a while."

"Then we'd best leave." The strain in Yrsa's voice more than hinted at her impatience, and even anger. "As soon as may be."

"It grieves me that I cannot help you. And I understand your haste." The sorceress-queen shifted her gaze to Gnorn and then Volund before returning it to Yrsa. "But please stay at least to sup. You are most welcome to remain for the night as well, or as long as you need."

"The lass is right. We must be heading back for Grimrik." Gnorn patted his stomach. "But a decent meal on land before we set out would be welcome. Especially for those of us with no sea legs."

"Good." The queen nodded. "You have five men waiting within the palace, I'm told. They too are welcome. The meal will be ready shortly. In the meantime, I will arrange for baths and rooms for you to rest in." She turned back to the girl sitting on the bench, whom Volund had all but forgotten. While still a southerner, she appeared fairer than most Asdralae, and she seemed close to Volund's age, though often southerners looked younger than their years. "Riall, please tell the cooks to ready a meal for our eight guests. I will be joining them."

The girl rose from the bench and nodded. "Yes, my lady," she answered in the Northern Tongue. As she passed by on her way into the palace, she seemed not to notice Gnorn tugging at his beard while watching her with widened eyes, leaving Volund to wonder what the Dweorg saw.

$\maltese$ 6 $\maltese$

Sucking in a deep breath, Volund winced and eased into the copper tub of steaming water with his hands clenching the rim. His flesh reddened as the hot water welcomed it and rose around him with a tickling burn somewhere near the edge between pleasant and painful. He sank further down until only his head remained unsubmerged. The long breath leaked out of his lungs, and his limbs floated as if attached to nothing. Aches he had not even been aware of seeped out of his muscles, and weeks of tension seemed to dissipate. Despite all the fears weighing on him, Volund allowed himself a small smile as his eyelids fluttered closed.

The door to his room flew open and banged on the wall, and Volund's eyes popped back open as wide as they could go as the water sloshed with his startled movement.

"Shit!" The girl who had burst in closed the door with exaggerated care, turned around, and, facing Volund, put a finger to her lips. "Shh-hh," she hissed, as if the din had not been of her making. It was the girl from the garden.

Volund gawked at her, unable to speak even if he could think of something to say.

"I'm sorry," she said in the Northern Tongue. "This was the only way I could speak to you without anyone knowing." Seeming to notice his unclothed state belatedly, she covered her eyes with one hand. "Sorry."

Volund sat up a bit in the tub and spotted a small black dog standing next to the girl, its little pink tongue poking out of its mouth as it stared at him. "What . . . What are you doing here?"

The girl kept her hand over her eyes. "I heard what you said in the garden. I'm going to help you. I can rid Grimrik of the dragon. And I'll get your sister back from the Ilarchae too if I can."

"What?"

The girl frowned in irritation, and Volund thought she might have peeked for a moment through a gap in her fingers. "There's little time. I can help. But we mustn't tell anyone. We've got to leave without Queen Sequara knowing."

"But . . . Who are you?"

The girl took a deep breath. "I'm Riall. I know you must have many questions, but there isn't time. The queen can't know we're leaving. She wouldn't . . . want me to go. And I think your Dweorg friend would tell her if he knew. And your sister scares me."

Volund shrugged, stirring the water a little. "Me too. But if we don't tell anyone, how will we leave?"

"I know a way out of the palace from here. We can make it unseen into Kiriath. Once there, we buy passage on a ship. I've a little silver. It should be enough, I think."

Volund shook his head. "Why?"

"*Because* . . ." The girl clenched her fists at the sides of her head and glared at Volund before covering her eyes with one hand again and speaking in a quieter voice. "Because I *want* to help. And there's somewhere along the way I need to stop first. That's my condition. But it would be best if you were to conduct me to Grimrik. I haven't . . . traveled much. Besides, with you accompanying me, people there will take me seriously."

"I'm not sure *I* take you seriously."

The girl's hands dropped to her sides, and her eyes opened to gaze at Volund with a stare that lacked emotion yet chilled him beyond description. At once, the air crackled around her while jagged, bright blue currents of energy buzzed and sparked to life, snaking and writhing all around her body and birthing eerie shadows that cloaked the room. The energy winked out a moment later, leaving a red after-image dancing before Volund's eyes.

Despite the hot bath, goosebumps covered his flesh. His mouth hung open as he gawped wide-eyed, and his arms drooped at his sides, one outside the tub. "Wizard's fire," he gasped in a choked whisper.

"We call it *almakhti* here." The girl's stern expression did not change. "Few have enough strength in the gift to summon it. I may be the only one who doesn't even need a song of origin to do it. I am stronger in the gift than Queen Sequara, or anyone else in Andumedan. Much stronger. I *can* wield that dragon. And I will."

Still slack-jawed and staring, Volund realized something soft and slimy was slopping against his dripping hand. He turned to see the dog licking him.

"You're wet," explained the girl. "Probably salty too." She gave a small smile and a quick giggle. "And she likes you." The smile disappeared. "Well? Will you take me to Grimrik?"

❧ 7 ☙

Riall slumped on the railing of one of Kiriath's docks with her head in her hands. Belu sat beneath her, wagging her tail and looking up at her with eyes eager to comfort and to play, as if that would solve the world's problems. *Play?*

The girl let out a long sigh. "I thought I had enough silver." One ship's captain had actually laughed at her and walked away without another word when she showed him how much she had for their passage to Grimrik. It was not enough even for Caergilion. "I'm an idiot." Another sigh. "It's just that I've never had to pay for anything up in the palace."

"Might be we should head back there." Volund's shadow loomed over her as he stood nearby. His voice was kind, but she suspected he more than half believed she was mad. The usual market crowd was milling around them as mongers at their carts competed with their shouts over whose wares were freshest and cheapest.

Riall shook her head. "No. We've got to find a way to Grimrik. It's too important. And I need to reach Caergilion as soon as may be."

"My shipmates will see me soon. They'll tell Yrsa." They had narrowly avoided several Thjoths at another dock.

"Damn. We're losing time. It won't be long before someone in the palace notices we're missing. There *must* be a way."

"Pardon me."

Riall's head jerked up, and Volund spun around. A slender young man had appeared out of nowhere next to them, or he had snuck up on them without making a sound. He was clad in expensive silks and a black cloak. Like Riall, he was fairer than most Asdralae, with his dark, curly hair showing hints of brown, and his jaunty smile said he knew something that no one else did.

He had spoken in the Northern Tongue. Riall wondered for a moment if he might be Caergilese, like her. But first she needed to find out how much of their conversation he had heard. "How long have you been standing there?"

Ignoring her, the newcomer flourished a parchment and held it out to Volund. "You dropped this earlier."

Volund responded with a puzzled frown, and then he felt inside his cloak. "My design for a small winch." He reached in haste for the parchment and unfolded it before gazing at it as if to make sure it was intact.

"A small wench?" The boy winked at Riall. "I prefer mine tall."

Volund did not look up from his parchment. "Not a wench. A winch. For my stirrup bow."

The young man raised his eyebrows at Riall as if they were sharing a jest and shrugged before his smile returned.

Riall looked at Volund and pointed at the newcomer with her thumb. "Do you know him?"

Volund finally glanced up from his parchment, which he tucked into his cloak. He turned to the boy with narrowed eyes, not bothering to hide his suspicion. "We ran into each other. He gave us directions."

Riall frowned at the young man. "Well, it sounds like you've been quite helpful. Unfortunately, we're unable to give you proper thanks since we have urgent business."

Instead of taking the signal to say his goodbyes, the young man stood there gazing at the two of them with his smile, which was becoming more irritating. "I couldn't help but overhear a bit of your conversation. Did you say you're seeking passage to Grimrik?"

Riall's heart squirmed in her chest. If Queen Sequara should find out where she was, everything would be ruined. She pointed a finger at the newcomer's chest. "Listen, I don't know who you are . . ."

The young man grasped her hand as if she had proffered it like a noblewoman, and then he kissed it. "My name is Khel. My mother is well known in the palace. Perhaps you've heard of her."

Riall blinked at him. How did he know she had come from the palace?

The boy continued as if unaware of Riall's rising anxiety. "She's a merchant and tavern owner here in Kiriath. Dalriana is her name. You must know *her*." For some reason, he looked at Volund when he said his mother's name, but then he turned back to Riall.

She saw no point in pretending. "Yes. I've heard of her. She's the one who loaned Queen Sequara all that silver to rebuild Kiriath after the war."

Khel's smile widened. "The very same."

Riall gritted her teeth together. Every passing moment increased the risk of their discovery. "What do you want?"

"I want to help you." The young man winked again at Riall, who suppressed the urge to punch him or worse. "You want to go to Grimrik. As it happens, I've a fancy to travel. You need a ship. As it happens, my mother owns several. I'm sure she wouldn't mind if I used a small one for the three of us. You also have need of silver." He shook the fat purse at his hip, and it jingled. "As it happens, I have plenty."

"And what do you get by helping us?"

"Why, the pleasure of your fascinating company, of course."

Riall's eyes narrowed as she glared at him. "Why do you want to go to Grimrik?"

"My reasons are my own."

"There's a dragon there."

"So I've heard."

"You know who we are?"

"Of course. He is Volund, son of Orvandil Dragonbane, king of Grimrik. And *you* are the freak they keep locked up in the palace."

Riall's mouth quirked into a half smile at his description of her. "You've been following us, haven't you?"

"Yes."

Volund looked at Riall and shook his head. "I don't trust him."

Riall kept her gaze on Khel. "I don't either. But he knows who I am. I'm the *dangerous* freak they keep locked up in the palace. And that means he should know I can kill him with less than a thought if he betrays us. Better to have him with us, anyway, since he knows too much." She held out her hand to Khel. "Very well. Let's see this ship of yours."

His grin as wide as ever, Khel grasped her hand and shook it.

❦   8   ❦

"Are you sure we'll need so much?" For the hundredth time, Riall glanced all around the market crowd to make sure no one from the palace had spotted her.

Khel pivoted around and raised a skeptical eyebrow. "You two were not even prepared for an afternoon stroll, let alone a voyage of the sort we're undertaking. It's a good thing you fell in with me." He turned toward Volund and slipped the straps of the water skins he had just bought around the young Thjoth's shoulder. Several packets of food and bags of gear already weighed down the lad, who protested only with a glare at Khel. In addition, at a weaponsmith's shop, Khel had procured a slender Asdralae curved sword, which he wore at his hip in a scabbard. He had pronounced it passable steel, though not the equal of Volund's heavier Dweorg-wrought blade.

Oblivious of Volund's glare, Khel loaded Riall with the last two water skins and smiled at her. "Now, some salted fish, and we'll be on our way." He led them toward one of the carts near the docks.

As they approached, Riall could not help but notice the fishmonger scowling at Khel. He was not the first dockside merchant to direct sullen looks toward the young man. "What do you want, you thieving whoreson bastard? Stay away from my cart."

In response, Khel reached into his purse and drew out a silver piece, which he proffered to the fishmonger. "We require two casks of salted fish. This will more than cover it. Be quick about it, and you may keep your coppers."

The fishmonger glared at the coin before snatching it. Without a word, he hoisted a cask from the back of his cart and handed it to Khel, who tucked it under one arm. Once he repeated the process, Khel took the second cask under his other arm and put on a teeth-baring smile. "Pleasure doing business with you."

The fishmonger's scowl did not change, and he kept his hard eyes on Khel. "I'm watching you, bastard."

Sketching a bow and grinning in a way that made a mockery of it, Khel headed for the docks without a word in reply.

Wondering what he had done to earn such infamy among the dock-side merchants and if it ought to concern her, Riall followed with Belu at her side. At this point, she appeared to have no better option. What mattered most was that she reach Seren. She glanced behind her to check on Volund, who peeked over the packages of food and gear he lugged. Without speaking a word, Riall grabbed two leather bags from the top of his pile, and he nodded his thanks.

Khel led them to a dock where a small, one-masted fishing boat was tied up and tossed the two casks of salted fish into it. Even to Riall's unpracticed eye, the boat appeared old and worn, almost rotten in places, with obvious recent repairs here and there. A set of oars lay at the bottom along with ropes and nets, and the square sail was furled and tied up to the yard.

His eyes wide, Volund stared at the vessel. "I suppose your mother couldn't spare one of her better ones?"

Khel grabbed a packet from the Thjoth's arms and threw it aboard. "Well, it's not one of her fine merchant ships. But we need something small enough for the three of us to handle, don't we? She'll ride the Great Sea like a dolphin, trust me. Besides, you Thjoths can sail anything, they say." He peeled the straps of the water skins off Volund's shoulders and flung them in the boat.

Volund kept staring at the boat. "Anything that doesn't sink."

Khel slapped Volund's shoulder. "That's the spirit." He turned to Riall and took her two bags, which he lobbed into the boat.

Throwing in the water skins, Riall took a deep breath. Her stomach was roiling. She tried to ignore it, and she wiped her sweaty palms on the long tunic she wore over her baggy trousers. It had been many years since she had come to live on Asdralad, and in that time she had never left the island. In truth, she had hardly been outside the palace, and she did not remember much from before her arrival. She was not certain if she was more terrified of leaving or of Queen Sequara discovering her before she could escape. "Alright, Belu. Let's get on with it."

"Who's Belu?" Khel stood next to her with a puzzled frown on his face.

Riall gestured toward Belu, who wagged her tail as she peered into the boat, probably scenting the salted fish.

"The cur? I thought it was a stray following you around." He made a sour face when he glanced at the dog. "We can't take it with us."

Riall glowered at Khel. "*She*. Not 'it'. And she's coming with us."

For a moment, he looked like he might protest, but then he held up his hands. "Fine, but you'll have to feed it out of your own stores."

"Fine."

"And teach it to shit over the side of the boat."

While Riall glared at Khel, Belu made a noise that was half alarmed whine and half impatient growl.

The young sorceress did not dignify Khel's last comment with a response. "Let's go. Come on, Belu." She climbed into the boat, which bobbed and shifted a little under her weight. After crouching and emitting another high-pitched growl to muster some courage, the little dog hopped in after her and wagged her tail while moving in playful circles.

Without a word, Volund stepped in with his long legs and placed the oars into their locks while Khel untied the boat from the dock. Khel leaped in and took a seat at one of the oars, and he and Volund rowed them away. With her insides lurching, Riall bid a silent farewell to Kiriath. She wondered if she would ever return, or if Queen Sequara would even allow her back. She had never quite felt like she belonged, but it had been home. She held on tight to Belu.

Once they were clear of the docks, Khel and Volund made quick work of untying the sail. After it was secure, it luffed for a moment until Volund positioned it with the practiced skill of a seafarer, and then it went taut as the boat creaked and lurched ahead. The wind seemed eager to fill the sail as they skimmed further into Halion Sound, whose clear, azure waters glistened beneath the warm sun. The city grew smaller with each moment, and Riall allowed herself a long sigh.

Distant shouts coming from Kiriath's docks snatched her attention. At first, she feared someone from the palace had spotted them, or perhaps one of Volund's fellow Thjoths. But when she squinted at the figure waving his arms at the end of the dock where the boat had been tied up, she thought she recognized the fishmonger who had seemed to dislike Khel so much. Realization hit her like a punch to the gut.

She turned to Khel, who wore a satisfied grin as he gazed back at the shouting and cursing fishmonger. "This isn't one of your mother's boats."

He shrugged. "Well, he called me a thief, didn't he?" He looked at Riall, and his face grew serious for the first time since she met him. "But I would have let him be if he hadn't called my mother a whore."

Riall sighed and shook her head. "As if I wasn't in enough trouble already."

Khel laughed. "Oh, I imagine we'll find plenty more of that before we're done."

$$\text{❧} \quad 9 \quad \text{❧}$$

Queen Sequara laced her fingers together as she watched Gnorn and Yrsa approach her throne, a beautiful work of art with scrolls and vines carved in the polished wood in likeness of the former seat of Asdralad's sorcerer-monarchs. The Torrlonders destroyed the old one along with the rest of the palace during the war, but Sequara had ordered everything remade as much as possible like it was in former times. Her throne was not the one that her beloved predecessor, Queen Faldira, sat upon, but Sequara had wanted the resemblance as close as possible. Even so, she never felt comfortable on it.

The servant who conducted Gnorn and Yrsa to the throne room bowed and departed before closing the doors, leaving the three of them in privacy. Gnorn and Yrsa bowed when they were ten feet from the throne and halted. Sequara was as impatient of the courtesies as she imagined they must be.

The day had been frantic enough when Volund turned up missing. When no one could find Riall, it had been a strain to hide the panic welling up in her. She blamed herself for not immediately sensing the girl's absence, but there had been distractions. The absence of Riall's power seemed a terrible, ominous void to her now as she reflexively reached out to sense it. At least she had tidings to share with her guests. They would need to move with great swiftness, but she deemed they would be able to catch the youths before they caused too much harm.

It was not hard to see the worry in Gnorn's expression and the anger in Yrsa's. Sequara decided to be as direct as possible. "They've left the island."

"You know this?" Yrsa gripped the hilt of her scabbarded sword. She appeared ready to dash down to the docks that very moment.

The queen nodded. "I can no longer sense Riall, which means she must be miles away. My servants have gathered enough information from witnesses that we can piece together what happened with reasonable certainty." She released a sigh. "It appears that, after sneaking out of the palace, Volund and Riall left the island by their own will on a stolen fisherman's boat."

Gnorn's face wrinkled in confusion. "That makes little sense. Why? And where are they bound?"

"Several ships' captains informed us that they were attempting to buy passage to Grimrik."

"What?" Yrsa shook her head. "We were returning home anyway. Why wouldn't Volund wait for us?"

Sequara took a deep breath. "It is not Volund who didn't wish to wait. Most likely Riall convinced him to help her find a way to Grimrik. She knew I would not allow her to journey there."

Yrsa's frown deepened. "Who is this girl, and why would she go to Grimrik?"

Queen Sequara paused. She had debated how much to reveal to Gnorn and Yrsa, but there were certain things they would need to know to make sense of what the two youths had done. *I owe Gnorn at least that much.* "Riall came to us from Caergilion. It was Seren who made us aware of her abilities."

"Seren?" Gnorn's face lit up with a smile. "It's been so long since I've had word of her. How's the lass?"

Sequara wrung her hands. "Gnorn, I'm so sorry to add to all the ill tidings, but we just learned that Seren is unwell." She cleared her throat. "In fact, she may be close to dying."

The Dweorg's face fell, and he staggered backward a step. "No. It's not possible." He shook his head. "Too young." The pained look in his eyes cut Sequara's heart. "I've seen so many lost when they were too young. In the war. My brother. The Prophet. So many, and so young. But not Seren. Her lovely voice." His lip quivered, and he tugged at his beard. "By the ancestors and Edan, I've lived beyond my time. Is there nothing you can do for her?" A sob broke free with his last word.

"I'm so sorry, Gnorn. As soon as I learned of it, I arranged to send one of my best healers. But Riall . . . You must understand that Seren raised Riall back when she lived with her uncle, Duke Imharr. She was an orphan whom Seren took in, but when she saw what the girl could do, she sent word to me. It was a good thing too. Riall is . . . powerful."

"Powerful in the gift?" Yrsa frowned.

Sequara sat straighter on her throne. "Yes. More than powerful enough to wield dragons."

"But you said . . ."

"I will explain, and when you know the facts, you may judge me."

Yrsa paused and then nodded, and, after wiping a tear from his eye and sniffling, Gnorn nodded as well.

"After you made your request for aid, I thought for a moment of accompanying Riall to Grimrik. I almost wish I had decided to do so. I could have asked her to use her power to subdue Gorsarhad, and she would have done it. But, in doing so, I would have risked unleashing something far more dangerous than any dragon."

Sequara turned to Gnorn. "Do you recall the Prophet of Edan's power? Whence it came? How dangerous it was?"

The Dweorg's eyes widened for a moment, and he shivered. "I'm not likely to forget the dread and the terror of it. Freezes my bones just to think of it still."

Sequara nodded. "The whole of Andumedan believes the Prophet saved us all from a terrible power after the War of the Way. And he did. But few know the terrible power came from within him."

Yrsa shook her head. "I don't understand. What does this have to do with Volund and this girl?"

"Listen, and you will see. No one knows whence the gift comes or why it is present with enough strength in a few of us to give the power to influence the energy in what is living, what most call magic. But, in the depths of the eldest forests and other untamed places, there are rare concentrations of the gift outside of human minds. They are not so much living creatures as presences. Such presences are doorways into the realm of origins, and they are so powerful that anyone who encounters them never comes back, at least in spirit. Most often they appear to those who behold them as a sublimely beautiful person or creature, but that illusion may only be a creation of the victim's failing, desperate mind to ease their passage."

"Elves." The haunted look had not left Gnorn's face.

"Yes. Since Riall has been my ward, I have tried to make a study of elves. Even our most ancient lore says little to nothing of them. No song of origin exists for them. It's possible they have some connection to the gift's existence, but I cannot be certain. It helps little that those who find themselves close enough to one for observation never return. So far as we know, the Prophet of Edan was the first person to encounter an elf – to look one in the eyes, so to speak – and live. Not only that, but the power he displayed afterwards came from the elf, or a piece of it dwelling in him. He used that power to stop the Supreme Priest Bledla from wielding the dragons and to end Torrlond's War of the Way. However, in using it to defeat Bledla, he unleashed the presence within him, and it hungered to end all suffering – to end all human life. It slew thousands, especially among the Ilarchae of the Wildlands, but it might have slain many more. The Prophet's greatest gift to us was to sacrifice himself in order to end that threat and return the elf's power whence it came."

Gnorn shuddered and shook his head. "I remember it well. We were there that day. Among the few who survived. But it was an end to the war. An end to the madness."

"So I believed. But, one day, Seren sent me a message from Adanon urging me to see an orphan child she had taken in. This was before she occupied her home in Caergilion, back when Seren still lived with Imharr. Riall was only four years old, far too young for the gift to manifest itself. What Seren described gave me cause to wonder, so I journeyed to Adanon. When I came close enough, well before I even saw Riall, I knew, and I feared. You must understand: We with the gift feel one another's presence with an intensity in accordance with our strength. We are like stars – some brighter and some dimmer – twinkling across the night sky to each other. Riall's power blazes like the sun. Yet it thrusts an all too familiar chill through me every time I come near her. It is the same presence that drove the Prophet to madness and death. The same power that snatched away scores of thousands of lives with less than a thought. Somehow, within the child dwells an elf's presence."

Gnorn nodded as if recalling something. "The Prophet encountered the elf in the forest near his home in the Mark. You and I know this, though few others do. What of the girl? Do you know aught of how it came to pass?"

Queen Sequara paused and then shook her head. "Seren found Riall as an infant in Caergilion soon after rebuilding her parents' home, which had been destroyed in the war. The Prophet spent much time in Caergilion in that very area, near the coast, healing the wounded from the war and the sick. Perhaps he passed on a piece of his power to someone. Perhaps it happened the same way it happened to him, a chance encounter with an elf."

The Dweorg frowned. "Unlikely. In all our chronicles and lore, no one ever survived a meeting with an elf until the Prophet did. It must be connected with him somehow."

"So it seems. However it happened, two choices lay before me when I met Riall: slay the girl out of mercy for her and those around her, or take her with me in an attempt to train her to control her power. I took a terrible risk and chose the latter."

Yrsa gazed at the queen with a flat stare. "I see why you lied."

"You do *not* want Riall in Grimrik. Should she use enough of the strength within her to wield Gorsarhad, it could awaken the elf's hunger and overwhelm her, just as it happened to the Prophet. She would become an elf-dwola, a creature of such fearful power that it could turn Grimrik and even all of Andumedan into a wasteland."

"You should have killed her." Yrsa said the words without a hint of anger, but with plenty of conviction.

Sequara lacked the luxury of conviction. She gazed at the younger woman for a moment. "Perhaps. Had I tried, it's possible the presence of the elf within her would have defended itself, and I would have unleashed the very thing I feared. At times mercy and wisdom are the same. I pray so in this case, but it has meant that Riall and I both have been prisoners here on Asdralad. I have never dared to allow her to leave, and I have never dared to leave her side."

Gnorn grunted. "That explains much. But surely the lass knows the risk. Does she believe she can help Grimrik by wielding the dragon and then contain the elf's presence within her?"

"She has no doubt convinced herself that is the case. She is aware of what might happen should she draw too much on her power. I believe she might not have disobeyed me had it not been for Seren."

"Seren?" The Dweorg tugged on his beard.

"Riall and Volund will not sail straight to Grimrik. She will go to Caergilion first to heal Seren."

Yrsa's eyes narrowed. "Do you know this for certain?"

"I am as certain as I can be. I know Riall. She has a healer's instincts. Her wish to help is also what convinces her that she can wield the dragon without losing control of her power. But we must stop her, and we must sail as soon as possible. Your ship is swiftest. If you'll allow me, I'll sail with you."

Yrsa made a slight bow. "Of course."

Queen Sequara took a deep breath. "There's one last thing you should know. Volund and Riall are not alone. Another young man is accompanying them. His name is Khel, and his mother is a widowed noblewoman here on Asdralad. I might add that she was of great service in rebuilding Kiriath after the war, and I doubt she is aware her son has departed. Her service is one reason we have tolerated him. Some have accused him of thievery, though no one's ever caught him before. Also, there was an incident last summer, a fight in which the other young man died, though witnesses confirmed Khel slew him in self-defense. Some would call Khel troubled. Others would say he's dangerous."

Yrsa snorted and smirked. "He'll find *himself* in danger if he tries to harm a son of Orvandil Dragonbane."

Sequara gazed at Yrsa with a pensive frown before turning to Gnorn. "His mother's name is Dalriana."

It took a moment, but Gnorn's mouth opened as his eyes widened. Sequara knew he remembered the name.

Yrsa glanced at the Dweorg. "What is it?"

Gnorn swallowed and gazed at Sequara, who nodded to him. The Dweorg cleared his throat. "This lad . . . Khel, you say?"

Sequara nodded again.

Gnorn let out a long sigh and looked at Yrsa. "If his mother is Lady Dalriana, and he's the right age, it's an easy guess who sired him."

"Who?" Yrsa's frown spoke of her confusion.

The Dweorg looked uneasy as he swallowed and then raised both eyebrows. "Orvandil Dragonbane."

Yrsa's eyes widened as her mouth popped open, though no words came out.

"Long before he was a king, before he wed your mother, during the time we stayed here in Asdralad, training the troops for Queen Faldira, he and Lady Dalriana . . ." Gnorn sighed and shook his head.

Sequara looked at them both with a sad smile. "Dalriana asked me to keep it quiet. She never sought attention for herself or her son. But there is no doubt Khel is Orvandil's, and he knows who his father is."

The Dweorg nodded with a worried frown. "Which means he also knows he's Volund's elder half-brother."

$\text{❀}\quad\text{I O}\quad\text{❀}$

"What's it like?" Khel lounged in the boat with his legs extended in front of him, one crossed over the other. As the salt-laden sea breeze ruffled and tossed his long, curly hair, he gazed at Volund with an intensity in his eyes belying his casual posture.

Riall found it strange, but she pretended not to notice and continued scratching Belu behind the ears. The little dog huddled inside Riall's cloak for protection against the constant wind, but the bright sun shone overhead and warmed them.

Asdralad was no longer even a distant speck on the water. Surrounding them was the Great Sea, an endless expanse that somehow called out to Riall's power and filled her imagination. Considering the state of their boat, it was just as well that the sea was not too rough, though the steady wind kept pushing them further north. Volund had said it would take three days to reach Caergilion's shore, and though it was still the first day, Riall felt a world away from Asdralad already.

The further they sailed, the more the dread in her had dissipated, giving way to a yearning to see new things. Distant shores waited out there.

She could explore the whole of Andumedan, find the land of her forest dreams, and perhaps even discover faraway kingdoms. Or so the wind whispered to her. At any rate, this journey was just a beginning. She would heal Seren and save Grimrik from the dragon. And then? She did not know, but, for the first time she could remember, the possibilities excited her.

It took a long moment for Volund, who was keeping the boat on course, to realize Khel had been addressing him. He always seemed a bit surprised when someone spoke to him, as if he preferred to be alone with his thoughts. "What's what like?"

Khel grinned. "To be the son of a great hero. Orvandil Dragonbane. The warrior. The dragon slayer. The king."

Volund shrugged. "It's alright."

Khel raised an eyebrow. "'Alright?' Nothing more? Don't you want to be just like him? To do great deeds the shapers will sing of for many a winter to come? To be king of the Thjoths someday?"

Volund frowned for a long moment, as if it was a matter he had often considered. "The Thjoths pick the worthiest among them to lead." He looked down at his lap and mumbled, "I make things."

"Oh." Khel nodded with exaggerated seriousness. "Like your wench?"

"Winch." Volund set his jaw and turned his gaze north.

Khel's smirk wavered a little as he gazed at the younger boy, and he looked as though he might say something more, but then he turned to Riall with a predatory smile that suggested he was about to make some jest at her expense. "And what of you? You must have made Ma and Da proud, being such a powerful sorceress."

"I don't have a mother or father."

"No? An orphan, then. Likely you're a bastard, like me. There are more than a few bastards on Asdralad from the war. Lighter skinned, like us. Torrlonder fathers and Asdralae mothers. They let some of the women they raped live."

"I'm from Caergilion."

Khel's mouth popped open in mock surprise. "Oh." He grinned once again. "Well, they say all Caergilese are bastards."

"Don't." Volund was gazing at Khel with fury in his eyes.

Khel's smirk gave way to a bewildered frown, all pretend innocence. "Don't what?"

Volund's face reddened, as if he had surprised himself by speaking, but the strain remained in his face and voice. "Don't mock her."

A laugh escaped Khel's throat. "Perhaps you'd prefer it if I mock you."

Volund's gaze hardened. "Don't. Mock."

"Or you'll do what?" Khel maintained his casual posture, but Riall sensed tension in him, as if he were coiled to spring. "Oh, I see. The hero comes to save the maiden from the vile, mocking fiend. Is that it? So you *do* want to be like your father, then."

Riall watched with a sense of dread as Volund took his hand off the tiller and moved toward Khel, who sprang up and faced the other young man in a balanced posture, like a trained swordsman. Volund was taller and heavier, but, having seen how light he was on his feet, Riall suspected Khel was quick. Without anyone steering the boat, the sail began to luff. The boat lost speed and began to list as the wind pushed the sail, causing Volund to stumble a little while Khel adjusted his footing. Riall grabbed the side of the boat and held on to Belu. She tried to think of something to say to soothe everyone, but her tongue was stuck. She thought of reaching for the gift.

Just then, a dim awareness pierced her dread. It was yet distant, but there was no mistaking the presence that whispered in a deep place of her mind. She sat up straight. "Stop! They're following us."

Khel and Volund, who had closed in on each other, turned toward her with puzzled frowns. Khel relaxed his posture, and his arms dropped to his sides. "Who?"

Riall swallowed. "Queen Sequara. She's behind us, on a ship. And gaining on us."

"How do you know?"

"She's right." At the boat's stern, Volund was peering southward with his hand shielding his eyes from the sun. "That's a Thjothic warship. Yrsa's there too."

The dread had returned with a vengeance to twist at Riall's stomach, her dreams of seeking new lands all fled. "Can we outrun them?"

Volund glanced at her for a moment, and then he shook his head. "They'll catch us before nightfall."

They all remained frozen in the boat for a moment, the two young men looking at Riall. She took a deep breath. She petted Belu one more time, and, ignoring the little dog's whimper of protest, she stood. Keeping careful to maintain her balance in the rocking boat, she walked aft until she stood next to Volund. "Steer us north. And tell me when it's enough."

Volund frowned at her. "Enough?"

"You'll see. I don't want to put them in danger. Just slow them down."

She turned southward, focusing on the distant white speck on the horizon. She had known this would happen, but knowing did not make it any easier. *I'm sorry, my lady. But I won't go back.*

Once Volund had the boat back on course, Riall untethered her mind to float into the realm of origins and chanted a song of origin:

Voromar in dharu khirgan an ulumo,

Dagathar im ghuishu noldan di khurono.

Husharu ingharno an toronu yondalwy,

Indwinu sturono ni bhaladu fandinwy.

Unlike others with the gift, she did not need to chant a song of origin to influence the energy inhabiting the world of forms. But Queen Sequara had shown her that the songs of origin made it easier for her to focus her power and to keep *her* energy tied to her body, decreasing the risk of something terrible. Also, she thought it best to give Volund and Khel fair warning that she was about to do something.

Riall became a conduit between the eternal and the string of moments plucked from it, what mortals experience as the present they cling to. From the timeless realm of origins, power coursed through her and exerted her bidding on the energy in the realm of forms. Her will, anchored in the realm of forms, shaped the energy.

High above the water's surface, vapors began to form, snaking and coalescing. The sky darkened. In mere moments, a huge shadow swallowed their little boat as a grey maelstrom took shape and swirled in the sky like an immense disc. Jagged flashes of lightning crackled and illuminated the blackening clouds. Something enormous began as a distant rumble and, within a few breaths, expanded into a monstrous roar.

Riall gestured downward with her hands, again not from necessity but as a way of focusing her purpose, a reminder of her present intentions. As if tracking the motion of her hands, a vast column of wind spewed from the center of the spinning clouds and plummeted from the sky like a giant, invisible fist. It plunged into the Great Sea midway between their boat and the Thjothic ship pursuing them, producing a massive explosion of water whose boom made Khel cringe and cover his ears. The water pattered back down as a thick, eddying drizzle.

"Hold on!" commanded a voice that, within the serenity of the realm of origins, Riall dimly recognized as hers. She was the wind, and her will was its will. She spread her hands apart, sundering the gale into two halves. One gust howled northward over the water, churning it and capping the waves with white foam as it swept toward their boat and struck it within heartbeats. The wall of wind nearly picked up the boat, which jerked forward and creaked as the sail billowed and tightened, and they sliced through the sea at a dizzying pace. Khel, who had been standing and staring open-mouthed up at the sky, lost his balance and fell on his back. Volund clutched the tiller, while Riall crouched and held on to the boat's side with her cloak whipping behind her and Belu huddled beneath her. The little dog barked with excitement, and Riall understood that, through their bond, Belu felt the power coursing through her.

The squall propelling them was only half of the wind Riall had called. The other half was howling southward to buffet the Thjothic ship, which was struggling to tack in the sudden headwind and soon disappeared behind the horizon. Riall kept both halves of the wind at full force a while longer, until a dim voice entered her awareness.

"Enough! Enough! You'll kill us all!"

She realized it was Volund, and she severed her connection to the realm of origins so that her full awareness returned to her body in the realm of forms. Belu whined in disappointment. *More! Play!*

After a few moments, the wind lessened and returned to normal, a mere caress across the skin. Their ship slowed under a brighter sky while the clouds dissipated with the same suddenness with which they had formed. There was no visible sign of the Thjothic ship, but, now that she knew to seek it, Riall could feel Queen Sequara's lingering presence, though dimmer than before. The queen might call the wind as well, but she well knew she was no match for Riall, who hoped their pursuers would take this as a warning to stay back. If not, she would repeat the process.

"Sorry," she said to soothe her companions. "They're alright back there on their ship. I can sense them. I'll be gentler next time if I have to do it again."

But it was too late. Both young men stared at her with a look that was all too familiar from her years of training among Queen Sequara's pupils. Her fellow students had always been able to sense her power, and though they grew used to her as they trained together and strove to conceal their fear, she often caught their horrified glances when she exercised the gift. Even others with the gift feared her; or rather, they feared her more than other folk did, for they could sense the monstrosity within her, whereas others could only see it when she used her power. Khel had been right. She was a freak.

Struggling up from the bottom of the boat, the older boy fixed her with his dark eyes, and for the first time since she met him, his easy confidence seemed to have fled. He shook his head as if in disbelief of what he had witnessed, and then he gawked at Riall again like she was a dangerous animal. "Right. No more mocking."

Riall sighed and sat down. She would have preferred the mocking.

Belu whined and nuzzled her leg. *Sad?*

She gave the dog an assuring pat on the head. Belu's trusting eyes gazed at her. Riall smiled at her companion and massaged the soft fur on her neck, scratching behind the ears. *Always I pretend I'm comforting you when you're the one comforting me.* The little dog's warm pink tongue darted out to lick Riall's hand. At least she had one friend in the world who was not too frightened of her to come near.

Riall wore a man's corpse. Flesh, bones, and tissue housed her awareness, but their former owner was gone. She more than suspected it was the body of the man she had killed on the northern forest's outskirts. It was hard to tell while looking out from his eyes. But she knew that *he* was no longer in this frame trudging over the undulating landscape of green hills gilded in dawn light. His flesh was a garment, a means of exiting the forest and going . . . Where was she going? East, to judge by the blinding rays emanating from the sun, which peeked over the hills before her path. Some purpose she could not wrap her mind around bore her on.

The man's body was hungry and tired. She had been walking in it without sleep for a long time. Days, perhaps? Thirst was less of an issue since she had stopped several times to drink from the river that paralleled her path. She could not remember drinking from the river, but she was certain she had done so.

Though she dwelled in the body, she was aware of its hunger and thirst only as abstract things, needs she must tend to in order to use such a primitive tool. Removed from its former occupant's fate, she felt no connection to or distress over the nerves signaling pain in its legs and bleeding feet. Its bowels were writhing and cramping with tiny parasites that produced the brown, watery fluid leaking from its anus, but this caused no discomfort or disgust in Riall, only a sense of inconvenience. Lungs and heart too were working hard to keep it moving. Without proper nourishment, the body was beginning to break down. A weak, fleeting tool subject to measureless pains.

Thus, when she spied a few dwellings nigh a bight in the river, she headed for them. The path she followed broadened into a muddy road as she approached the village, which seemed for the most part still abed. At least one villager was stirring, however. A figure appeared ahead on the road, someone leaving the village and heading toward the corpse Riall walked in. The person, who did not appear to notice the approaching stranger, whistled a cheerful tune. As the figure drew closer, it became a boy clutching a staff, and he continued whistling until his head jerked up, finally alert to the unexpected presence nearing him. The boy adjusted the grip on his staff and slowed his pace, but he kept coming all the same.

A vague sense of unease for the boy sprang up within a dim part of Riall, but she moved closer to him nonetheless.

When he came within hailing distance, the lad stopped walking and nodded. "Morning, sir." He was pale-skinned and a bit younger than she was.

Riall knew he had used language – and one she recognized at that, the Northern Tongue – but her mind fumbled to recall the purpose of speech. Like the sound any animal makes, the words, the tone behind them, and the almost imperceptible quiver in them expressed an array of meanings. *You don't belong here and I'm afraid of you, but I'll pretend all is normal and perhaps, if I observe the customary rituals, it will be,* he seemed to convey all at once. The fear for him grew in her, but she could not grasp whence it sprang. Some urge drove her closer to him. She did not respond to his words, though the distant part of her knew it would have been the appropriate thing to put him at ease. Something told her it would not matter soon anyway.

"Morning, sir," he tried again. "You looking for . . ."

As she drew nearer, his voice went dry and his eyes widened. "You don't look right, sir." He halted and then stepped backward. "What happened to you?"

She kept approaching in silence. The protest deep inside her was dim and futile. *No. Don't hurt him.* A much stronger and older part of her whispered, *No more pain.*

The boy held his staff in front of him. "That's close enough. If you need help, you . . . Oh."

His mouth gaped open as a bright light emanating from her bathed him, and the expression in his eyes − locked onto hers − transitioned from horror to ecstasy and then emptiness.

No!

But he was gone.

With no warning, Riall's viewpoint shifted. Before her stood an emaciated, filthy version of the man she had killed by the forest, still naked from the waist up, and his beard a tangled mess. His lifeless blue eyes stared at nothing, and then he collapsed to the muddy road as if boneless. That corpse was empty and free to return to the soil.

The new body she occupied let its staff drop to the road with a clatter and turned about to walk east, with the blinding sun shining in its face.

Riall blinked, and the red of her eyelids alternated with the bright light. There was something hard beneath her, and she swayed. The world was all wrong, tilted on its side. It took her a moment to realize she was lying down.

She shook her head, and then it came to her. *Only a dream. Only a dream. I'm in the boat with Belu and Volund and Khel.* A long sigh escaped her. Just as in her dream, it was dawn. But she was in the boat, with the hiss and moan of it cutting through the water as the cool sea breeze plucked at her. Wood creaked, and the pregnant sail snapped. She was lying on her side, huddled beneath her cloak and a blanket, facing the rising sun. *Oh, merciful Edan. I'm in the boat.* She gazed at her hand and wiggled her fingers to make sure she was in the right body, and then she sighed again. The dream left nausea in its wake, and she took deep, steady breaths until it dissipated. *I'm in the boat.* She willed herself to forget the vision of the boy's startled eyes along with the guilt and horror of what she had done to him. *Only a dream.* At length, she told herself the dream felt less real, and she was ready to rise.

Something was missing, though. There was no ball of warmth

cuddled up next to her, and no one had wakened her from her nightmare or comforted her when she stirred. *Where's Belu?*

Suppressing a stab of panic, Riall sat up and took her bearings. She breathed a sigh and felt a bit foolish as she sensed Belu near the boat's tiller. Her back and limbs were stiff from sleeping on the wooden strakes. Nearby, another form slept unmoving, and from its size she reckoned it was Volund. He had taken the first shift steering them during the night, while Khel was supposed to relieve him. Riall, who knew nothing of sailing, had the luxury of sleeping the whole night, unless one of them had wakened her with news of pursuit, which had not happened.

Her gaze slipped past Volund and rested on the tiller, where Khel sat smiling in the early morning sun while the wind tossed his dark locks. This was not his usual ironic smirk, but rather a look of honest mirth. He was looking down and, with one hand on the tiller, holding out something in his free hand. Belu's small form sat beneath him, and she opened her mouth as he gently guided a piece of what appeared to be dried meat into it.

When the little dog took it with a wag of her tail and began chewing on it, Riall felt her deep satisfaction and found herself salivating in response. Khel's smile broadened, and he dug into one of his bags of provisions. After he withdrew his hand with another piece of dried meat in it, he waited for Belu to finish the first. When the dog gazed up expectantly and wagged her tail again, he put his index finger over his mouth and winked at Belu, as if this was to be their secret. He gave her the meat, and his almost childlike smile blossomed again.

Riall watched with a growing grin of her own, remembering how Khel had insisted she would have to feed Belu out of her own stores. When he reached into his bag again, she shook her head. *He's going to spoil her.* She cleared her throat noisily, and Khel's hand jerked out of the bag. While she stretched and yawned in imitation of awakening, he looked out at the horizon as if he did not notice Belu sitting beneath him waiting for another piece of food.

She got up, tiptoed past Volund's still form while holding on to the mast and lines for balance, and approached Khel. When she was near enough, she whispered, "Good morning."

Khel's usual jaunty smile greeted her, so he was at least pretending he had gotten over her display of yesterday. "Good morning, indeed. A fine day."

"I hope Belu was not disturbing you."

Khel looked down and feigned a look of mild surprise. "The cur? Hadn't really noticed it."

Riall worked hard to suppress a smile. "Oh. Good."

"No sign of our pursuers." He seemed eager to change the subject, and he looked south to verify what he had just said.

"Good." Riall knew better, but she did not care to correct him. The sense of the gift in Queen Sequara still lingered, but it was dim. The Thjothic ship must have been keeping its distance, but the queen would know exactly where Riall was even if she was staying away for the moment. Yesterday's ploy with the wind had worked. At least their pursuers seemed to have understood the message. But they had not given up the chase. Perhaps the queen would allow her to reach land unhindered and would then attempt to intercept her. She knew better than to hope the woman would simply turn back to Asdralad. *But I'll make it to Seren. She can't stop me. And then I'll keep my word to help Grimrik. I just hope we arrive before more harm comes to the Thjoths.*

❧ 12 ❧

Orvandil Dragonbane slid the sharp steel of his long dagger out of the man's neck. A dark gush pumped from the gash in the flesh, and the iron tang of blood mingled with scents of oil, leather, sweat, and the mead that had permeated his victim's last gasp. The Ilarchae's mouth made a smothered, burbling cough as he thrashed, but he could not break Orvandil's embrace as he grasped him from behind, for the Thjoth was larger and far stronger. Wet, sticky warmth seeped on the hand Orvandil clenched over the guard's mouth, and he held it there until the body shuddered one last time and went limp.

The man's eyes – wide and panicked just a moment ago while he struggled with his neck craned to glimpse his attacker – were still gazing into Orvandil's, but they saw nothing. Holding it up from behind, the king of the Thjoths lowered the warm corpse gently until it rested on the ground, which would drink the rest of its blood.

With as little noise as possible, he dragged the body under a nearby thicket. He wiped his hand and his dagger on the dead man's kirtle, pausing only to take note of how his hands were trembling, and then he sheathed the weapon. His heart hammered in his chest, and he made an effort to slow his breaths. He was not sure if it was fear or keenness. Perhaps both. He had not reacted this way since the kill on Vargholm all those years ago. Of course, that had been his best friend when they were little more than boys. He shook his head to banish the memory and focused on the present.

Remaining in a crouch, he scanned his surroundings to make sure no other guards had overheard the brief tussle. It was hard to see since the moonlight penetrated the forest canopy in only a few spots, but he waited a long while, hearing nothing but the breeze's hiss in the leaves and distant cries from the encampment.

He exhaled a long breath. It had been years since he had killed anyone. The War of the Way seemed another lifetime ago, and he was not the same man he had been, thanks to the Prophet of Edan. He had become the man the Prophet had shown him he could be: no longer a killer, but one who labored to preserve life. It was a sort of penance for his bloody youth, a redemption he had worked hard to earn. And yet, the old battle lust was kindling to life within him, the thrill he had so often sought in war, which was the only time he ever felt alive back then. He shook his head and stomped it down. *Too old for that shit.*

Many things had happened since the war. He was a king now. Most importantly, he was a father. His cousin Vols's daughters were just as much his as Volund was. He had loved the girls like a father the moment he laid eyes on them, even before Vols had died. He would find a way to get Sigra out alive, and not just for her mother's sake, though he did not want even to imagine the queen's grief if he should fail. *I'll get her out, Osynia.*

King and father: Those were the two reasons he was here. Perhaps that was why his hands trembled. Unlike his younger self, he had something to lose, making him both weaker and stronger. He would do whatever it took to fulfill his duty to protect his folk and his children. Even kill again. Surely the Prophet would have understood that. If not, Orvandil was damned no matter what he did.

In fact, he had not wanted to kill the guard. The poor fellow had stumbled on him where he hid in the darkened forest, forcing Orvandil to deal with him before he understood what he was seeing. He had hoped to approach the Ilarchae camp undetected. But Bolverk was taking few chances, having posted roaming guards around the camp's perimeter, including some at the edges of the Ironwood. Folk reckoned him the wariest and craftiest war-leader in the Wildlands, which was likely true since his Raven Eyes were among the few tribes to survive the War of the Way and the mass destruction of the Ilarchae. The Prophet had seen to that too, though he never meant to.

Still, this gamble the Ilarchae were taking with Orvandil and his folk was a big risk. At full strength, the Thjoths could crush Bolverk's Raven Eyes and the few other remnants of tribes he held sway over. In fact, the whole thing seemed out of character for the reportedly cunning but cautious war-leader. However, things had gone hard for the Ilarchae at the war's end, and perhaps they were desperate. Knowing the dragon prevented the mustering of Grimrik's forces, these folk of the Wildlands were scavengers taking advantage of a situation. With the potential to rule the Wildlands with Dweorg-wrought weapons, Bolverk must have convinced himself the rewards were worth it. Orvandil aimed to prove otherwise. He would avenge his people, free his daughter, and teach the Raven Eyes never to come within sight of Grimrik again, and he would do so in the wisest manner possible.

But first he needed to arm himself with a leader's most important asset: knowledge. One thing he had learned as a captain of war and a king was that there was nothing like seeing a situation for himself. No need for the Ilarchae to know he was there while he gathered an understanding of their strengths and weaknesses. Thus, he had come alone, commanding his small following of warriors to await him deeper in the Ironwood and leaving Duneyr to help Osynia rule back in Grimrik. When he had departed from home, Osynia had asked him to take a vow either to save Sigra or avenge her with the blood of Bolverk and all his Raven Eyes. Her tears had hardened into cold rage, and he could deny her nothing, this woman he had spent most of his life longing for. Even in their youth, long before she wed Vols . . .

Orvandil shook his head. *Must be old. I keep returning to the past.* The truth, though, was that all this indulging in nostalgia was just delaying what he had to do, and he knew it. *Best get on with it, then.* He rested his hand on Seeker's hilt. An old habit. The sword, wrought by Gnorn all those years ago, was a reminder of the man the Prophet had inspired him to become. He could not help but feel he had failed somehow, and that this failure had led him to this moment. He released a sigh and crept closer to the encampment.

One thing he had not lost was his stealth. Patient and quiet were his steps. He wore no byrny lest its clinking give him away, and mail would only slow him if he needed to run. Through trees and brush he stole until the glow of campfires grew brighter up ahead. Cries that could have been revelry or argument grew louder. Orvandil stopped and scanned the area for guards. *Need to get closer.* He moved nearer to the forest's edge, where, through the trees, he could make out the silhouettes of guards against the campfires.

Crouching behind a large oak that was as close as he could get without exposing himself to the firelight, Orvandil watched. Several guards stood no more than fifty feet from him, on the Ironwood's outskirts. Beyond them was the encampment, which, to judge by the number of hide tents and fires in his view, held thousands of Ilarchae. Above some of the fires loomed the tall poles from which the various clans of the tribe hung their grisly totems – some animal or monster's hide or skull, and in some cases a foe's corpse, or part of it. The Ilarchae would die before allowing the capture of their totems, whence they believed their strength came.

He did not know what he was looking for exactly – some weakness, some suggestion of a plan for finding Sigra. It would be folly to try to enter the camp, but if he waited long enough, perhaps something would present itself for a future plan. At least his hands had stopped shaking, and his breaths were steady. Whatever was coming, Orvandil was ready.

His gaze flicked from campfire to campfire until it rested on one of the largest, which blazed outside a big hide tent. A great bustle was taking place around that fire. It was too distant to make out the finer details, but he could see a large circle of people taking seats around the fire, which licked higher and showered sparks as someone fed it more wood. Something important would be happening there, he reckoned.

A nearby shout startled him, and he jerked back behind the oak. Laughter followed the shout, and there were no sounds of anyone crashing through the forest towards him. He exhaled a long breath as he leaned his back on the tree. Peeking out again, he saw one of the guards nearest him still chuckling and slapping another – a female warrior, Orvandil thought – on the back. He observed them a moment longer to be sure their attention was not on him, but they were watching whatever was happening at the large fire. He too turned his gaze back to the gathering.

Orvandil held his breath. Illuminated by the fire and standing up were two figures that seized his attention. Since the others around the fire were sitting, he had a good view of them. His sight from afar was still excellent, and so he could just make out that the tall, white-bearded man wore a patch over one eye. A good match for the descriptions he had heard of Bolverk. He needed no descriptions to recognize the second standing figure, though she had her back turned toward him. The old war-leader of the Raven Eyes grabbed Sigra by the hand and thrust out his other hand to grasp her face. He forced her gaze toward the fire.

With a red-hot wave of wrath boiling inside him, Orvandil tensed his muscles to sprint from the forest. A moment later, however, he saw what Bolverk was compelling Sigra to look at, and he remained behind the oak. Grinding his teeth and clutching Seeker's hilt, Orvandil watched, reminding himself that a rash move on his part could end in his death or, more importantly, Sigra's.

Two large warriors held a figure between them. She appeared to be a young woman, and she was naked. Orvandil had no doubt the victim was one of the other Thjothic hostages, likely one of Sigra's companions, and he knew what they were about to do to her. An old woman, some sort of priestess by the look of her robe and what might have been bone necklaces dangling from her neck, stood before the helpless hostage with something gleaming in one hand.

The young woman's scream reached Orvandil's ears over the encampment's din just as the priestess lunged toward her throat with the gleaming object. Red rivulets washed down her pale body from her neck, and her head lolled to the side. A moment later, the naked body slumped, but the two warriors held it up and then heaved it into the fire. The fire lessened for a moment, but then it mounted higher as it consumed its new fuel. The priestess held up her arms and, in a croaking voice, led the throng around the fire in some kind of chant. All the while, Bolverk forced Sigra to watch.

Orvandil too beheld it all unfold, as helpless to look away as Sigra, and he cursed himself for staying put even as he knew he could do nothing. He was supposed to protect his folk, and one had died before his eyes, slaughtered like a sheep. Sigra's face was too far away for him to see her expression, but he knew she would confront the spectacle with courage. Bolverk released his grip on her, and two warriors approached to grasp her arms and pull her into the large tent.

Orvandil watched a long time after the sacrifice as the crowd dispersed and the flames lessened. He knew they had given the young woman to their gods to win their favor. Those gods were not so different from the ones some Thjoths still worshipped alongside Edan. It was not so long ago that Grimrik's folk had committed such gruesome sacrifices. Certainly Orvandil's grandfather had done so to his captured foes and the occasional thrall. The Ilarchae likely even counted the victim much honored, though she would not have seen it that way. But Bolverk had also staged the event in order to intimidate Sigra. He wanted to break her. The fool did not know her well, then.

A new group of guards came to relieve the ones nearby, and still Orvandil observed in silence. He needed the deadly calm of the old days, the lethal clarity he had always wielded in a fight. The moon rose higher in the sky, and the king of the Thjoths brooded.

So. Sigra was alive and unbroken. Beyond that, he was uncertain of anything save that the guilt he had felt for slaying the guard was gone. He would exact much fiercer vengeance still. For now, he decided it was best to return to his warriors in the Ironwood. There was little so few could do in the Wildlands. Mostlike he would return to Grimrik. Perhaps Gnorn, Yrsa, Volund, and the rest would be back from Asdralad before he reached his kingdom. Once there, he would seek the counsel of Duneyr, Osynia, Gnorn, and others, and form a plan of attack. With Gorsarhad ever watchful, he did not yet know what that plan would be, but, as a cold and hard resolve grew in him, Orvandil kept in mind the vow he had made to Osynia.

❧ 13 ☙

Sigra was not surprised when, shortly after the guards pulled her into the dark tent and shoved her down onto the sleeping mat, Bolverk entered bearing a torch. She squinted up at the light in a manner that she hoped showed more of her defiance than her fear. Of course, he would try to intimidate her in the wake of the grisly sacrifice. The shock still left her numb and uncomprehending, but she could feel a rising reservoir of tears that she dared not release. *Whatever they have done to her body, she has returned to Edan now.*

Emmi had been her maid and one of her closest friends. No doubt Bolverk had selected her for that reason. Sigra knew she could never erase the memory of Emmi's scream, the blood washing over her chest, and the sizzling and crackling of the fire as it devoured her body. She did not wish ever to smell roasted meat again, let alone eat it. She suppressed a shudder and the urge to retch.

Bolverk barked something to the two guards in his rough voice, speaking words she could almost understand as orders to depart the tent, which they did. The fact that their language was so similar to Thjothic was an unpleasant reminder that the Thjoths had only a couple hundred years ago left the Wildlands to raid the territory that would become Grimrik after they wrested it from the Dweorgs. It made Sigra sick to think of her people's kinship with the Ilarchae.

The tall, white-haired war-leader stood before her, frowning and staring down at her with his one pale-blue eye. The torch he carried cast a ruddy light on his face. They were the only two in the tent. Not for the first time, Sigra wished she had been a warrior like her little sister. Had Yrsa been in her place, she would have killed this old man and taken a few of the other Ilarchae with her before the end. Lacking Yrsa's ferocity and courage, Sigra was using every bit of her wits to keep alive and unharmed. This game of survival was becoming more difficult with each passing day, and she was not even sure she wanted to keep playing it. Emmi's death might have been the breaking point, but she refused to weep in front of her captor or show him the slightest sign of weakness. She would offer at least that much defiance, and she hoped she would not scream as Emmi had in her last moments, though she was not sure she would not. *As the Prophet taught, I am one with Edan. My death will only be a full awakening to that fact. I need not fear it.*

Bolverk stood in silence above her for a long while, and in his unrelenting scrutiny Sigra read his desire for power at war with his lust. At first, after the Ilarchae had captured her on their raid, the war-leader had made it clear that he intended to trade her for Dweorgs to make weapons for the Ilarchae. Later, after the Thjoths rejected his offer, his attentions to her had changed, and his gaze had become more predatory. And then, three nights back, he had given her an alternative: Wed him, and he would drop his demands and free the rest of the hostages.

Emmi had been the first to die for her refusal. No doubt Bolverk wanted her to believe the blame for Emmi's death lay on her. Perhaps there was some truth to that, but she well knew who had murdered the young woman as well as others dear to her during the raid, and she could never consent to be with him. The fact that her friend had insisted she never give in to Bolverk did little to console her.

The red glow on Bolverk's face deepened the lines etched on it and the shadow around the patch he wore over his missing eye. His long white beard appeared ruddy, reminding her of the blood all over Emmi's chest. He rested his free hand on the hilt of his scabbarded sword as if he was thinking of drawing it. She gazed back at him, refusing to cower though her body almost betrayed her, and only the greatest effort kept her from trembling.

The flap of the tent's entrance pulled back, and someone else entered. If there was anyone Sigra could have wished to see less than Bolverk, it was the man who took a place by the war-leader and leered down at her. Tall, slender, and grinning like a fierce wolf, Unnar had been a wealthy fur trader whose journeys over the years took him all the way to Ellordor and Torrhelm, where he had picked up the Northern Tongue, which Sigra of course spoke well. It was he who had led the initial raid in Grimrik, which Sigra's outnumbered guards almost beat back. Unfortunately, Bolverk had shown up with additional warriors, and they slew the surviving guards defending Sigra. In one way at least she was glad the old war-leader had arrived, for she shuddered to think of what Unnar might have done to her in the absence of Bolverk, who had taken possession of the hostages.

Unnar served as translator between her and Bolverk, but Sigra suspected the man embellished or altered his renderings to fit his own ends. Unnar was also Bolverk's youngest and only remaining son, and he possessed more than his fair share of his father's cunning. Both of his elder brothers had died in a suspicious manner, one while hunting and the other by choking on his own vomit after a feast. Unnar had as much as boasted to her that few believed the deaths had been accidents.

The war-leader rumbled something, all the while not blinking or moving his gaze from Sigra.

Unnar's grin widened. "Father says we will give another of your folk to the gods each night until you wed him."

Sigra stifled a gasp. "You mean *murder* another of them each night."

Unnar shrugged. He did not bother to translate her words.

Sigra gathered her courage and took a deep breath before speaking to Unnar. "How does he know I won't murder *him* in his bed on our wedding night?"

Unnar's grin grew fierce. "Kill him. Then *I* will have you. That thrall of yours was not bad, but I'd rather have you warming my bed each night."

"I'd sooner warm my hands in your blood. And she was no thrall. Emmi was my friend."

Bolverk's harsh voice lashed the air, wiping the leer from Unnar's face. The younger man spoke in his native tongue to his father, translating Sigra's response, she supposed. When Unnar finished, Bolverk laughed. The old man crouched down, and his mirth disappeared as his free hand shot out to grip Sigra's face with wiry strength. His fingers dug into her cheeks, and he forced her to look at him. Sigra's breaths came faster as his eye gazed into hers. Words grated from his throat, and the stench of mead on his stale breath was strong.

"He likes your courage," said Unnar. "He says you will give him strong sons." The younger man scowled after he spoke, perhaps not as pleased with the latter notion as his father was.

Bolverk released his grip and stood. Sigra felt sure his fingers must have left marks on her cheeks, but she refused to show any pain. Time. She needed to buy time, and for that she needed to stay in command of herself. "Tell him not to slay any of my folk, and he'll have his answer in a month."

After Unnar translated, Bolverk scratched his beard and spoke two words.

"A week," said Unnar.

"A fortnight." Sigra tried to look stronger than she felt.

Unnar grinned and said the word in the Ilarchae tongue.

In response, Bolverk's eyes narrowed, and his gaze did not waver from her. At length, he spoke, and Unnar rendered his words soon after. "A fortnight. And if you refuse, you will join your thrall with the gods, but we will not slit your throat. You will die screaming in the fire. But first you will watch the rest of your folk die the same way."

Sigra did not need to feign her anger, which surged in her and emerged in fierce words before she even thought of what to say. "Kill me, and my father will avenge me. Before it is over, you will beg him to end your life, and your people will be no more." When the Ilarchae first took her, Sigra had dared to hope rescue would come. Perhaps her father, or perhaps Halvard, would come leading an army. But the dragon would have made that impossible, which, of course, Bolverk had counted on.

She and Halvard had been set to wed in mere weeks. That was before Gorsarhad had turned up, and before the Ilarchae raid. She spared a thought for her betrothed and the agony he must be suffering. He had wanted to accompany her when she left with her party, but her father had needed his best warriors for their defense of Valfoss. They would not have heard of her abduction until well after the Ilarchae had departed with her and the others. The outcome had always been inevitable.

No one had come. As she, her fellow thirteen surviving hostages, and their captors sailed over the Gulf of Olfi and journeyed through the Wildlands and past the Ironwood, her hope had dwindled with each mile, and the cruel truth finally withered it. But there was one thing she knew: The Thjoths would never leave her death unavenged, and that knowledge gave strength and ferocity to her words.

Unnar's eyes had widened when she spoke, and when he finished translating her words, Bolverk paused. Then he smirked at her. He spoke once more, turned, and left the tent with his torch before Unnar even translated what he said in the ensuing darkness: "Orvandil Dragonbane is far away, and he cannot help you." Unnar paused and seemed to leer at her one last time before he too exited the tent, after which the silent guards returned.

❧ 14 ❧

The small fishing boat's keel sliced into a sandbar not more than fifty feet from where waves groaned and lapped the shoreline. On both sides of the small beach loomed green hills sheared off by water and wind into rocky cliffs, above which seagulls keened. The heavy breeze was laden with the scent of salt and seaweed. When a wave smacked the boat's side, its spray sprinkled Riall's face. She breathed in and stretched.

A fine drizzle hung in the air. When Riall thought of Caergilion, she brought to mind the rain and the rugged hills often dotted with the white specks of sheep flocks. They had sailed deep into Culvor Sound before beaching the boat in this little bay, and she felt certain they could not be too far from where Seren dwelled. She had fuzzy memories - little more than impressions - of a stone house and a barn tucked in a valley, the place where Seren had grown up and where she had brought Riall in the warmer months of summer, when they traveled from Duke Imharr's castle in Adanon. It might not be easy to find, but the locals could at least point the way.

Riall took her bearings while Khel and Volund tied up their boat's sail. It was strange to be back. Though she could not say she remembered much other than a vague impression of the landscape, just the notion that she belonged here gave the place weight in her mind. Had she not been eager to find Seren, she might have thought further on the odd sensation of simultaneously feeling native and foreign to this land.

Fortunately, she had kept up her Ondunic over the years, having spoken it with Kara and Iwan, Queen Sequara's Adanese pupils, all the time back on Asdralad. There were also the letters that Seren wrote, sometimes in Ondunic and sometimes in the Northern Tongue, which Seren had taught her. As she thought of Seren's letters, she grew more anxious. *What if she's already gone? We need to hurry.*

She turned toward Khel and Volund, who were discussing how they should push the boat further ashore and tie it up.

"We'll leave it behind."

The two young men turned toward her with puzzled looks that suggested they were still trying to work out what she said. Volund squinted at her. "What?"

Riall took a deep breath. "Your sister's ship is not far behind us. They've kept their distance, but they'll find our boat well before we reach where we're going."

Khel raised his eyebrows. "And just where *are* we going?"

"To see an old friend." Riall hesitated and swallowed the lump in her throat. Her eyes watered up a bit, but she hoped they would not notice with all the moisture in the air. It took a moment before she could speak. "Seren took me in and raised me when I was little, before I went to Asdralad. She's dying, but I'm going to save her." She faced the two young men, bracing herself for their objections.

"Oh." Khel nodded, but he did not mask the incredulity in his eyes.

There was a long moment when no one spoke, and the only sounds were the moaning of the waves and the seagulls' cries. Volund fidgeted and frowned. Riall decided to answer the question on his face before he spoke it in words. "We'll reach Grimrik by the overland route. I know it'll take longer, but . . ."

"There's a mountain range in the way, you know." Khel was speaking in a tone reserved for a child, a simpleton, or a lunatic. Perhaps he thought her all three.

"I *know*. As part of my training, I've studied maps."

"Maps?"

"Yes. You know: vellum with squiggly lines written on it that show you where things like mountain ranges are. And the Marar Mountains have a pass. Balnor Pass. It's close to Caergilion's chief city of Iarfaen."

"It'll take a long time on foot."

"We'll get horses. Perhaps Seren will loan us three. If not, we'll buy them in some village. You have plenty of silver, remember?"

Khel laughed. "I've not forgotten." He shook his head. "But how much do your maps really tell you about the world? Do they say what lies between here and Grimrik?" There was no bitterness in his words, which he spoke almost gently. "Not only will we need to journey the length of Caergilion and cross the Marar Mountains, but we'll need to pass through Torrlond and likely Ellond after that. And Edan knows what we'll find on the way. Have your maps prepared you for all that?"

Riall glared at the young man and put her hands on her hips. "I thought you had a fancy to travel."

"So I do. I just like to know where I'm going and what things I'm likely to meet. Some of them might be dangerous."

"Don't fret." She winked at Khel the same way he had often done to her. "There's not much out there more dangerous than I am."

Khel's eyes widened for a moment, but he recovered quickly, and he smiled at her even as he shook his head. "Are you certain?"

Riall took a deep breath. "No. I'm not certain of anything. But it's not as if we have much choice. Queen Sequara is behind us, and she won't give up easily. So is Volund's sister, and I suspect she's every bit as stubborn. Believe me when I tell you it would be best if the queen and I did not meet." She did not mention she feared to use the gift oftener than she needed to. Every time she exercised it of late, her dreams of possessing someone else's body grew more vivid. She did not understand what the dreams meant, but there was no need for them to know what danger she could unleash by losing control of the power within her.

Khel seemed unsure for several heartbeats as he gazed at her and frowned, and then he released an exasperated sigh. "Very well." He raised his hands in surrender and glanced around at the rocky cliffs and the drizzle. "This place seems full of interesting things to see anyway." He rolled his eyes.

Riall looked at Volund, who had remained as silent as usual. "We *will* get to Grimrik. We must. I know I can wield that dragon. And I have an idea about how we might get your sister back."

He gazed back at her, seemed to weigh her, and, without a word, nodded.

Taking that for consent, Riall let out a long, relieved breath. "We'll need to carry as many supplies and food as we can in the packs."

Khel was still looking up at the overcast sky as the drizzle thickened to rain. "The spare cloaks will come in handy."

They made short work of packing, and then they took off their shoes and rolled up their trouser legs to wade through the waves. From the boat, Riall handed Belu down to Volund, who carried the little dog to shore. Riall winced when she jumped into the cold water, which jostled her and crept up her legs, awakening goosebumps all over her flesh. Once they reached the pebbly beach, Volund gently deposited Belu, who wagged her tail, darted in little circles, and crouched as she growled at all three of them. She was ready to play after being penned up in the boat.

Riall reached down and mussed the wet hair on Belu's head. "Don't worry, little one. We'll be stretching our legs plenty. We're going to meet Seren."

Belu let out a high-pitched bark in response, which made Riall smile despite the dread building in her that she might be too late.

More than once Volund had wondered why he let this strange young woman talk him into all this madness. He did hope she could help Grimrik, but that was not the whole truth. She *was* pretty, but it was much more than that too. Beyond how powerful she was, there was some kind of intensity within and all about her that whetted certain emotions in him. Not that he dared to think of her in *that* way – in his awkward and shy manner, he had fancied a girl or two back in Grimrik, but Riall was too frightening for that sort of thing.

Still, she exerted a weird sort of compulsion on him, as if he could not help but want what she wanted. He did not think she was producing this compulsion with a purpose so much as exuding it without even knowing, though he was not certain. She was a sorceress, after all. As hopeless as he deemed himself with words, he did not think he could say it rightly, but Riall was at once the most remote and the most alive being he had ever encountered, and somehow he felt both scared and protective of her.

That was never more true than now. With Riall setting a quick pace, they had trudged through the rain on the coastal path for a fair part of the day before meeting a local. When she spoke to the man in

Ondunic, he became friendly. Fortune had smiled on them, even if the sun would not. The man informed them they could reach the valley where Riall's friend dwelled before day's end. Just as they arrived at the stone house, the rain had let up. The dark-haired woman who answered the door knew Riall after she told her who she was, and after much embracing and enthusiastic fussing that Volund could not understand since it was in Ondunic, she conducted the three of them through the front room to the candle-lit sleeping room in the back.

This was how Volund found himself standing and dripping in a room that smelled of sickness with Riall, Khel, Belu, the woman who met them at the door, and a dying woman lying in a bed. He and Khel stood near the fire crackling in the fireplace, for which he was glad. Belu shook her body, flapping her ears and tail and sprinkling droplets all over him before flopping down next to the fireplace with a contented grunt.

Volund was torn as to whether or not he ought to stay. Riall was trembling and weeping as she embraced her friend, who sat up in her bed with several pillows supporting her head and back. The woman rested her bony hand on Riall's head. It was strange, but Riall's tears brought a lump to his throat, and he swallowed a sob. Somehow he could not look away from the scene, though he felt the guilt of an uninvited spectator.

Volund glanced at Khel, but the other young man showed no sign of moving. He had just about made up his mind to leave the room when Riall sniffed, turned, and gestured toward them. "These are my friends: Khel and Volund." Using the Northern Tongue, she spoke in a shaky voice.

The woman called Seren nodded slowly as she gazed at Khel and him in turn. "Welcome," she said in the same language. "I am sorry I cannot be a proper hostess to you." Her voice was raspy, and it seemed a trial for her to form her words, which were as frail and insubstantial as a spider web. She appeared old and gaunt, but Riall had told them Seren had seen around thirty years, not many more than his sister Sigra.

Khel stepped forward a pace and gave a slight but graceful bow. "We are content, my lady. All that matters is that Riall is here."

Volund wanted to say something as well, but, feeling clumsy next to Khel, all he could think to do was nod his agreement.

Even the smile Seren gave them seemed to take an effort. "You are gracious." She turned her eyes toward Riall, and her smile trembled. "And I am so happy to see you." Her voice cracked as she said the words, and Volund reckoned she would have wept had she possessed the strength.

Riall sniffed as fresh tears ran down her cheeks. "I came for you. I came to save you."

The dying woman winced with obvious pain as she raised a quivering hand to wipe Riall's cheek. "You already did."

"I'm going to heal you." Riall shook her head. "You can't die."

Seren gave another weak smile. "Everyone dies, my love. It's enough that you came."

Riall acted as if her friend had not spoken. "I can't stay long after I heal you. I'm going to Grimrik to help them. A dragon has been attacking. I can help."

"Yes. You can." Seren seemed to be looking for something as she gazed into Riall's eyes. "I've heard about the dragon. Of course you can help."

"Volund is King Orvandil Dragonbane's son." Riall gestured toward him, and Volund felt his face flush. He made a stiff and awkward bow.

Seren nodded at him. "You have your father's look."

Volund reminded himself not to fidget when people were speaking to him. "Many say so, my lady." He did not think those were the right words, but no others would pass his lips. Everyone was staring at him, even Khel, as if expecting him to say more. He blushed and glanced at the wooden floorboards.

"You've met King Orvandil, my lady?" Khel rescued him by raising the question he should have asked.

"Before he was a king. When I was a bit younger than you are. He was kind to me." Seren looked at Riall. "Does he know you're coming?"

Riall swallowed before speaking. "No."

"And what of Queen Sequara? Is she aware of what you intend?"

This time Riall looked down at the bed. "Yes. I think. She's following us. Along with Volund's sister and some others. They sailed behind us."

Seren exhaled a quick breath that might have been a laugh, and her mouth quirked into a smile. "I ran away once too, in a manner. So, if she's behind you, you'll be traveling overland, then."

It was not a question, but Riall nodded all the same.

Silence took hold of the room, and then, after a few labored breaths, Seren nodded as if she had reached a decision. "I have friends along the way who can help you. In South Torrlond, Torrhelm, and Ellordor." Her eyes turned to Volund and Khel. "On that writing table you will find a sheet of parchment, ink, and a quill. Kindly bring them to me."

Before Volund could think to follow her instructions, Khel was already at the table. He handed the items to Riall, who held the ink bottle and gave the parchment and quill to Seren. The latter dipped the quill in the ink bottle Riall held and scratched something onto the parchment.

She spoke as she wrote. "In a town called Alndon, a couple leagues south of Torrhelm, there's a carpenter called Edgelaf. His wife is Nelda. Remember their names."

Riall nodded, and Seren continued to speak as she wrote. "Give them this, and they will help you. Show the letter as well to the man who cares for the books and scrolls in the library of the New Way's monastery in Torrhelm. Bagsac is old now and a bit odd, but he can be helpful. And if you go by Ellordor, there you will find in the king's court a bard called Abon. He will assist you if you show him this. Give each of them my fond greetings. Oh, and take provisions as well as three horses from the barn. There are saddles and everything you need in there. The red mare is the gentlest."

When she finished writing, Riall nodded again. "Thank you." She slipped the parchment away from Seren and blew on it before Khel approached to take it as well as the ink and the quill. He too blew on the parchment before folding it and returning the ink and the quill to the table.

Riall looked at her friend and tried to smile. "Now, let me heal you."

Seren gazed at her for a long while. "If you heal me, will my voice come back?"

Riall bit her lip, and new tears sprang to her eyes. She shook her head. "Perhaps, had I known earlier . . . I can keep this disease from taking you away. And it might be you'll grow stronger and your voice will improve with time. It might not ever be the same, like when you used to sing to me. But you'll be alive." The two of them clasped hands, and a single tear freed itself from Seren's eye to track down her sunken cheek.

"The Prophet of Edan healed me once." Seren stroked Riall's brow with her free hand. "Brought me back from death. But some things never heal. Life leaves us marked and scarred."

Riall nodded and spoke through a sob. "I'm going to make you better."

"I wish you had met him. The Prophet. He was . . . beautiful. I used to wonder why he saved me. I saw my mother and father murdered during the war. I named you for my mother. Remember?"

Riall sniffled and nodded.

Seren's eyes grew distant with memory. "When I lost them, it destroyed everything I knew. I fell sick. So many people died until *he* came along. He came and called me back. I was one of the first. And I always wondered why." She released a deep sigh. "When he died, the world grew empty. I didn't know why he left me behind. Until you came. My child. How I wanted you to be mine."

Riall's lips trembled, and her breaths grew heavier. "I *am*. You're the only mother I ever had."

Volund glanced down and shifted his feet, feeling ever more the intruder but unable to move lest he disturb what he was witnessing. He would never be able to explain the aching tenderness he felt for Riall in that moment, and he sniffled as he held back his tears.

Seren smiled up at the younger woman. "Not the only one. She always loved you."

Riall sat up. "Who?"

"She who gave you life. She *loved* you."

Riall was shaking her head as if denying something. "How could she? Why did she give me up? Who was she?"

"I've said too much." Seren shook her head. "I swore a vow." She winced in agony, closed her eyes, and groaned.

Riall stroked the older woman's head. "You're in pain. Let me heal you."

Seren gazed at her for a moment as if in a daze, and then she shook her head. "So much pain." She brushed Riall's cheek with her fingers before her hand fell to the bed. "So much beauty. I've had my fill. But it all hurts so much. I'm tired."

The woman who had met them at the door, whom Volund had nearly forgotten, sobbed and and covered her mouth with her closed fist. Tears tracked down her cheeks. Volund looked away from her raw grief, which threatened to overwhelm him.

"Please." The word came out as a sob as Riall grasped Seren's hand.

The frail woman shook her quivering head. "There are times when I want an end. When I want to join Ma and Da. My friends who died in the war. The Prophet. He let me live so I could take care of *you*. You're all grown, ready to save the world. I know you will, my dear."

Riall shook her head as if in denial and blinked and sniffled as the tears streamed from her eyes.

Seren trembled with the effort to speak. "Is it wrong of me?" She gasped and grimaced as another stab of agony seized her.

"I don't know." Riall shook with sobs and embraced the older woman, who moaned with her eyes closed.

At length, Seren opened her eyes. Her labored breaths came as faint gasps. She gazed at the woman who was weeping next to Volund, who wanted more than ever to disappear but dared not budge. "And yet," said the dying woman, "there are those for whom I would remain. Those I love." Her voice was little more than a hoarse whisper, but she seemed to beckon to the woman with her eyes. "*Cariad*."

Volund did not know if the word was the woman's name, or if it meant some other thing in Ondunic, but the woman rushed to the bedside on the opposite side of Riall. She took Seren's other hand in her own and kissed it.

"My Uncle Imharr." Seren managed a weak smile.

"Does he know?" Riall sniffled. "That you're . . ."

The woman opposite her nodded. "I sent him a letter. Against her wishes." She looked toward Seren. "He was here just two days ago. He was . . . upset. Went to fetch a healer from Adanon."

"He always wanted what he thought best for me. But when I wanted something else, he had the grace to be happy for me." A little smile broke through Seren's pain, and she glanced at the woman holding her hand, who returned the smile even as she sobbed.

The dying woman's eyes turned to Riall. "And you, my dear."

"Will you let me heal you?" Riall's voice trembled with grief and fragile hope. She sat up. Though tears still tracked down her face, her shaking ceased, and her eyes grew determined. "Or, if you want me to free you . . ." Her face nearly crumpled, but she inhaled and mastered her emotions. "I love you."

Goosebumps crawled all over Volund's skin as a chill and a strange energy filled the room, which seemed to darken except around Riall.

The dying woman gazed into the eyes of the young sorceress, something Volund knew in that moment he would not have had the courage to do. She closed her eyes and, as if it were her last breath, released a long sigh. When she opened her eyes again, she spoke. "I will try to live." With a will that she mustered from some place Volund could not fathom, she nodded to Riall.

The young sorceress nodded back and placed her hands on Seren's temples.

Everything in the room fell away except for Riall's eyes, in which Volund beheld something more beautiful and terrifying than anything he had ever imagined, and he was glad they were not focused on him. His mouth gaped open, and he was as helpless to flee as he was to look away. The energy charging the room found its focal point in Riall, as if she were drawing it all toward her. Volund almost took an involuntary step toward her, jerking back his foot and planting it with an act of sheer will. If she had called him or so much as glanced at him, he would have walked into the void without hesitation to disappear into the peaceful and still darkness looming behind her.

Seren gasped and then released a long breath. Her mouth formed a slight smile before going slack. Her body seemed to sag and lose all its tension, all its pain. Everything went still. Seren's eyes were closed, the gentle rise and fall of her chest the only movement in the room. The strange energy was gone, and the room felt emptied.

Riall inhaled a deep breath. "She is healed. The malignancy that wasted her body is gone. She will need much rest." She turned to the woman opposite her. "She will be very tired for a few days. Feed her well. I cannot stay now. Please tell her my task was too urgent, but that I will return here once I am done if I can."

The woman smiled through her tears and clasped Riall's hand across the bed. "Thank you." She collapsed onto Seren and trembled as she embraced the still woman.

Released from the spell, Volund staggered back a step. He did not know which was greater in that moment: his joy or his fear. Perhaps there was no word for what he felt. It was simply too vast. His mouth was still wide open.

Riall turned to him, and a pained expression widened her eyes, which seemed to plead. "Please don't look at me like that."

Khel took a few slow steps forward and put his hand on her shoulder. He made an obvious effort to control his breaths. "It's alright. You did a beautiful thing." There were tears on his cheeks that Volund had not noticed before. Even Belu whimpered and padded close to Riall, putting her front legs up on the bed to lick Riall's hand.

Volund shut his mouth and tried to regain control of his face. He wanted to embrace Riall. He wanted to run away. What he did was nod. "I'm sorry." He wasn't sure if he was apologizing for gawking at her or for being terrified of her or for lacking the courage to approach her. Perhaps all at once. He managed a smile. "I'm happy. For you. And her." He nodded toward Seren and the woman who was still embracing her and stroking her hair.

Riall nodded and managed a quick smile. "Thank you." With that smile, she suddenly became an ordinary girl again before crumpling onto the peaceful and sleeping form next to the woman that Volund understood was Seren's beloved. The three of them formed something sacred in Volund's eyes, something that gave him great peace and wonder to behold. His friend wept and embraced the one who had been a mother to her as sobs racked her.

❧ 16 ☙

Rays of sunlight pierced rents in the clouds to illuminate swaths of the wet, rugged hills. Caergilion was much how Sequara remembered it. During the war, it had been an afflicted and dreary place, filled with disease and the horrors and death that the invading Torrlonders visited upon it. It was as damp and green as ever, but it seemed to her the land was somehow less weighed down, as if it had been healing over the years.

She wished she could say the same of herself. Though she tried not to dwell on it, she could not help but shudder as recollections prompted by the landscape flooded her. She glanced down at the scars on her palms, but the worst memories were not the ones where she almost died. She had taken so many lives here and in Adanon, and more while defending Asdralad and then many more in the east.

Never would she be able to erase the scent of burnt flesh from her mind. Jagged currents of almakhti had erupted from her hands to slay rank upon rank of Torrlonder soldiers. Sometimes her victims had been local Caergilese and Adanese that the Torrlonders had conscripted. It was easy to say she had done it all in order to save many others, but the war had disfigured her from a healer into a killer, and she had never forgiven herself. She shook her head and put one foot in front of the other as she climbed the coastal path up a steep hill.

Behind her walked Gnorn, Yrsa, and three of the Thjothic warriors from the ship. The rest had left them ashore and sailed for Grimrik to report to King Orvandil. There was a pleasant ache in her legs from walking the hills, and it felt good to wear her traveling clothes again after so many years. No stranger who encountered her in her long black tunic and trousers would take her for the queen of Asdralad, and she could almost forget the duties that defined her life. But nothing could distract her for long from her purpose here.

Like a lodestar, the vast presence of the gift in Riall drew her on. Sequara reckoned the young woman must be close to Seren's home by now. Grief twisted inside her at the thought of what Riall might meet there, but the girl had made the risk of approaching her at sea too great, and there had been no safe way to prevent her from reaching Seren.

In one sense at least, Sequara was glad. Riall deserved to be with the woman who had raised her and loved her so much, and Seren more than deserved the solace of her company. It was cruel to deny them this. And yet, there was a terrible possibility that Sequara did not wish to dwell on: In seeking to heal Seren, Riall could unleash death upon thousands or more. A moment's pity could endanger many. Sequara cursed the choices life gave.

The best chance now was to overtake the girl by land, and as soon as possible. Perhaps Riall would allow her to catch up once she healed Seren – if Seren was still alive. And if their dear friend had already departed the realm of the living, she would mourn alongside the girl once she joined her, and at least there would be no reason for Riall to use her power in Caergilion.

As if in answer to Sequara's thoughts, the sense of the gift in Riall so many leagues ahead erupted. The sorceress-queen gasped at the immensity of it, and she staggered backwards.

"Your Majesty, are you well?" asked Gnorn's gruff voice behind her.

Sequara shook her head and stared off in the direction of the eruption. "A healing spell." It was dreadful in its vastness. "Edan's mercy." She allowed herself a slight smile. *She arrived in time to save her.*

A chill suffused her body, and it seemed to her that a measureless shadow veiled the sky ahead of them. Darkness awaited them, the timeless void that touched the fleeting realm of forms, which was a thin veil behind which loomed eternity. This was the power that exploded from the Prophet of Edan, taking scores of thousands with it. Had the Prophet not sacrificed himself, it might have swallowed every living soul in Andumedan before the end.

And then, as abruptly as it announced itself, the elf-power diminished. Once again, Sequara detected the gift in Riall — huge but steady and far away. The girl had contained it. *Thank the Mother and Father.* But had the girl succeeded? If anything went amiss, anyone near Riall might be gone. Not just Seren. Volund and Khel. After suppressing a spike of fear for the young men, Sequara made a quick decision not to tell Yrsa and Gnorn yet — not until they discovered more at Seren's home.

"Queen Sequara? Are you well?"

The sorceress-queen steadied her breaths and then turned to face Gnorn. "We must hasten. I must know what she's done."

"What is it?" asked Yrsa. "What do you sense?"

Sequara sighed. "Riall has awakened her power. We will first go to Seren's home to see what she has wrought. They will likely be gone by the time we arrive. If that proves true, we must find a way to outdistance them and head them off."

"We could use some horses." Gnorn winced, and Sequara well knew how little the Dweorg liked riding. "But where do you propose we should spring the trap?"

"They're bound north, to Grimrik I don't doubt. There's only one way: east to Iarfaen and then north through Balnor Pass."

"You mean to catch them in the pass." A thoughtful frown took over Gnorn's face, with a hint of sorrow escaping his eyes.

I'm not the only one whose memories haunt them. "Yes. There will be nowhere to hide or run." Sequara put her hand on the Dweorg's shoulder. He would be remembering his brother, who had long ago died in the Battle of Iarfaen as the War of the New Way began. In Balnor Pass too there had been great slaughter. "After we take Riall and Volund and

Khel in hand, we may pause to honor the fallen. I have not forgotten where you lost Hlokk."

Gnorn's head lowered and he gave a solemn nod. He looked up at Sequara with the saddest of smiles. "And where you saved the Prophet's life. Let us not forget that."

Sequara nodded. "Yes." *But if I had not saved him, we would not be here now.*

Hundreds of strange hummocks lay all over the grassland. On a crisp, sun-drenched day like this, the surrounding plain offered a clear view for miles in every direction. The wind moaned as it kicked up, and the sea of grass bowed in waves. Though the land appeared fertile enough, not a soul was visible, as if folk shunned this haunted place.

Something did haunt this land. The hummocks: They were barrows. Each and every one was someone's final resting place. The body she walked in was weary – she was fairly certain it had once belonged to a boy who was carrying a staff, though the staff was gone – but it was not through any physical sense that Riall understood she was trudging through a mass grave. The barrows *spoke* to her. By the reckoning of mortals, the folk within them had long ago rotted and turned to soil – hundreds of years ago, in fact.

For her, the passage of time mattered naught. She could hear the suffering of those within the barrows as if it were happening before her: the brutal loss of their loved ones, their land torn from them, exile, and a wearying path leading to an uncertain existence. It had been too much for many – the old, the young, the wounded, and the sick at heart. Rather than linger in such desolation, they had succumbed along the journey, leaving their kin to bury them according to their rites. Something had broken these folk of long ago, and the land still echoed their suffering.

Such was the lot of mortals. A life was a flash of narrow awareness with a distorted and inflated sense of a self. Not only mortals' lives, but their tribes and kingdoms came and went with few lasting traces. Surrounded by darkness on all sides, they would cling to kin, wealth, fame, or whatever they pretended gave meaning to their fleeting moment in the light. Caught within time like flies in a web and ever dreading their moment of return to the energy dwelling in all things, they left their misery etched in the land. Such was their terror of ripping away the illusion that they were anything more than flickers of the one energy, passing waves on an infinite sea of existence. Over and over again they clawed and tore, inflicting their fear onto the other lifeforms around them. To what end? Would it not be better to rid the world of such suffering?

Riall pitied such creatures.

She blinked.

When she opened her eyes, a far different landscape of rugged hills greeted her, and the sky was overcast. No barrows in sight. Caergilion. That other place had been somewhere far away. But real.

She was not walking after all, but riding a horse – the gentle red mare that Ceri, Seren's beloved, had saddled for her. Little used muscles in her legs and back were already aching. Belu sat before her, cuddled up against her in the saddle. The little dog's warmth brought her fully into her own body, but the strangeness of the waking dream lingered. It had been so vivid. *It's getting worse. I wasn't even sleeping. Not a dream at all. What, then?* In some ways, it had been more real than what she was experiencing now, just as the realm of origins was truer than the realm of forms. She had a sinking feeling that using the gift would result in more such unwelcome visions.

She thought of the suffering of the barrow people, which had been so present for her, and it made her see the act of saving Seren's life in a different light. *She will live through more suffering. More loss. But more beauty too. More love. But did I have the right to do it? She chose it in the end.*

"Did I do the right thing?"

"Yes." said a voice to her right and just behind her. Khel.

Riall had not realized she spoke the words aloud. She turned toward Khel, who rode up beside her and gazed at her before nodding.

Volund rode up on her left. He too nodded at her.

Something in the affirmation the two young men offered lifted a weight from her, and she smiled. "Thank you."

Belu nuzzled against her, burrowing into the comfort of her warmth, and Riall grinned at the little dog. They rode in near silence as the only sounds were the plodding of their horses and the creaking of their leather saddles.

At length, Riall felt the need to speak again. "I would have given her peace as well . . . If she had asked it of me. I didn't know that when we arrived there. But in that moment, I would have done it."

"If she had asked it of you, it would have been right." Khel's eyes were intense as he gazed at her, and there was no trace of his usual irony.

Riall shook her head. "But is it my place? To make someone live or die?"

Khel's smile returned, but it had a rueful edge to it. "*Make* someone live? For her sake, or for yours? Even you can't make a person live. Or *want* to live." He paused a moment as if gathering his thoughts. "You did the right thing because you did it for her."

Riall put on a suspicious frown as she gazed at Khel. "Where have you been hiding all this wisdom?"

"Ha! Not my fault if you've been blind to it all along." Khel winked at her.

She rolled her eyes and turned to Volund. "Can you believe this? One compliment, and his head swells like a ripe melon."

The young Thjoth looked at her and nodded once again. And then he smiled. Riall could not recall him smiling often, and though it was tentative and shy and brief, it said more than he could have expressed with words.

She took a deep breath. "Thank you. Both of you. I'm glad you're here."

"I wouldn't want to be anywhere else." The sarcastic bite returned to Khel's voice. "Just look at all the hills and . . . clouds. Lots of clouds in this place. I always wanted to see such clouds. We don't have enough of them in Asdralad, I say. And the rain. All *sorts* of rain here. Sometimes it patters. Sometimes it drizzles. Sometimes it just mists when the clouds come down for a nice wet visit. Sometimes there's a steady downpour. And then it downright pisses. Who knew there were so many ways to rain?"

Volund shrugged. "It's all wet."

Khel swept his arm toward the young Thjoth. "Precisely, my eloquent friend. With such an observant companion to point out its merits, how could we fail to appreciate this land as we ride beneath its hills and its clouds?"

Volund frowned and squinted at Khel as if doubting the latter's sincerity.

Khel's smirk grew larger. "Between you and the mongrel she carries everywhere," and here he gestured at Belu's rump poking out of Riall's cloak on the saddle, "I'm sure we could hear an adequate summary of Caergilion's finer points."

Riall rolled her eyes and put more annoyance into her voice than she truly felt. "Belu is *not* a mongrel." The little dog's tail wagged at the mentioning of her name.

"No?" Khel raised his eyebrows with exaggerated skepticism. "Funny. I took it for part dog and part mouse. Well, you should know I have a tender place in my heart for mongrels, being one myself." He placed a hand on his chest.

Riall could not help smiling. "I think your heart is more tender than you'd like anyone to know."

Khel opened his mouth and closed it, gawking at Riall and looking as if he had swallowed a fly. His face flushed.

"No more words?" Volund appeared serious as he considered Khel, but then a broad grin broke out on his face. "Now I *know* she's a sorceress."

Riall burst out laughing just before Volund did. With a half-hearted glower, Khel feigned annoyance for a brief moment before joining them. Beyond all reason and feeding off their companions' mirth, the three of them laughed louder and longer than Riall had in a long time. At one point, Volund nearly teetered off his horse. They made such a ruckus that Belu poked her head out of Riall's cloak to growl and let out some playful barks. Then, as they all kept laughing, the little dog howled in accompaniment, which fanned the laughter further until Riall's belly ached and her lungs were tired and tears leaked out of her eyes. It was just what she needed.

After the laughter gave way to giggling and snorting, which in turn diminished into intermittent chuckling, she took a deep, relieved breath. With unspoken agreement, they continued on their way, each of them breaking out in titters from time to time as their horses trod along. Riall realized her companions had needed to laugh as much as she had.

When there had been no outbursts for a while, her smile sagged into a thoughtful frown. She stared ahead at the hills in the distance. "Speaking of mongrels . . . There's something else I need to tell you."

The two young men were quiet, but she could feel their gazes on her. In her love and relief for Seren, she had put aside this matter, but it was not something she could long ignore, and she needed to tell someone.

She let out a long sigh. "When someone with the gift enters a person's mind to do something to them . . . like I did with Seren . . . she sees some of the person's memories, especially what that person was thinking about in the moments before. It's a bit confusing, almost like you think you *are* the person, though at the same time you feel like you're no one at all, outside of everything and in everything at the same time." Realizing she was delaying, she swallowed. "I didn't mean to pry, it's just that this one thought was so strong in her. Perhaps she just wanted me to know." She shook her head, and then she took the leap. "I think I know who my father was."

A long pause. The silence that followed was deep in its contrast to their laughter of a moment before.

"You don't have to tell us if you don't want to." Khel's voice had gone gentle and kind again. She almost wished it had not since it made her want to cry.

Riall worried they would think her mad, but she had to say it aloud just to hear if it sounded as absurd as she feared it would. And yet, it explained so much, and Seren's memory could not have been stronger or clearer as it was nearly all she thought about in the moment of her healing, before she lost consciousness. But still . . .

"The Prophet of Edan," she blurted out. "He was my father." She looked at Khel and forced a smile even as Queen Sequara's warnings over the years about her power rushed back to her mind. "Which, since he was from the Mark, makes me a mongrel too. And likely more dangerous than I ever realized."

$\maltese$ 18 $\maltese$

Bolverk accepted the wooden cup of mead from the slave – a former member of the shattered and vanished Cleft Skulls. "Return to me with Unnar."

The slave – a thin, quiet man by the name of Ottil – bowed and retreated from the fire, leaving Bolverk with his three bodyguards. Atzil, Inger, and Uga were among his loyalest, deadliest, and most unimaginative warriors, which was what made them perfect body-guards. The two men were huge, even among the Folk of the Tribes, while Uga, smaller than most of the other female warriors, was quick as a viper.

The Cleft Skulls, Bolverk recalled with a whiff of nostalgia, had always sought the front lines in battle. Their war-leader Graen was one of the ugliest and bravest warriors he had ever met. *Damn fool.* The Raven Eyes had fought them more than once, and Bolverk had always outsmarted Graen. Still, the man had been brave, and it was a shame he and the best part of his folk were gone.

Bolverk shook his head when he recalled how many tribes – worthy foes and allies, all of them – had disappeared because of the stone-dwellers' war. The Night Trolls, the Stone Fists, the Strong Axes, the Boar Tusks, the Tall Spears, the Bear Fangs, the White Foxes, the

Bright Shields, the Snow Bears, the Black Elks, the Hawk Claws, and so many more. And, of course, the Fire Dragons, along with their leader Surt, the one who had forged the ever-bickering tribes into one folk and led them to their doom. Gone. Scores of thousands of warriors. Their grand dreams of conquering all of Eormenlond shattered in a moment. And it was all because of that damned other-worldly sorcery. He still got shivers when he dreamed about that day.

He had always known it was a bad idea for the Folk of the Tribes to get involved in the stone-dwellers' affairs, but there was little he could have done to stop it. As it was, he was lucky to have led his Raven Eyes out of it, and every bit of his cunning had served to keep them alive.

This was why he found Unnar's stupidity so vexing. The young fool was determined to get them all killed, starting with his own father.

Bolverk's youngest and only remaining child approached the fire along with Ottil. Putting one hand on his knee, the war-leader pushed himself up with a grunt and stood to face his son. Unnar was of a height with him and had his slender build. He also had his father's cunning and ambition. A shame he had his dead mother's wits.

Unnar glared at him with every bit of insolence he could muster. "You called for me, Father?"

He gazed at Unnar in silence until the young man shuffled a bit and then looked down. "Boy." He held out the untouched cup of mead to his son. "I find I'm not so thirsty this evening. A pity to waste such fine mead."

Unnar did not move.

Bolverk smirked. "Drink. It."

A long silence followed in which Unnar stared at his feet.

The war-leader pushed the cup closer to his son. "Come now. Drink." He waited another long moment. "No? Well. At least hold it for me."

Unnar glanced at him, his confusion and fear written on his face.

"You can do that much, can't you? Hold the cup for your father." He held it still closer to his son.

Unnar sulked and delayed as long as he could, but in the end he had no choice. He reached out for the cup. Just as he was about to grasp it, Bolverk jerked it back, startling both Unnar and Ottil.

"Don't spill it, now." Bolverk grinned at his son and held out the cup again.

Unnar grasped it and glared at him.

"Good. Was that so hard?" Bolverk unsheathed the long dagger at his hip and, with the swiftness that saw him rise to war-leader in his youth, plunged it up into the soft part of Ottil's jaw, severing his tongue and shoving it up through the roof of his mouth. He clenched his teeth as he drove the steel up further into the man's brain. The slave's eyes bulged wide as he jerked and quivered and opened his mouth to cough out a gout of blood, which spattered Bolverk with red droplets. After the old war-leader withdrew the blade, Ottil collapsed. He twitched on the ground and made wet, gasping noises while his blood leaked out of his mouth and nose and the large gash behind his bearded chin.

Unnar's hand was trembling, and a bit of the mead sloshed out of the cup onto it.

Bolverk bent down to wipe his dagger on Ottil's kirtle and, after sheathing it, he released a sigh of disappointment. He nodded at his son's hand, which was dripping with mead. "Told you not to spill it, boy. What am I to do with you?"

Unnar glanced behind his father at the three bodyguards. That seemed to put a stop to whatever stupidity the boy had been thinking of committing next.

Without looking back, Bolverk knew that all three of his warriors were gazing at Unnar with their hands on their sword hilts since he had ordered them to stand thus. "Well, what am I to do with you? Did you think I didn't know Ottil was a poisoner? A true war-leader must know follower and foe alike. Most of all, he must know his kin for what they are. Wouldn't you say so?"

Unnar opened his mouth, but no words came out. The only sound for a long moment was Ottil choking and noisily dying. At length, the war-leader's son gathered the courage to speak. "I'm sorry, Father."

"You disappoint me, boy. Poison is a coward's way. I'd shove that cup down your throat if you weren't the last of my sons. Still, you tempt me. First your idiotic raid on the Thjoths, and now this. You think you're ready to take over? You think the Raven Eyes would have *you* as war-leader?" He pointed backward with his thumb. "Atzil there would be a fitter leader than you. He's braver, and he's got more sense, though he only speaks three words. Gods, my fecking *horse* would be better than you."

Bolverk shook his head and grinded his teeth, and then he slapped the cup out of Unnar's hand, spilling the poisoned mead onto the ground. "Gods damn you, boy! Are you trying to end the Raven Eyes? After all I've done to keep us alive? We survived because of *me*."

"I want more than survival." Unnar scowled at his father with obvious contempt. "We scratch out a living here while the stone-dwellers scoff at us. We're wild dogs to them."

"So, that's it, is it? You've seen the stone-dwellers' great cities, and now you want a taste of something more than hide tents and mud huts. We went down that path, and few came back." Bolverk shook his head. "Dreams of glory! I've outlived plenty of glory-seekers, boy. They're all feeding worms – every last one. Sailing for Grimrik to raid the high and mighty Thjoths. Has lording it over the other tribes here in the Wildlands grown too easy? Grimrik? Did you think we needed the Thjoths for foes to prove our courage? You're not wise enough to know the difference between courage and stupidity, and that's why you're not fit to lead. Here's the truth: If I hadn't come after you, you'd all have died on your raid like the glory-seeking fools you are. Worm food! As it is, I'm trying to make the best of your fecking disaster."

Unnar sulked and scratched his head. "I took hostages. Sigra is worth . . ."

"She's bound to cost far more than she's worth. Trading her for the Dweorgs might have worked and given us a real edge out here in the Wildlands, but Orvandil Dragonbane's no fool. We've got one last chance: I've got to wed her to make allies of the Thjoths, even if they're reluctant allies. Even just to keep them from slaughtering us. No other way out."

Defiance returned to Unnar's eyes, though he did nothing more than frown at his father.

Bolverk smirked at his son. "Is that the way of it, then? You want her, don't you?" He shook his head and rolled his eyes. "Gods damned idiot." He lunged forward, reached down under Unnar's kirtle, and grabbed his testicles, squishing them in an iron grip.

Unnar gasped and grunted as his father squeezed.

"Listen, boy." Bolverk spoke through clenched teeth. "Stop thinking with this." A sharp tug made it clear what he meant, and Unnar cried out. "Start thinking with this," and he tapped his son's forehead with his free index finger, digging it in and putting his face right in Unnar's. "Understand?"

"Yes, Father." Unnar just managed to wheeze out the words as his face went almost purple and a bead of sweat ran down a protruding vein in his forehead.

"And another thing you'd best understand: She's the only thing keeping us alive just now. Go near her without my leave, and I'll cut this off and make you eat it raw." He squeezed and wrenched one last time, and Unnar shrieked. When Bolverk let go, his son collapsed in a fetal tuck next to Ottil, who had stopped twitching.

Shadowed by his three bodyguards, Bolverk strode away from his groaning son.

❦ 19 ❦

Day gave way to the gloaming. Sinking on the horizon, the westering sun gilded the foothills of the Marar Mountains to the north, deepening the long shadows in their clefts and valleys, while its waning light coruscated on the playful, gurgling surface of the River Gilion, which paralleled their road. The further they journeyed from Caergilion's coast, the less it rained, and thank Edan it was a dry evening.

After feeding the horses and leading them to drink from the river, Khel rubbed them down while the others readied their little camp. He shook a slight cramp out of his hands and favored the beasts with a smile and a few whispered words of thanks. Breathing in their earthy scent – a somehow pleasant mixture of sweat, manure, and hay – he patted their bulging neck and shoulder muscles. He had always liked horses. They never betrayed him, never hurt him, and never called him a bastard or a half-breed or a thief.

He glanced over at the fire, which Volund was tending while Riall sat stroking the fur behind Belu's ears. Growing up as he had, he often found it needful to judge a person within the first few words of a conversation, and time rarely proved him wrong. Riall was different. Possessing one strange layer after another, she defied such deeming.

99

Never before had he encountered such a fascinating mess of contradictions as the Prophet of Edan's daughter. She was stronger than a mountain yet endearingly vulnerable. Perceptive yet naïve. Vibrant yet remote. Beautiful yet frightening.

Riall was watching Volund, and she said something to him that Khel could not quite hear. Volund looked up in that ever-startled way of his, making Khel wonder once again what was going on inside the boy's head. *Likely dreaming of winches.*

Volund rumbled a reply that made Riall giggle, belying the loneliness always lurking in her rich brown eyes. A shy smile crossed the young Thjoth's face as he stole a glance at the sorceress and then returned his focus to the fire. Riall's tentative grin disappeared, and she looked at Volund as if seeing something for the first time. He seemed unaware of her gaze.

Khel frowned at this interaction, feeling like an intruder in their adventure, though an intruder with a conveniently heavy purse.

He strode over to the fire and stood over it as he shook out his hands a bit more. There was a long silence in which the three of them gazed at the crackling flames. When the silence became nigh unbearable, Khel mustered up a smirk and stared at Volund. "I've heard of a custom among you Thjoths whereby two warriors at odds take sacred oaths, sail together to the island of Vargholm, and fight to the death. Is it true that the victor builds a funeral pyre for the loser?"

Volund's head rose slowly until he looked at Khel. He nodded.

In vain Khel waited for him to elaborate. "Well, that's quite civilized then, isn't it?" He barked a laugh, but there was no response from Volund.

Khel's smile sagged into a serious frown. "Ever done it yourself?"

"Khel." Riall's voice was calm, but the disapproval in it was evident. "What sort of question is that?"

He shrugged. "I was just asking. Perhaps it's some way to prove their courage."

"*Holmgang.* We call it that. Stops feuding. No one may take vengeance on the victor, who fought beneath the gods' eyes. Doesn't happen much now that we worship Edan." Volund gave a brief, almost apologetic smile. "And no, I've never done it. Told you: I like to make things, not break them."

Khel raised his eyebrows. "Not a fighter, then?"

Volund frowned and squinted at him the way he did whenever Khel touched a nerve. "We all learn to fight."

Khel gazed at him a moment and then rested a hand on the hilt of his scabbarded sword. "Of course. The legendary Thjoths." He stretched and rubbed his back with his free hand. "All this riding has me stiff all over. Some exercise would be good." He flashed a toothy smile at Volund. "How about a little sparring? Give us a glimpse of the fighting prowess of the Thjoths."

Riall sat up. "It'll be dark soon."

"Nonsense." Khel unsheathed his blade and swept it in a graceful arc. "There's still plenty of light." He gestured toward the setting sun, which set aflame the clouds with orange and pink glows.

"Still." Riall glanced around as if seeking some other reason for preventing their sparring. "Perhaps you shouldn't."

Khel forced a laugh. "Come now, we're not on Vargholm. No oaths. No . . . What did you call it? *Holmgang*?"

Volund nodded.

"And certainly no funeral pyres, I hope." Khel winked at Riall and swept his blade again before returning his gaze to the Thjoth. "Right. How about it, then? Care to help me stretch my limbs a little?"

Volund rose. "Alright." He unsheathed his Dweorg-wrought blade, whose distinctive wavy patterns reflected the slanted light.

Khel grinned at Riall as if to say, *See? I told you so.* He stepped away from the fire, and Volund followed. The two young men faced each other and gazed into one another's eyes. Khel's grin disappeared as he made a slight bow, and Volund nodded in return.

They raised their blades and assumed fighting stances.

It began. Khel probed with his blade to test his opponent. Volund did not retreat even a step as he parried, knocking Khel's thrust aside. Next, Khel feinted low and then brought his sword up in a diagonal slash, and once again the swords rang out when the young Thjoth parried. In the background, Belu was barking with excitement while Riall was scolding her, but Khel's focus was on his opponent.

He danced around, trying to keep his back to the sunset and to position Volund so that the younger boy would be squinting into the light. But the Thjoth was too smart and too solid for the ploy, and he managed to reposition himself with an admirable economy of movement. Khel began to suspect that his opponent might actually be quite good.

He darted in and unleashed a series of slashes and cuts. Without seeming to expend much effort, Volund made precise movements to either dodge or block each one. The Thjoth was like a thick wall, solid and immovable, and he used his longer reach to great advantage. Though larger, his blade seemed no heavier than Khel's as he kept up with every sweep and thrust. When Khel leaped backwards to disengage, his chest was heaving while he gulped in breaths. Volund, who did not pursue his wilting opponent but waited with a rock's patience, did not appear the least bit winded. *He's not just good. He's much better than I am. And he's not even trying to hit me.*

While he circled Volund, Belu's barking grew louder. He tried to ignore the distraction since he needed every bit of concentration. It dawned on him that, while he was an excellent swordsman back on Asdralad, where he had enjoyed all the lessons his mother's money could buy, here before him was something he had never fought: a warrior. The ease with which Volund flicked back his attacks spoke of training so thorough that the blade was not a tool but an extension of the Thjoth's body. He was not even attacking, but if he were, Khel knew he would be hard pressed to stay afoot. Volund was just as quick as he was, but he was also stronger, taller, fitter, and better. However, even as part of his mind took in all these facts, they also infuriated another part of his mind, which won over any trace of good sense. Having recovered his breath, Khel dashed forward to renew his attacks with greater vigor.

The results were little different, except that Khel grew more tired, his swings and thrusts more sluggish, while Volund still appeared as fresh as when they started. Sweat was making Khel's grip slip a bit, and he wiped his brow with his free hand to keep it from dripping in his eyes. He was almost gasping for breath. All the while, the confounded dog kept barking.

Khel gritted his teeth and dove forward again, only to glimpse a little black blur beneath his feet.

"Belu!" Riall's shout conveyed her alarm and distress, but she could not have been as alarmed as Khel, who shifted his feet to avoid stepping on the little dog and tripped over himself in the process. He let his sword fly out of his hands to avoid spitting himself on it, went down with a grunt, and rolled onto his back. Paws climbed onto his chest, and a little pink tongue darted out to slather his face.

"Ugh!" Khel grasped Belu's stomach with both hands and lifted her above his face so that her flailing limbs dangled under her.

The little dog appeared to be grinning at him in between her loud, high-pitched barks.

Khel groaned. "Defeated by a diminutive cur." He deposited the dog on the ground beside him, where she continued barking. Khel sat up and glared at her. "Not that I was doing so well before your arrival."

Riall knelt by her dog and put protective arms around her. "I'm sorry. She wanted to join in. She thought you were playing." Was she suppressing a smile?

Khel managed a weak grin. "So we were. Playing. Weren't we?" He looked up and winked at Volund, who stood over him.

Volund smiled. "Aye. That we were." He extended a hand toward Khel, who beheld the hand for a while before reaching up to take it. Volund hoisted him up, and they faced one another.

In that moment, Khel looked up into his little brother's blue eyes and ached to tell him who he was. His mouth opened, but no words came out until he said, "That's a fine blade you have, and you wield it well. May I?" He held out his hand. After a brief hesitation, Volund presented the sword hilt first.

Khel grasped the hilt, stepped back a pace, and swung the blade. His eyes widened. "Perfect balance. Lighter than it looks. Yet you could snap ordinary steel with it, I reckon." He gazed down at the wavy pattern on the blade. "Dweorg-wrought. First time I've held one." He handed it back to Volund hilt first.

The young Thjoth took the sword and sheathed it. He looked at his feet. "In truth, it's not quite Dweorg-wrought."

Khel frowned at him. "Of course it is. There's the telltale pattern. And it's . . ."

"I made it." Volund peeked at him before returning his gaze to the ground.

"You?"

Volund sighed. "Please tell no one. Gnorn would be in trouble if anyone knew, especially the other Dweorgs."

"Gnorn?"

"He's the Dweorg who was with you in Asdralad. Your father's friend." Riall stepped forward with a knowing grin on her face. "He taught you to forge, didn't he?"

Volund nodded. "He's likely with Yrsa and your queen now. I used to help him in the forge. Took an interest. When he saw what I could do . . ." He shrugged.

Khel's mouth dropped open. "*You* know the secret to forging Dweorg-wrought steel? No one but a highly trained Dweorg is supposed to be able to work it, and even then it's the most jealously guarded secret in Andumedan."

Volund looked worried. "Please tell no one. I shouldn't have spoken of it." He shuffled his feet. "It's just . . . There's no one else to tell."

Riall smiled and put her hand on Volund's shoulder. "Don't worry. Your secret's safe with us. Isn't it, Khel?"

Still in disbelief, Khel inflated his cheeks and blew out of puff of air. "Yes. Of course." He shook his head. He looked again at his little brother, this quiet warrior who could forge steel like a Dweorg, and both pride and despair filled him. *I'll never be like him. I'm not even half a Thjoth.* The moment to confess who his father was had passed.

"Thank you." Volund gave a brief smile. "If you want, we spar again on the morrow. Stay in form. And we both learn."

Khel debated a moment, embarrassed by Volund's generosity and ashamed of how part of him wanted to scream and rage at such kindness. He mastered his emotions and forced a grin. "Alright. But the cur can't help you again."

An amused snort escaped Volund, and they clasped hands in agreement.

20

Beneath the same sun that was setting upon Riall, Khel, and Volund but well south of the River Gilion in the kingdom of Adanon, Queen Sequara gazed northward. Many leagues back she had lost the sense of the gift in Riall. However, she was sure that the young woman and her two companions were following the road that paralleled the river on their journey east through Caergilion. Her plan was simple, though the risk was tremendous: take a more southerly route to skirt around her quarry and reach Balnor Pass before Riall did. There, within the inescapable confines of the pass, she would confront the girl. Everything depended on speed.

To that end, she and Gnorn and the Thjoths had traded the horses they had bought on a farm in Caergilion for fresh mounts in Harieth after crossing the river into Adanon. They were driving the steeds hard, but not quite hard enough to harm them. They would be depending on their mounts for many leagues to come. Thus, Sequara had expended a fair amount of energy soothing the animals and healing their tired muscles with the gift, murmuring the needed song of origin beneath her breath. A stone had injured one of their hooves, but she had seen to that too. It was as good as having fresh mounts, and healing always felt fulfilling to her, though it was draining and left her with little energy. She only hoped Riall would not think to take such a measure as well.

Given what could have happened at Seren's home, Sequara hoped Riall would have the foresight to refrain from using her power save in the most dire need. Unfortunately, the girl might perceive their looming encounter in Balnor Pass as warranting such an occasion. The sorceress-queen released a long sigh. She would cross that bridge when she came to it.

It had been good to see Seren, even if briefly. Though still weak and unable to rise from her sickbed, she had worn a mischievous smile when she confessed that she and Ceri had allowed Riall and her companions to take horses from their barn. Such was the sorceress-queen's relief at her dear friend's life being spared that she could not find the heart to scold her for aiding Riall's escape. And Gnorn had been so overjoyed to see Seren that the old Dweorg had wept. It was impossible not to share in that joy.

In truth, the part of Sequara that was not terrified of what Riall might do here on the mainland by using her power was proud of the girl. She had healed. The queen had checked Seren over herself using the gift, and she had found that Riall's healing had been most thorough and effective. Were it not for the nature of Riall's power, she would be everything Sequara wished she herself could be. Devoted, loyal, compassionate. Still, Riall's act frightened her beyond words, and Sequara could not shake the sense of foreboding that gripped her ever since the girl had embarked on this journey. But Seren was alive, and Volund and Khel appeared to be unharmed, which bespoke Riall's control of her power.

A hundred yards away, the Thjoths were preparing their camp. Traveling with them – and most especially with Gnorn – in Caergilion and Adanon brought back more memories of the events of the war. Not all were terrible. Some were even beautiful. None were without consequence.

Behind her, Gnorn cleared his throat to warn of his approach. "Your Majesty, Yrsa and her warriors are going to seek game in the little remaining light. I'll stay in your company if you wish."

Sequara put on a smile and turned around. "Your company is most welcome, old friend." She took a deep breath and let it out slowly as she gazed at the grassy landscape around them. "It's strange to be back, isn't it?"

"Aye." The Dweorg stood next to her and beheld the darkening plain. He tucked his thumbs into his belt and gave a solemn nod. "We saw a great many things in those days. Never expected to survive some. But we pulled through, didn't we? All that death and destruction. At times, it felt like an end to everything. But when I think about it all, what I remember most is the Prophet. In his gentle way, he changed the world, I reckon."

Sequara looked at Gnorn, who glanced at her with a sad smile on his weathered face. "Yes. He did." She returned her gaze to the plain.

The Dweorg shook his head. "Can't see a sunset without thinking of him. He was . . . beautiful."

"Yes." She continued her study of the shadow-steeped landscape.

"I miss him."

A single tear spilled from Sequara's eye and tracked down her cheek. "As do I." The words came out in little more than a whisper.

Next to her, Gnorn nodded. "The lass. Riall. She doesn't know he's her father, does she?"

With her years of training having become instinct, the queen betrayed little outward emotion. Even so, a fist clenched her heart. She could not think of what to say, so long had she kept this vast and sacred secret that her friend had just given voice to.

Gnorn's smile conveyed the sorrow and pain but also the wisdom of a long, eventful life. "Don't forget I knew him well. Not as well as you did, but better than most anyone else. The moment I saw the lass in your garden, she put me in mind of him. She has the same . . . Well, my clumsy old tongue won't find the words for it, but there's a kind of longing that comes in her presence, like when one gazes at the glow of all the stars on a clear night. And there's the way you look when you speak of her."

Sequara swallowed and licked her lips, tasting the salt of the tear that had ended there, but she could not master her voice yet. Her question must have been written in her eyes, for Gnorn answered it with his next words:

"Fear not. No one but I has guessed the truth, though I reckon Seren must know everything. Perhaps Imharr as well? Well, no one will learn of it from me unless you bid me speak of it. I know you, and I knew *him*. When you told us of the nature of Riall's power, it wasn't so hard to put it all together. It's a strange joy to see a bit of him still in the world, I tell you."

Another tear freed itself from Sequara's eye. She was nigh breathless, but she managed to speak. "I've carried him with me all these years."

"Aye, I know. And the secret of Riall's birth. Am I right in assuming the girl has no notion you're her mother?"

Sequara lifted her trembling hand to her mouth and bit her knuckle. Her eyes blurred with tears she willed not to fall. She nodded.

"So." Gnorn put his hand on Sequara's shoulder. "That's a heavy burden you took on. But I know why. Asdralad's throne. No Andumaic sorcerer-ruler may wed or have children, and your kingdom needed you after the war, especially with Queen Faldira gone. No one else could have healed Asdralad as you did."

Sequara bowed her head as she held back more tears and tried to steady her breaths. Gnorn too bowed his head and waited while the darkness thickened around them.

At length, the sorceress-queen cleared her throat and found her voice, which quivered only a little. "Give up my daughter or my kingdom. That is what I told myself. But I also feared . . . The war changed me. I was afraid I could no longer love a child the way a mother should, and so duty became my refuge. My excuse."

Sequara shook her head. "It was in the earliest days of my rule. Months before my time came, I journeyed to Adanon, letting it be known I was there to visit Queen Rona and procure supplies for the rebuilding of Kiriath after the war. Imharr and Seren knew. It was Seren who suggested I use her newly rebuilt home in Caergilion as a refuge where I could give birth without anyone knowing. She served as midwife. In the meantime, Rona kept the supplies coming to Kiriath, thus preserving the pretense of my journey."

Her sad smile was laden with memory. "Riall's birth was the most beautiful and painful moment of my life. I left my baby with Seren to raise, knowing she would love her. I swore her to secrecy."

Sequara looked at Gnorn, who nodded and waited for her to continue. She shuddered with a deep sigh. "But Riall . . . my daughter. She needed me. When Seren sent word about strange things happening around the child, I knew something was amiss. The gift should not manifest until a child is much older. And then, as soon as I saw her, I knew what was in her. Her father's power. The elf." She shuddered, whether in grief or in fear she was not certain.

The sorceress-queen ran her fingers through her hair and shut her eyes for a moment. "I did not lie to you back in Kiriath. My first thought was that I should spare her a life in which she would inevitably destroy many others, starting with those closest to her, as the power within her took over. My second was that I could not. I've tried so hard to keep her from harm, and to keep her from harming others. And now . . . I'm so afraid. So afraid for my girl." She paused to collect herself lest she succumb to the sob building in her. "I'm worn out. And I've failed." She shook her head and wiped her cheeks with her sleeve.

"No, you haven't." Gnorn drew himself up. "No harm has come to Riall yet, nor has she done any. The lass may surprise you. She has her father in her, I tell you. And more than a bit of her mother." In addition to wisdom, there was deep kindness in the Dweorg's smile. "Besides, we'll catch them up, and you will guide her, as you've done all these years. As only a mother could."

Sequara looked at Gnorn and sniffled before nodding. In the last rays of the setting sun, she embraced her old friend and, for the first time in many years, allowed her tears to flow.

21

"It's her," said Orvandil before he even reached the ship's bow to confirm Hakon's sighting.

"Heading straight for us." The veteran's gaze was frozen as he squinted toward the oncoming threat.

"Aye." The king of the Thjoths gripped the rail and peered skyward. In the midst of the blue streaked a speck that would grow larger with every heartbeat as it headed toward the ship. Far below it, Grimrik's rugged coast beckoned. There was no chance their ship would reach one of the fjords before the dragon swooped down upon them. Even had they been in one of the famed Thjothic warships, they would have been doomed.

Orvandil had hoped the merchant ship sent to pick up his small party from the Wildlands would be inconspicuous, and, in the darkness of early morning, they had indeed slipped away from the Ilarchae undetected. With smooth sailing on a cloudless day with nearly perfect winds, they had almost made it home without incident. Almost.

It was strange that the ancient serpent of the air would seek such quarry as a lone trading vessel. Since Gorsharhad had been making her attacks, the dragon had for the most part targeted populous areas or large gatherings. Perhaps the lingworm was turning to smaller prey since folk had abandoned many northern towns and cities.

Perhaps it was personal. Orvandil had more than once wondered if Gorsarhad somehow knew how he had earned the name "Dragonbane" during the war and was dealing out vengeance. That was, of course, nonsense – even in light of the cunning intelligence the beast possessed – and anyway the Torrlonders, Ellonders, and Sildharae had suffered the attacks too. Still, the name attached to him seemed a mockery, given his helplessness to stop the beast from terrorizing his kingdom.

Perhaps no longer.

He clenched his teeth and took a deep breath. The old battle lust was rising in him, and he made no attempt to suppress it. Here was another chance to repeat the deed of slaying a dragon. And, he reminded himself, a way to save his kingdom. Once free of the beast, he could bring Grimrik's full might to bear against Bolverk and his Raven Eyes. He looked around at his men, who were gawking up into the sky, some with their hands shielding their eyes from the bright sunlight. They would need to be swift.

"All of you! Flee the ship! Pair up! Help one another shed your mail. Leave your weapons behind save one dagger. Lose your boots too. It's a long swim to Grimrik. No unneeded weight." His warriors were strong swimmers. Some of them would make it.

However, none of them obeyed his command. Instead, they stood where they were, some gazing at him and some at their own feet.

His mouth quirked into a crooked smile. He had expected some resistance. As afraid as they must have been of the approaching death from the air, their fear of cowardice was greater still. That was the essence of courage. To flee would shame them, but, most of all, they could not live with the humiliation of abandoning their lord.

Orvandil cleared his throat. "Brothers! No king has ever had worthier or braver warriors than I. But hearken to me: A dragon is no human foe. This ship is doomed, and there's no shame in living another day to avenge ourselves on the beast. Swim for your lives, and I will see you on shore."

Only their stony gazes answered him, but he read what lay behind them. None of them wished to be first.

"Go on, then!" Orvandil slapped Halvard's shoulder to get him moving. The other men were still hesitating. "Into the water!" He pushed Halvard, who stumbled a couple steps. "Do you dare to disobey my command?"

A few began helping each other out of their mail, but Halvard planted his feet. "What about you?"

"I'll be along. Get moving."

Wearing a stubborn frown, Halvard stayed put.

Orvandil strode up to the tall warrior and stared straight ahead into his eyes. He was one of the few men the king did not look down at. "Gods damn it, man. I'll throw you in the water myself."

"Can't leave. Not until you're off the ship."

"You'll do no good here, unless you can fly and spout flames out your arse." He quieted his voice. "If I don't make it, Sigra will need you. I depend on you."

Halvard's eyes widened only a little. Even though he kept the stubborn set to his jaw, Orvandil knew he had him.

"I'll be right behind you. I swear it by Edan."

The younger man hesitated, and then he nodded.

"Good. Now help me out of my cuirass, and then I'll get your byrny off."

By the time they had performed those tasks, some of the men were already diving off the ship into the water. With each splash, Orvandil hoped another of his followers would survive. He glanced up at the sky. Gorsarhad was larger than a speck now, and he could see her outstretched wings as she glided on them with an occasional flap. She was still heading straight for the ship.

He bent to pull off his boots. When he looked up, Halvard was standing next to him barefoot. He nodded at the younger man. "Go on. Don't forget what I told you."

"Never. But I'll see you in Grimrik."

"Aye."

He gave Halvard a gentle push, and the last of his warriors heaved himself over the railing to leap off the ship.

Orvandil strode aft. The grain of the wooden deck was smooth beneath his feet. He felt light without his leather armor, but he still wore Seeker on his belt. He was willing to chance the extra weight to keep the sword Gnorn had forged for him, and it might come in handy against his approaching foe. Once he reached the ship's stern he bent down and removed a canvas tarp, which he cast aside. Among the spears stored there was one different from the others with its shorter, black shaft: one of the Dweorg-wrought iron-shafted spears they had recovered from Valfoss. Orvandil had ordered it stored aboard the ship in case of need. He was glad his foresight had allowed him another chance to use it.

One spear. One brief moment of opportunity. At least it was possible, and it was worth the risk.

He slid his grip along the spear until the balance felt perfect, and then he walked toward the ship's bow. Once he passed the mast, he gained a clear view of the beast plummeting toward him.

Her vast and awesome form was unmistakable. She was darker than most dragons, almost black instead of crimson. On a ship half the length of the eldest of dragons, Orvandil was insignificant beneath her enormity. He readied his grip. His smile was fierce and eager.

Gorsarhad folded her wings, each far larger than the ship's sail, and tipped downward into a dive, slicing the air and speeding straight for the ship.

Standing his ground not far from the mast, Orvandil abided her.

One hundred feet above the water, Gorsarhad unfurled her wings with a loud snap, ceasing her downward fall even as she careened toward the helpless ship. Huge muscles rippled and slithered along her neck. Her massive jaws opened, revealing yellowed teeth as long as Seeker. Preceding her on the sea's surface, her huge shadow slipped over and darkened the shimmering water.

Come, big lizard. His eyes locked onto the monstrosity hurtling toward him, Orvandil tightened his grip on the cold iron shaft of his spear and hoisted it above his shoulder. He took one slow step forward. Then another. Several more came in succession until he was walking, and then, before Gorsarhad's shadow swallowed the ship, he broke into a sprint toward the bow, his feet pounding on the boards.

A ruddy-orange light kindled to life deep down Gorsarhad's dark gullet. The black slits in her amber eyes bespoke the cunning and triumph of a predator about to devour her prey. Air-bending heat rushed from her mouth, and a roar like an avalanche blasted everything before her.

Gaze fixed on that vast maw, Orvandil dashed at full speed to the ship's bow, where he leaped up, landed with one foot on the railing, and pushed off with all his might into the air, his legs still pumping as if he trod on invisible steps. At the same moment, with every bit of momentum from his sprint behind the thrust, he hurled the spear into the jaws of death, whence a horrific torrent of flames exploded forth. The spear's shaft glowed bright red before the inferno enveloped it. A blinding flash and wave of heat swarmed the king of the Thjoths, who plummeted downward.

❧ 2 2 ❧

Riall gazed down at the empty husk she had walked in for countless miles. Sprawled on the ground where it had fallen, the boy's body had been too broken to continue much longer in it. She glanced at the unfamiliar hands attached to her. With the palms facing outward, she held them in what must have been a protective and alarmed stance on their previous owner's part. They were dripping water. A woman's hands, plump and light-skinned, though chafed and red on the knuckles from the cold of the water and much hard use. She wore a brown woolen frock.

Beside her on the ground were two piles of clothes, one dry and one wet. Worn leather shoes lay nearby. A burbling sound drew her attention, and she turned around to see a broad river behind her. She stood on the riverbank at a bight where the water eddied in a small, shallow pool perfect for bathing or washing clothes. A washerwoman, then. Well, no longer.

No need for the shoes. Thick callouses covered the bottoms of her feet. Good for walking, though these mortal bodies were so frail.

She took a step, and the soft grass of the riverbank became a busy cobbled street, full of people and animals and buildings and smells, an all-out assault on her senses. The people were talking and shouting, mostly in Ondunic, but the familiar cry of merchants boasting of their wares would have been similar in any language. Horses snorted, dogs barked, and chickens clucked. A giggling little boy ran in between the legs of a man, who scolded the child loudly. In the shadow of one building slumped a hooded beggar, probably an old woman. The buildings were of grey stone, and several spires and domes were taller than anything she had ever seen in Kiriath. Even more overwhelming than the noise were the rotten stenches of dung, sweat, and human waste of all sorts.

A distant part of her mind awakened and remembered. *Iarfaen. Caergilion's chief city.* Here was the seat of her native kingdom's monarch, King Moradoc, though she was no longer certain she was in fact Caergilese if her father was the Prophet of Edan.

Riall's head jerked down to gawk at her hands, which she flapped in front of her to shake the water off. But they were, of course, dry. And brown, which seemed strange for a heartbeat because she had expected them to be white with reddened knuckles.

She looked to her right, where Khel stood gazing at her, wearing a worried frown. "You alright?" He had to almost shout for her to hear him above the din. He glanced at her hands, which she still held before her.

Her hands dropped to her sides. She nodded and tried to smile. "Just . . . too much noise."

"What?"

"Too much noise!"

Several passersby turned to her with scowls that plainly said they thought her mad. Riall flushed and pulled up her hood, but the citizens of Iarfaen, no doubt accustomed to the sundry forms of lunacy that cities evoke or attract, moved on without a backward glance.

Khel did not look convinced by her answer, but he jerked his head to indicate she should follow. Ahead of them, Volund was waiting with Belu in his arms.

As she walked behind her companions through the jostling throngs, everything rushed back to Riall's mind to displace the fleeting amnesia and confusion that always gripped her mind after each waking vision. They had reached Iarfaen that morning. Since their horses had been bone weary, they had agreed to sell them to a courser and use the silver to buy fresh mounts on the other side of Balnor Pass, in Torrlond. She would repay Seren for the steeds when she returned to visit her. They had also bought thick wool cloaks for the cooler mountain air, especially at night. Each of them wore a pack stuffed with provisions since they no longer had their horses to carry everything.

With the notable exception of her disturbing and increasingly vivid visions where she occupied someone else's body, the journey to Iarfaen had passed pleasantly. They had ridden for hours each day until her riding muscles grew used to it. Volund and Khel practiced their swordsmanship each evening, and sometimes Riall joined in, using Khel's blade since it was similar to the one she had trained with under Queen Sequara's weaponsmaster. Volund remained their teacher, but she and Khel had learned much. More importantly, the three of them had grown closer and more trusting of each other, though she knew they each held on to some secrets. It seemed almost a miracle to her that, for the first time in her life, Riall enjoyed the affection of open friendship with someone her own age, which she pondered with a secret smile each night as she drifted off to sleep.

But for the visions, it would have been beautiful. When she was not trying to forget them, Riall acknowledged that her waking dreams were becoming more powerful − somehow closer to her, as if she were drawing nigher to the thing she was seeking in them. What haunted her most was how the theft of each victim's body mirrored the mercy she would have given Seren if the woman had asked it of her. *But none of these people wanted to die.* She swallowed a lump of guilt. *I have no control of these visions. What can I do?* But she could not shake the conviction that the visions were in some way connected to the exercise of the gift in her, and so she resolved to avoid using her power. Of course, she said nothing of them to Khel or Volund, whose friendship was too precious to endanger.

There was also one other worry. It had been a long while since she felt the presence of the gift in Queen Sequara. Here in Iarfaen there had been someone with the gift, but he − Riall thought of the person as a "he" for some reason − had not been nearly as powerful as the sorceress-queen, and he was likely too far away to sense the gift in

Riall. In the midst of her banter with Khel and Volund, at times she forgot to worry about the queen's absence. But there were little reminders, like the fellow with the gift in Iarfaen, that made her wonder when she would encounter her mentor again. Knowing Queen Sequara as she did, she did not doubt that she would.

Such were her thoughts as she followed Khel and Volund's backs through the loud, clogged streets. Volund went first. Crowds parted for the large, pale-skinned young warrior, making it easy for him to clear a path for the companions. Though many stares lingered on him, Volund did not seem bothered as he led them north through the city. Being a broad-shouldered, fierce-looking Thjoth had its benefits, though the fact that he carried a little black dog added a slightly comic effect to his ferocity, which made Riall grin. She sensed Belu's contentedness in Volund's arms, and she was glad her little companion was sharing in her new friendships too.

However, her grin faded as they approached a large cobbled square before the city's northern gate, where they gained an unobstructed view of the landscape outside the city. Over the wall in the distance loomed jagged, snow-capped peaks that dared to pierce the clouds. Beneath the snow, massive slabs of grey rock soared upward as if the earth had thrust them there in some ancient cataclysm. The Marar Mountains. Such a marvel alone would have given Riall pause. But the view was not the reason she stood in the middle of the square gazing northward toward the mountains.

Khel looked back toward her, his worry written on his face. "Riall? Is something amiss?"

She took a deep breath. "I knew she wouldn't give up. She's *ahead* of us."

"She?" Khel shook his head. "Who's ahead of us?"

"Queen Sequara. She's up ahead somewhere. She'll be waiting for me in Balnor Pass." The sense of the gift far ahead was the faintest of whispers, but it was enough for Riall.

Khel's frown deepened. "You're certain?"

"Yes. No mistake."

"And you still wish to avoid her?"

Riall nodded. She could not allow Queen Sequara to stop her

before she made it to Grimrik to rid the Thjoths of the dragon. She had promised she would do it, and she knew she could help them. If the queen forced the issue, Riall would use her power, but she wished to avoid this for two reasons. The first was that she had no desire to confront her mentor, for whom she held the deepest respect and even awe, even though the woman's considerable power could never match her own. The second reason was the dire warning that her visions seemed to give.

Khel's wonted grin returned, full of mischief that warmed Riall despite her worries. "Well, then. We'll simply find another way through, won't we?"

❧ 23 ❧

"That's where they piled the dead."

As if he could still see the corpses, Gnorn's wide eyes were gazing at the interior of the southern wall of the fortress occupying Balnor Pass. Consisting of a northern and southern wall, each dozens of feet high with a thick gate in the middle, the fortification also included a small castle to house the garrison. Folk had considered it an impregnable barrier since so few could approach it in the confines of the pass. That was before the War of the Way.

The Dweorg shook his head, seeming to break the spell of the past, and then he sighed. "In truth, it was no battle. It was a massacre. The Torrlonders hardly even needed to engage. The trolls, aglaks, and pucas had already broken the Caergilese garrison."

One of the frequent gusts that careened between the rocky cliffs surrounding the pass kicked up and moaned, seeming to give voice to ghosts haunting this place where soldiers shed their blood in the name of their kingdoms. Sequara squinted into the chill wind and brushed aside her loose hair before pulling her woolen cloak tighter to her body. She stifled her old anger at how the Torrlonder priests of the Way had enslaved the beasts to use them in their war, visiting horrors upon the people they sought to conquer. Even years later, the Marar

Mountains were said to be full of escaped and cast off trolls and pucas, making any route over the mountains other than the well-guarded Balnor Pass too dangerous to risk.

Yrsa snorted her contempt. "That's a coward's way to fight. Making other creatures do the work for you."

Gnorn looked at her with a sad smile. "So the powerful have always done."

"Not the Thjoths. We fight our own battles."

"Aye. There's no braver folk. But even Thjoths take what advantages come to them." Gnorn nodded meaningfully at the Dweorg-wrought blade scabbarded at Yrsa's side.

Yrsa looked down at the sword and, seeming to understand Gnorn's meaning, opened her mouth to retort. But then she seemed to think better of it, for no words came out.

Gnorn chuckled without mirth. "No shame in it where both parties profit. Your father's a wise king, and we Dweorgs cherish the place he has honored us with in Grimrik, which was our homeland before your ancestors took it long ago. Dweorgs and Thjoths alike gain from his wisdom. But the leaders of the Torrlonders back during the War of the Way, King Earconwald and the Supreme Priest Bledla, were not so wise. They used and tortured living creatures, including the dragons, in worse ways than anyone has ever done to a sword, and the beasts gained nothing but death and misery from it. I sometimes wonder if Gorsarhad's attacks might not be her idea of vengeance. Such an ancient beast must have long memories, and who is to say that she might not inflict such sorrows as the feuds we lesser creatures wreak upon each other?" He nodded and frowned as he gazed again at the wall.

Sequara glanced at her old friend. Gnorn had been melancholy ever since they reached Iarfaen. On the slopes outside the city, his younger brother Hlokk had died in the first largescale battle of the War of the Way. Their haste to save the Prophet of Edan on that day had prevented Gnorn from giving his brother a proper burial. Sequara knew the Dweorgish rites for the dead were sacred since Dweorgs believed the spirit of the departed needed them to journey to their ancestors. Perhaps Gnorn's failure to conduct them for Hlokk was one reason why the old Dweorg seemed so troubled, as if he expected to see his brother's ghost lingering in the mountains.

The past weighed on the sorceress-queen as well. Iarfaen was where she first met the Prophet and saved his life, back when he seemed so young. In the process, she sealed their fate, though she resisted it for a long time. In a sense, then, Iarfaen was where Riall's story began. She wished she knew more about where and how it would end. But one thing she did know: She would do everything in her power to save her daughter from whatever threatened her, including herself.

A group of Caergilese soldiers in their red tunics walked past their party, casting quick but curious glances at her and Gnorn and the Thjoths. Sequara was glad she had taken the time in Iarfaen to secure permission from King Moradoc to await Riall and the two young men in Balnor Pass. Moradoc had asked no questions of her and generously forgiven her the haste she was in, even going as far as giving her party fresh horses as well as warm clothes and supplies.

It helped that Asdralad and Caergilion enjoyed close ties after the war, especially in consideration of everything Sequara had done while serving alongside Caergilese rebels against Torrlonder rule. She had also met Moradoc's father King Malruan before the latter died in the same battle that took Gnorn's brother. In view of such a long friendship, Caergilion's current king had gladly written orders to the garrison's captain to admit Sequara and her party, allow them to stay as along as needed, and assist them in any manner the sorceress-queen requested.

The trap was set. All that remained was to wait and to deal with Riall when she arrived.

Sequara quieted her mind, slipping into the realm of origins to listen for Riall's presence. She had sensed it when Riall must have been in or near Iarfaen the way one senses the sun before it rises in the predawn. Of course, the girl would also detect the gift in her, but there was no sensible way over the Marar Mountains other than Balnor Pass. Riall would have to come this way. Certainly no Caergilese guide would risk another route.

And yet . . . Sequara closed her eyes to eliminate all distractions. At first, as dim as it was, she did not believe what she was sensing. But then, as her heart seemed to constrict in her chest, she could not deny it. Almost beyond her perception, Riall's presence was more distant than it ought to be. And further east. The sorceress-queen opened her eyes and shook her head. "Well, I can't accuse her of being too sensible, I suppose."

"Your Majesty? What is it?" Gnorn was looking up at her with his brow wrinkled in a frown. Yrsa drew nearer and waited for the sorceress-queen to reply.

Sequara released a sigh. "It seems our young friends have decided to risk another way over the mountains."

Yrsa frowned. "What other ways are there?"

"Only dangerous ones."

"The trolls and pucas they speak of?"

Sequara nodded. "Yes, but the creatures pose little threat to Riall." She did not tell the younger woman her true worry. What might happen if Riall used the gift to master the beasts? Would she maintain control, or would the elf-power escape? Such creatures would not be difficult for the girl to wield, but she could not shake the feeling that Riall had been on the razor's edge of disaster at Seren's farmstead.

"All the same, we should pursue them. Cut them off in the mountains. It's time to end this chase." One of the other three Thjoths nodded at Yrsa's words, but the whole party looked to Sequara to answer.

Realizing that Yrsa's impatience stemmed from the abduction of her sister by the Ilarchae, the absence of her brother, and the danger to them both, Sequara nodded at younger woman. "That is good counsel. But I fear that the closer I get to Riall, the further I will push her away. She will always know of my approach. And yet, I *must* reach her. If I could mask my presence somehow, prevent her from knowing I am coming . . . But she will sense me before I sense her." Again the queen left unsaid her chief concern. The last thing she wanted was a contest of power against her daughter.

Yrsa shrugged. "The answer is simple. Stay here and send us on. We will catch them and deliver a message to the sorceress girl from you."

"Easier said than done. What if they resist? And how will you track them without me?"

Yrsa pursed her lips and rubbed her temple. "Well, we know they're going to Grimrik."

Gnorn cleared his throat. "Your Majesty, if I may?"

"Yes, my friend?"

Wearing a thoughtful frown, the Dweorg tugged his beard. "At Seren's farmstead, I noticed something. While you were tending to her, I happened to glance at the writing table in her room. Seeing ink on the quill, I picked it up. The ink was fresh enough to smudge my finger, as if someone had recently written something, but there was only blank vellum on the table."

"You believe Riall, Volund, and Khel carried a message with them."

The Dweorg nodded. "Aye. We already know Seren aided them with the horses. Would it not have been like her to think of friends along the way who might speed them on their journey, supplied with a letter of introduction? So. We both know Seren well enough. Who would she think of? Someone on the young ones' path to Grimrik, of course."

Sequara thought for a moment. "Riall, Volund, and Khel must travel through Torrlond, and all roads lead through Torrhelm. There's Lieutenant Edgelaf, of course. His town is south of the chief city. And there's Bagsac in the Way's monastery. Seren is devoted to them both."

The sorceress-queen froze in place. The answer to her problem of encountering Riall leaped to her mind, and her mouth opened as her eyes widened in realization. At last, she knew where they must go and how they must arrange everything. "Of course. Gnorn, you're brilliant."

Yrsa and the other Thjoths looked on with confused stares, but the Dweorg returned Sequara's expression of sudden hope with a big grin.

❈ 24 ❈

Sigra jolted sideways as something snatched at her dress, and only the greatest self control stifled her scream. She held stone-still in the moon-lit dimness of the Ironwood, trying in vain to quiet her heavy breaths. With a gentle tug on her dress, she realized its hem was caught in a briar. *Only a briar.* The dress refused to budge any further, so she pulled harder, and there was a snap as the briar began to give way. Cloth ripped, and she staggered, almost falling over when the garment came loose. She moved on as quickly as she dared, taking uncertain steps in the near darkness. Her desperate need to remain undetected and her fear of the forest competed with frantic haste to flee as far and as swiftly as she could from the Ilarchae encampment.

Surely by now her guard had noted her absence and had organized a party of warriors to search for her. She expected them to pounce on her at any moment, but somehow she had evaded pursuit thus far. Perhaps the forest would hide her long enough. Perhaps she would make it. She could not begin to think of what she must do once free of the forest or how she must somehow journey many leagues to the shores of the Wildlands and then find a way over the Gulf of Olfi to home. She did not even know what direction she was going in. If she succumbed to such thoughts, she would be lost. *Just find a way out.*

125

Trust in Edan. She forced her legs to keep moving as branches slapped her face and scratched her outstretched hands.

With blind panic threatening to grip her, fragments of thoughts competed in her mind. It was hard to recall what had happened even a moment ago, let alone how she had escaped. She had not planned it. The female warrior called Uga had conducted her to the edge of the woods after sunset to relieve herself before retiring for the night. When Sigra pulled up her dress and squatted within the privacy of the trees, Uga had turned her back. A sort of madness seized her that very moment, and, after a few tentative steps, she bolted into the forest.

It was impossible to believe that Uga had not realized her absence, but there was no sound of pursuit behind her – no cries of anger or dismay, no armed warriors crashing through the trees – only the eerie silence of the forest. The Raven Eyes seemed to believe the Ironwood was an effective barrier, turning their backs to it without fear of attack from behind. It served as a prison wall in her case. Not many dared to pass through it. Of course she had heard of the legendary monsters dwelling within its trees. Few who wandered beneath them lived to tell of it. However, Sigra was willing to risk such horrors to escape the torture of her imprisonment. The worst monsters by far walked on two legs.

She willed her body to keep moving, still half refusing to believe there was any pursuit and half convinced it was right behind her. The further she could flee, the more secure her escape would be, with every moment that passed in her favor. Dim shapes of branches lurched at her in the moonlight, which penetrated the canopy in small patches. Anything might come at her from the darkness, and she would not know until it was upon her. She pressed on.

A hundred tickling itches sprang to life on her face as something almost insubstantial clung to it. A moment later, she realized she had walked into a large spider web. Her hands reached up to claw it off, but it stuck to her face and hair, and the itches persisted in several spots. It felt as if spiders were crawling all over her flesh and down her neck, and she spat strands of web out of her mouth.

The next moment, she grunted when the ground slammed into her back, knocking the breath out of her, and bright pinpricks of light flashed in her head when it smacked something hard. In the darkness, it was difficult to tell which direction was up, but tree roots dug into her right side, while the ribs on her left side throbbed where something large had punched into her. Whatever it was, it was lying on top of her, its heavy weight pinning her to the forest floor. She cried out, fully expecting sharp teeth to tear into her throat.

Instead, a hand covered her mouth, smothering her cry. Something cold and sharp pressed against her neck.

"Be silent," hissed a voice in the Northern Tongue. A man's voice.

Willing that voice to belong to anyone other than the man she recognized by it, Sigra whimpered.

"Quiet, bitch!" Unnar's face was so close to hers that she could smell his sour breath. "I'll slit your throat here and now if you make another sound." The dagger pressed harder against her throat, and the skin there stung as it made a tiny slice. A drop of blood tickled her neck when it ran down it. In addition to her bruised ribs, her right elbow smarted like it was scraped, and her wrist ached from stopping her fall.

Hurting in more places than she could count and struggling to get her breath back, Sigra went motionless, save for a tremble she could not suppress.

"No one's coming for you, so don't get any stupid ideas. I gave that cunt Uga a little trail to follow. She'll be running through the Ironwood in the wrong direction all night." He sniggered, and his heavy weight shifted on top of her, forcing her onto her back. "She'll keep running too. She won't dare show her face again after losing you. My father would have her skinned alive if she comes back. You and I will have a nice long night together."

Filled with paralyzing terror, Sigra shuddered as she realized he must have been stalking her the whole time. She did not resist or speak. It was as if something had severed the connection between her mind and body. As in a nightmare, she could not muster the will to move. Even her shallow breaths came with great difficulty, and dizziness sapped her little remaining strength. *Edan help me. Give me strength!*

"Good." Unnar seemed to take her lack of movement as compliance. He removed his hand from her mouth. The dagger remained at her neck. "Now, lie still." His weight shifted, and some of the pressure left her body. A moment later, the cool night air caressed Sigra's body as Unnar lifted up her dress. His loathsome hand reached toward her, and she let out a cry as she tried to shift away from him.

His weight on her increased, pinning her down. "Be silent! You're mine, bitch. *Mine*. Move or cry out again and I'll take out one of your eyes first." His breaths were hard and rapid. He pressed the cold steel of his dagger on the flesh of her cheek, right below her eye. It was the flat of the blade, but it made her wince all the same, and goosebumps spread down her neck over her body.

She froze in terror, which seemed to satisfy him as he removed the dagger from her face. All his weight came off her, and he sat up so that a patch of moonlight shone on his chest. His hand seemed to be quivering as he pulled up his kirtle and fumbled at the tie on his breeches. "Gods damn it. Come on. Come on."

While Unnar was struggling with his breeches, Edan seemed to answer her prayer. Anger sparked within Sigra and exploded into rage at once, shattering her fear and freeing her from her paralysis. Every place on her body where he had touched her seemed afire. Her wrath at this filthy creature's violation of her was so sudden and so powerful that she forgot any regard for her life.

Growling in triumph, Unnar managed to tug down his breeches.

With all the force she could muster, Sigra drew back her leg and smashed her foot into his ugly face. Bone snapped, and she could feel something sharp even through the leather of her shoe. Unnar grunted and tumbled backwards, clutching his nose and cursing.

He rolled, stood, and pulled up his breeches with dismaying speed. One of his hands held his nose, whence streams of blood visible even in the dim moonlight streaked and darkened his lower face. The dagger gleamed in his other hand. "Fecking bitch! I'll kill you!" He lunged toward her.

She screamed defiance, welcoming death. But even as she pushed herself up to leap at her attacker, her hand grasped something hard. A rock almost as large as her hand came up in her fist, and instinct allowed her not a moment to think. Unnar was a mere three feet away when, with a feral yell, she hurled the stone at his face, so it was no surprise when it made a loud crack, jerking back his head and sending him flailing backwards. He landed with a thud on his back. In the ensuing eerie silence, his body lay still.

Sigra stood grinding her teeth and clenching her fists, ready for him to rise. Her shoulders rose and fell with each rapid breath, and her heartbeats thumped so hard in her chest that they seemed to throb in her ears. She stood there waiting, prepared to pummel him and dig strips of flesh from his face with her nails.

Still he did not move. When something like rational thought returned to her, she debated whether to find his dagger and make a sure end of him. But she almost retched at even the thought of the deed, and she did not believe she could force her feet any closer to his body. Perhaps the stone had finished him.

She spat in his direction, and then she turned around. She walked several paces, still having no idea what direction was best, and she even worried she might be heading back toward the encampment. *Be brave. Like Yrsa.* A few more paces, and her hands began to tremble. *Edan save me. I'm not Yrsa.* She thought she might start weeping, but she held in the sobs and forced her legs to keep going. Her breaths were still heavy, but the feeling of suffocation was gone. *I'm going to make it.*

Something gleamed ahead of her in the moonlight, and a figure rose before her, eliciting a startled gasp from Sigra as she froze in place. She recognized the silhouette of Uga. The woman was holding a sword out, pointing it at Sigra's chest. She also thought she could see the white of Uga's teeth. The warrior was smiling at her.

Uga's head jerked to the side, indicating the direction in which Sigra should walk. Back to the encampment.

No panic rose in Sigra. The fight with Unnar had drained her, and there was no defiance left in her. She also hurt in several places, especially her ribs, and the peril of the forest no longer seemed worth it even if she could find a way to fight Uga, who stared at her as if reading her thoughts.

There was something hard and lean about this woman that reminded Sigra of her sister. If Bolverk trusted her to be one of his bodyguards, he did so with good reason. Her head drooping, Sigra began walking in the direction her captor had indicated, and the warrior fell in behind her. She only hoped that, from a desire to stay out of trouble, Uga would not report the incident to the war-leader.

As they began the slow march back to the encampment, they passed the scene of the horrible assault. Sigra forced herself to look for Unnar's body. However, where she thought his form should be lying, she could make out nothing but brush. She glanced back at Uga, who seemed to be staring at the same spot. The warrior turned to her and shrugged, and then she pointed with her sword.

With numbness spreading over her, Sigra obeyed the unspoken order and walked back toward her wretched prison among the Ilarchae.

❈ 25 ❈

"Might be we should stop." Volund looked up and frowned. It was growing dark and cold, and the wind howled in gusts that knifed through his wool cloak to cool his sweaty body. Though the tips of their white summits glowed pink in the last light of the westering sun, the jagged peaks above him were becoming starless blots on the lower portions of the sky as twilight succumbed to night.

By way of answering him, Belu whimpered and squirmed a little in his arms. She was tired too, no doubt, having trudged into the mountains on much smaller legs than his. He had carrried the little dog for much of the way, and his arms were weary.

He smiled down at the pup. "Little mountain wolf."

Belu whined at him.

Volund turned and waited for his companions, who were little more than shadows clambering on the rocks just below him. He was feeling the climb in his legs, but Khel and especially Riall had been slowing down for a while, and he could hear their heavy breaths in the thinner, crisper air. They had stopped a couple times to eat and to wait for the young sorceress to rest and regain some strength. When they stopped again, it would be for the night.

Khel arrived next to him and, instead of starting up with his usual banter, took some deep breaths.

Riall crawled up to them a bit later. "Need to . . ." She hunched over with her hands planted on her knees and panted heavily. "Get as far as we can." She gulped in a few more breaths. "Just a bit further." However, instead of taking another step, she collapsed onto a large rock and sat there.

Khel squinted at her. "Why the almighty haste? Is Queen Sequara hiding behind that rock over there?" He pointed downslope.

The sorceress shook her head. "I haven't . . . sensed her in a long time. I'm not sure where she is. But we must reach Grimrik . . . as soon as we can." She looked at Volund in appeal as if he should confirm her words, but he could see how exhausted she was.

Volund set down Belu, who padded over to Riall, and he waited a moment. "We can make camp in the lee of that boulder." He pointed with a thumb at the spot he had picked out while waiting for the others. It would shelter them from the worst of the wind, which was growing chillier by the moment. "I'll make a fire."

"And invite all the trolls to dine with us? Or *on* us?" Khel had found his usual voice. "A fire's just the thing we need to announce ourselves."

Volund frowned and scratched an itch on his sweaty scalp. "Are not trolls shy of fire?"

"How do I know? Do I look like a troll?"

Volund was tempted to answer in the affirmative, but Khel was already irritable enough. They were all tired, and they were lost. Riall was right: They were losing precious time in these mountains. Still, they had to stop.

His silence did not discourage Khel from going on. "Miserable, troll-infested mountains. Who put them here anyway? Who needs all this rock?" He kicked a boulder. "Ouch. Damn it." The wind gusted, giving him new fuel for his litany of complaints. "And why does this damnable, confounded wind blow so hard all the time? My balls are shrinking by the moment. We're likely to freeze to death."

"So, a fire, then?"

"No! Do you like trolls so much? Perhaps some pucas will come along as well. And throw in some wargs for good measure."

Volund released an exasperated sigh. "Better to fight a troll than freeze."

"Oh? And how many trolls have you fought? From your vast lore of troll combat, enlighten us on the proper techniques for keeping them at bay, if you will."

"Well, for one thing, they don't like fire."

"Everyone knows that fire attracts them!" Khel waved his hands in the air and turned toward Riall. "Please tell him that a fire will bring the trolls."

"Make the fire." Her features were indistinguishable in the dimness, but Riall's voice was firm, as if she had reached an important decision. "I'll deal with what comes."

Khel went still.

Volund too did not move for a moment, but then he shrugged out of his pack, in which he had stowed his flint and tinder and a couple pieces of dry wood. They would need to gather more wood for the night, but the tree line, where a few scraggly pines clung to the rocks, was not far below them. "Right."

A short while later, all three of them and Belu were sitting in the lee of the boulder around the fire, which cast a ruddy glow on their faces. Even Khel was smiling as he rubbed his hands over the flames. A small pile of wood lay off to the side, waiting to provide more warmth for the night.

Volund cast an occasional look at the surrounding darkness, wondering if Khel had not been right after all. However, having witnessed her power, he put his faith in Riall. He stole a glance at her, and she seemed calm as she gazed into the fire and stroked Belu.

A loud but distant bellow jerked him up onto his feet, and he put his hand on his sword's hilt. The deep, animal growl echoed from the rocks, and the silence that followed was profound until Belu responded with a yip that would not have intimidated a squirrel. Volund exchanged glances with Khel, who was also standing wide-eyed and open-mouthed with his hand ready to draw his blade.

Volund swallowed. "You were right. Fire brings trolls."

Khel gave a quick nod in response.

"Be at peace." Rather than sounding like a confused girl like she usually did, Riall spoke like a queen, or perhaps like an imperturbable ethereal being that was beyond mortal concerns. Her voice gave Volund a chill that sliced right through his mundane fear of the troll, and goosebumps covered him. The sorceress was still sitting and gazing into the fire. Her eyes, however, seemed to see something far away.

Belu stopped growling and wagging her tail. The little dog moved back by the fire, circled a few times until she decided the spot was right, and plopped down as if unconcerned by anything. Volund decided to follow her example. He and Khel both eased back into a sitting position and waited. They stole nervous glances at each other but said nothing as Riall's posture did not change.

They did not need to wait for long. Loud thuds sounded from the darkness. Volund reckoned that if an ancient and huge tree grew legs and went for a stroll in the mountains, its steps would sound the same. They grew in volume until he could feel the rock under him vibrate with each boom. He almost gasped when something impossibly massive stepped out of the darkness to emerge into the firelight.

More than twice the height of a tall man and thicker than an old tree, the troll loomed over their encampment. Long, matted hair that had once been dark but was streaked with grey framed a bare face furrowed with a web of deep lines. Save for patches on the upper arms, hands, and feet, the same hair covered its enormous body. Where pale flesh showed, the hide appeared thick, and though thick muscles bulged in the arms, its wrinkled skin sagged. The large nostrils on its wide nose flared, and the yellow canines jutting from its mouth gave its frown a hostile cast. But its amber eyes gazed blankly at Riall, who sat before the fire unmoving.

Volund gazed up at the beast in near disbelief. Its potent stench was musty and damp and at the same time acrid like old sweat and piss. A longer look revealed what appeared to be two broken arrow shafts protruding from its hide, one from its right shoulder and one from its left thigh. There was a nasty looking scar that might have come from a sword slash on its right arm as well. This was one of the famed trolls that escaped the Battle of Iarfaen to dwell in the mountains. It would not be inclined to like humans, then.

Fortunately, Riall appeared to have firm command of the creature, which stood still as if tame and awaiting her orders. The sorceress returned from her trance, at first blinking and then smiling at Khel and Volund. "Gentlemen. Meet our new guide." Volund was not certain, but there seemed to be some relief in her smile, as if she had been unsure of something.

Khel's eyes widened. "You want to keep it?"

Riall giggled. "He's rather nice, and he'd make a fine playmate for Belu." Her face grew serious. "But no. Trolls aren't meant for pets or slaves, and this fellow's seen enough horrors. If we weren't in such need, I'd set him free right now." She yawned and stretched. "As it is, he'll keep watch over us tonight. At first light on the morrow he'll guide us on the quickest paths down to Torrlond."

Khel's jaw dropped even further than it had before. "You want us to sleep with *that thing* standing there?"

Riall shrugged. "He won't harm us. And we need the rest. I'll have him stay outside the firelight if that helps. He doesn't like the fire anyway."

As if obeying an unspoken command, the troll turned around and lumbered into the darkness.

"Well, now I feel much better." Khel turned to look at Volund with his eyebrows raised. "So, you were right too. Doesn't like fire, she says."

Volund acknowledged him with a nod. He shared Khel's unease with their guest, but he trusted Riall, and he was bone weary. Still, perhaps it was best to be cautious. "I'll keep first watch."

Riall gave him a gentle smile. "That's kind of you, but you needn't." She nodded toward where the troll must have been standing guard. "His scent alone will keep away other trolls, pucas, wargs, and anything else we need to worry about."

Khel wrinkled his nose and waved his hand in front of it. "I believe *that*."

A big yawn split Volund's face. "Alright. We rest, then."

Khel shrugged. "Very well. I don't have the energy to disagree, but if we're all at the bottom of a troll stomach by the morrow, don't blame me." He lay down and curled up in his cloak. "Sleep well, then. Good-night, Riall. Goodnight, Volund. Goodnight, Belu. Goodnight, nice troll." He raised a hand and waggled his fingers in a wave before drop-ping it. A moment later, his steady breaths indicated he had fallen asleep.

Riall smiled at Khel's form, and then she lay in her cloak with Belu folded inside.

Volund took one last glance at the darkness where the troll was stationed, shook his head, and lay down, tucking his wool cloak tight around him. Within a few weary breaths, he drifted into a half-awake state in which he worried for his sister Sigra and wondered how folk back in Grimrik were faring against the dragon. A little while later, he succumbed to deep sleep.

❧ 26 ❧

After dismissing Halvard and the other warriors guarding him, King Orvandil Dragonbane took a deep breath and stared at the door of the wooden hall. Tucked in a valley of the Fyrnhowes north of Valfoss, the hall had long served the rulers of Grimrik as a summer residence when a fancy for hunting took them. It was much smaller than Skjold had been, but it was adequate to house Queen Osynia, her serving women, a fair number of refugees, and the warriors who kept watch over them all. Thus far, it had escaped Gorsarhad's notice, unlike Skjold. The ancient royal hall of the Thjoths was nothing but ash now, along with the rest of Valfoss. Orvandil had vowed to rebuild it all, but first he had to deal with the dragon so he could confront the Ilarchae on stronger terms and get back Sigra and the other hostages.

Before any of that, though, he had to reckon with Osynia.

He raised a hand to scratch one of the scabs on his shoulder and then, recalling the healer's firm instructions, resisted the itch and lowered his hand again. Gorsarhad had left him with many marks all over his body from their encounter. His clothes and hair had been singed, his body burned in several places. Fortunately, he had plunged into the cool waters of the Gulf of Olfi a moment after the dragon's flames washed over him, and the burns had not had time to reach deep into his flesh. However, the reddened skin all over his body had felt as if he had spent far too many hours exposed to the sun, and itchy scabs covered the worst areas.

In truth, he had been less nervous confronting Gorsarhad than he was at the moment. His eyes still locked on the door, he flexed his hand the way he often did before drawing his blade for combat. *Nothing's fiercer or stronger than a mother's love.* He did not relish telling Osynia he had seen her daughter but still had no notion how he would free her. His memories took him back to the grim time in the wake of Hallgerd's death. A fever had taken Osynia's middle daughter seven or eight winters back. Orvandil feared to witness such grief and pain ever again. The loss had shattered the queen, who took years to become something like her former self. He would do almost anything to spare her another such ordeal.

There had to be a way to get Sigra out of the Wildlands alive. Racking his brains during every waking hour had produced no convincing ideas that would keep her from danger. He would sit with his counselors, and they would form a plan. The messages had already gone out to Duneyr and the others. It seemed that Gnorn was still away on his errand, however. He would sorely miss the Dweorg's wisdom.

Releasing a long sigh, the king of the Thjoths grasped the latch, pulled open the door, and then gasped. Osynia was standing in the doorway, frowning at him with her arms folded across her chest. Brought out all the more by her green dress and golden brooches, her striking green eyes fixed him with their gaze. With streaks of grey in her curly auburn hair and dark circles under her eyes, she was beginning to look a bit like a woman who had seen nearly fifty winters. But she was still as tall and lithe as she had been in their youth, and her beauty took his breath away, just as it always had – even in his memory during his years of exile, when she was wed to Vols.

At the moment, it was also evident she had lost none of her fire. "How long were you going to make me wait?"

"I . . ." Wanting to tell her how much he loved her and missed her and how he was so sorry he could not rescue Sigra all at once, he said nothing whatsoever as his tongue seemed stuck in his mouth.

"Come here, you big lout." Osynia rushed toward him and embraced him.

Even though it stung his burns in several places, he returned the embrace, resting his chin on top of her head and breathing in the familiar, precious scent of her hair. They squeezed each other and disengaged only to kiss, and then they embraced again. He sniffled a bit as he suppressed a tear. He did not trust himself to speak just yet.

After a while, Oysnia broke off the embrace and, reaching up to grasp his shoulders, squinted up as if inspecting him. "Your hair is shorter."

"Had to cut off the scorched bits."

"You were wounded."

"It's nothing." He dismissed his injuries with a wave of his hand. "A few little burns. The healer gave me a salve."

She pursed her lips as if skeptical of his assessment. "I heard about it." She frowned. "How many of our warriors died?"

He hung his head. "Five did not make it to shore."

"And the dragon?"

Orvandil sighed. "Gorsarhad carries a reminder of our meeting. One of the Dweorg-wrought spears. The tip and a couple feet of the shaft are sticking out of her lower jaw. It won't slow her down much. Might serve to make her angrier."

Oysnia nodded at this information, and then she too sighed. "Come inside and tell me of my daughter."

Orvandil swallowed and followed her into the hall. Wooden columns carved with vines, animals, and depictions of the old gods reached up to the rafters, and the louver at the top was open to allow some light and air into the dimness of the interior. There were only ashes in the long stone fire pit occupying the center of the hall, which appeared to be empty at the moment. Most folk would feast and sleep in the main hall, and there was usually some activity within, but Osynia likely had ordered her folk away to ensure her privacy when she heard tidings of Sigra from him. She had never liked to weep before anyone.

At the back of the long structure was a sealed off chamber where the king and queen slept. Osynia led him there. After she opened the door, he followed her within and closed it behind him. She sat on the bed. He sat next to her, sinking into the furs and wool blankets on top of the down mattress. He faced her. They looked into one another's eyes for a moment, and he could see the tears forming in hers, which brought a lump to his throat. He reached up to caress a curl of her hair away from her face and tuck it behind her ear.

"Tell me." Osynia blinked as a slight tremble passed through her body.

Orvandil took a deep breath. "She's alive. I saw her."

Osynia's eyes widened for a brief moment. She gave him a slow nod that spoke of nearly intolerable fear and hope held in check by an iron will. "Where?"

"In the Ilarchae encampment, on the border of the Ironwood."

"How did you find them?"

"It was not hard once I entered the Wildlands. Most Ilarchae avoid the Ironwood as a cursed place, but the Raven Eyes are different. Though the other tribes deem them mad for it, they use the forest as a barrier against their foes, living hard on its southwest fringes. But the trees also allowed me to get close to them at night. Alone, I stayed hidden and watched, though there were guards all around. I bade the others to await me in the forest, where they stayed safe." He decided not to tell Osynia about the man he slew.

"Was she well?"

"She appeared unharmed. By chance, I saw her from a distance as they led her into a tent, but I know she's alive." He paused and glanced down at his lap. "We were too few to free her. Any attempt would have ended in our deaths and likely hers." Once again, he thought it best not to tell his wife the entire truth. The sacrifice of one of Sigra's maids would have enraged and distressed her.

Though the intensity in her eyes revealed she was starving for more information about her daughter, the queen composed her face and merely nodded at his tidings. "They guard their encampment well?"

"Aye. Bolverk is no fool."

"And how many warriors do they have?"

"About half as many as we have, from what I could see. Perhaps a few more. If we could muster our strength and sail for the Wildlands, we would defeat them."

Osynia sat up straight and frowned. "And the dragon prevents this." Her voice gave only the slightest indication of her anger, but Orvandil well knew the signs. "If we had allowed Gnorn and the Dweorgs . . ."

"You know we could not." Orvandil tried to make his voice gentler. "The Dweorgs would have died and even undergone torture and slavery for us, but to surrender friends in such a manner would shame us forever. And what would come next? Had we given over our friends, the Ilarchae would only have learned to attack us again for hostages and ask for more. Give a dog meat at your table, and he'll return for your next meal."

She glowered at him and clenched her fists. He was prepared for her to strike him or pound on his chest. Instead, with a slight quiver of her lip, she lowered her head. "I know. I only want her back. Sometimes nothing else matters. There is a certain madness that comes from grief and uncertainty. Forgive me."

He stroked her hands, which relaxed beneath his touch. "There's nothing to forgive, my love."

She looked at him, and at last a tear fell from her eye as she gave vent to her suffering. "Why? Is Edan punishing us? Or are the old gods angry at us for abandoning them?" Her voice quivered with emotion and sorrow that tugged at Orvandil's heart.

He knew he had to tread carefully here. Osynia had never known the Prophet as he had, and she had not ceased to worship the old gods without regrets. "Gorsarhad is a beast. Her vengeance has naught to do with Edan."

"Her *vengeance?*"

Orvandil scratched his beard, which itched him where it was growing back in. He hesitated to explain his theory, but he had already let it slip. "The Supreme Priest Bledla used dragons as pawns during the War of the Way. The Prophet seized them to end the war, using Gorsarhad to achieve it. The destruction she wreaks now is her response. This is what my heart tells me."

"After all these years?"

"Not so many if you've lived a thousand or two."

Osynia's eyes narrowed, and she frowned as she pondered his words. Her chin came up when she next spoke, and the controlled fury was evident in her wet eyes. "Then let us learn from the beast if we must. Her vengeance won't be half so fierce as mine if I don't have my daughter back, no matter how long it takes. Either she returns to us, or we destroy the Raven Eyes. Do not forget your vow."

"You know I will not."

She took a deep breath, and her shoulders drooped as a sad smile briefly crossed her face. At once, the years and her sorrows seemed to weigh on her. "Yes, I know it."

He grasped her shoulder with one hand and held her chin with the other. "We'll find a way. When we hold the moot, we will decide what to do. I'll do everything in my power to have Sigra and the others back."

"Good." She began unclasping the brooches that held together her dress. "Now, comfort me. I've missed you."

Bending to kiss her, Orvandil did as she bade him.

❧ 27 ☙

Riall frowned as she watched the large, hirsute form of the troll disappear behind an outcrop of rock in the distance. He was returning to the mountains whence he led them, where he belonged. Before he departed, she had conveyed her thanks to him not in words but in the feelings – *gratitude, comfort, safety* – she gently placed in his mind. He had responded with a huff from his nostrils, which she understood as a gesture of friendship. It was a sad farewell for her, not only because she would miss him, but also because she sorrowed at the memories she had peeked at in his mind and the pain that had plagued his life – pain wrought by humankind, the most dangerous, vicious, and needlessly cruel predator of all.

For a short while she continued to watch in case she might spot him lumbering a bit further in the distance, but when it was obvious she had seen the last of him, she released a sigh. She turned around. Belu, who had been waiting next to her and was also sad to say goodbye to her big friend, turned as well with a soft whimper.

Khel and Volund were watching her, each showing a bit more concern than he likely realized in his frown. Behind them, the gentle knolls and vineyards of South Torrlond rolled on into the horizon. All they needed to do was descend this last foothill of the Marar Mountains they stood upon, and they would enter Torrlond, the mightiest kingdom of Andumedan, or what they called Eormenlond in the Northern Tongue. It was also, of course, the kingdom that had waged the War of the Way, which had forever changed all the kingdoms. Not one escaped unscathed from the bloodiest conflict in the continent's history.

It was her father, the Prophet of Edan, who put an end to it. He had transformed Torrlond and the rest of Andumedan in the process. Torrlond had a new ruler, King Ethelred, a man everyone said was just, and a different Supreme Priest, Osfrid, who was as gentle as his predecessors had been violent. Still, Riall could not help shuddering at the idea of entering Torrlond.

Khel, who must have perceived her nervousness, put on a smile. "Alright?"

Riall nodded. "Yes. Just a bit anxious about traveling through Torrlond."

"Not to worry. It's a marvelous place. And there's nothing in the world like Torrhelm. You can find anything you want there." Khel had already told them he had been to Torrlond's chief city once with his mother on trading business.

"Doesn't it make you uneasy, being a stranger there?"

Khel shook his head and grinned. "We're all strangers in Torrhelm. All sorts of folk from all over Andumedan. No one will give even you or me a second glance. Everyone is different, so everyone fits in." He glanced at Volund and frowned, putting his hand on his chin with mock concern. "Though, come to think on it, I'm not so sure about Volund."

Volund's mouth quirked into a half smile. "Very funny."

Khel laughed and faced Riall. "There's nothing to worry about. We didn't even lose much time in the mountains, thanks to your troll. Of course, he would have been a deal less helpful had you not been wielding his mind."

Riall winced. "Well, about the troll . . ."

Khel tilted his head and wore a puzzled frown. "What?"

"I wasn't wielding his mind. Not since last night, anyway."

Khel's eyes widened. "You mean . . ."

"We had an agreement."

"You and the *troll?*"

"Yes. I told him what we needed, and he was happy to guide us. No compulsion needed."

"And you believed him?" Khel swallowed and put a hand on his chest. "What if he had eaten us?"

"Trolls don't like human meat. We taste bad."

"He told you that?"

"Yes. In a manner. Besides, he liked us."

"He *liked* us?"

"Yes. Though, come to think on it, I'm not so sure about you." Riall put her hand on her chin and frowned before grinning at him.

Khel squinted in annoyance at her, and then, while Volund burst out laughing, he rolled his eyes and chuckled. "I suppose I deserved that. I yield to you, mighty Mistress of Mockery. Shall we head for Torrlond, then?" He bowed and swept his arm in front of his chest to gesture the way for Riall.

The three of them and Belu began walking down the hill, which had a gentle slope to it. Every once in a while, Khel would complain or make a jest, but Riall said little. She was debating whether she should tell her friends of her visions, which were becoming stronger and more vivid than ever. There had been a point that morning when she startled out of one waking dream with her foot hovering over the edge of a boulder. It would have been a nasty surprise if she had taken one more step in the body of the washerwoman only to find herself lying at the base of the boulder with shattered bones. Since she had been last in their company as they filed down the rocks, she did not think Khel or Volund had noticed.

She was worried how they might react if they knew of her wanderings in other people's bodies. The two of them had become more dear to her than she could express, and the last thing she wanted was to lose them. However, the longer she was with them, the more she felt as if she was betraying them by withholding the whole truth. It was unfair not to tell them of the risk of being near her. She might also need their help.

Khel was in the midst of complaining about his feet. ". . . aching in more places than I can count. How many bones do feet have, anyway? Enough walking, I say. Let's get horses in the first decent-sized village we come across."

Riall took a deep breath. "There's another reason I released the troll last night."

Khel went quiet, and both young men turned to her.

"I'm trying to use the gift as seldom as possible."

Khel and Volund waited. There was no judgement in their gazes, only concern. She loved them for that, and she hoped they would somehow remain the same after she revealed her secret.

"I've been thinking. If I am the Prophet of Edan's daughter . . . No, I know I am. He *was* my father. Queen Sequara always spoke of him with reverence, but sometimes she let slip that there was something unstable about his power. Something dangerous. He was different from others with the gift. And so am I. For one thing, I have no need to chant a song of origin to use the gift. The same was true of him, the queen has told me."

Khel nodded. "That makes sense."

Riall swallowed. "There's more. It's the dangerous part. When I use my power, I often have dreams. They used to be dreams of a forest somewhere in the north. For years I had them, as far back as I can remember. It was a peaceful place, my refuge. I never told anyone about it. But something changed. Just before we set out from Asdralad, in my dream, I left the forest . . . in the body of a man. I killed him by removing his spirit and took his body. I walked for miles in that body, and then I took another. And another. Each time, the body I leave behind is empty. I don't know where I'm going in these bodies, but I'm looking for something. I don't know what it is."

Khel pursed his lips in thought. "Dreams are strange. I've often been someone else in my dreams. And often enough I'm seeking something I can't find."

She shook her head. "It's not like those dreams. Mine are *real*. It's as if they're really happening somewhere. And I don't just see them when I'm sleeping."

Khel's eyes narrowed as he frowned. "You mean . . ."

"Sometimes I wake up from a vision. One moment I'm walking in some poor woman's body that I've stolen in some place I don't know, and the next I'm back with you, riding on a horse or walking in the mountains. It takes a moment to remember who I really am. I never know when it will happen. But I know one thing: Whenever I use my power, the visions worsen. They become more real. That's why I didn't want to stay in the troll's mind for too long. I don't know why it's happening, but I'm afraid. Queen Sequara tried to warn me for years about something like this."

Khel nodded. "Sometimes you get a strange look about you, like you're not with us." He glanced at Volund, who nodded in confirmation. Both of them seemed nervous.

"Yes. I suppose that's when I'm gone, in another body." She looked at Volund. "I'll do everything I can to wield the dragon and help Grimrik. But I need you to know that something is happening, and I'm scared I might fall over the edge. Perhaps I won't come back from one of those visions. But I'm going to try with everything I have. If we can make it to Grimrik, I know I can do it."

The two young men stared at her. This was the moment Riall dreaded. Perhaps they would be different towards her now, more cautious. Perhaps they would do the sensible thing and abandon her.

Khel beheld her and gave her one of his gentle smiles, the kind she liked the most. "Well, if one of those visions happens, we'll watch over you until you're back. Won't we?" He looked at Volund, who gave one of his serious nods that was as solid as a vow.

At first, Khel's words surprised Riall, and then she struggled to hold back tears. She was not sure if she was more relieved or grateful. Perhaps she was simply glad for such friends. "Thank you." The words came out in a strained whisper.

But Khel and Volund heard them. Walking on either side of her, they each put a hand on her shoulder as they continued on their way into Torrlond with Belu trotting along in the lead.

28

Bolverk smirked when Atzil and Inger led Unnar into the tent. His son's hands were tied behind his back, which the whole encampment would have seen as his guards conducted him. More shameful still, however, were the marks on his face: a broken, swollen nose and a bloody wound surrounded by a bruise in the dead center of his forehead. These marks told the truth that Bolverk already knew from Uga, who stood by his side. Also, the pure hatred in Unnar's eyes as he glanced at Sigra, who sat behind Uga with bonds on her wrists and ankles, confirmed everything Bolverk suspected. Still, he was interested to know what sort of tale the fool would spin in his defense.

Unnar stood in between Atzil and Inger, thrusting out his chest and sticking out his jaw with all the bravado he could muster.

Bolverk knew how shallow his son's courage was. He locked eyes with him until Unnar lost his nerve and looked down at his feet. The war-leader snorted. "Well, boy. You've returned."

Unnar's head snapped up. "Why have you put me in bonds?" He likely meant to sound angry, but he sounded more petulant.

"What else should I do with a sneak who disobeys my orders? And a rapist?"

"A rapist?" Unnar's surprise almost seemed genuine.

"Aye. Do you deny forcing yourself on her?" He pointed at Sigra, who glared at Unnar as if she was ready to kill him. "After I told you I'm to wed her. That makes her *my* betrothed. And what is the punishment for raping another's betrothed?"

Unnar went pale and wide-eyed. He licked his lips and shook his head. "I never did."

Bolverk scoffed. "Perhaps not. But you tried to."

The young man shook his head more vigorously. "No. There's no proof. No witness."

"Uga says you did."

Rage flashed in Unnar's eyes, and he glared at the bodyguard. "She's a lying bitch. She never saw me in the forest."

Bolverk shook his head and sighed. "Who said it happened in the Ironwood?"

Realizing his slip, Unnar's eyes went wide again with panic. "Uga's lying, I tell you. She's a vicious cunt. She's setting me up. She wants your place as war-leader, and she's bringing down her rivals."

Bolverk glanced at Uga, who was directing a contemptuous smile at Unnar. "You think you're Uga's *rival?* Bloody fool. The Raven Eyes would do well to choose her for war-leader when I'm gone or too old to know what the feck I'm doing. You, on the other hand, will be nothing more than a cockless idiot."

Unnar jerked backwards, but Inger and Atzil held him firm. "I tell you I didn't do it."

"Oh? Then what were you doing in the Ironwood when the trackers found you? And how did you get those pretty marks on your face?"

"I . . ." Unnar looked around as if seeking some manner of escape. Seeing none, he fixed his gaze on Sigra and nodded toward her. "*She* tempted me. She promised to lie with me in the forest. I was a fool. I didn't suspect her real plan was to escape. She picked up a rock when I wasn't looking and struck me in the face. When I awoke, I was afraid because I had allowed her to escape, and so I stayed away in fear. I didn't know Uga had found her. Thank the gods you captured the treacherous bitch. She must have bewitched me, and I lost my wits. I've learned my lesson now. I won't go near her again."

"He lies."

Bolverk turned around.

"He *lies*."

This time he saw Sigra say the words in the tongue of the Folk of the Tribes, and the fury in her eyes as she gazed at Unnar confirmed her meaning. Everyone else in the tent was looking at Sigra as well, but the surprise that she had understood their conversation and spoken in their tongue was most evident on Unnar's face.

Bolverk smiled. "You speak our tongue?"

Sigra glared at him, looking all the fiercer with the scratches on her arms and face and the one curious nick on her neck. "Your tongue like mine. Thjothic. I learn."

The war-leader nodded. "So. Did Unnar try to rape you?" He spoke the words slowly to make sure she would understand.

"Yes."

"Did you tempt him into the forest?"

"No. He lies. I run. He follows."

"And you struck his face when he tried to rape you?"

Sigra's grin was fierce. "Yes."

Bolverk chuckled as he looked down upon his Thjothic captive. "I'm pleased that you're learning our tongue. You *will* give me fierce sons, won't you? I'm in need of some, to be sure." He turned to Unnar, who was paler than before. "Well, it seems we have our witnesses. Your word against Sigra's and Uga's."

Unnar gawked at Sigra and trembled. "She's a captive. A slave. Her word means nothing."

"Mind your tongue. She's your future mother. And what of Uga?"

Unnar turned toward the bodyguard and, though his mouth hung open, he seemed to have run out of words.

The war-leader grinned. "You could always challenge her, of course. The gods grant victory to the truth-teller."

Unnar seemed to weigh this option as he looked at Uga, whose broad smile revealed what she thought of her chances. Evidently,

Unnar thought less of his. "They're lying, I tell you. Uga must have put her up to it. Uga put those vile words in her mouth."

Bolverk shook his head slowly. "No, boy. You won't slither out of this one. I've given my *life* to the Raven Eyes. Nothing's more important. Not me. Not you. And not your gods-cursed pride. You never would learn that."

Unnar snarled and glared, but he said nothing.

Bolverk stood straighter and, stepping forward, shoved his index finger into Unnar's face, which made the young man flinch. "You've put us all in danger one too many times. This time, you'll take the punishment you earned. If you're too great of a coward to challenge Uga, then one of two things must follow. The gods have decreed the punishment for a man who forcibly lies with another man's betrothed: lose your manhood, or leave the Raven Eyes and never return upon pain of death. Since I once called you son, I give you the choice. What will you have, then? Castration or exile?"

Unnar's eyes widened, and his lips trembled while a spasm of fury and terror crossed his face. He spat. "If I am no longer your son, you are no longer my father, and I renounce you all. I choose exile."

Bolverk smirked at him. "Always the coward's way. So be it."

29

Alndon was something between a large village and a small town on the outskirts of Torrhelm, where it was becoming increasingly hard to tell where one town ended and another began. It had been easy, however, to find the way to the carpenter shop of Edgelaf, who seemed to be well known or even some sort of local celebrity. Most folk had looked at Riall, Khel, and Volund with curiosity and even a hint of hostility, making Riall conscious of her brown skin in a place where everyone else save Khel was pale. But when she asked about Edgelaf, the folk of Alndon smiled in understanding and pointed the way. When the companions arrived at their destination, they beheld a modest shop and home that spoke not of fame or wealth but of solidity and comfort.

A low stone wall with a gate enclosed the two structures, which were wrought of timber with white stucco on the exterior. Though it had a roof, the shop was open to the elements on the front side, and so there was no need for a doorway. Within the shop were pieces of furniture in various stages of completion as well as scraps of wood and shavings littering the floor. There was also a very large man with hair and a beard that were mostly silver-grey but had once likely been blond. The man was kneeling and frowning as he banged a wooden mallet on something that seemed on its way to becoming a chair.

Leaving her horse and Belu with Khel and Volund, Riall opened the gate and stepped toward the shop until she stood just outside its open front.

Noticing Riall, the man ceased pummeling the chair. He stood, and Riall had to look up to see into his eyes. Save for the leather apron he wore and the wooden mallet he held, he could have been a tall Thjothic warrior like Volund. The frown remained on his face as he glanced behind Riall at her companions and then returned his gaze to her. "You don't have the look of someone ordering furniture."

"You are Edgelaf, are you not?"

"Aye." He nodded, but he also squinted as if suspicious of her. "Who are you, and what's your business with me?"

Too intimidated to speak, Riall held out the letter of introduction Seren had written for her.

Edgelaf frowned down at it. "I never did read well, and my eyes aren't what they used to be. Just tell me what it says."

Riall swallowed and licked her lips. "It's from Seren. She said you might help us."

"Seren?" The carpenter's eyes widened. "You've come from Seren? How is she? It's been . . ."

Breaking off, he must have noticed that Riall was trying not to cry. And failing. She wiped a tear from her eye and sniffed before mastering herself. "I'm sorry. She's fine now. It's just . . . Well, it was a near thing. But she's well now." She managed a broken smile.

Edgelaf stood with his mouth hanging open for a moment. "Well, thank Edan." Looking away from Riall, he tugged at his beard and sighed. "But I see you have a tale to share." He shook his head and cleared his throat. "Oh, but pardon me. You must be Riall. Seren told me about you so many times. I reckon you and your friends better come in. Nelda will fix something up for you."

A short while later, after Riall had told Edgelaf everything that happened at Seren's farm, she, Khel, and Volund sat at a table with the old carpenter, who had insisted they call him Edge. Tail wagging, Belu sat beneath Riall's chair. Nelda, a pleasant, heavy-set woman as grey-haired as her husband, was preparing food over the fire. As soon as Edge had told Nelda who Riall was, the woman had embraced her and Khel and Volund as well for good measure, fussing over each of them and welcoming them like her own grandchildren.

Edge was telling them how he had met Seren during the war, when the Torrlonders occupied Caergilion. He had been a lieutenant in the Torrlonder army. "When the king ordered us to search the barn, I found her. Just a scared girl hiding. I knew what King Earconwald would do to her. The worst king that ever lived, and I don't mind saying so. Might be that's why I whispered to her to stay put. To this day I can't say for sure, but that was the moment that changed me, thank Edan. So, the way I reckon it, *she* saved *me*. You see?"

Riall, Khel, and Volund each nodded.

"But you were always a good man, dear." Stirring something that smelled of meaty stew in a black pot, Nelda glanced over at them with a smile.

"No." He shook his head. "When everyone around me was doing wrong, I lacked the courage to do what was right. It took a brave girl to show me what right was." His sad smile seemed laden with memory. "At any rate, I told the others I found no one in the barn. That's how Seren escaped, but her father and mother weren't so lucky. They burned her place, and I came back and found somewhere to hide her. She was sick with the plague by then, but the Prophet of Edan saved her. I brought him to her."

"You met the Prophet of Edan?" Riall tried to keep some of the curiosity out of her voice.

"Met him? I was the first Torrlonder to follow him. By the end, almost our whole army down in Caergilion and Adanon was on his side. War never would've ended otherwise."

"Why? Why did you all follow him?"

Edge took a deep breath and stroked his beard. "He saved us. Body and spirit, he saved us. Saved us from disease. Saved us from war. Saved us from ourselves. He showed us the Caergilese, and everyone else, were our brothers and sisters. We all come from Edan, see?" His eyes were bright with belief.

"That's right," said Nelda by the fire.

A brief, small smile crossed Riall's face. "What was he like?"

"The Prophet?" Edge pursed his lips in thought for a moment. "Just being near him made you want to be the best you could. He could see into anyone, but he never seemed to judge. He was pure. And wise, like he'd lived a thousand years, though he was only a young man. And gentle. The kindest person I ever met."

Riall nodded and smiled even more at this description of her father.

Edge's eyes widened as he raised his eyebrows. "But make no mistake: He could scare the breeches off you too. Sometimes I still get chills thinking about it. There was a mighty power inside him, something beyond the understanding of the likes of me. At times he was far away somewhere in his mind. That's when he could frighten you the most. And he always seemed in pain, like he was trying to hold in all that power somehow."

Riall's smile slipped away, and her gut twisted at the familiarity of Edge's description.

Wrapped in his memories, he did not seem to notice her reaction. "Anyway, that's how I met Seren. She came to live with us here for a bit, before Queen Sequara took her to Adanon, to her uncle, the Duke Silverhand, with the war's end. She and Ardith, that's our girl – well, she's a woman grown now, with little ones of her own – she and Ardith were of an age. Like sisters, they were." He turned to look at his wife. "Were they not, dear?"

"That they were. Like sisters."

Edge nodded and smiled. "Ardith will be glad to hear of her." He looked again at Riall. "But you didn't come here to listen to an old man ramble on, did you? Seren sent you, which means I'll do whatever I can to help you."

Riall blinked for a moment, pondering how much she should tell him. "We're on our way to Grimrik. We have important business there, and we'd like to arrive as soon as may be."

Edge waited for more, but then he nodded. "Sounds simple enough, though there's a dragon wreaking destruction up north these days. I reckon you know your business." He looked at Riall for a moment as if hesitating, but then, to her relief, he continued. "Quickest way is the road to Torrhelm. From there you ride the northeast road and cross the river over to Ellordor, chief city of Ellond. There you should sell your horses and take passage on a ship going up the Theodamar, which opens into the Gulf of Olfi. Not far to Grimrik then."

"Seren mentioned someone named Bagsac in Torrhelm and Abon in Ellordor." Riall held up the folded letter. "She said we should show them this too."

"Bagsac." Edge nodded. "Good fellow, though a bit cracked, if you take my meaning." He tapped his head with his index finger. "He can get you fresh horses in Torrhelm and speed things up a bit. And Abon would help you arrange passage on a ship from Ellordor. Yes, you should see them both. They'll want to aid you for Seren's sake." He smiled. "She always thinks of everything. But you would know that. Always speaks of you as a daughter."

Not trusting her voice, Riall merely nodded, and then she looked down at the table as she held her tears in check.

"Your pardon, my dear. I've upset you."

Riall shook her head and wiped her eyes with her sleeve. "No. It's good to hear you speak of her. I'm just happy . . . happy she's alive. Happy for her." She smiled. "I would hear more tales of her from you."

Edge smiled. "And so you shall, for I'll be accompanying you to Torrhelm, and you'll have to hear me ramble the whole way. I can get you into the monastery of the Way, where old Bagsac stays." He looked down at the table as if a bit embarrassed. "I'm known there to a few, on account of being acquainted with the Prophet and all. The priests asked me all sorts of questions. Wrote down everything I could recall about the Prophet and made books out of the stories he used to tell. The Supreme Priest Osfrid himself even came once. Now there's a decent fellow."

"Thank you." Riall nodded. "You are kind. We accept your help, and we'll be glad for your stories as well."

"Good. It's settled, then, and we can leave after we eat." The carpenter grinned, but then he looked at Riall with narrowed eyes and a thoughtful frown. "One thing does occur to me, though. It might be a bit tricky getting you into the monastery, seeing as how you have the gift. You might draw some unneeded attention." He smiled. "We'll need a little help from Bagsac, but I think I know what to do."

+ 30 +

Torrhelm was like nothing Riall had ever seen or imagined. It could have swallowed twenty Kiriaths. Even Iarfaen down in Caergilion was a provincial town in comparison, though the same stench of human and animal waste predominated in both places, as well as a cacophony of shouts, neighs, barks, clucks, and all manner of sounds made by living creatures. Tall buildings of grey stone vied with one another to block the sun, casting shadows that darkened swaths of the cobbled streets. Those thoroughfares swarmed with activity, though their enormous width allowed enough space for the flow of horses, carts, and people of all sorts from every part of Andumedan. Most of them were pale northerners, but Khel had been right: There were enough folk from the eastern and southern kingdoms that no one looked twice at Riall.

They had experienced no difficulty as Edge led them through the busy checkpoint of the city's towering southern gate, where the captain of the guards recognized him, into the prosperous western half of the city. On the other side of the River Ea lay East Torrhelm, the squalid, filthy sibling of West Torrhelm, though Edge explained that King Ethelred had done much to improve the slums where the poorer denizens of the great city dwelled.

Riall had spent most of the time walking and leading her horse through West Torrhelm with her mouth open as she gawked in a mixture of amazement and unease, while Khel sometimes glanced back at her with a smile. Cradling Belu in one arm, Volund brought up the rear and said little. It had been a relief to stable the horses at an inn that Edge knew, and thence he led them to the walled complex of buildings that made up the Temple and Monastery of the Way. Once they had arrived at the august headquarters of the Way in Torrlond, he bade them wait across the street while he went inside to find Bagsac.

Riall stood with her mouth agape and head craned back, gawping up at the vast ribbed dome atop the Temple of the Way. Enormous marble columns surrounded the building's circular façade, while huge friezes above the columns portrayed old stories of the Prophet Aldmund, who had founded the Way centuries earlier. Beyond the temple, ornamented spires and an abundance of statues decorated the outer walls of the monastery. Above those walls loomed more spires and impossibly lofty buildings with soaring buttresses and majestic windows. Riall was confident the entire complex alone was larger than Kiriath. "You could fit thousands inside there."

Volund stood next to her, gaping up in a similar manner.

"Could you two act just a bit more normal? At least pretend for a moment? We're not supposed to be drawing attention to ourselves, remember?" Khel spoke from behind them.

"Oh. Right." After snapping her mouth shut, Riall turned around to face her friend. Khel's arms were crossed as he leaned his shoulder and hip in a graceful pose against the wall of a bookbinding shop that formed one side of an alley. He was also smirking at her and Volund.

Riall walked over to Khel and, jutting out her hip, leaned in a similar but slightly exaggerated manner on the wall that formed the other side of the alley. She crossed her arms and smirked at him.

Khel frowned at her. "What are you doing?"

"Acting normal."

Volund, who was still holding Belu in his arms, strode over and leaned his back on the wall next to Khel. He grinned. "I too."

Khel rolled his eyes and shook his head. "I knew it was too much to ask."

Just then, Riall spotted Edge heading toward them from across the busy street. "He's back." Behind the carpenter limped a man in one of the white robes of the priests of the Way.

In the kingdoms of the north – Torrlond, Ellond, and the Mark – most of the small number of people with the gift became priests or priestesses of the Way and donned the white robe that was the mark of their devotion to Edan. The greater part of the gifted by far had only a trace of it, just enough to influence a small creature by chanting a song of origin again and again. Very few were strong enough to control fire or produce almakhti like Queen Sequara. The Supreme Priest Bledla had been even more powerful, but his sort of strength in the gift was something that came only once in a few hundred years. Of course, there were also the Prophet and Riall herself, but they were special cases.

Anyone with the gift could sense it in anyone else who had it. Most people held no trace of it, or so little that it made no difference. If someone with the gift were close enough, however, it produced a feeling that Riall thought of as akin to having someone just outside her line of vision watching her. It was a presence distinct from the person it dwelled in, and the stronger it was, the greater the person's power. Even at this distance from the monastery, she could feel inside it the presence of the gift in more people than she had even known to possess it.

The man hobbling toward her in the white robe was different. Within him was something Riall had never sensed before: a gaping hole where the gift had once been, as if it had been ripped out of him, leaving behind not a scar but a nothingness. He was hunched and thin, and the long, wiry hair around his bald crown fluttered in the breeze like the white puff around a dandelion. His deep-set eyes watched her over his beaky nose, and he grinned as he came closer.

Riall stood straight. She could not take her eyes off the man and the horror he embodied.

"Yes, yes," said Bagsac in a raspy voice. He kept his squinty gaze on Riall. "They always look at me that way when first they meet me. Those with the gift, that is." He glanced at Edge. "This is the girl, eh?"

Edge smiled. "That she is." He was holding a sack bulging with something, and he pointed with his free hand at the priest. "This is Bagsac." He gestured at the companions. "Here are Riall, Khel, and Volund. And Belu."

Bagsac seemed to wink repeatedly while he opened his mouth wide, and it soon became apparent that a series of involuntary convulsions and twitches had seized his face. "Pleased to make your acquaintance. Lieutenant Edgelaf has informed me of everything. Ahhh!" His body jerked backwards, making Riall flinch, and he held his hand to his backside, wincing and spluttering as he limped in a circle. Then, he ceased as suddenly as he had started. "Seren was kind. A very kind girl. Kind to me when others were not. I will be of service to you, yes?" His face began twitching again as his head bobbed up and down in a nod.

Riall tried not to stare at him. "Yes. I hope so. And thank you."

"Right. Into that alley there." Edge fished inside the sack and pulled out a white robe. "Here you go." He threw the sack at Khel, who caught it. "Each of you put on one. We tried to find your sizes."

Khel frowned down at the sack. "White's not my usual color."

"Good." Edge grinned. "Yours are yellow. You're to be novices."

After Edge and the three companions donned their robes, Bagsac led them to the monastery. On one side of the front gate, a massive statue of an ancient king glowered down at them. On the other side was an equally imposing statue of a stern holy man with a long beard and a robe much like those they were all wearing. Nodding to Bagsac, the soldiers in white tunics guarding the front gate paid little attention to the group. As they walked beneath the tall arched doorway, Riall reminded herself not to gawk. Next to her, Volund gazed upward. Still holding Belu, the young Thjoth looked about as much like a novice priest as a robed troll might. Riall caught his attention and tugged at her hood. He looked puzzled for a moment, but then he nodded and pulled up his hood like the rest of them.

Limping and dragging one foot, Bagsac led them through a capacious foyer, into a broad hall, and along several shadowy corridors, not once glancing back. They passed many closed doors on either side, and the hallways seemed to go on for a long way. All the while, though they met no one, Riall could sense the gift in a number of individuals behind some of the doors, and she wondered what they must have thought of her presence. At length, their path ended before a large door. Bagsac dragged it open, allowing light to spill into the dimness from it. After blinking and gesturing for them to follow, he walked through the doorway.

Riall squinted as she emerged into a large, sun-lit courtyard surrounded by columned cloisters. A gravel path led straight through the grassy lawn, amidst which two large oaks spread their branches. The breeze hissing in the leaves was pleasant after the stuffiness of the passageways. They passed beneath the shade of the trees and crossed to the other side of the courtyard, where a door identical to the first awaited them in the cloister's wall. Bagsac opened it and, lips spread in a rictus, put his index finger to his mouth while one of his eyes blinked. He made a hissing sound that Riall took for a request to keep quiet. Following this, a series of twitches took over the priest's face, and then he ducked inside. The others passed within after Bagsac, and Riall stepped inside last.

It took a moment for her eyes to adjust to the relative dimness of the large chamber. In the sunlight streaming through the high, arched windows danced motes of dust. At each one of the hundred or so desks in the room, a candle provided more light as well as some of the thin smoke drifting up to the vaulted ceiling. Only the faint sound of a hundred quills scratching on vellum intruded on the scriptorium's silence. At every desk sat a white-robed priest or a yellow-robed novice copying a book, and one older priest stood over a novice supervising her work. Riall could feel the gift in all of them.

One hundred faces looked up, turned her way, and gawked at her. They held their quills as if frozen in mid-thought. Bagsac was convulsing and gesturing for her and the others to follow him. He hobbled straight through the room, his teeth showing in what was perhaps meant for a smile but looked more like a grimace. The others followed with Riall still last.

As they passed the desks, every pair of eyes stayed locked onto Riall. One novice whispered, "It's all coming from *her*."

"Shhhh," scolded the priest who was supervising the room. That broke the spell, and they all returned to their work, or at least pretended to.

The priest in charge nodded at Bagsac, who returned the gesture. At last, to Riall's relief, they reached the other side of the room, where Bagsac opened the door. When they entered this next chamber, Riall had to stifle a gasp. Even with its vaulted ceiling and walls high enough for three levels of arched windows, the vast chamber they had entered seemed to have no more room for books and scrolls. Shelf after shelf was brimming with them, and several ladders leaned against the walls for those needing access to the higher shelves. Only a few white-robed priests occupied the monastery's library, but they too gazed Riall's way in obvious shock.

"Perhaps this wasn't the best idea," she murmured under her breath.

With the others tailing him and Riall again bringing up the rear, Bagsac hobbled through the maze of shelves until he reached a small door tucked in a corner on the other side of the monastery's library. He turned around and, after smiling at them, spoke in a loud whisper. "Down this hallway lies my room. You'll be able to wait there while I find your new horses. Shouldn't take long at all, and you'll be on your way. Oh yes, almost there." His head bobbed up and down, and then he turned to open the door. He entered without waiting for a response.

The hallway he led them along was dark. However, when Bagsac turned a corner, high windows on one side of the hall permitted a little light to spill within. Also, from the other end of the passageway, two figures in white robes with their hoods up were walking toward them. From their forms, Riall supposed they were priestesses. They were stronger in the gift than any of the other priests or novices she had come across thus far, and one was rather tall.

Their group went in single file behind Bagsac to give space to the two priestesses to pass by in the narrow hallway. As they grew closer, Riall frowned at the priestesses. In fact, the strength in the gift was coming from only one of them, the shorter of the two. This woman was powerful, and her presence felt strangely familiar.

When she came alongside Riall, the shorter priestess stopped and turned toward her. Riall froze and stared at her, her thoughts slow to catch up with her screaming instincts.

The white-robed woman removed her hood. Queen Sequara gazed at Riall.

❧ 31 ❧

Sequara beheld her daughter and suppressed tears of relief. Knowing the girl was about to reach for her vast power, she held up her palms to forestall any catastrophic misunderstanding. "Peace, Riall. I only wish to speak with you."

Riall had been gaping at her, but she collected herself and, with a cautious frown on her face, made a slight bow. "Very well. Your Majesty." The girl still seemed on edge and ready to strike. Sequara knew she would not have a chance even to finish a song of origin before it happened.

Everyone else in the narrow hallway, including Bagsac and Edge, had been watching the two of them. However, before the sorceress-queen could speak again, Yrsa removed her hood and scowled up at her brother, whose yellow robe ill fit him. "Why are you holding that cur?" Volund was cradling Riall's dog as if she were a baby.

"Her name is Belu." It was Dalriana's son who had spoken. He grinned at Yrsa and bowed. "And I am Khel. You must be Yrsa, of whom Volund speaks so warmly."

Yrsa's eyes narrowed as she gazed at Khel. "I know who you are. Does he?" She pointed at Volund.

Khel's eyes widened and his mouth was stuck open for a moment. He closed it and looked at the floor. "No."

Riall directed a puzzled look at the young man. "What does she mean, Khel?"

The young man kept his face down. "I was going to tell you. Truly, I was."

"Tell us what?" Volund too was frowning and watching the other young man.

Khel opened his mouth, but no words came out. He shrugged and then shook his head as he looked at Riall and Volund. "I'm sorry." His shoulders drooped, and he released a sigh.

"Sorry for what? What is this?" Riall's voice betrayed her worry.

Yrsa pointed at Khel and spoke to Volund. "He is your father's bastard from the days when he and Gnorn trained the troops on Asdralad."

Khel sagged and looked at the floor again. Sequara felt a stab of pity for the young man. Perhaps harboring her own secret added to its poignancy.

Riall's eyes widened. "You're King Orvandil's son?"

"No. Only his *bastard*." Khel looked up and smirked at her, and in that expression Sequara read years of pain and loneliness.

"Is that why you wanted to come with us to Grimrik?"

The young man blinked several times and directed a sad smile at Riall. "Yes. But only at first. I don't know what I was thinking. I had a ridiculous notion that I might challenge Orvandil Dragonbane to holmgang and tell him who I was as I lay dying. Like in a story. Perhaps I only wanted to see him. Just once. It doesn't matter. I'm a fool."

"Your mother is worried for you, Khel." Sequara tried to keep her voice gentle.

Khel directed a bitter smile toward her. "You see, your Majesty, I've managed to hurt her too. Too many times."

Yrsa frowned at the young man. "Then you should go back to her."

"Yes. I should." Khel sighed. Not moving his gaze from the floor, he shook his head. "I'm sorry. To all of you. Riall. I know you'll wield the dragon and help find Volund's sister. You *will*. Volund. You . . ." He swallowed and waited a moment, but he left unsaid whatever he had been trying to express. "I'm sorry. I'll find my way out." He moved as if to return the way they had come.

"No."

Khel froze, and everyone looked at Riall, who had spoken. She blocked his way and gazed at the young man. "Don't leave. I need you." Sequara was both touched and alarmed at her daughter's reaction, and she wondered what had been happening among the three young companions during their journey together. It was obvious they had grown close. *Later. I'll find a way to speak to her.*

Looking in Riall's eyes, Khel frowned for a long moment until a gentle smile broke out across his face. He nodded.

Volund stepped forward and held out Belu to Yrsa, who scowled but took the little dog in her arms. The young Thjoth then turned to Khel, stood before him, and peered down at him with a hard frown. A sudden, bright smile broke out on Volund's face. Putting his left hand on Khel's shoulder, he clasped his right hand. "Brother."

Khel stared at him and blinked, eyes wide in seeming disbelief. Finally, he grinned and nodded. "Brother."

Riall sniffled and beamed with a smile as she watched her friends. She put a hand on the shoulder of each. The trio stood there in their yellow robes, safe and ready to defend each other from the world.

Sequara could not help allowing a small smile to cross her face as she reached a decision. She cleared her throat. "Perhaps, Khel, you could write a letter to your mother before we move on to Grimrik. Bagsac would see to it that it reaches Asdralad, I'm sure."

Bagsac bowed and then jerked before grasping his backside. "Ahhh! To be sure, your Majesty. I'll see it done."

Riall turned to the queen with her surprise written on her face. "Your pardon, Queen Sequara. Did you say, 'before *we* move on to Grimrik'?"

This was the moment Sequara had prepared for. In some ways, she had been waiting years for it. "You were right to heal Seren. And you are right to want to help Grimrik in its time of need, for you have the power to do so. Besides, I could not stop you anyway."

Riall opened her mouth and began to smile, but the queen held up her hand. "*However*, there is great danger in what you're attempting, and not only to yourself. Therefore, I will allow you to proceed only if you agree to two demands."

Riall's nascent smile disappeared, but she nodded. "What are they, my lady?"

"The first is that you allow me to accompany you. Yrsa and Gnorn will be with us as well."

"Is Gnorn here, your Majesty?" Volund looked down after addressing her, having spoken with excitement but then showing his wonted shyness.

Sequara smiled at him. "Yes. We would not have caught you without his cleverness. He's here in the monastery, but we could find no robe to fit him, and we did not think you would take him for a priest in any case."

"So, this was a trap? Edge and Bagsac *led* us to you?" Riall eyed the two men with more than a hint of accusation in her frown.

Bagsac looked away and quivered, but Edge met her gaze. "I'm sorry, my dear. Begging your pardon, but Queen Sequara's a wise woman, and she's not someone I can refuse."

"Edge and Bagsac have long been my friends as well as Seren's. They are faithful and good-hearted." Sequara directed a grateful nod their way, and then she turned back to Riall. "You will not hold their part in this against them, I hope, since I convinced them it was all for your good. So, do you agree to my first condition?"

Riall thought for a moment, but then she nodded. "Yes. It is well if you are with me."

"Good." Sequara nodded, impressed by her daughter's poise and a little intimidated by her formality. *She's grown since we've been chasing her, or have I been missing something?* She took a deep breath to prepare for the next and hardest part. "The second condition is that you must allow me to do something in the event that you feel you are losing control of your power."

Riall frowned and took a while to consider her words. "What is it you would do, my lady?" Sequara sensed there might be something the girl was holding back, something she almost spoke of but dared not.

The queen waited a moment and then decided she could question Riall about this later as well. She released a sigh. "There is a song of origin from before the days when the Andumae came to these shores. Very few have heard of it, and fewer still have used it, for good reason. I may be the only one living who knows this song. However, in my lifetime, it has been used at least twice. One of those times, the man who used it performed it on Bagsac." She looked over at the old fellow, who was hunched over but was baring his teeth in a wide grin.

Riall glanced over at the wizened, white-robed man, and something like fear entered her eyes. Sequara understood how the girl was repulsed by the void she sensed in the poor former priest. Riall turned back to the queen. "And the other time?"

"The Prophet of Edan." Sequara swallowed her grief and kept her face impassive. "He allowed someone to perform it on him in an attempt to save the world from the power that was erupting from him. In the end, he sacrificed himself."

Riall gazed at the queen for a long moment. "What does this song of origin do?"

Sequara took a deep breath. "The gift is something that dwells in those who have it, but it is not a fundamental part of them. It can be removed. This song of origin allows anyone powerful enough to wield it to cut away the gift from another. Done with care, it leaves the subject alive and of sound mind."

Riall glanced over at Bagsac and raised an eyebrow.

Sequara nodded in understanding. "When the subject is unwilling or resists, things can go wrong. Even death can result. It is also impossible to perform it if the subject is both unwilling and more powerful in the gift than the one using the song of origin. That is why you must promise me that you will willingly allow me to use this song of origin on you in the event that you begin to lose control of your power. I would use it only in dire need, but you *must* allow me. I ask this not only for your sake but to protect the lives of everyone around you. That is my second condition. Do you agree?"

Riall frowned at the queen. "If you perform this song of origin, where does the power go?"

Sequara was prepared for this question, and so she lied without blinking. "The one using the song of origin may channel the power where she will. That will be my concern. I must also tell you that, should I need to use the song of origin on you, you might no longer have the gift at all. However, some amount of it also *might* remain in you."

"How will you know?"

"I won't know until I use the song of origin. Of one thing I am certain: The majority of the vast power in you does not belong there. It may be that some amount of it is native to you. Such was the case with the Prophet of Edan. It may hold true of you as well. If it does, I would try to preserve that portion of the gift in you if possible, but the rest is what endangers you."

Riall nodded. "I know. It came from my father."

Sequara blinked, and a fist squeezed her heart. She shut her open mouth and tried to compose her face. Without her years of training to rein in her emotions, she might have gone weak in the knees.

Riall continued. "It was in Seren's mind when I healed her. I didn't mean to pry, but I saw it . . . felt it like my own memory. I know the Prophet of Edan was my father. What you've said of him over the years . . . It makes sense. He had the same power I have. Whatever is in me, it came from him."

Attempting to keep her face collected, the queen nodded. "Yes, I suppose it does make sense."

"Seren also knows who my mother was."

Sequara's heart was throbbing in her chest, and her throat constricted so that not a word could emerge. Her jaw muscles tensed as she tried to swallow.

"But she wouldn't speak of her. She said she swore not to."

The queen forced herself to nod. "I see." Under the white robe and her traveling clothes, sweat was running down her back. "Perhaps she was someone from Caergilion, where you were born. There is much we don't know of the Prophet from his days there." Feeling a coward, Sequara told herself there would be a better time to tell Riall. *Too many secrets spilled in one day already.*

Wearing a thoughtful frown, Riall nodded. "I thought the same. I suppose I'll never know." She smiled at the queen. "Very well. I accept your conditions."

Sequara caught her breath and sighed. "Do you promise?"

Riall looked her in the eyes. "Yes. I promise."

Hoping she was not betraying too much relief, Sequara forced a smile. "Let us travel to Grimrik, then, and see what you can do about that dragon."

❦ 32 ❦

"**D**ragon!"

Orvandil jerked out of troubled sleep and fumbled for his swordbelt in the dark.

A flash of orange-red erupted in the night. The blast of heat was at least a couple thousand feet in the distance but bright enough to illuminate for an instant the features of the riverbank and the awed faces of his warriors, which were painted an eerie crimson. A moment later darkness returned, but a roar like an earthquake broke the stillness, so deep and loud that it vibrated in his chest.

After the space of a few breaths, a dull glow appeared over the top of the riverbank.

"The village is in flames!" said one of his warriors.

"Quiet. The beast has keen ears." This made the sixth village along this stretch of the Mjothelf that Gorsarhad had attacked in the last two days. All the folk in the first two villages had perished. Following that, everyone had fled the other villages in the area, and even Osynia and the refugees she had gathered around her had abandoned the summer hall in favor of a safer, more secret shelter. They had evacuated this particular village yestereve, thank Edan. *Just a few empty huts.* Nevertheless, the king's heart was thumping and his hands trembling as he finished buckling his belt. It was heavy with the quiver of arrows attached to it. "Bows ready, then up the bank. Pass the word."

Bodies all around him scrambled in the dark. Orvandil found his bow, wrapped his leg around it, and grunted as he bent it to string it, feeling the smooth notch for the loop at the string's end with his fingertip since it was too dark to see. Grasping the strung bow in one hand, he crouched low as he crept up the riverbank and pushed reeds out of his face with his other hand. As his boots sank in the wet soil, he tried to tamp down his excitement. *This could be our chance. Or our deaths.*

When he reached the top of the riverbank, he beheld the conflagration that was already devouring the entire village. Bright flames crackled and roared and surged as they swarmed all over the huts, and sparks spiraled in the air around them. A ruddy aura surrounded the doomed village, but the sky above it was murky. *Damn the beast. Where is she?* He scanned the darkness above him, well knowing the danger since the dragon possessed far better night vision than he did.

It was worth the risk. Gorsarhad needed to know there would be a price for the wanton attacks that she had wreaked upon the villages of Grimrik with more ferocity than ever since he wounded her. If the lingworm had not undertaken a personal sort of vengeance before, she seemed intent on doing so now.

The cunning monster had heightened her attacks to the point of waging all-out war. No one slept without fear. She seemed to be picking any target where humans might dwell, making her message clear: Sooner or later, all of Grimrik would burn.

Orvandil intended to respond with his own message.

Shadowy forms joined him atop the riverbank, and the king recognized the silhouettes of Halvard, Bodvar, and Hakon. Each had his bow ready, and so did the other forty or so warriors that were joining them, the most he could gather at short notice. Orvandil nodded to the men nearest him. "Remember to hit the wings. The arrows will pierce no other part of her, save the eyes."

A loud and sudden gust passed in the darkness overhead. Orvandil winced, and most of his warriors flattened themselves. He tightened his grip on the bow with his sweaty hand and peered skyward. He could see nothing, but his instincts were screaming at him.

"Nock arrows!"

Yew creaked in the darkness. The village was groaning in its death throes as the bright pyre ascended into the night. The king of the Thjoths and his men waited, but there was no other sound, no sign of the terror from above.

A vast, shadowy form winked by as another blast of air rumbled overhead, and this time the wind in its wake plucked at Orvandil's cloak and hair. A few warriors cried out, and they all were jerking around as they tried in vain to glimpse the massive predator above. The darkness defied them.

Orvandil could almost smell the panic rising in his men. "Steady! Keep your arrows nocked and ready."

A longer silence followed. The king began to wonder if the serpent of the air might have departed. *She's toying with us.* He peered up into the darkness, which yielded no answer.

Other than the growling of the flames behind him and the breathing of his men, there was no noise. The king strained to listen until he almost believed he could perceive his own heart beating. But then, at first faint, something like the sound of the breeze around a swift ship arose just at the edge of his hearing. With terrible speed, the soughing grew louder and deeper until it rolled like thunder. The very darkness seemed to be roaring at them. Orvandil raised his bow and pointed the arrow in what he hoped was the right direction. "Pull!" Once again, forty bows groaned as the warriors all prepared to speed their missiles.

Aloft, an orange-ruddy glow leapt to life, illuminating glistening teeth set in an enormous maw. Protruding from the lower jaw was the tip and part of the black shaft of the Dweorg-wrought spear Orvandil had cast. Hurtling closer to him and his warriors, Gorsarhad bellowed just before an inferno erupted from her vast throat.

"Loose!" Strings twanged, and their missiles whistled as they sought their target above. Having aimed to the right of the dragon's mouth, the king prayed his arrow would rip a hole in the leathery wing. One arrow wound would not slow her down, but forty tears in her wings would at least hamper her. He took heart when the stream of fire from the beast guttered out and she released an ear-piercing scream of pain and frustration, but his triumph was short-lived.

The giant burst of fire the dragon had disgorged before the storm of stinging missiles reached her exploded into the ground where some of his warriors knelt. Orvandil rolled, and a wave of blistering heat passed over him. He stood, snatched an arrow from his quiver, and nocked it. The dark forms of several of his men flailed like drunkards inside the flames, which withered a broad swath of the reeds, and the men's shrieks bore witness to their agony. Those shrieks and the stench of burning flesh would haunt his nightmares, he knew, but there was no time to dwell on that.

The fire's glow revealed the backs of many men fleeing for the river with their long shadows preceding them. Several warriors remained beside the king, however. Among them, Halvard stood and squinted up at the sky, his bow ready as the uncanny light reddened his face.

"Steady! Let's see if she makes another pass." Orvandil scanned the sky. He turned around to behold the burning village. Illuminated in the ruddy glow above it, a giant reptilian form materialized as it sundered the veil of smoke, careering in the air toward the king and his remaining men.

"Nock and loose! Then run for the river!" Orvandil showed his teeth in a mad grin and drew his bow as death's shadow loomed and swallowed him.

※ 33 ※

"Good. Very good." Sitting on a cushion opposite Sigra, Bolverk smiled at her, causing the wrinkles branching from his good eye to deepen. "You learn swiftly."

The afternoon sunlight bled through a gap made when the breeze outside toyed with the tent's loose entrance flap. Light also streamed down through a hole at the tent's apex, but it was still dim inside. Dust motes spun in the shaft of sunlight from the smoke vent, with the light pooling on the tent's floor in between where Sigra and Bolverk sat.

She bowed her head slightly in acknowledgment of his praise. She was walking a very narrow line. In order to keep the other remaining Thjothic captives alive, she needed him to be pleased with her, but not too pleased lest he take her compliance for a sign of resignation to their wedding. Though the war-leader did not allow her to see her folk, he assured her whenever she asked after them that they were well and being treated with the same dignity the Ilarchae accorded all slaves. He still promised their freedom as a wedding gift.

Sigra took such assurances in silence, but inwardly she wondered if it would not be better to save her folk by relenting. Perhaps she would. For now, it was possible to imagine that rescue still might come from Grimrik, and so she was buying as much time as she could.

But time did not seem to be her friend. With each passing day, she felt a little more remote from the kingdom of her birth and her people, including Halvard, her mother, and her siblings, as if they were part of her fading past. Each day, even Emmi became a less substantial memory, and at times – such as when she caught herself enjoying her lessons in the Ilarchae tongue with the war-leader – she forgot to be angry over her friend's horrible death, which Bolverk accounted a great honor since he had given her to the gods. Each day, it grew harder to nurse her dwindling hope, and it did not help that the only company she received was Bolverk's. One thing, however, represented a vast improvement in her circumstances: the absence of Unnar.

Since the would-be-rapist had departed, she had been surprised at Bolverk's reaction. After all, she had tried to run away. Also, she would have thought the exile of even a hideous son like Unnar might have kindled his anger against her. However, rather than punish her, the old war-leader had become kinder, and he visited her often to teach her the Ilarchae tongue. He had even ordered her free of her bonds, though she had not failed to notice the watch on her tent had doubled.

"Now, heed me." He pointed at his hand, which was spotted with age. "Hand."

"Hand," she repeated. Obedience was so automatic that she almost had no need to feign it. It was also not difficult since the word in Thjothic was almost the same.

"Arm." His finger moved up to his forearm, covered in white, bristly hair.

"Arm."

"Yes. Good." He wiggled his fingers and smiled. "Fingers."

"Fingers."

He paused a moment, seeming to consider something before grasping the top of his head. "Head."

"Head."

Taking a lock of his long white hair between his fingers, he tugged on it. "Hair."

"Hair."

With a smile and a chuckle, he pulled on his white beard. "Beard."

"Bee-erd."

"No." He shook his head. "Like thus: beard."

"Beard."

"Yes. Good." His fingers brushed over his face. "Face."

"Face."

He pointed with his index finger at his remaining eye. "Eye."

"Eye," she repeated, but she was gazing at the patch over the ruined one. A bit of scar tissue the patch did not cover ran down his cheek. Sigra did not know why, but the missing eye was the part of her captor that frightened her most.

Bolverk frowned at her as if guessing her thoughts. He blinked, and then he reached up to the patch and pulled it up over his head, strap and all.

Sigra stifled a gasp. Where the old man's eye should have been, there was a hollowed out space covered with taut, uneven scar tissue. A jagged, pink scar also claimed part of his eyebrow before running down across the ruin of the eye hole to his cheek. The strap of his eye patch left a line on his forehead where it dug into his flesh.

The smile Bolverk gave her was almost gentle. "I'll tell you the story one day." His smile sagged, and he looked in her eyes. "You find me ugly?"

Sigra found it difficult to look away from the puckered scar where his eye should have been, but she forced herself to gaze into his good eye, which was pale blue. Perhaps it was the lack of the patch, or perhaps it was the old man's seeming vulnerability without it, but a sudden shift occurred in Sigra's perception. He seemed frailer to her, weary and subject to doubt. She had also understood something since the encounter with Unnar: Bolverk might be a monster, but he was a monster who loved his people and feared for them. He might even be a good leader, at least according to the old ways. *He's not so different from a king of the Thjoths a couple generations back.*

"No." She shook her head in answer to his question.

Something beyond her desire to keep him pleased seized her, a feyness that welled up in her and took over her body. She felt Edan's presence in all things, even in this brutal and rigid man whose harsh life had formed him. Before she understood what she was doing, her hand was reaching toward his scar. With the gentlest of caresses, she brushed it with her fingertips, and it seemed to her that a strange and intense blend of feelings – pity, sorrow, pain, and empathy – leaped out between them. In that moment, her fear died.

Bolverk flinched a little, and his good eye widened in shock.

The sense of transcendence ended. In disbelief at what she had just done, Sigra dropped the offending hand, enclosed it in her other one, and looked down at her lap, hoping she had not gone too far.

Trembling slightly, his hand reached up and felt his scar where she had touched it. Somewhere beneath the lines graven in his rough face lay a hint of the anxiety weighing on him, a desperation he strove to conceal. "I lost it for the Raven Eyes long ago, when I was young."

Sigra nodded to show she understood.

Bolverk gave her a sad smile. "All I have done is for my tribe. I have lied, stolen, betrayed, murdered, and worse so that we would *survive*. Life in this world is hard, and nowhere is it harder than in the Wild-lands. Do you understand?"

She nodded again, and for some reason she could not explain, a tear freed itself from her eye to spill down her cheek.

Bolverk frowned at her. "I too sorrow for your pain. You do not know how it grieves me. I am scarred, but not unfeeling."

Sigra gazed in his eye, no longer pretending to be submissive or afraid, for she felt no trace of dread for this battered old man who seemed in as much need of comfort as she. He was right. The world was full of pain. Her own suffering was part of it all, somehow less terrible in light of this revelation suffusing her. She sorrowed for the Raven Eyes and their hardships, for Bolverk and the choices that had disfigured him. His face blurred as unshed tears filled her eyes. She was not certain if it was courage that took hold of her, but her fate no longer troubled her in that moment.

Bolverk kept his gaze locked on her. He swallowed and then narrowed his eyes as a hardened expression took over his features. "I must wed you. My fool of a son has doomed us otherwise."

Sigra continued to gaze at him, not understanding whence her tears came, or whether they were for him or herself or the world. She could not help smiling at the peace and strength welling in her.

Bolverk blinked at her, uncertainty furrowing his brow. He released a long sigh. "The only way we can avoid the Thjoths' vengeance is to make allies of them. The dragon won't torment them forever. Orvandil Dragonbane will find a way. I have seen men like him before, one or two. And after he does, he will come for us. Before that happens, I must be your husband, and you my wife." His words were slow and soft, almost a whisper. "You are our sole hope. Peace-weaver. Thousands of lives, many of them Thjoths, depend on you. As war-leader, it is my duty to wed you. Our children will guarantee the Raven Eyes' survival."

Sigra heard his words but did not acknowledge them. Instead, she looked him in the eye and held his gaze until he blinked again and looked down at his lap as if ashamed. When he glanced back up at her, he wore a puzzled frown. His mouth opened as if to speak, but no words came out.

With the last shreds of her fear and hate for this man dissolving, she understood him at last and what he wanted. With that understanding came an uncanny compassion. "I will think on your words. And pray to Edan." Her own voice sounded strange to her, strong and commanding.

He studied her for a long moment as if trying in vain to comprehend the change in her, but then he inclined his head in a slight bow to acknowledge her words. Bolverk stood at once and turned away to leave. The tent flap parted with a ruffle, allowing a momentary surge of the daylight within the tent, and then he was gone.

Sigra stared at the flap for a long while before her shoulders drooped and a long sigh escaped her. She was no wiser as to the path she would follow, but it seemed to her that much had changed. Somehow, she had unshackled herself from the fear. With a small and fleeting smile, she acknowledged the first small victory she had tasted in a long time.

❧ 34 ❧

The gloaming was gilding the green landscape with its aura and setting the clouds afire with pinks and oranges when they halted to make camp. They had left the River Ea behind and were journeying northeast on the road to Ellordor. To the east loomed the northernmost of the Osham Mountains, their peaks tinged pink in the twilight. Therein lay, it was said, the dragon Gorsarhad's lair. To the west, a lone mountain towered far above the rest of the land: the mighty Ormetberg, where, in yore-days before they worshipped Edan, the Torrlonders and Ellonders once believed their gods dwelled.

Khel and two of the Thjothic warriors were taking care of the horses while Yrsa and the third Thjothic warrior sought game. Volund and Gnorn busied themselves making a fire. Sensing imminent warmth, Belu was sticking close to Volund. This left Riall alone with Queen Sequara. The two of them stood some way off from the camp peering out at the Ormetberg and, all around it, the westering sun's brilliant display.

Riall gazed at the sunset but was thinking more of the vision she had experienced while they were riding, not long before they stopped to make camp. In the waking dream, she had approached a stone bridge spanning a broad river. In the distance lay a great city, wherein twilight's long shadows would soon fade into night's darkness. Though it was much thinner and on the verge of collapse, she had still been walking in the body of the washerwoman.

Two brown-skinned soldiers in helms and gold colored tunics stood before the bridge bearing long spears, and two more sat on stools in front of a small stone dwelling that appeared to house the bridge guards. In contrast to the pale-skinned people she had seen in her previous visions, these men appeared to be Andumaic, but their garb was unlike that of the soldiers of Asdralad. They must have been from one of the eastern kingdoms of Andumedan.

As Riall approached them, the two standing guards straightened their postures and appeared to frown at her, squinting into the slanted light behind her. Wariness became alarm when she came within twenty feet of them. Clearly, something about her had frightened them – perhaps the filthy, emaciated state of the body she walked in. They pointed their spears at her and commanded her to halt in Andumaic, though with an accent that differed from that found on Asdralad. The other two guards rose from their stools and grabbed their spears.

All four soldiers froze at once. Each went wide-eyed, and one moaned in horror and ecstasy. Without a word or a gesture, Riall emptied their bodies. Spears clattered on stones. Three of the bridge guards' corpses fell along with the washerwoman's. Riall looked out from the fourth soldier's eyes. She dropped his spear and began crossing the bridge.

She shuddered as she recalled the vision. Somehow, having Queen Sequara nearby made her a bit less afraid of it, though she was still not sure how she felt about her mentor's presence for the rest of her journey. Her relief was perhaps most prominent, but not far behind it was disappointment that was not quite resentment. The queen and their other older companions threw into confusion the rhythm that had developed between her and Khel and Volund. Also, her two friends were in the process of understanding their relationship since it emerged that they were half-brothers. Riall was happy for them, but she missed having them to herself. She released a quiet sigh.

Glancing at Riall, the sorceress-queen seemed to take the breaking of the silence as a chance to speak. "Would you like me to tell you about him?"

It took a moment for Riall to understand whom the queen meant. "My father?"

"Yes." Queen Sequara nodded. "The Prophet of Edan."

"You knew him well, my lady?"

One of the queen's familiar, sad smiles crossed her face. "Yes. Queen Faldira trained him in Asdralad. I was there for many months with him, but I left for Adanon and Caergilion to fight in the war while he continued learning to use the power that was in him." She shook her head. "We lost the southwest, and I returned to Kiriath. Not long after that, the Torrlonders invaded Asdralad, and few of us escaped. Gnorn, Orvandil, the bard Abon, whom you will meet in Ellordor, the Prophet, and I. The Prophet's control over his power was . . . unstable, and he was unable to defeat the Supreme Priest Bledla at that time."

Queen Sequara frowned at Riall as if she were seeking the same instability in her, but then she smiled. "But that's not what I meant. Everyone knows the stories of the Prophet and how, riding upon the dragon Gorsarhad, he defeated Bledla at the Battle of Thulhan. I would like to tell you about the man."

Riall nodded. "Yes. I'd like that."

The sorceress-queen gazed at her for a moment, and then she nodded in return. "His name was Dayraven. In truth, he was little more than a boy, perhaps three or four years older than your friend Khel." The queen glanced over at the horses, where Khel was rubbing one down.

Riall followed her gaze and, knowing how Khel enjoyed the horses' company, allowed a half smile before returning her attention to the queen.

Queen Sequara smiled and continued. "Dayraven was the son of Edgil, a thegn of the village of Kinsford in the kingdom of the Mark. His mother Eldelith died giving him birth, but she also gave him the gift, which ran strong in her family. Her aunt, Dayraven's great aunt, was a witch-woman of great power and wisdom, and she was my friend. She died along with Queen Faldira when the Torrlonders invaded Asdralad, but I will tell you more of her another time."

"So, the Prophet was born with his power, like me?"

"No. He was born with the gift, and he might have been a strong wizard or priest had he learned to use it. But he did not. He was not even aware he had the gift."

"Then how did he become so powerful?"

The queen sighed. "One day, in the Southweald, the ancient forest near his home, he met an elf. As you know, when someone gets close enough to an elf, they do not live to tell of it."

"The elf-sleep."

"Yes."

"He met it in the forest?" The northern forest of her dreams sprang to Riall's mind, and she almost believed she could envision the place where the Prophet encountered one of the ethereal presences that mortals, lacking knowledge of their nature, feared and named elves.

Riall knew that Queen Sequara had made a close study of elves over the years, and sometimes she had shared what little lore she found with her pupils. The queen nodded. "Yes. And he *lived*. For the first and only time that we know of, someone survived a close meeting with an elf. But it left something inside him: the vast power that made him the Prophet of Edan. He gained enough control over this power to defeat Bledla at the Battle of Thulhan, but he paid a terrible price. When he wrested control of the dragons from the supreme priest to end the war, he used too much of the power within him. There on the battlefield, the elf emerged from him, taking over his body and mind. It sought to end all the pain around it by eliminating its source: humanity."

"He would have killed *everyone*?" A tightness in Riall's chest began to expand as she realized what the power inside her could do.

The queen nodded. "It was a near thing. But Dayraven returned and contained the power for a little while. A few days later, he disappeared. No one knows much of his wanderings, save that wherever he went, people began to follow him. Lacking his memories or any knowledge of who he was, he ended up in Caergilion, where he healed the sick, made peace, and somehow transformed Torrlond's occupying army into followers of the Edan he preached."

"And met my mother."

The queen paused a moment. "Perhaps. In the meantime, taking advantage of the chaos and weakness in the wake of the war, the Ilarchae broke out of the Wildlands. They fought all the way to Torrhelm, where the Prophet had traveled to secure the peace he sought. Unfortunately, he lost control of the elf-power just as they arrived to savage the city. In fulfillment of its intent to end humanity, the elf seized the Ilarchae army as its weapon."

"The entire army?"

"Yes. More than one hundred thousand lives gone in an instant."

"Edan's mercy." Riall shuddered at what she heard and what she realized she might do.

The queen continued. "Tearing away the energy that constituted their spirits, the elf took their bodies and filled them with its will, thus creating an army of elf-dwolas. They were animated corpses intent on one thing: to slay all in their path. Very few of the Ilarchae escaped that fate to return to the Wildlands. However, through the song of origin I spoke to you about, the Prophet survived the separation of the elf's power from him. He became Dayraven again for a brief time, and the gift that was native to him remained within him."

"What happened, then? How did he die?"

The sorceress-queen released a long sigh. "He refused to allow the army of elf-dwolas to destroy everyone in its path. It was heading for the Mark, Dayraven's birth kingdom. Using the same song of origin that saved him, he attempted to return the elf to the Southweald, the forest whence it came. In the end, he succeeded in this, but he died in the process. He sacrificed himself to save countless others." The queen looked Riall in the eyes. "He was a good man. Gentle and loving. You should know that."

Riall nodded. "So, the elf and all its power returned to the Southweald?"

The queen gazed at Riall for a long moment. "Perhaps not all."

Riall swallowed as everything fell into place in her head. "You mean the Prophet passed it on to me. When my mother was carrying me inside her womb, it was already there. I was born with the elf-power."

Queen Sequara beheld Riall with such intensity that she seemed to tremble. "Yes. I'm so sorry."

Riall looked at the ground for a long moment until she reached a decision and returned her gaze to her mentor. She had a foreboding that she would be needing the sorceress-queen's help, and she needed to tell someone what she had realized anyway.

Queen Sequara stared back at her, the beginning of a puzzled frown indicating she saw the conviction on Riall's face.

Riall took the leap. "There's something about my dreams I must tell you. What you call an elf-dwola walks in them." She swallowed and licked her lips. "I think the elf is coming for me."

❅ 35 ❅

After Khel finished rubbing down Riall's horse, Volund's, and his own, he gave the two Thjoths nearby a polite nod. He thought their names were something like Flosi and Njal, but he was fairly certain he could not pronounce them correctly. He had said little to them. Speaking the Northern Tongue less well than Volund and his sister, they had talked even less to him. However, ignoring him as they attended to the other horses, they had spoken plenty to each other in Thjothic. An occasional glance his way convinced him they had been speaking about him the whole time.

It made sense that they might want to measure up a son of Orvandil Dragonbane, even if he was hardly a half-Thjoth in body or spirit. They did not seem terribly impressed. Then again, perhaps he was just being too self-conscious. *They might have been speaking of their grandmothers, for all I know.*

He made his way to the fire that Volund and the old Dweorg had just kindled. It was beginning to pop and crackle and smoke. Khel sat beside Belu and rubbed the little dog's head and neck the way he had seen Riall do a thousand times. With Queen Sequara around, he found himself unable to enjoy Riall's company as often or as freely. He tried

187

not to resent the queen since he knew the woman was keeping Riall safer.

Belu rolled on her back and, front legs sticking up, seemed to demand that he rub her belly. Complying with a smile, he took a moment to poke the little dog. "You need more exercise. You're getting fat from Volund carrying you around everywhere." He would have to make do with Belu for company, though the pup never teased back the way Riall did. *We mongrels better stick together, eh?*

Volund was smiling. "She's fat from you feeding her when you think no one's looking."

Khel put a hand on his chest in mock innocence. "I? No chance. I don't even like curs." Even as he said it, he continued to rub Belu's belly with a stupid grin on his face.

Volund chuckled, as did Gnorn. The web of wrinkles on the old Dweorg's face deepened when he laughed. He looked at Khel when he finished. "I was acquainted with your mother back in the days when King Orvandil and I stayed on Asdralad, before he was king. Queen Sequara informs me she's done much for the island kingdom."

The grin fell away from Khel's face, and he nodded. "She helped finance the rebuilding of Kiriath after the war. Queen Sequara has always been grateful, but some of the larger noble houses – or what was left of them after the war – grew a bit resentful. Of course, their feelings might have had something to do with her having a bastard as well."

Gnorn nodded. "It's not easy to live where folk treat you like you don't belong."

"And what would you know of that?" Khel had not meant to sound so bitter, but the Dweorg had hit on a sore truth.

The old Dweorg frowned and tugged at his white beard. "King Orvandil has given the Dweorgs of the Fyrnhowes an honored place in Grimrik, which was our ancestral land many winters ago, before the Thjoths wrested it from us in war and sent the remnant of our folk into exile. Before our recent return, however, we few hundred survivors eked out a sorry existence in Torrlond, the land of our long exile, in the city of Etinstone. The wealthiest of the Torrlonders were happy to buy what we made, but most folk treated us as vermin. In all the years we dwelled there, we were never welcome. We were a folk without a land, watching our slow extinction creep upon us." Gnorn's sorrow was most evident in his eyes, which fixed Khel with their gaze.

Khel nodded. "I suppose some of us have a hard time finding our place. But at least you have a home now."

"Aye. The best possible. I never thought I'd see the Fyrnhowes, and now I am content to die there. The last of us will be buried next to our ancestors."

"The last of you?"

Gnorn looked at Khel with the saddest of smiles. "We are still a dying people. In one, perhaps two generations, we will be gone. Most of us are old. The few who are young have no one to wed according to our laws, being too close kin. When we are gone, our secrets will go with us." The old Dweorg stole a glance at Volund.

Pretending not to notice the look Gnorn gave Volund, Khel held his mouth open for a moment. "No more Dweorgs?"

Gnorn smiled. "Oh, there are other Dweorgs still. We Dweorgs of the Fyrnhowes are the only ones to have lived among you newcomers. The others are few, to be sure, and they keep to their ancient hill forts and caves in the remotest parts of Eormenlond. They are stubborn as rock, and they will live out their days in the places where their ancestors were born. Long before the coming of the Andumae nigh two thousand years ago and the northerners somewhat later, we Dweorgs had dwelled here for countless centuries. We are part of the land, and someday we will return to it."

Khel paused in scratching Belu. "It seems rather sad."

"It is the way of life. For now, we are here, and our task is to find what we are to do and with whom we shall do it."

Khel sighed. "I'm not sure I'm up for it."

"You may be closer than you think." Gnorn put a hand on Volund's shoulder and, raising his bushy eyebrows, gave Khel a meaningful stare.

Khel shook his head. "Volund is my brother, but I'll never be a Thjoth."

Gnorn smiled. "Nor will I, but I've found a place among them."

"How?"

The Dweorg scratched his beard. "Well, King Orvandil was a great help."

"He doesn't even know I exist."

Gnorn nodded. "True. But that is a lack we will remedy."

Khel frowned. "I'm not sure. Perhaps it's better that he remain ignorant of me."

"Nonsense. Volund and I will speak to the king." The old Dweorg turned to the young Thjoth. "Won't we, lad?"

"Aye."

Gnorn turned back to Khel. "It might not be easy at first, but I counsel you to be brave and stubborn. The Thjoths respect nothing more."

"Brave and stubborn." Khel nodded. "Right."

Just then, the sound of metal ringing out drew their attention. Flosi and Njal were sparring with swords, rushing at each other with abandon and grinning as they displayed great skill with their blades. It did not take Khel long to see that either of them would best him in mere moments.

Gnorn chuckled as he watched them. "Ha! You see. Look at them. Brave and stubborn. That's how King Orvandil slew a dragon during the Battle of Thulhan. It was not because he was bigger and stronger." He turned to Khel and gestured toward the combatants. "You and Volund should each challenge one of them."

Khel's eyes widened. "You think so?" He turned to Volund. "Perhaps I'd be better off taking on your sister. Do you fancy my chances there?"

"No." Volund shook his head.

Khel frowned at the decisiveness of his brother's reply, which did not encourage him.

Gnorn looked Khel in the eye. "It doesn't matter if you win or lose. The Thjoths respect a brave loser more than anything. Courage in the face of certain doom: What could be more noble?"

Khel gazed back at the Dweorg until a sudden resolve sparked to life in him. He stood and drew his blade, and then he nodded at Gnorn. "Brave and stubborn, then. Perhaps a little stupid as well. Are you ready, Volund?"

Volund stood, drew his blade, and smiled at his brother.

✣ 36 ✣

In the early morning mist, Orvandil found him lying behind a large rock on the rugged hillside, not far from where the broken and charred corpses of his other warriors were strewn. His eyes were closed, his body still. From the trail of blood on the rocks, the king could see how he had dragged himself there. The rest of his blood had pooled beneath him, having flowed out of his body from the ragged gash running from his left shoulder straight through his leather armor, flesh, and ribs to end all the way down at his thigh. A claw wound. Gorsarhad's claws were just as dangerous as her teeth when she fought on the ground. Burns covered the other half of his body. Hair, beard, and ear were gone on the right side of his face, which was a mass of raw, seeping wounds. His right arm had withered to little more than blackened bone.

He had died a brave, terrible, and agonizing death. And the blame lay with Orvandil.

The ambush the king had planned had, as in a nightmare, veered with terrible and unstoppable suddenness into a death trap for the Thjoths, not the dragon. To be sure, they had wounded the beast, even to the point where she had difficulty flying away when it was over. But the cost was too high.

More than a hundred of his warriors had become mutilated corpses. Another hundred who had been part of the ambush escaped with their lives, but of those many were wounded. Orvandil had been unable to help anyone while he struggled to avoid Gorsarhad's flames, teeth, and claws. He and his men had been like ants crawling all over the lingworm, and they had hacked her with their blades, but too few of them pierced those hard scales.

Every one of the Thjoths' deaths weighed on the king, who mourned them all. But this one broke him. He sank to his knees next to the body and gazed upon it.

"Halvard."

He had been set to wed Sigra, a future union that had been a source of joy and contentment to Orvandil and Osynia. They had already begun to think of Halvard as a son. Long before that, the warrior had proven himself many times, even as far back as the War of the Way, when he had been a headstrong young man, hardly more than a boy, though a big one. Halvard had grown into his strength by developing wisdom and kindness. He had also been close to Gnorn, who would take his death hard. There was no more loyal and brave warrior among the Thjoths or any other folk.

All lost. How life could change with such terrible swiftness. How fragile dreams could be, if one event could shatter them beyond recovery. All because he, Orvandil Dragonbane, had failed.

He had failed to keep Halvard safe. He had failed to protect Sigra as well. He had failed to save his folk from the dragon. Everything he had done had only aggravated the beast and spurred her on to greater heights of vengeance. What sort of king put his people in more danger by his decisions? He could not help but think about what the Prophet would have thought. He imagined him as a ghostly visitation shaking his head with disappointment and sorrow. For the king of the Thjoths, there could be no stronger rebuke.

"Halvard. I'm sorry, son. I failed you. How could I lead my people to such hideous deaths?"

Halvard's eyes opened.

A small gasp escaped Orvandil. He grasped Halvard's blood-spattered left hand. "Oh, merciful Edan. I'm so sorry."

Somehow, what remained of Halvard's lips on the left side of his face trembled into a smile. Blood coated his teeth. "To follow you . . . was my life's glory." His voice did not rise above a hoarse whisper. "Greatest of kings. Bring . . . bring her back."

Orvandil nodded. "I will. I swear it. By Edan and all the old gods, I swear it."

Halvard smiled again. He closed his eyes and seemed to drift into unconsciousness. But he opened them again for a moment to speak. "Burn my body."

Followers of the Way in Torrlond and Ellond buried their dead. Most Thjoths, even those who worshipped Edan, still followed the old way, which the Prophet himself sanctioned when he burned his own father's body after the Battle of Thulhan. That death too still weighed on the king, for in combat he had killed the man himself, though not willingly.

Orvandil nodded. "You'll have a glorious pyre, my son."

Halvard's eyes were closed again, his mouth slightly open.

Keeping ahold of the younger man's hand and gritting his teeth to contain his despair, the king of the Thjoths bowed his head and watched over his dying warrior and friend.

❦ 37 ❦

On the eastern bank of the Theodamar River lay the city of Ellordor, chief city of the kingdom of Ellond. The City of Spires they named it, for hundreds of them soared above the cobbled streets and tree-lined parks within its walls. Many of them belonged to the city's famed schools of learning, which dated back to the days long before the Prophet Aldmund first proclaimed the Way of Edan.

Fewer spires graced the skyline now, however, and, like the rest of the city, the schools of learning were for the most part empty. Gorsarhad had razed many buildings in her attack on Ellordor, and many others she had blackened with her flames. Most of the citizens had fled the city for safer quarters in the countryside. Thus abandoned, the city became a haunted place, while its beauty had yielded to a sense of eerie foreboding.

It was Riall's first look at the fearsome destruction the dragon had wrought. It was not only sobering, but also frightening. For perhaps the first time, what she was attempting became real in her mind. When she had been far away, the dragon's predations were mere stories. Witnessing the devastation left in their wake made them material, and it gave her an indication of Gorsarhad's power. Swaths of the city were rubble, whereas large sections were untouched. She wondered how many people perished when the serpent of the air attacked. King Fullan had ordered most folk away, but many soldiers and some priests – those few with enough strength in the gift to wield fire – had remained to defend the chief city, and some citizens refused to leave their homes no matter the threat.

Whether by chance or because it was well defended, King Fullan's palace escaped largely unscathed. Stithfast it was called, but it was in truth a network of centuries-old buildings, the oldest ones being solid and thick and suited for defense, whereas spires, columns, buttresses, and arched windows graced the later additions. Cloisters surrounded green courtyards among the buildings, and stately old trees stood guard on their lawns, giving the whole place a sense of airiness and grace. While walking through it, Riall could almost forget about the ruin elsewhere in the city.

Queen Sequara's name gained them swift entry to Stithfast, leaving Riall to wonder how she and Khel and Volund would have managed on their own. When he heard that the queen of Asdralad had arrived with a party, King Fullan had ordered rooms prepared for all of them. After bathing and resting, Riall left Belu to nap in her room. She and her companions went to meet the king, followed by a sumptuous meal at a long table in an elegant hall. The king, a kind-looking man with a grey-blond beard, kept them company. Also seated there was Abon, a squat, bald fellow with a nasty scar across his face and a sparse, grey beard. On the table next to him was some sort of harp, for Abon was a bard, or what the folk of the northern kingdoms called a shaper. From the conversation during and after the meal, it was apparent that both the king and the shaper had known Queen Sequara for many years.

After servants cleared the table, there was a little polite conversation before King Fullan looked at Queen Sequara and turned to more serious matters. "So, you've come to deal with the dragon. On behalf of my people, I offer you my thanks. If it is within my power to give it, I will deny nothing you request to assist you in your mission, including strength of arms. My army is at your disposal should you require it."

Queen Sequara bowed her head in acknowledgement. "You are generous, and I knew we could count on your help. However, all that we would ask of you is a ship for passage to Grimrik as soon as may be. I apologize for our haste."

King Fullan smiled. "Do you recall the last time you were here, during the war? You made the same request for a ship back then, and you were in just as much of a hurry."

For a moment seeming to look far away, the queen nodded. "Yes, so I could return to Asdralad. It was after the Battle of Thulhan. Earl Elfwy and his men accompanied me."

The king's face grew thoughtful with some old memory. "Earl Elfwy. He was a good man. One of the many we lost in those days." He returned to the present with a melancholy smile. "Yes, our reports indicate the dragon has been ravaging Grimrik far more than any other kingdom of late. From what we've heard, it's an all out war up there. You will find Gorsarhad in Grimrik, and of course you shall have a ship. The swiftest I have is yours."

Riall spotted Yrsa shifting in her seat. A cord of muscle stood out on the woman's jaw as she seemed to grind her teeth. She also noticed Volund stealing a glance at his sister.

"I am grateful. But you should know it is not I who have come to deal with the dragon." Queen Sequara looked at Riall, who thought she perceived something like pride in the sorceress-queen's slight smile, and gave her a nod. "That task is Riall's. She alone has the strength in the gift to wield the song of origin, and she came here of her own will to help. It is she who deserves your thanks, and, should she succeed, the thanks of every soul in the northern kingdoms."

The king's eyes widened a little as he shifted his gaze to Riall, who felt her face flush and looked down at the table. "You would think," said King Fullan, "someone so powerful in the gift would be known in all the kingdoms of Eormenlond. You've kept her well hidden, Queen Sequara."

"She is young still." The queen smiled again at Riall, and this time there could be no doubt of her esteem. "But the kingdoms of Andumedan will hear of her soon, I think." Her smile fell away, and she released a sigh. "Another matter comes to mind, however, which concerns our friend Abon." She turned to the bard, who sat across from her. "Seren sends you her greetings. She suffered an illness recently, but she is well now thanks to Riall."

The shaper peered at the queen for a moment before turning to Riall and nodding in acknowledgement. "Then I already owe you my thanks, young lady. The world would be a poorer place without Seren and her voice."

There was an intensity in his gaze that Riall understood, having always treasured Seren's voice. Being a shaper, this man would appreciate it as well, but she had not known Seren was so well loved outside of her humble home in Caergilion and her Uncle Imharr's castle in Adanon. It seemed she had much to learn about the woman who raised her. Not trusting her voice as her emotions stirred at the thought of Seren, she nodded back to Abon.

As if those emotions tossed her to another place, with her next heartbeat Riall beheld all around her endless fields of wheat. On the horizon loomed a vast mountain range with white peaks. She was walking in the body of the young Andumaic soldier she had taken at the bridge. Some aloof part of her mind recalled that Queen Sequara had told her the soldier's golden tunic meant he was likely from Sildharan, but that conversation seemed so unimportant now, belonging to a distant, insignificant life. The soldier's identity mattered naught, nor even did the kingdom of Sildharan, for, like all other kingdoms, it was but a fleeting thing, the collective fiction of mortals, who deluded themselves and were less enduring even than their fictions. Long after they and their kingdoms and their religions and the other illusions that held them together would be gone, the land would abide.

Swaths of the wheat bowed in a gentle wind. It was peaceful in that place. No mortals appeared to remind her of pain and suffering. Nothing but the breeze, the wheat, and the bright sun overhead. Life breathing in and out. She was walking toward the mountains, she knew. She would find what she sought beyond them.

On and on she walked, and she was at peace knowing her oneness with the wheat, the wind, the mountains, and the sun.

She blinked, and a woman's face appeared before her. Though scarred with small burn marks, it was a beautiful face with dark brown eyes.

"Riall?"

It took a moment for her to realize that the word the woman had uttered was her name. After another moment, she associated the face with Queen Sequara, who was leaning over her.

Riall came back in scattered pieces that began to fit together. Behind the queen stood Khel with a worried frown. Volund appeared next to him in a similar posture. Riall's body was sitting in the chair at the long table where she had dined, but someone had shifted the chair so that Queen Sequara could look straight at her as she leaned on the arm rests. Other than the queen, Khel, and Volund, everyone was still seated, but they were all staring at her in obvious concern.

She blinked again. "I'm back. I'm fine."

"What did you see?" The queen's frown spoke of her apprehension.

Riall shook her head. "Wheat. Lots of wheat. Huge fields of it, with tall mountains in the distance. I was . . . The soldier I told you about was walking toward the mountains." She shook her head again. "That's all, I think."

Queen Sequara's frown deepened. "He could be in Sildharan, heading east or north toward the Amlar Mountains. But why? We're headed for Grimrik."

"It . . . He knows what he seeks. He will find it where he's going. He's seen it. Or, it's more like he's living the moment when he finds it all the time. I don't know how to say it, but there's no sense of past or future for him. All is present. What he seeks cannot escape him. He knows it."

Khel and Volund appeared puzzled, and the faces of the others betrayed their utter confusion.

Queen Sequara, on the other hand, looked ready to fight. "Then we'd best be ready for him."

❊ 38 ❊

The first sighting of Grimrik's craggy coastline lifted Volund's heart. Etched deep into the green coastal fells were the fjords where he had learned to sail as a little boy. Gnorn stood next to him on the ship, an Ellonder vessel that almost might have kept pace with one of the famed Thjothic warships. Though he disliked any body of water larger than a puddle and never had acquired sea legs, the old Dweorg loved to gaze at the shores of the land where his ancestors dwelled.

Volund glanced to his other side, where Khel was leaning on the railing as he took in his first view of Grimrik from the ship's deck. His brother was quiet, which was how Volund knew how nervous he must be. The intensity in his eyes betrayed a yearning that Volund, who had always known where home was, did not think he could understand, though he wished to. As always, he could not find the right words of assurance. So, instead of speaking, he put a hand on Khel's shoulder, a gesture his brother returned with an anxious smile.

With no dragon in sight, they made an easy landing on the pebbly beach of one of the fjords, where they bid farewell to the sailors from Ellond. Volund did not worry overmuch about Gorsarhad attacking their party since he put his faith in Riall. He believed with all his heart that the daughter of the Prophet would wield the beast the first time she encountered her. Dreams or no dreams, she was more powerful than any other sorceress or sorcerer, witch or wizard, priestess or priest in all of Eormenlond. She would rid Grimrik of the lingworm, and then they would be able to get his sister and the others back from the Wildlands. Such was his bright hope when they landed.

The first dent in his optimism came when they sighted the long hall at the fjord's end, or rather, when they sighted what was left of it. Naught but ashes remained of the shelter built to receive Grimrik's sailors when they returned from the Gulf of Olfi. In days of peace, the king kept the hall provisioned and manned to welcome all, but not a soul came to greet them.

The eerie quiet continued as the nine of them walked through the rugged fells of Grimrik's countryside. Not even the sheep remained. No hawk circled in the blue sky overhead. The creatures of the land were in hiding or gone. It was as if Grimrik had become a haunted wasteland. And then they came across the first of the ruins.

In truth, there was too little left even to call them ruins. Only charred blotches on the earth told where the dwellings once stood. All that remained of the villages were muddy pathways running in between the debris that had been shelters where folk led their lives. Blackened skeletons lay in many of the ash piles, some of beasts and some of people. Volund tried not to, but he could not help imagining what their agonizing deaths had been like. From his own encounter with Gorsarhad, he could feel the helpless dread rising up in their throats as the flames descended from above to engulf them, and he almost retched more than once.

Their company encountered one former village or farmstead after another, all of them reduced to ashes drifting in the breeze. They spoke almost no words, for there was nothing to say in the face of such horror and devastation. With every village they found, Yrsa's face grew angrier. Gnorn trembled, and his widened eyes filled with tears. Riall could not disguise her shock, especially at one point when she stood transfixed before the remains of a family huddled together in the ashes of what had been their home. Three small skeletons lay in between two larger ones that faced one another in an embrace. Almost everyone in their company seemed to share the sense of despair. Even little Belu seemed cowed. Whenever he put her down to rest his arms, she stuck close to them instead of exploring like she usually did. Only Queen Sequara observed it all with steady determination, and it seemed to Volund that, alone among them, the sorceress-queen had witnessed such nightmarish destruction before.

Volund had almost come to fear that all of Grimrik was gone by the time they encountered signs of life. Hoofbeats sounded in the distance. Like the others, he rested his hand on the hilt of his scabbarded sword. They waited on the hillside as the sound of approaching horses grew louder, and he thought he could feel the vibrations from their pounding hooves beneath his boots. At once, a party of six mounted warriors crested the hilltop. Thjoths. Volund released a sigh as the horsemen slowed their steeds and approached.

The lead warrior raised a fist, and they came to a halt. He alighted from his steed and walked up to Volund's sister. "You are Yrsa, daughter of Queen Osynia, are you not?"

"I am. And here is her son, my brother Volund." Just as he had spoken to her, Yrsa answered in Thjothic.

The warrior nodded to Volund. "Well met, son of Orvandil Dragonbane. The king and queen will be glad of your return. There are many ill tidings since you departed."

Yrsa nodded. "We have seen many signs of them. But we are in haste. Where are the king and queen?"

"In the caves behind the falls at Valfoss. King Orvandil has called a moot of all the leaders among his warriors."

Yrsa's eyes narrowed as she gazed at the man. "You have my thanks. What is your name?"

"Grani."

"Grani. Very good. We need your horses. All six." Yrsa pointed at Riall and Queen Sequara. "These powerful witches have come to rid us of the dragon, and we are in great haste to reach King Orvandil. I will see that your steeds are returned to you or pay you their value in silver."

Grani's eyes widened as he gazed at the queen and Riall, who seemed to realize they had become the subject of the conversation. He gave a slight bow. "Of course. You may take them."

In short order, Volund, Yrsa, Queen Sequara, Riall, Gnorn, and Khel were mounted. Volund was pleased to see Flosi, Njal, and Runolf say farewell to Khel in particular. The three warriors had become fond of his brother during their sparring sessions, and they respected the way he learned from them. Only Yrsa remained cold to him, but winning her over was like the melting of the stubborn winter snows in the shadow-filled clefts of the fells in the spring: It took much time. And even she had directed a grudging nod his way the last time he practiced his swordsmanship with Flosi. Khel was making a good beginning to understanding the Thjoths and Grimrik, which made Volund happy. He just hoped there would be something left of Grimrik waiting for them.

❧ 39 ❧

Bolverk strode on one of the muddy pathways through the encampment, his long legs almost breaking into a jog at times. Even huge Inger was having trouble keeping up with him. Past hide tents and cookfires he weaved his way, returning the greetings that came at him with a curt nod. *Gods damn me if I'm not sweating and trembling like a green boy.* He shook his head to dismiss his foolishness, but his hands were clammy without a doubt.

"Did she tell you what she wanted?" He took a quick glance back at Inger as he asked the question.

"No," came the deep-voiced answer. "She said nothing save, 'Summon Bolverk. I would speak with him.'"

Bolverk stopped so abruptly that Inger almost bumped into him. He turned to face his big bodyguard and squinted at him. "What did she look like when she said it?"

Inger's large jaw hung open for a long moment in puzzlement. He put his hand up to his chest and frowned. "About this tall. Red hair."

Either his companion was too stupid for words, or he possessed a depth of wit that Bolverk had not hitherto suspected. Either way, the war-leader cast a withering glare at the bodyguard.

Inger shrugged.

Bolverk rolled his eye. "Gods damn me." He turned around and marched on toward Sigra's tent without bothering to see if Inger followed. The entire way he racked his brain in flustered wonder about the reason for the summons. It was the first time *she* had asked to see *him*.

Perhaps it was the tidings that had reached them two days ago that prompted her request. A trader had come from one of the coastal tribes bearing news of Grimrik's affliction. It seemed the dragon had settled on destroying the Thjoths, giving Orvandil Dragonbane more than he could handle for the time being. Bolverk had made certain that Sigra heard the trader's account. He was not certain, however, if these tidings favored him or not since the woman was more of a mystery to him than ever.

A change had come upon her, leaving him in awe of her courage and poise. It was no longer only for the Raven Eyes' survival that he wished to wed her. As ridiculous as he felt about it, she had awakened deep admiration in him. Perhaps she truly was channeling her god. He shook his head at his own stupidity. *Unmanned by a captive who could be my daughter. This is for the Raven Eyes.* He summoned a commanding expression on his face and strode on.

When he reached the tent, he nodded to the warriors standing guard outside it. Hardly breaking his stride, he flipped the entrance flap out of his way and ducked inside. He almost started as he stopped short, and the imposing look he had worn fled from his face, yielding for a moment to witless bewilderment.

Sigra stood before him, fists at her sides as if awaiting his arrival. Though it was dim inside the tent, he could see her green eyes gazing straight at him, and he perceived from the stubborn set of her jaw that she had arrived at an important decision. The first thought that flashed in his mind was that he lacked the courage to give her to the gods if she refused his demand.

Bolverk flicked a glance at Uga, who was standing guard in the tent. "Out."

Uga obeyed without a word, though she directed one of her knowing grins at Sigra before leaving.

The war-leader took a deep breath and frowned at his captive. "You summoned me?"

Sigra's eyes continued to hold him. Standing straight and tall, she frowned back at him like she was one of the stone-dwellers' beautiful queens and he her humble petitioner. She blinked once, and then she put a hand to her chest. "Peaceweaver. I will wed you." She nodded to make her meaning clear.

Bolverk could do nothing to stop an idiotic grin from blossoming on his face. His people were saved. *Thank the gods.* He took a step toward his betrothed.

Continuing to frown at him, Sigra held up her palm to halt him. "I worship Edan, not old gods. Our sons and daughters worship Edan." Her hand still up, she waited for a response.

The old war-leader considered her for a moment and scratched his beard. "So, you would begin to make us like the stone-dwellers. A hard bargain. And clever. But it could cost us much in years to come. I foresee strife between followers of the old gods and your new one here in the Wildlands. The Folk of the Tribes cleave to the old ways. We dislike change."

He released a long sigh and nodded. "But all things change, and we have survived by adapting when others have perished. Oftentimes the changes are slow, and we don't perceive them as they creep into our lives. At other times they are swift and bring hardship. Who can say if the changes are good or ill? The sons of our sons and daughters of our daughters will deem us right or wrong, but what will they know of the choices facing us? All I know is that I must save the Raven Eyes in this moment so that I will have descendants to judge me."

He shook his head. "Edan was always going to come, I reckon. Let it be thus. You may worship Edan, and you may teach our children to worship Edan, and anyone else who will listen to you. Does that satisfy you?"

Sigra stared at him, and then she nodded. Her hand trembled slightly as it came down, and she cast her gaze at the floor. It was the first time during the meeting she betrayed any nervousness.

Bolverk stepped toward her and put one hand on her shoulder.

With his other hand, he gently lifted her chin until she looked up at him. He smiled down at her. "Thank you."

She met his gaze with her fierce green eyes, and it struck him how truly courageous this young woman was. He had not broken her or frightened her into submission. She had decided to sacrifice herself to prevent war and death. And, with her god, she would transform the Raven Eyes in the bargain. She nodded in acknowledgement.

He went down on his knees and nodded to her. "Peaceweaver. Brave one. You've saved thousands of lives. You have saved my folk."

The roar of the falls dimmed enough at the far end of the network of caves to allow everyone at the moot to speak in normal voices. Closer to the entrance, the sound of the Mjothelf plummeting from the cliff to slam into the rocks waiting below was deafening, like constant thunder. Just before Gorsarhad's plague of attacks began, Orvandil had ordered many of the caves filled with grains, produce, and other essential items to keep his folk alive. Refugees from Valfoss occupied most of the other available space. However, this chamber served as the king's meeting room. Torches were set in sconces bolted to the walls, filling the cave with smoke. Their ruddy light glistened on the slick rock, and from the roof the occasional fat drop of water plopped into a puddle.

Around a long table they all sat on benches: King Orvandil, Queen Osynia, and the most respected leaders remaining among the Thjoths – Duneyr, Arinbjorn, Kialar, Asgrim, and Gudrun, the last of whom was a shield-maiden like Yrsa. Orvandil could not help noticing that, with the exception of Gudrun, who was still a young enough woman, each of them was looking more haggard than he remembered them. Of course, they were all older than they had been when last they met, but he could not help wondering if the war with the dragon was not also taking a toll. Certainly he felt he had aged decades since the beast arrived to torment his kingdom.

There too at the table were Bur, Kol, and Ilm to represent the Dweorgs. Ilm was Gnorn's cousin, and Orvandil had often found her as wise as his good friend. Still, he missed the old Dweorg, and he experienced a pang of worry for Volund and Yrsa. Wherever they were, he hoped they were faring better than he was. Perhaps sending them away had been the only good decision he had made in a long while.

Bodvar and Hakon stood guard at the chamber's entrance, but they were not the last of the company present. Arinbjorn had brought a man with him who claimed to be an escaped Ilarchae slave. Speaking the Northern Tongue rather well, the man had appeared on the coast just before Arinbjorn set out for the moot, and he said he could help the Thjoths. Calling himself Ottil, he said he had been a member of a tribe called the Cleft Skulls. Like many other tribes of the Ilarchae, the Cleft Skulls had suffered much from the War of the Way. It had only been a matter of time before the Raven Eyes overran and enslaved what remained of them in the Wildlands.

Ottil also claimed to have spoken with Sigra since he had served as a translator between her and the war-leader Bolverk. He said he ran away from the Raven Eyes because of their cruelty, most of all from their one-eyed war-leader. A large scab and bruise on his forehead and a recently broken nose that still appeared a bit swollen seemed to confirm this part of his story.

It was toward Ottil that Queen Osynia directed an intense gaze. Knowing why, Orvandil intended to open the moot by addressing the matter of their Ilarchae guest. He took a deep breath. "Friends, let us begin." For Ottil's benefit, he spoke in the Northern Tongue, which everyone present could understand.

They all cut short their private conversations with those seated nigh them and peered at him in expectation. The burden of their hopes and fears was almost palpable.

After looking at them each in turn, he gestured with an open hand at the newcomer. "We have here among us a man of the Wildlands, one Ottil by name. He has escaped from the Raven Eyes, our foes, and thus we may learn something of use from him." The king directed his gaze at the Ilarchae man. "You have offered knowledge of our foes, and for that we are grateful. However, it would be unwise of us to accept it without questioning you. I'm sure you understand if we are wary."

Ottil smiled. "I do. And I vow you will find me eager to aid you however I can."

The king nodded. "You say you were a member of the Cleft Skulls."

"I was. Most of our warriors perished in the war in the west. Being cowards, the Raven Eyes avoided such a fate by fleeing. But that gave them greater numbers than ours, which is how my folk and I became slaves."

"And how is it that an Ilarchae slave speaks the Northern Tongue?"

This time Ottil's smile was almost a smirk, as if Orvandil's question had somehow touched his pride. "Before the Raven Eyes conquered us, my father was a fur trader. When I was a lad, he brought me with him. Being clever and young, I picked up the Northern Tongue faster than he did, and so I served as his translator."

Before Orvandil could ask his next question, Queen Osynia leaned forward. "You have seen my daughter?" Her chest heaved with her heavy breaths, and she stared at Ottil as if she were trying to see through him.

Ottil paused before responding to her. "Seen her and spoken to her. Aye."

"And how is she being treated?"

The Ilarchae frowned and glanced down. "Bolverk is a cruel man. I don't like to say what he does with women in his power, but much of the camp could hear her screams when he was with her."

The knuckles on Osynia's tight, trembling fists were turning white. "You will tell me everything. After the moot is finished."

Ottil looked up at the queen and made a deep nod. "As you say, your Majesty. But Sigra was alive when I escaped. She's a strong woman."

Orvandil cleared his throat. "She is. We will speak of her later, and then you may tell us all you know of her: her condition, where they keep her, and how well guarded she is to begin with. You say you have knowledge of the Raven Eyes' encampment. How many warriors can they field?"

"Nigh four thousand." Ottil scratched his beard and seemed to consider something. "But of those, I deem only three thousand reliable. The rest are freed slaves from other tribes and could turn against the Raven Eyes with some prodding."

The king raised an eyebrow. "That is good to know." He clasped his hands before him and fixed his gaze on the escaped slave. "Is there a way to take them by surprise? Say, through the Ironwood?"

Ottil shook his head. "I would not lead an army through the Ironwood, even though I made my escape by hiding in it. There are *things* in there you don't want to go near. Others who fled like me have never come out again. Besides, Bolverk is too cunning for such an attack to work. He keeps guards at the forest borders at all times. They would know your attack is coming long before you reached the encampment. But you have the strength of numbers, and everyone fears the Thjoths. Perhaps there's no need for surprise."

He doesn't know how many warriors we've lost to Gorsarhad. Orvandil nodded. "What you say may be true, but strength of numbers alone does not win every battle." He considered for a moment. "You said the freed slaves might turn against the Raven Eyes."

The Ilarchae nodded. "Yes. If you come with enough force, they could break and flee the battle. They might even help us. They have little love for the Raven Eyes. I think I could help with that."

"How?" Orvandil watched the man for signs of treachery. He did not trust the fellow, but he was also desperate for help, for some way to tip the balance his way.

Before Ottil answered, however, Bur spoke up. "Your pardon, my king, but we're trying to shape the steel ere we heat it, are we not? Before we can fight these Ilarchae, we have the dragon to deal with. We can't even muster our warriors without the beast descending on us, let alone sail for the Wildlands." Of course, the Dweorg was right, and Orvandil knew it, but he had little heart to discuss Gorsarhad since he had no idea how they could defeat her without great losses. The serpent of the air was the harder problem, but also the one that needed solving first.

Gudrun banged her fist on the table. "Let the beast come, I say. Muster the warriors, and we will fight the lingworm. When she's dead, we sail for the Wildlands and teach the savages never to set foot on Grimrik's soil again."

Duneyr shook his head. "Throw our warriors against Gorsarhad, and we won't have enough of them left to fight the Raven Eyes. We *might* slay the lingworm, but not without great cost."

Arinbjorn narrowed his eyes as he gazed at Duneyr. "Are we not Thjoths? Gudrun has the right of it. Even if the Raven Eyes outnumber us, we'll slay every last one of them. Let us fight the beast and then set sail."

"We *have* been fighting her." Asgrim threw up his hands. "And losing. Open your eyes. We cannot charge straight at this foe as we do in battle against other folk."

Arinbjorn scowled at Asgrim with contempt. "Do you fear the dragon so much?"

Asgrim's jaw tightened, and he leaned toward Arinbjorn. "Aye. I fear her. I have fought her. I have seen how she burns and tears apart men. And I say that if you do not fear her, you're a greater fool than I ever took you for."

Arinbjorn's face went red, and he stood up from his bench.

"Sit." Not needing to shout his command, Orvandil spoke it in a stern voice that conveyed just enough of a threat for them to know he would brook no more squabbling.

Arinbjorn sat down, but he continued scowling at Asgrim.

"Peace. We must be together. Now more than ever." The king scanned their faces and waited until they all gazed at him. Arinbjorn and Asgrim had the grace to look ashamed. Unfortunately, Orvandil had no idea what they could do, nor even what he might say next. *Edan help us. There's no way out of this.*

A disturbance rescued him from the need to speak. There was a sound of several footsteps approaching the chamber, and Bodvar and Hakon turned to block someone from entering. However, a moment later, they stepped back and allowed the newcomers entry.

Despite all his despair and sorrow, Orvandil's heart leaped to see Yrsa and Volund and Gnorn, each alive and well. There was also a pair of southerners with them, a boy and a girl, each of which stared at him. A little black dog accompanied them, which struck the king as curious.

But he did not dwell on it since the sight of the last person to enter made his mouth drop open.

"Sequara. Queen Sequara." Orvandil smiled and stood up, and it seemed to him that a large weight fell from his shoulders. At last, here was some sliver of hope. "You've come to help us against the dragon."

Sequara returned his smile, but she shook her head. "Not I, old friend." She pointed at the southern girl. "But she has."

$\clubsuit$ 41 $\clubsuit$

Riall blinked as every face in the chamber turned toward her. The Thjoths and Dweorgs around the table stared at her, their gazes betraying their curiosity. Though they hid it well behind their pride, there might have been a measure of desperation in their expressions too. Certainly they appeared worn and tired. Having seen the horrific destruction the dragon had wrought upon Grimrik, she did not wonder at such desolation, and she hoped she would prove worthy of the spark of hope that kindled in some of their eyes, most especially the king's. In that moment, the task of wielding the dragon became more real and pressing than ever. Lives depended on her.

Orvandil Dragonbane – Khel and Volund's father – appeared every bit as formidable as the tales made him. He was tall even for a Thjoth, perhaps the tallest man Riall had ever seen. Silver streaked his blond hair and beard, and wrinkles framed his blue eyes, but his muscular body suggested a much younger man.

But it was not the king of the Thjoths who seized her attention at first. Seated among the Thjoths and Dweorgs was a man wearing eerily familiar garb. Riall knew the man with the wounded face for an Ilar-chae. She was certain of this because he was dressed the same way as the man whose body she had taken over in her last vision – wool tunic of a coarse weave, thick leather belt, fur cloak, and a bone pin tying back his long hair. Seeing this man at the table brought back the vision for an intense and confusing moment.

In the Sildharae soldier's body, she had crossed the mountains onto a grassy plain, where a group of pale-skinned warriors approached her on horse. Based on Queen Sequara's guesses about where the elf-dwolas were heading, she believed she was in the Wildlands, and these warriors' appearance seemed to confirm that. Though their nervous horses whinnied in protest, the mounted warriors surrounded her and pointed their spears at her, screaming in a harsh language she did not understand.

Not even a flicker of her eyelids had betrayed her response, and she had not flinched when all but one of the Ilarchae warriors tumbled as if boneless from their steeds. The riderless horses neighed and galloped away. From horseback, she watched the Sildharae soldier's corpse she had walked in for so many miles collapse as well to its final resting place. She dropped the spear in her hand.

She had swung a leg up over the horse she was on and alighted from it, and that horse too screamed before running off. There had been no need to involve the beast since she would arrive where she needed to at exactly the right moment. Then, in the body of the Ilarchae warrior, she had begun walking in a direction that might have been north, away from the mountains. Whatever direction it was, the elf knew it for the right one.

The Ilarchae seated at the table in the cave must have caught her staring at him since he leered at her and smirked. Still in wonder over his presence, she decided she did not like him and turned toward Queen Sequara, who continued speaking of her.

"Riall is one of my pupils in Asdralad. She's the orphan from Caergilion that Seren brought to my attention some years ago, and we have good reason to believe she might be the Prophet's daughter."

The king of the Thjoths frowned and squinted at Riall. And then, after his eyes widened for a brief moment, he glanced at Gnorn. The old Dweorg kept his face blank, but he made a barely perceptible nod.

Queen Sequara seemed to follow this exchange, but she kept

speaking. "She is more powerful in the gift than anyone alive. If there is someone who can help you against Gorsarhad, it is Riall."

King Orvandil Dragonbane gazed at Riall, who thought it strange to have him gawking at her as if *she* were the living legend. "The Prophet's daughter?" He shook his head. "I have too many questions to ask at once, but they can all come later. It is the greatest of honors to meet you. Your father was my friend and my teacher."

Riall made a slight bow, though Volund had told her the Thjoths did not hold to the same formalities that folk in the other kingdoms did. "The honor is mine, King Orvandil."

The king's smile made him appear a bit less fierce. "You are kind to have come, and I will be forever in your debt for it, as I am in your father's. I cannot begin to tell you all the things he taught me and the things he forgave me."

"Forgave you?" Riall frowned, wondering what the king could mean.

King Orvandil glanced down at the table, and then he looked up with a bitter smile on his face. "Queen Sequara perhaps did not tell you out of kindness to me, but you must know one thing: I slew the Prophet's father, your grandsire, at the Battle of Thulhan."

Queen Sequara stepped forward. "That was not your doing, old friend. You did everything you could to prevent it. The Markmen fought alongside the Torrlonders, and fate put the Prophet's father in your path. No one knew that better than the Prophet. As you said, he forgave it."

"Perhaps. But she must decide for herself." The king frowned at Riall. "Do you still wish to help us after knowing I slew your kin?"

Riall considered before answering. "Yes. That's why I've come here. But I have one request."

Orvandil Dragonbane raised his eyebrows. "I will grant it if I can."

Riall gave him a gentle smile. "When it's over, please tell me what happened at the Battle of Thulhan. And also, I would hear all you know of my father."

The king hesitated, and he glanced at Queen Sequara as if seeking her permission for something. The sorceress-queen nodded to him, after which he turned back to Riall and nodded to her. "So be it."

Queen Sequara put her hand on Riall's shoulder and gave her a nod of encouragement before turning back to King Orvandil. "All that remains is to find the dragon. We journeyed from Grimrik's coast to Valfoss, and though we saw the destruction Gorsarhad left in her wake, never did we spy her."

The king wore a rueful half smile. "She is licking her wounds from our last battle, mostlike. But she'll return as soon as we muster our warriors. She is not hard to rouse these days."

"You are in haste, are you not, to have done with her so that you can sail for the Wildlands to free your folk held hostage there?"

"Aye." The king released a sigh and glanced at Queen Osynia. "We are."

Queen Sequara gazed at him for a moment, and Riall saw the determination in her mentor's face. "Muster your warriors, then. Gather them to sail east to the Wildlands. Riall will take care of Gorsarhad when she comes." At that moment, Riall took heart from the queen's courage and her faith in her. She reckoned she never would have possessed the strength for what lay ahead without Queen Sequara by her. Other than herself, the sorceress-queen alone understood the risks involved in what she was undertaking, and still she spoke for her.

King Orvandil turned to Riall. "What will you do with the beast once you wield her?"

Riall cleared her throat. "I've given some thought to that." She nodded in a likely vain attempt to look as determined as Queen Sequara had a moment before. "The greater the Thjoths' strength when you encounter the Ilarchae, the more likely they are to surrender the hostages without a fight. Is that right?"

"Aye. True." The king stroked his beard and frowned. "But the dragon has slain many of our fighters and wounded many others. We won't be fielding many more warriors than the Raven Eyes can. In their lands, it will be an even fight at best."

"But you won't be alone."

King Orvandil's eyes widened just a little. "You and Queen Sequara mean to come with us to the Wildlands?"

Riall nodded. "I swore to Volund I would help him free his sister." She knew what was waiting for her in the Wildlands, but she also knew deep in her bones that the elf would find her no matter what she did or whither she went. Not only had it seen the moment, but it lived out their meeting in the eternal present in which it dwelled. What the elf knew, then, was fated, and nothing could change it. All she could hope was that she would be able to help the Thjoths before it happened.

"You swore to Volund?" The king glanced at his son.

"Yes. I wouldn't be here without him and Khel."

"Thank Edan." Queen Osynia's voice quavered. She released a long breath and sagged in her chair. The woman seemed beyond exhausted.

Riall swallowed her sorrow at the look of desperate hope on Queen Osynia's face. For the sake of the mother and her obvious anguish, she hoped she would succeed in her task. She turned back to the king. "But you'll have something even more persuasive than two sorceresses on your side, and the Raven Eyes will find it hard to gainsay you."

King Orvandil's eyes narrowed as he gazed at her. "And that is?"

Riall allowed herself a small smile. "A dragon."

❧ 42 ☙

Khel could not help grinning with affection and pride at Riall, and then he turned his gaze back to the man who had fathered him. Unsure of what he had expected in coming to this place and whether he wanted to make known his identity at such a dire time, he had watched the king during the whole exchange with a strange and intense mixture of excitement, fascination, and dread churning in his stomach, as if its contents were trying to batter their way out. Fortunately, no one had paid much attention to him. Like him, everyone else was waiting for the king's response to Riall.

King Orvandil Dragonbane stared at the young sorceress until a fierce smile broke out across his face. "You heard the young woman. Muster the warriors! We gather on the eastern shore, nigh Rykinsvik. There you must bring all your remaining ships. We sail for the Wildlands three days hence."

For a moment, everyone was still, and then they all rose at once, speaking in excited tones to their neighbors as they prepared to leave.

The king turned to the man dressed like an Ilarchae. "Ottil, I will seek you out later. For now, remain with Arinbjorn."

Despite his wounded face, the man smiled and nodded as he stood up. "As you wish." Following the warrior who must have been Arinbjorn, the Ilarchae walked by Khel on his way out, all the while wearing the same self-satisfied grin, as if he alone understood some obscene jest. Perhaps it was just that he looked like someone had used his face for a battering ram, but Khel thought there was something ill about the fellow. To be fair, many people had thought the same of him, and he knew what it meant to be an outsider.

King Orvandil turned toward Khel's companions. "Yrsa, Volund, Gnorn. Come. Tell me in brief of your journey." He gestured over the two warriors guarding the door. "Hakon," he said in a quiet voice after they came near, "go and tell Arinbjorn I want Ottil watched at all times."

The warrior nodded and walked off.

The king turned to the other guard. "Bodvar, find private spaces, food, and drink for Queen Sequara, the Prophet's daughter, and our other guest." He looked at Riall and Queen Sequara. "We have much to discuss. Perhaps, after you've rested, we may begin?"

Riall smiled. "I'd like that."

"Yes. First, greet your children." Queen Sequara nodded toward Yrsa and Volund, who stood near Khel.

When he saw how the queen's gesture might have included him, Khel jerked a pace away from Yrsa and Volund without thinking, and then he winced as he realized he had drawn attention to himself by moving. Deciding he preferred being simply the "other guest," he took a sly step closer to Riall.

Queen Sequara smiled gently at him before turning back to King Orvandil. "We'll be ready when you've finished."

"It's good beyond words to see you." The king directed a warm smile at Queen Sequara. "My thanks for coming." He looked again at Yrsa and Volund. "Come. You too, Gnorn. I need your counsel."

Queen Sequara and Riall moved to follow the guard toward the cave's exit, whence everyone from the council had departed save King Orvandil and Queen Osynia, who rose to greet her children. Khel took a step to follow the two sorceresses, but a strong hand grasped his shoulder and stopped him. He turned to find Gnorn looking up at him.

The Dweorg smiled and nodded toward King Orvandil, who was embracing Yrsa at that moment.

Fully understanding Gnorn's intention of introducing him to the king, Khel stood frozen on the spot with his mouth hanging open. He closed it to swallow, but his throat was dry and tight. Uncertain if he could even make his feet work, he glanced back toward the cave's exit as if seeking to escape.

Riall was waiting there, gazing at him with a grin. She made a quick shooing gesture with her hands to encourage him or to tease him or both, and then she ducked out. Belu trotted after her mistress with her little tail wagging, leaving him to face what was coming.

Khel turned back again, and everyone – King Orvandil, Queen Osynia, Yrsa, and Volund – was staring at him. The king and the queen appeared slightly puzzled by his presence, and Yrsa frowned at him. But Volund nodded, and somehow his brother's gesture gave Khel courage.

Gnorn's smile broadened as he grasped Khel by the arm and pulled him along. Feeling like pieces of wood attached to his trembling legs, Khel's feet shuffled to keep up.

By the time they reached the group, the king was speaking to Yrsa and thus postponing Khel's humiliation. "I had not thought to see you so soon."

Yrsa's brow lowered in a puzzled frown. "Did they not tell you we were coming?"

"They?"

"Some of us took an . . . unexpected way home. I sent our ship ahead while we journeyed by land. It should have reached Grimrik long before us."

"It never came." The king released a weary sigh. "The dragon has been preying on any ship nearing our shores. Were all the other warriors on board?"

Yrsa's eyes widened, and she shook her head. "All save Runolf, Flosi, and Njal."

The king grasped her by the shoulders and looked down into her eyes. "If they are lost, we must grieve them when we can, along with the hundreds of others the beasts have slain. But thank Edan you have returned."

The king released her and turned to Khel, much to the young man's dismay. "You are the one Riall says helped her here, along with Volund. I owe you my thanks."

Gnorn stepped forward and cleared his throat. "My king, this is Khel. He is indeed Riall's friend from Asdralad. I had hoped to introduce you to him at a better time, but I deem there will be nonesuch in the busy days ahead."

The king frowned at Gnorn, but then he forced a curt smile as he nodded at Khel. "Well met, Khel. I wish we could have given you a more cheerful welcome."

"I . . . I've . . ." Khel took a deep breath, though it seemed a tremendous effort to get air in his lungs. For the first time he could remember, words seemed to have abandoned him. His hands were clammy, and his mind spun with sundry notions of what he might say, none of which seemed coherent, and none of which could escape his mouth in any case.

Gnorn stepped in. "I beg your pardon, King Orvandil, and yours as well, Queen Osynia. I should also mention that Khel is the son of an old acquaintance of ours. I'm sure you recall Lady Dalriana, my king."

King Orvandil frowned again at Gnorn, but a moment later his eyes widened as they focused on Khel. His mouth dropped open for a long moment before he said anything. "Do you mean . . ."

"Aye." Gnorn nodded. "I see you do recall her."

The king gawked at Khel. "Gnorn, what is this?"

Queen Osynia stepped forward and put a hand on Khel's shoulder. "*This* is your son." She looked at Khel and, amidst all her obvious weariness and anxiety, she somehow found a brief smile for him. "The king has told me of your mother, Khel. He did not tell me of you."

"I . . . I didn't know." King Orvandil blinked as his face flushed red. "After I left Asdralad . . ."

"Yes." The queen looked at her husband and raised a skeptical eyebrow. "Men are wont to forget what happens afterwards. We mothers rarely do." She turned again to Khel. "Welcome to Grimrik. We will make your stay here as comfortable as we can."

Though the queen said the words kindly, Khel heard the unmistakable message beneath them. He was accustomed to such subtleties among the noble families back on Asdralad. Finding himself in familiar territory, he discovered his voice. "I thank you for your kindness, Queen Osynia." He gave her a slight bow. "I cannot stay long, unfortunately. I came here for Riall, for the most part. When it's all over, I plan to return to Asdralad, though I'm glad for a sight of Grimrik. Truly, being in your presence is more than I hoped for."

Queen Osynia smiled at him and gave him a slight nod, thus communicating her agreement to their understanding. "Nevertheless, perhaps you will visit us from time to time in happier days."

"It would make me happy to be your guest, and may those days come sooner rather than later." Khel did not blame her. She was protecting her children's interests while remaining as courteous as possible to him. In return, he had made it clear he was no threat.

King Orvandil was still blinking at him. "I'm sorry. I didn't know."

Khel nodded at him. "I know you didn't. Mother didn't want you to. She's done well on her own. Queen Sequara can tell you. She helped rebuild Asdralad after the war. And she had *me*." He grinned, but the grin faltered after a moment. "Though I've given her a bit of trouble over the years. I didn't tell her when I left Asdralad with Riall and Volund. I suppose I just wanted to see it once. You know, Grimrik. I've read a bit about it."

The king nodded. "Good. I hope you'll come to learn more in those happier times the queen spoke of. You might enjoy getting to know the land. Yrsa and Volund . . . Your sister and brother would show you around. If you'd like, I could as well."

"He's not my brother." Yrsa folded her arms in front of her chest and scowled at Khel.

"He's mine." Volund put his hand on Khel's shoulder. "And he's welcome wherever I am."

Khel smiled at Volund, and then he nodded at his father. "I would like that."

King Orvandil gave a half smile. "It is well, then." He narrowed his eyes as he looked at Khel. "Will you be coming to the Wildlands with us, then?"

Khel nodded. "Where Riall and Volund go, I go."

"There could be fighting there. How well do you wield the blade you wear?"

"He can spar well enough, but he's no warrior." Yrsa stuck out her jaw as if challenging Khel to gainsay her.

Khel glanced down for a moment, and then he looked up at his father. "She's right. I'm no warrior. Not like the Thjoths." He swallowed, feeling an odd compulsion to explain himself to this stranger who sired him. "But I did kill a man once. He was a friend. Or, at least I thought he was. He was a few years older than I was. Growing up, I had few . . . well, no true companions. This man befriended me and taught me . . . how to steal. When I found out he was using me to rob my mother the whole time, I confronted him. He pulled steel on me, and I followed. The next thing I knew, he was lying on the ground with his blood leaking out of him. It was the worst day of my life, to tell the truth, and it haunts me still. I suppose he took some of me with him."

He released a long breath and looked at Yrsa. "I may be no warrior like you, but I'll do what I must with as much courage as I can find." He turned to Volund. "Please don't tell Riall. I'll tell her myself."

Volund nodded.

King Orvandil also nodded with seeming approval. "I too killed a friend when I was young, and with less justice on my side." He glanced at Queen Osynia, who frowned at some shared memory between them, before turning back to Khel. "We have tales to exchange. Later. For now, I must make preparations." He glanced at Volund and then looked back at Khel with a smile. "Stay by your brother."

Khel nodded and returned the smile. "I'll be sure to." He turned to Gnorn, who favored him with a broad grin and clapped him on the shoulder. Khel shook his head but couldn't help grinning back, thankful to the Dweorg for forcing his introduction to his father. *That went better than I imagined it would. And no* holmgang. *Now all we need to do is capture a dragon.*

"Thank you, Queen Osynia. It means more to me than I can say. I don't know what I would have done otherwise." Riall made a slight bow to her, and then she rubbed her stinging eyes. Torches shed dim, ruddy light in the small cave that served as the queen's chamber, making it smoky as they burned.

"It's the least I can do, considering what you're undertaking for us." The queen nodded to her. Riall had not realized how tall the woman was until she stood next to her. She seemed an older, *slightly* less fierce version of Yrsa. "You might even have asked me for such a small favor as Volund's friend. He thinks quite highly of you."

The young sorceress glanced down. "Volund has a kind heart."

"It comes from his father." Queen Osynia smiled, but there was no mirth in the gesture. Riall supposed that worry for her missing daughter had gnawed the laughter out of her.

The young sorceress took a deep breath. "Well, we're to leave for Rykinsvik shortly. I suppose I'll say goodbye to her now." Her throat tightened, and her eyes blurred with tears from more than the smoke. Now that the moment had arrived, it proved much harder than she had imagined.

Queen Osynia must have noticed her distress. The woman put her hand on Riall's shoulder. "Don't worry. I'll take good care of her."

Riall could only nod in response as she struggled not to sob. She took some deep, shuddering breaths to steady herself. "It's just that I've never parted from her before. Not since I found her. She was a stray in Kiriath. Starving. Sick. And yet, I think she saved me." She shook her head. "I'm sorry. You must think me daft."

The queen grasped Riall's other shoulder and looked down into her eyes. Osynia's eyes were a startling green with gold flecks in the irises. "No. I don't. I know exactly what you mean."

Riall sniffled, and then she nodded again.

Queen Osynia nodded to her in return, and then she backed off to allow Riall a moment to say goodbye.

The young sorceress knelt and then sat on the floor next to Belu, who had been watching the entire exchange with her little pink tongue hanging out. As soon as Riall sat, the little dog rolled onto her back and poked up her front legs while the rear legs splayed out.

Riall laughed through her tears, and she complied with Belu's request by rubbing the pup's belly. After giving the dog vigorous scratches in all her favorite spots, Riall released a sigh. "Belu, sit."

The little dog rolled up and, assuming a sitting position, stared at her mistress with her brown eyes. A moment later, however, Belu rushed into Riall's lap and began licking the salty tears on her cheeks. *Sad?*

The dog's pink, soft tongue tickled, and Riall could not help giggling. A moment later, however, she attempted to put on a serious face. "Belu, sit."

Belu gazed at her for a moment, but then she hopped off her lap and, after circling a few times, plopped her hind quarters down. She watched Riall with great expectation in her little eyes. *Ready.*

"Good girl." Riall nodded. "I need to tell you something. I'm going away for a little while. I'll try to come back as soon as I can. Queen Osynia has agreed to look after you while I'm away, so you need to be on your best behavior. Will you do that for me?"

Belu's response was a high-pitched whine. Her tail began to wag, and she lifted one of her front paws as if to spring forward.

Riall pointed at her. "Sit."

The little paw came down, but Belu whimpered again in protest, and her tongue slithered out to lick her nose. *Go with you.*

Riall could hold back neither laughter nor tears. She held out her arms, and Belu bounced back up onto her lap. The young sorceress curled over the pup and held the ball of warmth close. At length, however, she sat up and looked at Belu.

"You can't come where I'm going. It's just too dangerous. There'll be a dragon, you know, and armies. It's not a place for little ones." She did not mention the thing she truly feared.

Staring into Riall's eyes, Belu whined again.

"You must stay here and be good for Queen Osynia. I'll come back." *If I can.* Though she had shared thoughts with Belu more times than she could count, she did not open her mind to the pup at that moment because she did not wish her deepest fears to distress her little companion. Belu would never allow her to leave if she knew what Riall was truly thinking. Besides that, she was determined to use the gift as little as possible to avoid the loss of control over her power and to prolong her inevitable meeting with the elf.

Riall looked at Belu a moment longer before the real tears came. She grasped the pup and put her gently on the floor, and then she leaned forward to kiss Belu on the top of her furry head, pausing only to caress the dog's soft ears.

After a long, shuddering breath, Riall stood. She took a scrap of dried meat from a pocket in her tunic and handed it to Queen Osynia. Belu followed the movement with her eyes, and then she padded over to sit before the queen in a hopeful stance.

"Give her that. She'll stay." Those were as many words as Riall could force out. She shook her head and peered at the floor of the cave.

"I understand." The queen's kindly voice spoke above her. "Go, Prophet's daughter, and may Edan be with you. Belu and I will be awaiting your return."

Riall nodded, and then, unable to bear looking at Belu again, she shut her eyes as she whirled around. She left the cave with hurried steps, not daring to speak aloud her thoughts. *I hope you'll see your daughter again, but I don't think I'll be returning. Volund will take care of Belu when he comes back.*

❧ 44 ❧

Sequara gazed up for what must have been the thousandth time along the march. Blue sky with a few wisps of cloud. No ominous speck in the distance. Even when she reached out with the gift, she sensed no approaching threat, and it was impossible that she could ever forget what a dragon descending upon her would feel like when her mind dwelled in the realm of origins.

She was not alone in her constant examination of the heavens. Almost every individual in the long column of warriors snaking over Grimrik's rugged green fells stole upward glances from time to time.

In their thousands they walked toward the coast, clinking in their byrnies and bristling with swords and axes and spears. Most also carried round linden shields and wore helms with depictions of fierce beasts decorating them. The Thjoths were not the most numerous fighters among the peoples of Andumedan, but they were the fiercest and the most feared. Sequara had witnessed their ecstasy in battle in the past, but today was a different matter. Theirs was a grim, determined company. A vast threat loomed over them, and only their courage kept at bay the edge of fear lurking and waiting to slice through them. No one embodied that courage more than Orvandil

Dragonbane, who led the march at the column's front, somewhere over a hill in the distance.

About the only person who never bothered to look up was Riall. The young sorceress stared ahead with blank resignation. Sequara knew her daughter had been brooding over leaving Belu behind, but there was a deeper matter as well. Even the fact that she had parted with her inseparable dog at all indicated something important. Her friends Khel and Volund, who walked on either side of her, glanced at her from time to time with worried frowns. The queen was grateful her daughter had made such friends. Khel especially was perceptive, but Sequara did not think either of them yet understood what she guessed – that Riall had accepted her fate, and at least some part of her did not expect to survive her inescapable meeting with the elf.

The sorceress-queen was less willing to allow that fate to pass. Guilt and sorrow for failing her daughter in so many ways weighed on her, but she would not fail to protect her from this. For years she had known this time would come, one way or another, and she had also known what she would do. The only real decision was to acknowledge that the moment had arrived.

She had grown not only prouder of Riall but also more awed by her every day. Perhaps it was because she had been born with it, but the young woman showed more control over her power than Dayraven ever had. Like him, she chose to use it to help others. They were both beautiful in their compassion.

She wished she could have told Riall how often she brought to mind her father. Oftentimes an unconscious gesture on the young woman's part would remind Sequara of him, and those were the moments when she had most longed to tell Riall everything. The queen had no doubt that Riall believed she was sacrificing herself to save Grimrik, and for that, she loved her with a fierce, painful love. No matter the cost, however, she would make sure that what happened to Dayraven would not happen to their daughter.

Sequara walked closer to Riall. When Khel noticed the queen, he moved aside to make a space for her, and she nodded her thanks to him.

"Riall."

Torn from her thoughts, the young woman looked over at her and forced a brief smile before nodding. "Your Majesty." They walked beside one another for a while.

"No sign of the dragon."

"Not yet. She'll come."

Sequara nodded. "When she does, I'll be chanting the song of origin of fire. I can keep her flames at bay for a short while if you need time."

"I understand. Thank you."

Several heartbeats of silence stretched out between them.

Sequara cleared her throat and waited until the young woman looked at her. "I know you'll succeed."

Riall nodded. "Thank you, my lady. It means a lot that you think so. Truly."

The queen waited another long moment. She took a deep breath. "I also wanted to apologize to you."

The young sorceress frowned at her. "For what?"

"For seeking to keep you from Seren. I was wrong."

Riall stared at her in response, and then she nodded before turning her gaze to the ground. "I know why you did it."

Sequara swallowed, tamping down her pain for her daughter and turning it into strength. "What you did was right. And I am . . . proud of you."

Without looking at her, Riall nodded.

The sorceress-queen watched her daughter. "If you'd like to talk about anything . . . There is much I must still tell you of your father. When this is all over, perhaps."

The young sorceress turned to her and gave her a quick, sad smile. "I'd like that very much."

"Good." Sequara nodded. "One last thing, then."

"Yes, my lady?"

The sorceress-queen made an effort to put on a regal face, the one she reserved for times when she would brook no argument. "You've kept the first of my conditions by allowing me to accompany you, and I thank you for that."

Riall nodded. "In truth, I'm glad you're with me."

"I would not be anywhere else." Sequara had to stop speaking for a moment lest her emotions break through the façade of her control. "But I would also like to remind you of the second condition you agreed to."

"The song of origin you spoke of?"

"Yes. You *will* succeed in wielding the dragon, and you will thus save thousands of lives. However, if, at any point, you feel a loss of control over your power, you must tell me as soon as possible. And then, you must allow me to use that song of origin to remove you and everyone else from danger."

Riall frowned and stared at her for a long moment. "Will the song of origin work? When you . . . take away the power and direct it elsewhere, will it leave me alone and harm no one else?"

It was only long practice that allowed Sequara to keep her face like stone. "It will work. I will not let the elf harm you or anyone else, but you must allow me to use the song of origin on you."

"And it will follow the power wherever you direct it?"

"Yes." Sequara put far more confidence into her voice than she felt. She hoped it was enough to convince Riall. "The elf seeks reunion with its power. Once it is out of you, it will leave you alone."

A measure of relief passed over Riall's face as she smiled gently, though she still seemed subdued. "Then it is well." She nodded. "I'll keep my promise."

Sequara could not help allowing a sigh of relief to escape. "Good." She put her hand on her daughter's shoulder for a moment. "Remember that I'm ready to listen if you'd like to talk."

Riall nodded. "Thank you. Perhaps when we make a halt."

"As you wish." When Sequara turned away to resume walking behind the youths, she caught Khel's eye for a moment. From his gaze, she knew he had been listening closely to her conversation with Riall. He gave her a nod that was almost a bow, and in it the queen could read his gratitude. Sequara answered with a brief smile. *That one's almost too perceptive.*

It made her glad beyond words that her daughter had friends who cared so much for her. Perhaps they would be able to give her what

Sequara never felt she could. For certain she would be needing them in the days ahead. *At least I can make sure she sees those days.*

❧ 45 ❧

Volund allowed a sigh of relief. It was good to breathe the salt-laden sea air, and the breeze caressed his skin like an old friend. A few seagulls keened overhead, a sign that not all creatures had abandoned the kingdom. They had reached Rykinsvik without incident, though the rear sections of the long column of warriors were still marching, skirting the burnt-out coastal village as they arrived. On the pebbly strand, about fifty of Grimrik's famed dragon ships abided the Thjoths who would board them. These were almost all that remained of the fleet.

According to his father's commands, he and Khel and Riall were on the king's ship, where some of Grimrik's best fighters were preparing to set sail. Like a few other full vessels, it waited at anchor out in the fjord to leave room for the remaining ships to be boarded. With the deck gently swaying beneath them and waves slapping the hull, the three of them leaned on the rail and gazed back at the fells and the line of warriors still arriving. A thin cloud of dust rose in their wake, and bits of steel glinted in the sunlight. Also aboard the king's ship were Queen Sequara, Gnorn, Yrsa, and the escaped Ilarchae slave who had offered to serve as a translator once they reached the Wildands. No vessel had ever seen a hardier crew, and yet the two sorceresses were the only reason Volund felt safe.

He thought back to the day in Kiriath when Riall burst into the room where he was taking a hot bath. She had seemed more than half mad. Why he had allowed her to drag him along was still a mystery to him, but he was glad he had. A smile tugged at the corner of his mouth, and he stole a quick glance at her.

Riall was gazing inland, but her mind seemed elsewhere. She had been strangely quiet along the march, perhaps even melancholy, to the point where he had grown concerned. But Queen Sequara's talk with her had cheered her enough. It was only natural that she would be nervous. Having witnessed her power, however, he knew she would wield the lingworm. He also suspected she felt Belu's absence, but he understood why she had left the dog with his mother back in Valfoss. Imagining the little pup waddling on the ship's deck and wagging her tail at all the warriors who passed by her, he smiled again.

"What are you smiling about?" Khel was looking across Riall at him.

"Belu. She'd like it here."

Khel grinned. "Lots of mischief to get into."

"I miss her." Riall's brief smile faded.

"We'll see her again soon." His grin replaced by a serious gaze, Khel nodded at Riall.

They looked at each other for a long moment until the young sorceress returned the nod. "I think we might."

They both returned their gazes to the fells, and Volund followed suit.

After a while, Khel sighed. "Well, here we are."

Volund nodded. "Aye."

"I wasn't sure we'd make it." Riall shook her head. "I wasn't sure I'd even get out of Kiriath." She looked at Volund and then at Khel. "I wouldn't have without you two."

Volund's tongue got all tied up, and even Khel seemed at a loss for words, though he directed a bow at Riall.

Riall turned back to the landscape. "I'm frightened."

Khel put a hand on her shoulder.

Volund hesitated and swallowed, but when Khel gave him a quick nod, he gained enough confidence to reach out and put his hand on Riall's other shoulder.

"Sometimes it feels like the darkness is closing in from everywhere." Riall shook her head. "It's going to swallow us no matter what we do."

Khel nodded and sighed. "Well, then, while darkness gathers, perhaps we'd best make a little light, so long as we're here together."

The young sorceress turned to him for a moment and stared as if she were seeing something in Khel she had not noticed before. She broke her gaze and looked out at the fells once again. "Don't leave me."

"Never." Khel spoke almost in a whisper, and he moved a step closer to her.

Feeling clumsier than ever, Volund squeezed Riall's shoulder.

Her eyes grew distant, and Volund had a feeling she was not looking at anything he could see. "She has come."

The brothers blinked at each other. A chill suffused Volund's body. He shielded his eyes and peered skyward, but he saw nothing save the same wisps of distant cloud that had drifted above them all day.

"Perhaps we'd best fetch Queen Sequara." Khel directed a questioning frown toward Riall, who continued to stare far away.

Volund did not think she would answer, but at length the young sorceress blinked. "Yes. Tell her."

Khel hurried off, but Volund decided to stay next to Riall.

Before his brother returned with the sorceress-queen, several cries erupted at once, and a number of hands on the ship and on shore pointed upward. Volund's eyes followed the direction they indicated until a tiny speck appeared in the distance over Grimrik. Nightmarish memories of the burning of Valfoss and the hideous deaths of men he had known flashed in his mind.

Gorsarhad had arrived. At once it grew more obvious how he and everyone around him were the bait. Whether they or the dragon ended up trapped depended on Riall.

A distant but familiar high-pitched bark tore his gaze from the sky. Volund scanned the shore and saw nothing but the Thjothic warriors boarding ships. *Must have imagined it.*

But then his eyes widened when they happened upon a small black shape darting and dancing in circles near a group of waiting warriors, who ignored the little dog. "Belu?"

Volund gripped the ship's railing and turned toward Riall, but his friend's eyes were blank, and he knew she was far away, perhaps beginning her sorcerous encounter with Gorsarhad.

He made his decision. As he stooped to remove his boots, he shouted toward the shore, "I'm coming, Belu!"

❦   46   ❦

D welling in the realm of origins and giving herself over to the power within her, Riall felt the presence of the approaching dragon as palpably as if her flesh brushed Gorsarhad's iron-hard scales. She grasped the beast's place in the infinite and ever-changing variety existing in the realm of forms, understanding the long span of her existence by the fleeting standards of mortal beings. Powerful and terrible, wondrous and beautiful, she was awesome to behold even in the midst of Riall's serenity. Deep and abiding were the lingworm's memories, much deeper than humankind's, whom she dwarfed in her enormity and in her life measured in centuries – even in millenia for Gorsarhad, eldest of dragons.

All around Riall flitted the smaller presences that were her fellow humans. A struggle between fear and determination displaced almost all other emotions in them at the moment. Every last one of their minds was wide open to her, their deepest yearnings and terrors there for her to read. Suffering from the illusion of their individuality, their greatest, most tragic, and most sorrowful failure was to lack understanding of their underlying oneness with all other creatures in the world. In the end, all songs of origin were one. But this was not the time or place to instruct them. Reminding herself of her task, Riall broke away from such thoughts to center her attention on the serpent of the air.

Her mind stretched like a waking cat as power surged through her. She had been suppressing it for too long. It felt good to release the rush of energy, to have something worthy of using it on. A dim memory reached her of words spoken by someone she ought to know. The memory took on sudden clarity, and she recalled the mortal woman Queen Sequara warning her to use the song of origin of dragons even though she might not need it.

According to the queen, the song would help keep her anchored in her body, which had become a curious object of observation, like all else in the realm of forms, as she hovered within and without it. She nearly dismissed the notion with a mental shrug, but a dim part of her screamed in protest at such a lack of caution. She decided to indulge that frightened girl who was her mortal self, though she seemed so far away. Thus, she reached back to the flesh and bones that housed the illusion of her identity and, with tiny explosions of energy running along the cells of that body, commanded the lungs to push forth the breath that her throat and tongue and teeth manipulated into the clumsy symbols that mortals called *words* when their vibrations hit the air.

Urkhalion an dwinathon ni partholan varlas,
Valdarion ar hiraethon im rhegolan wirdas.
Gholgoniae sheerdalu di vorway maghona,
Dardhuniae sintalu ar donway bildhona.

Thus she chanted, and her awareness of the dragon sharpened as it focused around her. She began to see from Gorsarhad's keen eyes. As her powerful wings cut the air, riding glorious currents of wind, the blue and green world spread beneath her. The puny ships and thousands of hairless, scaleless creatures that walked on two legs were little more than prey, though dangerous in enough numbers with their sharp steel and their cunning. But the glory of the flight was for her kind, and the fleshlings that dared to reach out to tame and destroy would rue their arrogance.

Such were her thoughts of vengeance. But Riall's energy wrapped around the mighty serpent of the air like a gentle breeze. When the beast grew aware of the sorceress, something she rarely felt spiked in her: fear. By the time she understood the enfolding presence, it was already too late, but that did not stop her from raging and gnashing. She attempted to bank in the air and flee the way she had come, but a will stronger than hers would not allow her prodigious thews to obey her. Onward she flew, straight into the embrace of the one who claimed mastery of her body. It seemed an impossible outrage that such a creature as a mere fleshling could contain such power and use it to wield a being so much nobler than it. But such had happened before.

Not only in recent times, but in an age when even Gorsarhad had been young, the feeble creatures that were humans had usurped strength far beyond their own. This was why the dragon had under-taken her desperate vengeance against the soft fleshlings, beginning with their strongholds, their greatest lairs. As impossible as it seemed, the arrival of the maggots walking on two legs meant the dwindling of the serpents of the air, for the land would support only one greatest predator. This was why Gorsarhad ignored the pain of her wounds – rips in her wings and the throbbing agony of the iron and steel embedded in her lower jaw. This was why she strained with such desperate but futile hate against the insubstantial chains binding her. Deep in her being, she fought not for the survival of her kind, nor to destroy those who would displace them, for she understood that the end was come. Chief among dragons in her might and fury, Gorsarhad wrought destruction for one simple reason: *despair*. Having lived a long and lonely life, she wished to perish from the world where she and her kin might fall under the sway of those who should quake in fear of them. She wanted to die.

While Riall held firm control over the lingworm, a portion of the beast's inward mind remained to her. It was there that she sensed Gorsarhad's futile rage at the loss of the era of her kind. Communi-cating not in words but in emotions and feelings, she sought to soothe the beast, and thus between the great dragon and the young sorceress an exchange of thoughts took place.

Fear not, eldest of dragons. I do not seek to harm you, but to prevent you from harming our kind.

One of the babblers. I knew another of you would come someday.

I have come.

Your stench in my mind is familiar. You are much like the last babbler that bound me against my will. You are kin to him.

He was my father.

He used me.

To make peace.

Peace among your kind? It will never last. You fleshlings will always make war upon each other and all other creatures. You destroy what you cannot enslave. You are a disease in the world.

And yet you too have made war against us.

I fight for two reasons: to eat and to survive. Among all creatures, only your sort slaughters for pleasure. You will destroy our kind and all others in your path.

There is a third reason why you fight. I know why you wrought your destruction. I feel your despair.

Do you? There is one of your kind down there who might have granted me my end. Almost he succeeded. The sharp iron he cast aches in my jaw. And you? Will you give me release?

If you agree to do my bidding, I will free you, and you may live out your days in the mountains, away from us.

Someday you will crawl even over the mountains, and you will steal the sky as well.

I cannot say that day will not come, but if it does, it is far away even by the measure of your life. If you would survive now, do my bidding.

And if I would not survive?

Then you will do my bidding anyway.

The best growled within her mind. *What is your bidding, fleshling?*

First, like my father, I would use you to make peace among us.

You would make me your weapon to bring your peace.

If all goes well, you will slay no one.

The more of you I slay, the better. Have I a choice?

No.

The eldest of dragons paused in her thoughts. *Who are you? I would know my conqueror so that I might curse you with my dying breath.*

Riall waited a moment to reply. *Don't you know? I'm one of the flesh-*

lings, a paltry thing that is fleeting before you. But I'm also the water and the fire. I'm the towering cedar and the lightning that strikes it, the deer and the raven. I'm the ray of sunlight and the dew on a flower petal. I'm the trout and the osprey that snatches it. I'm the troll and the thrush, the wind and the rain. I'm the gazelle and the panther that stalks it. I'm the salty wave and the cliff it beats. I'm the mountains and the sky and the sea beneath me. And, eldest of dragons, I am you.

Your father claimed much the same. But he also freed me when he said he would. Will you free me? Will you grant me my release when you are done with me?

The weight of the beast's thousands of years, most of them lonely, pressed upon the awareness that belonged to Riall's humanity. She remembered Seren — her friend's thoughts on the verge of death. *If that is what you wish.*

So be it.

Keeping her grip over the dragon stronger than Dweorg-wrought steel yet suppler than the wind, Riall withdrew her thoughts from Gorsarhad after leaving her with a final command to abide and then follow the ships.

Her senses returned to the realm of forms, and she blinked as a world both familiar and strange returned to her. Wisps of the dragon's ferocity, majesty, and sorrow still curled around her mind, and she could not help but perceive the fragility and smallness of the beings surrounding her. They were all gawking landward, and though she knew what so enthralled them, Riall directed her gaze there as well.

A shade of red so dark as to appear nearly black, the massive dragon descended from the sky, extending her claws to alight atop a fell in the distance, shaking the earth with her landing. Wind gusted as Gorsarhad folded her sail-like wings, which were veined and nearly translucent with the sunlight behind them. The mighty beast stood like a vast statue made by giants in some faraway age.

An anxious, brittle silence blanketed the army of Thjoths as they peered up at the serpent of the air, the most relentless foe they had ever known. Many warriors held their weapons before them. Others cringed where they stood.

A hand touched Riall's shoulder, and she turned. There on the ship's deck stood Queen Sequara, with Khel by her side. Behind them were King Orvandil, Gnorn, Yrsa, and a group of concerned looking Thjoths, their gazes flicking between the dragon and Riall for some sign of what was about to happen.

The smile that broke out on the sorceress-queen's face was the most free and happy Riall had ever seen on the woman, and yet her eyes seemed almost teary. "You did it." Queen Sequara rushed forward and embraced Riall, who stood stunned for a moment before returning her mentor's warm hug.

With a grin beaming on his face, Khel too approached and clapped the young sorceress on the back. Shaking with relief and joy, she could not help grinning back at them.

"The Prophet's daughter wields the dragon!" bellowed King Orvandil's bass voice. "Board the ships! We sail for the Wildlands! Gorsarhad will fly in our wake."

A great cheer began on the king's ship and soon spread to the others and then to the warriors on land until, as one voice, it reached the heavens.

Movement off on the ship's other side drew Riall's attention. Several Thjoths leaned over the railing and seemed to be hauling someone up onto the ship. When they had dragged up the person and parted to give Riall a view, Volund appeared on deck dripping wet in only his breeches. Though others were laughing at him, the young man only smiled down at what he was holding. The familiar presence — masked, no doubt, by her contest with the dragon — leaped into Riall's mind at the same moment that she realized what Volund was holding and scratching behind the ears: a bedraggled little black dog that barked her way in excitement. *Play?*

"Belu!" Trying in vain to sound stern, Riall shook her head and could not help grinning while her eyes blurred with tears. The Thjoths all around her were still cheering and exclaiming over their massive foe turned ally.

❦ 47 ❦

Leaving Sequara near the ship's bow while she tended to Gnorn, whose usual seasickness was getting the better of him, Orvandil walked aft until he spotted his two sons on either side of Dayraven's daughter. The girl's playful pup sat beneath her, content to be part of the pack again. The three youths were leaning against the railing at the stern, gazing either at the fleet sailing behind them in the Gulf of Olfi or at the dragon circling overhead. The eldest of dragons was an all too familiar sight that still awakened the battle lust in the king. He tamped it down and shook his head.

Still trying to make sense of how he felt about his erstwhile foe becoming his unwilling ally, Orvandil released a long sigh. No doubt it was an improvement over struggling to fight the lingworm. All that truly mattered was that the beast's attacks should end and that Sigra and the others gain their freedom. Neither of those things would have been possible without Riall, and he owed her his thanks and a great deal more. Besides that, there was so much he wanted to say to both Khel and Volund, and he did not know where to start. He was terrible with words, but, while Yrsa had charge of the ship, he would make a beginning at least.

He cleared his throat as he approached. When Riall, Khel, Volund, and the little dog turned around to face him, he nodded at them, focusing on the Prophet's daughter. "On behalf of my folk, I offer you my thanks, Riall. You've given us hope where there was none."

The young sorceress inclined her head in a slight bow. "I've finished only half of what I came to do. We must see your daughter and the other hostages free."

"Aye. I swore a vow to Sigra's mother to free them or avenge them, so I am bound to try. With your help, we have a chance." He squinted up at the serpent of the air. "Might be the old beast will sway the Raven Eyes to release them without bloodshed."

"That is my hope."

"It's a good plan." Orvandil's mouth quirked into a half smile as he nodded. "The sort your father would have thought of. He was forgiving and strong in his kindness."

Riall tilted her head. "But you see a flaw in it, do you not?" Orvandil felt she was gazing right into his mind and reading his thoughts. Though she seemed innocent, the young sorceress was also every bit as perceptive as her father had been.

"Flaws are part of every plan."

"And what are this one's flaws?"

Orvandil hesitated and then took a deep breath. "If the Raven Eyes choose to fight, will you unleash Gorsarhad on them?"

Riall's eyes widened. "I . . ."

The king gave her a gentle smile. "You needn't answer now. And I don't think it will come to that. But it's an outcome you must consider."

She glanced down at the deck. "I hadn't thought . . ."

"Where lives are at risk, we must think through all possibilities. Even then we doubt our decisions. Take it from one who learned that lesson far too late."

Riall nodded. "I will think on it."

"I know you will."

"Is there aught else I should consider?"

Orvandil waited a moment while he scratched his beard. "Well, there is one matter."

"And that is?"

"What will you do with her when it's over?" He nodded toward the distant airborne beast.

"I . . . I made a sort of agreement with Gorsarhad. I told her I would release her when this was finished. You may be sure she will cease her war against the kingdoms of Andumedan."

Orvandil gazed at the girl for a moment, narrowing his eyes as he sensed something she kept hidden. And yet he trusted her, just as he had trusted her father. "You will do what is right."

Riall swallowed. "And yet?" The girl seemed to pick up on his reservations.

The king waited a moment before answering. "Part of me seeks vengeance. The beast slew many dear to me, and the laws of my folk bid me to avenge them. For Halvard alone I would slay her if I could. He was Sigra's betrothed, like a son to me. And I am far from the only one bereaved."

Volund shuffled his feet and frowned. Halvard had been close to him, and, though he never showed much emotion, Orvandil knew the lad had taken his death hard.

Orvandil sighed. "And yet . . . The dragon is yours to command. She is a wondrous beast. Freeing her also sounds like your father. It's what he did after the Battle of Thulhan. Had he slain all those dragons instead, we would not be here today, but I do not question his wisdom. I know where slaying and vengeance lead." He looked at Khel. "I told you of my friend."

Khel swallowed. "The one you . . ."

"Aye. The one I killed. Thiodolf was my foster brother. We two were close to Osynia when we were children. When we grew old enough, we each began to fancy her. Years passed. We quarrelled more and more over her. Bitterness and jealousy poisoned us. It came to holmgang, though she swore not to speak to the winner. I lived, and I lost her. So, I left Grimrik, and she wed my cousin, Vols, who later became king. Thiodolf's was the first life I took, and the one I regret most."

For a brief moment, he wondered if his two sons harbored feelings for Riall beyond friendship. Their devotion to her was clear. However, even if they were both in love with her, he believed they would never settle things in the tragic way he had. Perhaps his story would serve as a warning, though he could see they were much wiser than he had been. "Many killings followed. I became a mercenary, and I sought out war. I never slew outside of battle, but with every death, my hunger grew until nothing mattered but killing."

He looked at Riall, whose eyes had widened in something like alarm. "The Prophet changed that. He never judged me, but he showed me the man I could be. He made me want to be that man." A wry smile tugged at his mouth. "I am still trying. 'Dragonbane' they call me after my most famed deed. For me, the name brings to mind my failings. Some have come of hard choices. Oftentimes there is no good path, only bad and worse ones, and someone will suffer no matter where you turn. In that way, a ruler has less freedom than others. I reckon Queen Sequara can tell you about that. Given your power, I deem it likely you'll face even harder decisions than I have." He sighed. "I cannot tell you what to do with Gorsarhad, Riall, but I will honor your choice."

Riall frowned at him. She tucked back some of her hair that the sea wind had been toying with, and then she nodded. "Thank you. You should know that the dragon . . . Gorsarhad . . . she too knows the hunger and despair that come from killing."

The king gazed at the young sorceress for a moment and then nodded at her with a gentle smile. Next to her, he took in his two sons, so different in appearance and personality. Volund looked much like Orvandil had as a youth, but he had always been far gentler, and Khel had the good sense to loathe killing even when he was forced to defend himself. "Well. Thank Edan you young folk have more wisdom than I ever had." He pointed at his two sons. "You two can each thank your mother."

The young men stared at him, seemingly at a loss for words. Riall, however, grinned at each of them and then returned her gaze to the king. "You might be right, though more of their wisdom might come from their father than you think."

In that moment, Orvandil saw a clear glimpse of the Prophet in the girl, and he felt the same desire to be a better man that Dayraven had always inspired in him. He smiled at her. "You are kind to say so." He bowed and then turned to go, leaving the youths to their counsels.

❊   48   ❊

On a rocky strand of the Wildlands the Thjoths beached their ships. Beyond the shore, the land extended in a broad, grassy plain with no barrier to break the moaning wind. Ten leagues or so east from where they landed, the plain ran against the eaves of the Ironwood and the territory of the Raven Eyes. Minor coastal tribes stood between the Thjoths and their foes.

The grasslands put Riall in mind of her visions. When she had first laid eyes on the grass bowing in waves at the wind's command, a fist gripped her heart. There was no doubt in her mind that somewhere in this land, the elf walked in the body of an Ilarchae warrior. *Soon. We will meet.*

The visions were growing more frequent. More intense. And it was becoming harder to separate herself from them. At times it seemed she was beholding the world from two pairs of eyes at once in two separate places. In such moments, even as she looked upon her friends, the elf in the body of the Ilarchae warrior walked through the wind-swept land, as indifferent to her dear ones as it was to the individual blades of grass it trod upon. She fought to stay close to Khel, Volund, and Belu, and even to Queen Sequara. Their familiarity kept her grounded, helped her to remain within her body. But her meeting with the elf was fated.

She did not know what would happen, nor even how she felt about it. In her fey moods, she almost welcomed the elf's coming. Once it happened, she would no longer feel as if she were hiding or running from anything. At the same time, of course, the idea terrified her, and not only for her own sake. Khel, Volund, and dear Belu would be with her, not to mention Queen Sequara and thousands of others. And yet, she did not feel there was anything she could do about when and where the elf would find her.

She glanced at Khel and Volund, each sitting across from her at a fire, one of many in the encampment. Belu sat beneath her, content to receive scratches behind her ears. *If only I could live like Belu and savor the moment I'm in.*

Queen Sequara was with Gnorn and some leaders among the Thjoths at another fire, perhaps thirty feet away. The sorceress-queen was never far from Riall, though she stayed back enough to allow her time alone with Khel and Volund. It was still afternoon, and the Thjoths had made camp upon landing that morning. They were waiting for the return of King Orvandil, who had brought thirty picked warriors with him to negotiate free passage through the coastal tribes' lands. With him also went the Ilarchae Ottil, who would serve as the king's translator. Ottil seemed to think the coastal tribes would grant passage gladly to the Thjoths, given how they resented the growing power of the Raven Eyes, which threatened to swallow them.

Riall released a long sigh. In addition to the looming matter of the elf, she had not decided whether she would be able to stomach using the dragon as a weapon of war. Should she do so, thousands would suffer horrible deaths at her command. On the other hand, thousands of Thjoths would live instead of dying in battle. No doubt the Raven Eyes felt they had just as much right to live as the Thjoths. Perhaps they even saw themselves and their ways as good. In such circles her mind went.

And then, of course, there was the matter of what to do with the dragon afterwards, should she live so long. She had given her word to Gorsarhad – in a manner at least, since there were no words involved.

And yet, King Orvandil had not been wrong to question the beast's fate. Would it be wiser simply to honor Gorsarhad's wish and rid the world of the dragon? Was she and her kind any more horrific than humans? Riall did not doubt which was the crueler predator.

She glanced up at the sky, where Gorsarhad glided in lazy circles, having rested earlier behind a dune some way apart from the encampment. King Orvandil had thought having the dragon aloft might send a less than subtle message to the coastal tribes to encourage their cooperation. Also, word of the beast would likely get to the Raven Eyes, who would think much harder about offering battle.

"Why are dragons harder to wield than other creatures?"

Riall looked at Khel, who had been following her gaze skyward before asking the question. She chewed her lip as she thought for a moment. "It's because they're more complex. Their age and their intelligence set them apart from all other creatures."

Khel frowned at her and then nodded toward Belu. "So, a dog is harder to control with the gift than a worm?"

"For the most part, yes. But a bond grows stronger with familiarity. With Belu, I needn't even think about it. There is so much of me in her, and her in me, that we are sometimes almost one mind." The little dog rolled onto her back, and Riall giggled as she rubbed Belu's belly. "Familiarity is one factor. Complexity is another. And distance: The closer the creature, the easier it is to wield it. Yet another is numbers. It's much easier to wield one dog than a hundred." She wrinkled her nose in mild disgust. "I've never tried a worm, though."

"In that case, nine dragons are harder than one. But nine dragons close up might be as hard as one far away."

"Yes."

"And someone you know would be easier than someone you don't?"

"Only if I had used the gift on that person before. More than once."

Khel nodded as he seemed to ponder this information. "When you use the gift on a person, do you see everything inside their mind? Their memories? Their fears? Their desires?"

Volund looked up, first glancing at his brother and then at Riall as he too waited for the answer.

Riall peered into the fire, thinking of Seren for a moment. "Yes. Especially the memories and thoughts at the forefront of their mind. That's why we rarely do so. When we heal a person, we try to see as little as possible."

"Because it's bad manners to snoop in other people's minds?"

Riall grinned. "That, and it's also dangerous."

Khel raised his eyebrows. "Dangerous?"

"Yes. It's hard to explain."

"Try me."

The young sorceress frowned for a moment. "When we use the gift, we hold in our minds two clashing ideas at once: One is that we remain ourselves, and the other is that we are the creature we are attempting to wield. We *become* the creature, and yet we do not release the sense of ourselves lest we become lost beyond recovery." Queen Sequara had spent years drilling that into her with countless speeches and exercises.

Khel pursed his lips and then frowned. "Sounds confusing."

"It is. Added to that confusion is the fact that dwelling in the realm of origins means perceiving that the boundaries separating the energy in you from the energy in everything else are temporary, or not even real."

"I'm not sure I follow."

Riall thought for a moment, and then she remembered something Queen Sequara once told her. "A person thinking they are separate from all else is like a wave thinking it's not part of the sea. The wave is here one moment, and gone the next. But the sea abides."

Khel's mouth hung open for a few heartbeats. He shook his head. "Now that sounds terrifying. Beautifully terrifying, though. And perhaps a bit mad."

Riall gave him a serious nod. "Many with the gift do go mad, or so other folk would say. They forget who they are. We've all heard or read stories of some sorcerer or wizard who thought he was a sparrow or a bear or some such thing. The danger becomes even greater between two people, especially if they both have the gift."

"Are you saying they might think they're each other?"

"That's one way of putting it, I suppose. They would share each other's memories, which are in a way who a person is."

"A person is memories?"

"Yes. Are you your body? It is only flesh and bones with no thought of its own. Your idea of who you are is tied up in a story you tell yourself. That story arises from the imperfect fragments of images, sounds, touches, and smells you patch together in your mind and call memories. What else are *you* but your memories?"

"But my memories are not trustworthy. I change them all the time to suit my fancy or just to live with myself. And they're imperfect to begin with. I can't even recall what I broke my fast on yesterday."

"Precisely." Riall winked at Khel the way he often did at her. "Now you see what a slippery, mutable, and fleeting thing you are. Permanence is an illusion. So is your separation from all else in the realm of forms."

Khel looked at Volund with a puzzled frown. "Did she just call me slippery? I'm fairly certain she did."

Volund pursed his lips and nodded with mock seriousness. "You *are* somewhat dodgy."

Riall rolled her eyes. "Not what I meant, but not necessarily inaccurate."

Khel put a hand over his chest. "You wound me." He smiled at her. "But, I thank you for the lesson. It helps me to understand a little."

Just then, a disturbance in the camp drew their attention. A crowd gathered, and, a moment later, it parted when King Orvandil emerged from it. Ottil strode at his side, and they were heading toward Queen Sequara and the Thjothic leaders. From the talk around them, it seemed the negotiations with the coastal tribes had been successful. The three friends stood up to gain a better view.

"Speaking of slippery, I don't like that fellow." Khel was looking at Ottil.

Riall nodded. "There's something wrong about him. Something broken, and I don't mean his nose. But he's helped us so far, and he seems to hate the Raven Eyes."

"Along with all their other neighbors, it seems. From the sounds of it, we'll be marching east. My guess is we'll be breaking camp in a bit.

We could reach the Raven Eyes as early as the morrow." Khel took a deep breath and released it as a sigh.

"Aye. On the morrow, we free Sigra and the others." Volund nodded, and he too seemed on edge as he glanced at Riall.

She shared their nervousness and felt the burden of their hopes, but she did her best to look strong when she nodded to them. "On the morrow." She did not say aloud what else she feared the morrow would bring.

❧ 49 ❧

They marched until long after day yielded to twilight. Once they halted and made camp, Volund lay awake for some while before anxiety succumbed to weariness. He drifted into troubled sleep. Before dawn's light seeped into the sky, they resumed their march through the endless grasslands. The sun rose, and they neared the territory of the Raven Eyes. All the while, the dragon flew high overhead, visible to anyone who might see the approaching army.

Walking next to his friends and not far from his father, Gnorn, and Yrsa at the front of the march, Volund had trouble making sense of his emotions. Chief among them was a deep sense of foreboding that sprang, as far as he could tell, from worry for Sigra, worry for the upcoming confrontation with the Raven Eyes along with the possibility of more deaths among his folk, and worry for Riall. A bit of concern for his own well-being was mixed in as well.

Whatever else might happen, he also realized that he was dreading the end for another reason. The time with Khel, Riall, and Belu journeying through Eormenlond and laughing together seemed so simple and pure when he thought of it, almost magical, and part of him wished it could have gone on forever. Just as Riall had said, though, nothing was permanent.

Added to all these emotions was guilt for indulging in even a bit of melancholy while his sister was still a captive. He tried to keep at the forefront of his mind their purpose there in the Wildlands. Sigra's freedom and wellness were more important than his foolish dreams. But perhaps there was nothing wrong with treasuring the way Belu jumped on his legs when she was tired of walking and wanted to curl up in his arms, or the way Khel and Riall teased each other. It made Volund smile when he recalled it, though he was a poor partner for either when it came to words.

Volund's smile disappeared as he yanked his mind back to Sigra and the other hostages for the hundredth time that morning. He shook his head and sighed. He could not afford to be so distracted when they encountered the Raven Eyes.

As if in answer to his thoughts, about a dozen horses with riders appeared in the distance. They approached across the plain, riding straight for the Thjothic army. Volund's father ordered a halt, and messengers carried the order down the line, yelling the king's command.

Soon enough, the Thjoths were awaiting the oncoming riders in silence, with the dust of their march settling around them. Like Volund, every last one of them seemed to be squinting to make out who was coming. Feeling a spike in his nerves, Volund glanced at Riall and Khel to assure himself. Even Belu seemed to understand the tension as she sat next to Riall and whined. Volund gazed over at his father, who stood with Yrsa and Gnorn and Queen Sequara nearby.

The riders grew nearer, and Volund saw that none of them were warriors. Some were old men. Most were women. A moment later, he realized they were dressed like Thjoths, not Ilarchae. A glimmer of joy spread like warmth in his chest when he recognized several of them as Sigra's folk. There were Gudni and Bryia, two of Sigra's maids. Other faces and names snapped into place in Volund's mind as the party began to slow their horses and approach.

He scanned the group to seek his sister, but he must have somehow missed her. He looked them over again, but still there was no sign of

Sigra among them. A sudden shadow fell over his mind. The hope that had blossomed in him just as swiftly wilted when he admitted to himself that she was not among them. His heart squirmed in his chest, and he found it hard to breathe as his worst fears for his sister surged in his thoughts. If Sigra was dead, the Raven Eyes would find themselves answering to several thousand furious Thjoths.

The mounted party halted some twenty paces away. An old man named Leifi, Sigra's attendant, alighted from his horse and walked toward Volund's father. With a worried frown on his face, he glanced skyward at the wheeling dragon for a moment. The old fellow appeared a bit thinner but otherwise unhurt, and yet he trembled as he came before the king.

King Orvandil spoke first. "Leifi. It makes my heart glad to see you and these others alive and free. But why is Sigra not among you? Where is my daughter?" The king spoke the words in a loud, strong voice, but Volund detected the slight tremble in it.

Leifi bowed his head and winced before looking at the king again and speaking. "Sigra is alive, my king. It was she who bade us come to you with a message, though the war-leader Bolverk granted our freedom first."

"What message is this?" The king frowned down at the old man with a sternness Volund seldom saw, and he was glad not to be in Leifi's place.

Leifi shook his head as if denying what he was about to say. "Sigra bids us to tell you that you must return to Grimrik with all your warriors. She has wed Bolverk, war-leader of the Raven Eyes, of her own free will. As a token of good faith and the union of their folk and ours, Bolverk granted us our freedom and sends gifts with us as well as a bride-geld." Volund noted that the horses were weighed down with packs.

His father fixed his blade-like gaze down at the old man for several heartbeats. "'Her own free will'? How can this be?"

Leifi tried to shrink as he stared at the ground. "It's not for me to say, my king. But she has wed him. We all witnessed it. She spoke in strong words, telling me to urge you to go home in peace."

With his mouth stuck open, the king appeared as if someone had struck him. His eyes looked all around him, but he appeared to find no help in what he saw. When he spoke again, it seemed to be more to himself than to Leifi. "I cannot go home. I swore a vow to her mother." He regained his composure and turned to Duneyr. "Find ten warriors to escort Sigra's folk back to the ships. They've seen enough hardship. Tell them to cast Bolverk's gifts and his bride-geld into the sea. If anyone takes even a coin of it, I'll cut off his hand myself."

King Orvandil looked around as if challenging anyone to disagree with his decision. No one spoke. The king took a deep breath and then spoke to those nearest him. "This changes nothing. We will free Sigra or avenge her."

"Death to the Raven Eyes!" Yrsa brandished her sword.

"Death!" shouted the warriors around her, and the cry spread until thousands chanted it again and again, shaking their weapons up toward the heavens.

Volund looked at Riall, whose eyes widened a little as she took in the spectacle. A moment later, she seemed dazed. Perhaps it was all the rage around them. She would be sensitive to so many high emotions. He needed to explain to her and Khel what had happened. Since the exchange took place in Thjothic, they could not know what was said, and yet it was obvious enough in the fury among the warriors.

Khel was frowning as he gazed toward their father. The chant was breaking apart into hundreds of excited conversations, giving the friends a chance to speak at last. Volund's brother tapped him on the shoulder. "Your sister?"

Volund took a deep breath. "They say she's wed Bolverk, war-leader of the Raven Eyes, and we should go home in peace."

Khel raised his eyebrows, and then he peered around at all the furious warriors. "I gather we're not following that counsel."

"No. We will free Sigra. She could not have wed him by choice." Volund glanced again at Riall, who took in these tidings with little show of emotion, though her eyes still seemed bewildered.

Khel nodded and, narrowing his eyes, returned his gaze to the group around the king. "Where'd that fellow slink off to?"

Volund looked in the same direction. "Who?"

"Ottil. He's been sticking hard by the king's side during the whole march. Where's he now?"

Khel was right. Volund could not spot the Ilarchae anywhere. "Must be nigh." There was a great deal of chaos at the moment, and perhaps Ottil had disappeared in the press of excited warriors.

Khel shrugged. "Of course, if I were an Ilarchae, this is not a crowd I'd like to be seen in just now." He turned to Riall. "Are you alright?"

Riall nodded, perhaps a bit too quickly. "Yes. I'm fine."

Looking as if he did not quite believe her, Khel frowned. "One of the visions?"

Riall blinked, and then she swallowed before nodding. "Yes." She looked at each of them in turn, and Volund thought he saw a trace of horror in her eyes. "We're getting close now."

Khel nodded. "We'll stick by you, then." He looked at Volund, who nodded in confirmation, trying to appear more sure of everything than he felt.

$$\text{\maltese} \quad 50 \quad \text{\maltese}$$

Sigra took one step, and then another, her heart trying to beat its way out of her chest. More steps, and she glanced behind her at the rows of warriors standing in formation. Bolverk had arrayed the full might of the Raven Eyes – some four thousand strong – to defend their encampment on the edge of the Ironwood, whose canopy loomed behind the hide tents and clan totems on their poles. A forest of spears rose above the warriors, and steel glinted among those with mail and blades. Bolverk stood out from the rest of the warriors, tall and white-bearded with his black eye patch. He had been wary of Sigra's plan and reluctant to let her have her way, but she had convinced him of the necessity.

She almost wished she had been less persuasive. As formidable as the Raven Eyes might seem, they were no match for the forces she beheld as she turned her gaze forward again. The Thjoths had come. Despite the message she sent with her freed folk to head them off, they had come, many carrying Dweorg-wrought steel. Tall and proud, fierce and strong, the most feared warriors in Eormenlond had come to free her by force or avenge her.

She would not allow it. Sigra had sacrificed too much in order to forestall this battle. There would be no vengeance on her behalf, no deaths of thousands weighing on her. Most important of all was the vision Edan had bestowed on her. *I am here for a reason. Edan will free these people through compassion.* All she needed to do was convince King Orvandil, the man who had been her second father, to turn around and go home to Grimrik.

As frightening as the Thjoths appeared – Sigra's birth folk, she reminded herself – what truly terrified her as she walked through the tall grass toward the waiting army was the vast beast towering behind the warriors. A dragon. A dark monstrosity that dwarfed all beneath it. And not just any lingworm. Gorsarhad, eldest of dragons. She stood as if tame and awaiting orders to devour the Raven Eyes or burn them to ashes. Somehow, her father seemed to have turned the beast from foe to ally. Sigra did not doubt it had something to do with the king's old friend from Asdralad, the legendary sorceress-queen. However it came about, Gorsarhad's presence meant a dire situation for the Raven Eyes had become certain annihilation.

There was but one way to prevent it. She would stop the slaughter before it began. *Peaceweaver.*

Sigra's feet carried her closer to the Thjothic army. She headed toward the formation's center, where she hoped the king would await her. Surely they had seen her by now, a lone woman approaching through the grassland lying in between two armies. She wore her Thjothic dress so that they would recognize her.

Save for the wind moving through the hissing grass, a strange silence hung over it all. Sigra began to discern individuals she recognized among the Thjoths. She had not been wrong. King Orvandil Dragonbane stood taller than those around him in the center. Near him was her sister Yrsa. Much shorter than the others and always staying close by her father, Gnorn was easy to spot. A woman with raven hair and the dark skin of the south also stood there in a long black tunic, confirming Sigra's guess that Queen Sequara must have been involved in the dragon's presence. Two other southerners were nearby, by their appearance a youth and young woman. And next to them was her brother Volund.

For some reason, it was the sight of Volund that made Sigra sob with the heavy realization of everything she would miss. Her gentle, strong little brother, looking suddenly like a man grown. Surely, among them all, he would understand why she was doing this. She took a deep breath and held her tears in check. She needed to be strong.

With each step her legs grew heavier, but she pushed on. Thousands of warriors stared at her as she approached. Would they see her as a traitor? A coward? *It matters not. Edan's will be done.* Still nearer she grew. At length, she made a halt and stood some twenty paces from her father, whom she faced.

King Orvandil's stern frown gave way to a sorrowful smile. "Sigra. Daughter. You live. Will you come home with us?" His voice quavered, sending a stab of painful regret through her body.

"Father. I have come to ask you for peace. Let there be no bloodshed or suffering this day. There is no reason to fight the Raven Eyes now. Return to Grimrik in peace, I beg you." She spoke in a loud, strong voice so that many could hear her.

The king's hand rested on the hilt of his scabbarded sword. "Will you come with us?"

Sigra glanced down at the grass, but she looked him in the eyes when she answered. "I cannot."

Her father's frown returned, and he shook his head. "I swore a vow to your mother to bring you home or avenge you."

"Tell my mother there is nothing to avenge. I have wed the warleader Bolverk to make peace between the Raven-Eyes and the Thjoths. It is done."

"I swore it on Halvard's body."

Sigra shuddered, her knees almost buckling. She could not deny the tears this time, and they blurred her vision. "Halvard is dead?"

King Orvandil bowed his head. "He died a brave death, fighting the dragon. Hundreds of others did as well."

She shook her head and wiped her eyes with her sleeve. "Then there has been enough sorrow already." She squared her shoulders and stood straight, and then she cleared her throat to master her voice. "You will keep your vow, Father. I will return to Grimrik in a year's time. Until then, I will remain with the Raven Eyes in a place of honor. I will abide here in the Wildlands, free to worship Edan and live as I will." Conviction welled in her, and her words grew powerful even in her own ears as some force spoke through her. "I am here for a reason. I will be Edan's messenger to the Raven Eyes. To the folk of the tribes. In time, there may be greater bonds between our two peoples. There is no cause for battle. Let there be peace this day."

The king frowned at her for a long while. Yrsa, Volund, Gnorn, and countless others stared at Sigra as well, and she felt the weight of their judgement. And yet the force that used her voice transcended the whole scene, serene in its certainty that all of this was meant to be.

Her father's frown faltered, and he shook his head as a trembling, sorrowful smile took its place. "I'm sorry. So sorry. I failed to protect you. My brave, wise daughter." He held his hands out and stepped toward her as if to embrace her.

But another figure not far from the king broke away from the Thjothic ranks at the same time, and it moved with terrible swiftness toward Sigra. Her eyes widened in disbelief and horror, and shock paralyzed her body as Unnar sprinted toward her with a rictus of hatred and madness distorting his face.

She could only stagger back one step. "You?"

Something gleamed in his hand, and he was upon her before anyone could react. His fist blurred into her chest, where a sharp and burning pain entered her as a huff of air pushed its way out her throat. When he withdrew the long dagger, her red blood smeared the steel, and she could take in no breath. Their strength gone, her legs collapsed, and she crumpled over as the world dimmed.

"Vengeance!" The Ilarchae who had called himself Ottil screamed the word in the Northern Tongue. He held aloft his reddened dagger with a crazed smile on his face.

As in a nightmare, Sequara had watched him rush toward Orvandil's daughter, her mind a step too late in grasping his intention. His strange behavior made sudden sense – disappearing when the freed Thjoths showed up and reappearing by the king's side once they had departed. Perhaps they would have known his true identity, whatever it might be. She had noticed him stealing behind a couple warriors while Sigra approached as well, but, caught up in the moment, she had not bothered to conjecture why. Such thoughts rushed into Sequara's mind all at once, but the realization was too late.

After the initial shock, a hush of disbelief fell over the Thjothic army. Yrsa was the first to react. The shield-maiden rushed forward, her sword flashing as she sprinted toward the man who had stabbed her sister. Ottil awaited her with his dagger ready, and they swung at each other as Yrsa growled. She dodged his dagger, but her longer blade carved through his forearm with a rope of blood trailing it. Even as he gawked at the gore spurting from the stump of his arm, Yrsa spun and wheeled her sword in a swift motion. Its edge bit through the man's neck with an audible crack of bone, and his head whirled off with crimson tendrils spattering from it. His headless corpse wobbled backwards and tumbled, its limbs flopping up once when it hit the ground.

A feral scream tore its way from Yrsa's throat, and she pivoted from the corpse to sprint toward the Raven Eyes arrayed across the grassland. That sparked the entire Thjothic army into motion. Warriors yelled as they hurtled themselves forward, and even Orvandil was swept up in the irresistible, mad rush.

For a fraction of a heartbeat, Sequara considered aiding the Thjoths in battle with *almakhti*. The jagged currents of energy could have torn huge rents in the Ilarchae line of warriors. But the thought of killing again in such a manner – a flash of searing agony, the stench of burnt, smoldering corpses – almost made her retch, and her healer's instincts had already kicked in. She found herself hastening toward Sigra's still body.

The young woman was lying face down. As swiftly as she could, Sequara bent to roll her over. Sigra's body was heavy since she was a tall woman, but the sorceress-queen grunted and managed to flop her onto her back. Blood soaked the front of her dress, and Sequara guessed from the wound's location that the long dagger had pierced a lung. Placing two fingers on Sigra's neck, the sorceress-queen felt the weak flutter of her pulse. Without a second thought, she began to place her hand over the still seeping wound.

She dodged aside, flattening herself on the ground as a large shape nearly collided with her. Like a raging river of flesh and steel, a chaos of screaming warriors swarmed all around her as the Thjoths dashed toward battle. A boot almost stepped on Sequara's head, and she cursed as she jerked away and tried to crawl back to Sigra.

Something slammed into Sequara's ribs, and she grunted as she rolled. When she pushed herself up on hands and knees, just off to her left in the grass, Ottil's shocked eyes stared at her with blood speckling his pale face. His headless body lay nearby. The warrior who had tripped on her was sprawled out next to her as well, but he was able to thrust himself up and continue his mindless rush toward battle. Pain flared in her side, and she gasped in a breath. She reached a trembling hand toward Sigra's still body, terrified that the fools would trample out the little life remaining in her.

A familiar voice growled above the din, and the stout form of Gnorn appeared. The old Dweorg planted himself before Sigra's body and screamed at Sequara, "I'll be your bulwark!"

He turned about and held the haft of his axe before him with both hands, bracing his legs in a wide stance, like a stubborn boulder in the midst of a frothing river. True to his word, he slammed aside first one and then another of the oncoming warriors, sweeping them away with a yell each time.

Above Gnorn and the oncoming warriors, Sequara caught a glimpse of the looming dragon, still sitting like a giant threat awaiting the command to unleash death. It seemed that, like her, Riall had decided not to throw her strength into the battle, which meant the situation still might be salvaged somehow.

There was no time for relief, however, as the sorceress-queen leaped toward Sigra and placed her hand on the wound gaping on the young woman's chest. Not bothering to check if she was still alive, she began the song of origin of healing, chanting beneath her breath. Trusting in Gnorn's defense, she allowed the chaos around her to recede from her awareness, and the realm of origins enfolded her like the sea receiving a diver from a cliff. Lending her energy and strength to Sigra's body, she focused on the flesh around the wound, willing it to knit together again.

Even in the serenity of the realm of origins, the sorceress-queen sorrowed and admired the young woman as she witnessed the flashes of her memories that bled into her mind. To judge by the fragments, Sigra had suffered terrible hardships in her captivity, but she had somehow found the courage not only to endure them, but to seize control over them. Sequara could not help allowing a sigh of relief as she perceived the torn flesh healing, experiencing the keen itch of rapidly forming scar tissue as if it were her own body. It cost her much energy, but it was working.

Just then, a loud grunt from Gnorn broke into her awareness, and she opened her eyes to see the old Dweorg lying still at the bottom of a tangle of bodies and limbs. More large forms rushed toward her, threatening to trample Sigra. Severing her connection to her, Sequara jerked out of the realm of origins and threw herself over the young woman, wincing in anticipation of bone-breaking pain.

Instead, there was a surge of the gift so vast that it leeched the very light from the world. An eerie stillness and silence took over the battlefield.

The sorceress-queen looked up and gazed all around her in every direction. The thousands of warriors had all frozen, every one of them stopped in mid-stride. With rage carved on their features, they filled the landscape like so many martial and life-like statues, caressed by the wind that pushed the grass in waves. Even the Ilarchae, who had been rushing to meet their attackers, stood motionless in similar poses across the grassland.

Though her mind had trouble wrapping around the truth, Sequara knew at once what had happened. She did not even want to think about the amount of power required to wield some eight thousand human minds at once.

In answer to the exertion of that power, the sky and the land darkened, as if some vast cloud had descended from space to blot out the sun and seize all color from the world. With that unearthly, all-enveloping shadow came a chill that made Sequara shiver. Though it had been many years since she felt it like this, it was terrible in its familiarity. The elf had come.

"Riall," she whispered, and she began a frantic search for her daughter among all the unmoving figures.

‏❧ 52 ❧

Like light from the sun, power coursed from Riall, who spread her arms out and trembled as she wielded eight thousand mortal minds. The memories, terrors, desires, lusts, and passions of eight thousand flooded her in a vast cacophony. In almost all of them, fear and rage – among the most primal of these mortals' emotions – had usurped their reasoning, and they were ready to kill and die in a screaming mass. Even gentle Volund had given way to the fury, burying his terrible grief for his sister beneath the red hot rage that screamed for vengeance. In this he joined the thousands of deadly Thjoths, the most feared warriors in all of Andumedan. But the Raven Eyes were no cowards. They too had been prepared to leap into battle to defend their own.

Riall's will held them all back. She commanded their bodies to stillness, and though they struggled within the innermost recesses of their terrified minds, they could not move a finger without her consent. Among the conscious, Riall had excepted three individuals from her command because they were the only ones not caught up in the frenzy for battle. One was Queen Sequara, who had rushed to heal Volund's sister. Another was Khel, who stood by Riall out of love and loyalty, and who watched her with his eyes wide and mouth agape. The third was little Belu, who whined as she trembled next to Khel.

"Riall! Are you alright?" Khel glanced around at the bizarre forest of still bodies before turning back to her. "How can I help?"

With the thoughts of eight thousand shattering her awareness into as many pieces, she found it hard to form words to answer him, but she managed to shake her head.

Something immense and numinous, world-encompassing in its presence, bled the light from the air. Belu's whining grew louder, more frightened. But she stood her ground, and her ears pointed backward as she tensed and emitted a high-pitched growl.

As the vast shadow blanketed the land, Khel gawked up. "What is that?" He shuddered and cringed. "Riall?" He too stood by his friend.

She turned southward, whence it came. Before seeing it with her eyes, she knew what was coming. Across the grassland it approached, clothed as a solitary figure. In the body of a tall Ilarchae warrior it walked with no urgency as it took step after inevitable step. Around it was a bright aura, as if it were drawing all the light into it. Behind it, Riall knew, lay eternal stillness and darkness. The elf.

Riall jerked back a step and snarled at it. Without a moment's reflection, she acted on her own terror and fury at the thing that had pursued her all her life, hurtling the mightiest weapon at her disposal toward her persecutor.

Gorsarhad roared. Greeting the darkness with a fey heart, the ancient beast unfurled her wings, stirring up huge gusts as she beat them with a thunderous din. She bounded into the air. Khel's cloak whipped behind him, and he stumbled backwards as he struggled to keep his footing. Belu barked with all the fierceness she could muster, turning in circles as if unsure where the threat lay. Up the mighty ling-worm launched her colossal body, catching a current and banking once before careering toward the elf.

"Riall! No!" Dodging and weaving in between the frozen warriors, Queen Sequara hurried toward Riall.

The young sorceress gasped, understanding her error. Death could not conquer the light-devouring darkness. Rather, it was of the dark-ness, the way into it. At the same time, she grasped that *she* had called the elf into being with the exertion of her power over thousands of minds at once. This was the moment she had long dreaded, and, in the end, she had summoned it. By seeking to thwart the battle, she had brought the elf into the realm of forms. Its long passage from the Southweald to the Wildlands had been simply a response to this moment, which it had always known Riall would beget. All along, with every decision and every step of her journey, she had doomed herself and those around her.

Too late did she recall Gorsarhad from her attack, for the dragon had already dived low and disgorged her flames. As the beast ascended again, a roiling conflagration cascaded upon the lone figure, who appeared so small beneath the river of fire. An inferno blazed for one moment of searing, blinding intensity, brushing Riall's face with its hot breath even as far away as she stood. When it was gone, it left a massive radius of blackened, smoldering grass. In the center, amidst curling smoke, stood the elf, no longer contained in mortal flesh, which had crisped and withered into ashes.

Without pausing, the figure wrapped in pure light walked toward Riall, and the chill behind it covered her flesh in goosebumps. It possessed the features of a man wearing a robe over a tunic and breeches, but it seemed insubstantial to her, almost translucent. Without so much as glancing behind it, the figure seized the dragon from Riall, who felt the severing of her connection to Gorsarhad like a lash on her mind. At the same time, she sensed the beast's energy winking out of existence to dissipate all over the realm of forms.

The eldest of creatures ceased beating her wings, growing limp with sagging limbs and neck before plummeting earthward. Her massive corpse shook the earth with its bone-shattering impact, and it raised a thin cloud of dust. Khel covered his ears as he stumbled, and Belu skittered behind him. Riall knew the dragon had been dead before her body collided with the ground, but she lamented such an end to an ancient life. The elf had granted Gorsarhad her wish. And it was not finished.

Even as it advanced toward Riall, the form containing the immortal elf beckoned all the light into itself, and a deeper shadow swallowed the land. Though it made no motion, Riall felt it calling her as well. It was coming for her, and with her it would take the eight thousand minds she wielded, but she was helpless to move or think of anything other than the eyes of the approaching elf, which fixed on her.

"Dayraven." Queen Sequara appeared next to Riall, her mouth open in shock. But then the sorceress-queen moved to block her view of the elf, standing before her and grasping her by the shoulders. "Don't look at it, Riall. Don't look at its eyes especially. Look at me."

Riall shook her head as she snapped back into her body. No longer the captive of the elf, she felt some of her self-control return to her. "Is it . . . Is that my father? The Prophet of Edan?"

The queen shook her head, her brown eyes wide with fear. "No. It has taken his form. That is all. They take the form of what we love, what tempts us most. Do *not* look at it."

"But . . ."

"Listen to me, Riall. It's time. Your promise. I must use the song of origin *now* to remove the elf's power from you."

Riall focused on her mentor. Still holding the minds of thousands under her control, she picked out among them the queen's and knew the truth of her intentions. Her mouth opened in shock, but no words emerged.

"Riall. I must use the song of origin." The queen's grip on her shoulders tightened. "You must allow me before it reaches you."

Riall swallowed, and her eyes widened in shock. "No. You lied to me."

"Riall! Listen to me."

"No. It will kill you. Won't it?"

"There isn't time. Please . . ."

"I can't let you. You lied to me." She frowned at her mentor. "And there's something else you lied about." Commanding the queen's body to stillness like the thousands of other living statues, Riall stepped back.

Her arms still held out as if she would grasp something, Queen Sequara stood frozen, helpless to move, the anguish and desperation fixed on her beautiful face. A single tear tracked down her scarred cheek. The sorceress-queen strove to hide her memories from Riall within the layers of her mind, but, as formidable as she was, she could not match Riall's raw power.

Riall peeled back the layers and saw it all: the loneliness, the guilt, the silent devotion, the longing, the sacrifice, the duty, and, more than anything else, the *love*. "All these years, you held it back. You watched over me, but you never told me. Why?"

Queen Sequara could not move her lips to speak, but her eyes were locked in entreaty. It was then that the woman ceased to resist, and she gave over everything.

Like uncountable shards of a broken mirror, each reflecting a glimpse of a person, years of memories poured into Riall. Some stretched all the way back to Sequara's youth, when a frightened farm girl went to train in Queen Faldira's palace alongside the young nobles with the gift. Images of war — horrific bloodshed and slaughter, torrents of fire from the maws of dragons, and the searing agony of using the gift as a weapon rather than to heal — all crashed into Riall. But there was much that was dear to the woman too, including the family of her youth, the queen who trained her, and the one who became the Prophet of Edan. By some miracle that Riall did not understand, some of the memories that reached her from Sequara's mind seemed to belong to the Prophet, as if they had been one person. Such was the intensity of their love. In a revelation that awed her with its sublimity, she perceived the woman before her as she never had before. Not as a remote queen or a wise mentor, but as woman — flawed and beautiful — who would give anything, including her own life, to save Riall.

Riall shook her head. "I'm sorry. I can't let you." Her own tears were falling, and she sniffled as she wiped them away. "I wish we had more time. I've got to go."

She would walk toward the elf and release the minds of the eight thousand before it took her. She hoped that would save them from it. Once it claimed her and reunited with its power, perhaps it would leave them all alone. Of course, if it did, they might resume killing each other, but she could do nothing about that.

Just then, Belu's barking intensified. *I'm sorry, my dear one. Stay with Khel and Volund.* There was a surge of emotion behind her, where Khel stood, and she perceived the feelings welling in him. Despite his fear, he too was ready to do anything to help her, but what could he do? Before facing the elf for her final moments of consciousness, she turned to say goodbye to her friend.

She had no time for surprise as the hilt of the dagger he held in his fist hammered into the side of her head. Bright streaks of light flashed before her eyes, and, almost as if her legs disappeared, her feet were swept from under her. Before the ground greeted her body, darkness took her.

Khel stood over Riall's splayed body, clutching his dagger in a white-knuckled grip. "Shit. Please tell me I didn't kill her." Belu was there licking the girl's face, but Riall's wonted scolding and giggling were absent. She did not stir. Khel's shallow breaths came hard and fast, and he fell to his knees next to her, gently putting his hand on her head where he had struck her. He winced as if he had received the blow rather than delivered it. "Riall. I'm so sorry."

Queen Sequara gasped and staggered forward, and when Khel looked up, he noticed that the thousands of warriors that had been under Riall's control were stumbling around while grasping their heads, many of them falling to the ground and groaning. It looked like a battlefield of reeling drunkards, and if there had not been a monstrous elf about to devour everyone's soul as it veiled the world in darkness, he might have spared a moment to chuckle at them. Having heard what Queen Sequara said to Riall about the elf, he resisted the powerful urge to look toward it, though the bright aura surrounding it seemed to beckon to him as it cast eerie shadows all around the grassland.

Seeming to recover faster than anyone else, the sorceress-queen knelt next to him and clasped Riall's head, causing Belu to step back and whine. The sorceress put her fingers on the girl's neck and then examined her scalp and temples with gentle movements of her hands. "She'll live."

The queen looked at him. "Thank you, Khel." And then she shocked him by leaning close and kissing him on the cheek, which did nothing for his already shattered composure. "Thank you for giving me a chance. Now, listen. If I succeed, you must find your father and tell him that Sigra lives."

Khel gawked at her and managed to nod.

"King Orvandil will be able to stop the battle. Tell him she lives, and then the Thjoths will have no reason to fight. Also, try to awaken Sigra."

"Right. Sigra." He nodded again. "And what if you don't succeed?"

She gave him a sad smile and shook her head gently. "Then you needn't worry about anything."

Unable to utter a word in response, Khel received this information with his mouth hanging open.

The sorceress-queen took a deep breath and looked down at Riall's unconscious form. "Stand well back."

Khel rose and obeyed the queen, stepping back a few paces. "Oh, shit." He could not help noticing the aura of light around the elf growing brighter as shadows deepened everywhere else, and he shielded his eyes from it with one hand.

Before Queen Sequara began, however, she glanced at him one last time. "Tell Riall I'm sorry. And I love her."

He stared at her for a moment, wondering how she could maintain such calm while death stalked closer to them all. "I will."

Returning her gaze to the young woman she knelt over, the sorceress-queen's eyes seemed to take in something Khel could not see, as if her mind had slipped somewhere far away. He recognized the same look Riall wore when she used her power. The queen began chanting in the strange tongue that those with the gift claimed was the primordial language, the one that gave all things their true name.

Druanil ecthonias an dharian gadalathon,

Abu mihil inghanias ni rakhyon abhularon.

Vardas diagol im parthas akwinway,

Shardas inkhathol an ghalas khalithway.

The queen repeated the chant again and again. At the same time, Khel noticed how the light emanating around the elf was growing brighter still, bleaching the features of the land as it neared them. Clotted shadows claimed everything outside its radiance. He still did not dare to look at it, though it called to him with sweet promises of bliss, and he forced his gaze to stay fixed on the illuminated form of Queen Sequara, in whom their desperate, fragile hope lay. He licked his lips and urged her on with a quiet whisper. "Come on, come on, come on."

As if in answer to his spiking urgency, twinkles of blue light sparked into existence between the queen and Riall's unconscious form, floating there like dust motes. The sorceress-queen continued to chant, and the sparks grew more numerous and brighter until a glow formed around them. The glow birthed more and more of the sparks until the light they cast vied with the unbearable aura from the approaching elf. He sensed the otherworldly entity in his peripheral vision, and its chill gave him shivers as goosebumps arose on his flesh. Gritting his teeth, he resisted the terrible need to gaze at it.

Khel's mouth dropped open again when the blue sparks intensified and rushed all at once from Riall to Queen Sequara, bursting in a bright flash when they hit her. Flinching backward in concert with Belu, he blinked several times before the dancing after-image receded enough to allow him to see again. He shook his head and took in Queen Sequara, whose distant eyes frightened him with their authority and the looming power behind them. The sorceress-queen rose to her full height and turned to face the elf. More hostage than witness, Khel was helpless to look away.

The elf stood no more than five feet from Queen Sequara, where it halted to observe her. It took the form of a man who reminded Khel of Riall in ways he would have found difficult to pinpoint, though he appeared to be a northerner. The light around him was so intense that relative darkness shrouded the entire landscape, leaving Khel feeling as if the world had shrunk to the small circle containing the elf, the queen, and Riall, with him and Belu teetering on the edge. The bluish-white radiance bathed all three of them, casting their features into stark chiaroscuro that made Khel squint.

Gazing straight into the elf's eyes, Queen Sequara spoke. "Long have I awaited you. Come with me. Leave these mortals to live out their days. Let us return together, and be whole at last." She reached out a hand as if offering it to the elf.

Like a puppet dangling from strings, Khel found his foot nudging toward the two of them, causing simultaneous alarm and ecstasy to pierce his mind in sundry places.

Cocking its head as if her proposal puzzled or surprised it, the elf hesitated for a long moment, during which Khel's heart slammed against his ribs as he jerked forward one more step. The otherworldly creature seemed to nod in silent acceptance before taking a step and reaching forward to grasp the hand the queen offered.

At the moment of contact, a silent explosion of blinding light threw Khel backwards, arms and legs flailing as he wheeled, and he landed on his back with a grunt.

The first sensation to return to him was Belu's tongue licking his face. "Ugh." He reached out and, to give assurance that he was fine, ruffled the fur on the little dog, who whined at him. When he shook his head and sat up, he thought he glimpsed a trail of light streaking toward the Ironwood, pulsing into brightness once within the trees. It was gone when he blinked.

The darkness had disappeared, or at least it had retreated for the time being. The world had returned to its wonted hues, which somehow seemed more vivid than usual, and the wind hissed in the grass. Khel took in a breath like it had been a thousand years since his last. Belu waddled over to where Riall's body lay and turned her attention to the girl.

Khel groaned and crawled forward until he reached the body of Queen Sequara lying on her back, her limbs askew where she had fallen. Her eyes were closed. "Queen Sequara?" He shook her, but there was no response. Putting his hand first on her neck, he felt for life the way he had seen her do on Riall. Nothing. His palm before her mouth felt no breath. Khel sighed and hung his head.

And then, jolting upright, he remembered her words to him. There were a few thousand angry Thjoths to placate, not to mention a battle to halt.

Khel whirled around to seek his father. All he could see were bodies lying in the grass, some moaning and some beginning to stir. In the distance, in the direction whence the elf had come, Gorsarhad's massive corpse lay like a giant mound on the otherwise flat landscape. Shaking off his wonder and dismay at the sight, Khel squinted as he searched in every direction.

He had to find his father. Taking off at a near sprint, he ran in the direction he last saw him. On the way, he caught a glimpse of Sigra shaking her head and beginning to rise from all fours. Others were starting to waken from their stupor as well, emerging from the grass as if rising from the dead.

Khel tossed aside all fear and dignity, and he began to shout at the top of his lungs. "Father! King Orvandil! Where are you? Sigra's alive!"

Heedless of any other thought, he ran until he reached a point where he saw no more bodies, and then, feeling at once frantic and absurd, he turned around to yell once again at the entire army of Thjoths, with every one of the warriors looking like the victim of a bad hangover. "Father! You've got to stop the battle! Sigra's alive!"

Dazed and wincing, several faces turned and squinted with puzzled and hostile frowns at Khel. He scanned all around him in desperation, but among the rising warriors he could not spot the king. "Damnation," he whispered. He prepared to scream even louder, though it occurred to him such an action might make him the most likely first target of the battle.

"Where is she, Son?"

Khel twisted around. There, not more than a dozen feet away, was Orvandil Dragonbane where he had risen from the grass, looking a bit wobbly but still as commanding as ever as he frowned at him.

A sigh of inexpressible relief escaped Khel, and his shoulders drooped as the rest of his body sagged. He pointed toward Sigra, who was already approaching their father through the grass in her blood-stained dress.

$$\maltese \quad 54 \quad \maltese$$

A wave slapped against the ship's hull, sending up a gentle spray that the wind pattered into Riall's face. She leaned on the rail and gazed back toward the distant, receding coast of the Wildlands. Much further inland than she could see, and not far from a huge mound covering Gorsarhad, was one lone grave that held the body of her mother. Thinking of all the questions she would never have answers to, she recalled how she had mourned back there.

Grief had torn her mind and soul into incoherent, wailing shreds. She had wept freely over Queen Sequara's fresh grave, realizing only then how much she had loved the woman even before she knew the truth about her. In some ways her mother had failed her. But not in the ways that mattered. In the end, the woman had given everything, perhaps only as a mother could.

Miraculously, the unbearable weight of her grief, something that had stolen her very breath at times, had settled into something she thought she might learn to carry someday. A calm had followed the storm of tears, and if dark clouds still loomed overhead, shafts of light pierced them in places.

Gnorn had told her all about her parents and also why Queen Sequara had felt the need to hide her birth from her and the rest of the world. She had understood all of it from sharing the woman's memories near the end, but it felt good to hear it from someone who had known her mother well. King Orvandil had supplied a few more details as well. And yet, she still longed to ask her mother so many things, to hear her voice give the answers that would explain her life. At times, the void was a fist clenching her heart, and sometimes memories of the simplest details about the woman — the scars on her hands, the sad smile with which she so often gazed at Riall — threatened to undo her again.

At least she had known her mother and even trained under her. Though stories abounded about him, her father was a legend she had never been able to meet. And yet, she had shared not only her mother's memories of him, but it felt as if many of those memories had in fact belonged to him. This was a mystery she could not understand, but she was glad to have something more of her father than the stories, and she almost felt as if she knew him. He seemed a gentle person, one who strove to bring peace to the world. The sorceress-queen, however, would always be in some ways what she aspired towards, a model of how one with the gift should handle her responsibilities in the world with dignity and compassion.

From what Riall could piece together, Sequara must have known for a long time what she would do when the elf came. Her final act was similar to what the Prophet of Edan had done, joining her energy to the elf in order to direct it with the last remnants of her will. The selflessness of it astounded her with both pride and sorrow, and she realized how alone the queen had been for so much of her life. Queen Sequara had been a great and wise leader, but for the first time, she thought she understood her mother. Now she was gone, and all she could do was try to live up to the woman who had trained her and given everything for her.

She would need her mother's example and her teaching, for the gift was still with Riall. True to her word, the sorceress-queen had taken from her only what belonged to the elf, leaving behind the gift that was native to Riall. She found that she was, in fact, a powerful sorceress, perhaps as powerful as her mother had been, or even a little more. Of course, that was nothing compared to what had been blazing inside her all those years, and though she was a bit wistful about the loss, for the most part it was an immense relief to be rid of it. No sense of being chased. No more horrifying visions. No danger of destroying everything she loved. She would just need to get used to depending on the songs of origin, like everyone else with the gift.

Riall released a long sigh. There were so many things to figure out, but she lacked the will to do much more than mourn at the moment. Chief among those things was Khel. At first, she had been furious with him, blaming him for her mother's death. Of course, she knew that was unfair. Had he not knocked her over the head, it was more than likely Riall would have taken everyone, including Queen Sequara, with her when the elf arrived to claim her. But knowing the injustice of her anger had not made her less angry, and Khel bore it all in stoic silence, infuriating her further.

She had not spoken to him since that day, except to tell him to leave her, and even that she said through tears without looking at him. She had said little to anyone else. As gently as they could, Gnorn and King Orvandil had talked with her about her mother, while Volund had tried in his shy, awkward way to console her. Others avoided her, perhaps out of respect for her grief, but also perhaps because they were afraid. She did not blame them. They had been in her power, and while she occupied their minds, she had faced the darkness of unbeing, almost dragging them all into it. It was not likely an experience they wished to be reminded of.

Only Sigra had gone out of her way to speak to Riall, thanking her for her role in stopping the battle, but Volund's sister was back in the Wildlands, determined to make the best of her new home. Though she was no warrior like her younger sister Yrsa, she had a different sort of strength. Doubting she possessed such courage and faith, Riall admired her and liked her as well. Of course, she herself was entirely homeless. Nothing tied her anywhere. She was not truly Caergilese, and she had never felt like an Asdralae in all her years there. She had never even seen the Mark, except in her forest dreams, which were gone now. Perhaps someday she would visit the kingdom where her father was born.

For the present, she had no idea where she would go after she reached Grimrik.

A shadow covered her as someone big loomed near. Riall looked up at Volund, who squinted as he followed her gaze back to the shores of the Wildlands. He was holding Belu in one hand and scratching the little dog behind the ears with the other. The two of them had grown close, and Riall was glad that the little dog had someone to be with while she faced her grief. Volund nodded at her and gave her a tentative smile.

Out of politeness, she tried to smile back and make him feel welcome. "What will you do when we get back to Grimrik?"

Volund frowned for a moment while he thought. "Make things."

Riall nodded. "I suppose there'll be a great deal of rebuilding to do. Your skills will be useful."

Volund considered this thought with pursed lips, and then he gave a quick nod of agreement. "Khel reckons he'll get his mother to help with some coin." He stole an obvious glance at Riall and waited for her to respond.

Riall decided not to take the bait and ask about Khel, though Volund was trying hard to insert his brother's generosity into the conversation.

Seeing Riall's silence, he held Belu a little closer to her. It was an invitation, but not an insistent one. The little dog's pink tongue hung out as she panted and gazed at Riall in expectation. Less patient than Volund, Belu whined as if to scold Riall for her neglect.

Though it was fragile and brief, a smile tugged at Riall's lips, and then she sighed as she reached out to pet the little dog. No one said anything as she took comfort from Belu's presence, scratching her in her favorite places and holding back tears. With a final ruffling of the dog's fur, Riall nodded to signal it was enough for the moment, and they returned their gazes landward over the vast water.

A silence extended itself between them, during which wind and waves and the creaking of wood made the only sounds other than distant conversations on the king's ship.

"He'd like to speak with you." Volund stared out at the waves, but Riall knew whom he meant.

She waited several heartbeats to respond. "Did he send you to tell me that?"

"No." Volund looked her in the eyes. "I came on my own."

Riall chewed her lower lip for a moment. She took a deep breath, and she realized she was ready. Part of her was eager, even, as she realized that it was cruel to keep avoiding Khel. Perhaps it was past time.

She nodded and turned to Volund. "You've convinced me."

Volund's eyebrows rose in surprise. "I have?"

Riall grinned at him. "You're a persuasive fellow, Volund. And more kind than I can say." She reached up and hugged him, squishing Belu between them. "Thank you."

She broke away and looked up at him. "Where is he, then?"

Volund motioned with his head toward the ship's stern, and then he smiled.

Trying to steady her breaths, she left him and Belu there. She dodged several warriors who were tending to the sail under Yrsa's firm directions, and then she made her way until she spotted Khel's back. He was alone, leaning on the rail and staring out at the Gulf of Olfi.

She stepped up behind him and took a long moment to gather her courage.

Riall took a deep breath. "Hi."

Khel jerked around and stared at her with his mouth hanging open. The wind toyed with the dark curls of his hair. "Hi."

"I was staring behind the ship. I thought I'd try the view out in front of it for a while." She gestured at the rail. "May I join you?"

Khel closed his mouth and blinked at her. He nodded.

She settled in at the rail, and Khel joined her at a polite distance. She glanced at him and scooted a bit closer. A long sigh escaped her. "I'm sorry. I haven't been very good to you these last few days."

"You're mourning. I understand."

"No. Stop being so damned kind, and let me apologize."

"Sorry."

One of her eyebrows arched up in mock contempt for his attempt at being less kind.

A grin spread across Khel's face with a hint of his old mischief in it, lifting her heart. "I am sorry too, you know."

Riall frowned at him. "For what?"

He pointed at her head. "For that. I worried I might have hit you a bit too hard."

She reached up to the spot and touched it with two fingers, wincing a little more than she needed to. "It *is* a bit sore still."

His face grew serious, and he swallowed.

She almost grinned at his look of contrition, but she cleared her throat instead and steeled herself. "I was angry with you, but I should not have been. The truth is that you likely saved everyone back there. I could not have done what Queen Sequara did. I would have taken you all with me. You understood what needed to be done, and you did it. I know you did it for my sake too."

He looked at her for a moment, and then he nodded. "Still. I'm very sorry about your . . . about Queen Sequara."

Riall fought back tears. She returned his nod and, after swallowing the lump in her throat, took a deep breath. "She knew all along. All those lives at risk. She always did what needed doing. I understand that now." One tear escaped her eye and tracked down her cheek, but she maintained control over her voice. "You gave her the chance she needed, Khel. You did the right thing."

He blinked at her. "Riall . . . I need to tell you something about me."

She wiped her cheek. "I know what you want to say. It wasn't your fault."

"You know?" He frowned at her.

"Don't forget I've been inside your mind. I know what happened back then, what that man made you do. And I know why you knocked me on the head." She rubbed her temple and winced, but then she smiled. "And thank you."

His mouth opened in astonishment for a brief moment. "Then . . . You know how I feel?"

She nodded and tried only a little to suppress a quick grin.

He cleared his throat and blinked at her. "Then you have me at something of a disadvantage, I suppose."

"And I aim to keep you that way. At least for a while." She winked at him.

A half smile tugged at the corner of his mouth, and he gave her a graceful bow before looking her in the eyes. "For as long as you like."

Riall looked up at him for a moment and then glanced downward before turning her gaze seaward. She rested against the rail, folding her hands in front of her. When he followed her lead and leaned on the rail next to her, she acted on an impulse, reaching out and taking his hand in hers. They moved closer together and gazed out at the water for a long while.

At length, Khel spoke. "Any idea where you'll go next?"

She waited a while to respond. "Not really. I'll need to return to Asdralad at least for a little while. Someone needs to tell Yudhiran what happened. He'll be king of Asdralad now. He'll do well, but I don't think he'll need me in the way there."

He nodded. "If you'll have me, I'll accompany you. But there's one place on the way I'd like to visit again with you, if you agree. And I think Volund might like to come with us." He grinned at her. "If nothing else, he'll enjoy carrying Belu a little longer."

Understanding brought a smile to Riall's face, and she nodded at her friend.

EPILOGUE

A herd of white clouds scudded across the sky, covering the deep-green rugged landscape in intermittent shadows. Though the wind whipped their hair and cloaks, it was what passed for a pleasant, sunny day in Caergilion. The salt-laden scent of the sea reached them from Culvor Sound, and seagulls wheeled overhead.

Sighting the familiar stone dwelling of the farmstead up ahead, Riall halted for a moment to compose herself. She glanced at her companions.

One standing on her right and the other on her left, Khel and Volund bided by her. The big Thjoth held Belu in one hand, letting the little dog nestle inside his cloak. Belu's nose and most of her face poked out, and even she seemed to be waiting for something to happen.

Riall took a deep breath and found that she could smile. Not a smile laden with memories or weighed with sorrow or regret. A genuine, full-hearted, and joyful smile. "Well. Here we are."

Khel smiled back at her and nodded, and that was all the signal they needed to proceed.

As they walked on the path snaking along the coastal fells toward

Seren and Ceri's home, something rose above the moan and hiss of the wind. Faint and indistinct at first, the sound grew louder as they approached the farmstead.

The door to the dwelling stood open to welcome sunlight and breeze, and from within came the sweet reverberations that lifted and swelled Riall's heart. Though it might have been a little rougher around the edges than it used to be, it was as beautiful as ever. Perhaps even more so for what it had endured.

Grinning in anticipation of their meeting, Riall stepped toward the sublime music of Seren's voice lifted up in song.

ABOUT THE AUTHOR

Rather than write about myself in third person, allow me to thank you for reading my book, dear reader, and to introduce myself. A medievalist with special interests in Old English, Old Norse, and various mythological traditions, I teach English composition and literature and run a YouTube channel ("Philip Chase" or "PhilipChaseThe-BestofFantasy") dedicated to the exploration of the fantasy genre. Feel free to visit me there and join the wonderful fantasy literature community that exists on YouTube. I can also be found puttering around on Twitter, Bluesky, and Instagram as "philipchase90," whereas Philip ChaseAuthor.com is my much neglected but soon to be updated website. Until next time!